Rose
Reason

Mary
Flanagan

BLOOMSBURY

First published 1991
Copyright © 1991 by Mary Flanagan
The moral right of the author
has been asserted

Bloomsbury Publishing Ltd, 2 Soho Square, London W1V 5DE

A CIP catalogue record for this
book is available from the British Library

ISBN 0 7475 0888 7

10 9 8 7 6 5 4 3 2 1

Typeset by Hewer Text Composition Services, Edinburgh
Printed and bound in Great Britain by Butler and Tanner Ltd,
Frome and London

For Michael Bleich

1942–1963

ACKNOWLEDGEMENTS

With thanks to Kenneth Lapides of New York City and John and Frances Nesbitt of Newmarket, New Hampshire.

CONTENTS

'And there are some things which
may not be advantageous, and
yet I call them good.'
– Plato, *Protagoras*

I promised to confess so I guess I'll have to tell you about the real Rose. The real Rose came to my school in the middle of the term, which was strange. She came in March when the ground was bare and the playground a fossil of our frozen footprints. She had been put back a year because Sister Mildred said she wasn't ready for fourth grade. There were no remedial reading classes in 1952. Children did not have learning disabilities, they were stupid. And Rose could hardly spell.

But that wasn't important to us. What mattered was that she had black hair and violet eyes and that the longest darkest lashes curled over her high cheekbones. Her father had been transferred from Lowell, or maybe there were other reasons why the family moved to Kittery. They had no relatives in the town. No one had heard of them. Her violet-eyed mother was pregnant, and she had an older sister who was not as pretty but had a contemptuous style. All this enhanced Rose's mystery. It was her mystery that was important.

The morning she arrived she stood alone on the Girls' side of the playground, watching us, shy and defiant, as we all walked towards her in our plaid skirts worn over snowpants and red rubber boots. Silently we approached her. Even I, who was not part of any clique and who was never chosen for baseball, even I was included in this posse. We hadn't planned to confront her in this way. No one had suggested we surround her. But suddenly we were doing it, just doing it as though we were under a spell, some force like spring, which was not resistible. We were greedy for her. We came up to her, nearer and nearer. No one spoke. We began to close the circle of which she was the centre.

She stepped back, turned on one foot and ran. We were amazed. We'd never seen a girl run so fast. She sprinted like a deer. She was an animal and yet not natural. Already she had crossed the yard and was at the top of the rise. We followed, running with all our might, but with no hope of catching her. (What we'd do if we did catch her we never thought.) She turned left at the fence and bolted for the sidewalk while we pursued her in silence as in an old movie. No shouts, no laughter. Only the sound of our breathing and of our twenty-two boots on the crusty ground.

We'd chased her three times around the playground before Sister Richard came striding towards us, ringing her bell with a ferocity that brought us all to a sudden stop.

'This is not the way little ladies behave,' said Sister Richard.

That afternoon when school let out we waited until we had turned the corner into Water Street where the nuns' eyes could not follow us. Then we chased Rose again. We chased her up Main Street along the canal and past the factory with its windows that reflected the sun like sightless eyes in a horror comic, too dangerous to look into. A few dead leaves still clung to the maple trees, rattling as we ran past, scolding us for our persecution.

She kept well ahead of us as far as the wooden tenement where she lived. We all stood in the street watching her take the rickety stairs two at a time and disappear with a bang of the storm door. We remained there like cats staring wistfully after our escaped prey.

Every day for three months it was the same. We chased Rose around the school yard until the nuns put a stop to it. After school we chased her home. Her mother complained but it did no good.

We chased her in all weathers. She never spoke to us, though we talked constantly of her, speculating about her past and developing fantasies of violent friendship. But we never questioned why we pursued her. She was simply one of those who fled, one of those who always flee us, escaping into wider space, fresher air, colours more intense, away from our obscene scrutiny and the staleness of our longing.

Summer vacation came and with it all the things I'll tell you about. I was banished to the Interior and given to my Aunt Bernie. I forgot Rose, or rather she slipped beneath my mental horizon. She lived for a while in the dark half of myself and then returned. I found her again when I became a Soldier of Christ and the Bishop announced to God and the world that from then on I, and not she, would be the real Rose, as though by taking her name I could capture her at last.

I know what you'd say. That I stole her soul. And you'd be right. It was the first of many crimes and is probably why my life has taken the wrong direction. And now you know. You are the only one to whom I'd tell this. You have my secret, I've given it to you. And he who has the secret has the power.

PART I

1

That Time

Childhood is a low fever. We cannot imagine a cure because we have only the present and a little immediate past. I know that because I am a child there is something wrong with me which must be put away or corrected. I rely on my parents to heal me, but I'm not sure when or how they will do this, only that they have the power. I love their power to heal me from the disease I do not know I have. I also love my disease.

In the house in Black Water Road the sheets are damp and the air is coloured. It is real air which rubs and resists you as you move through it. We live near the ocean though not on it. It is only a mile to Seapoint, where people come to collect seaweed for their vegetable gardens. In April and November there are fogs which when I wake up in the morning make me feel unreal and yet secure. I am in a world that holds me. It is the only time in my life I do not live in a city.

On summer Sundays we go to the beach in a convoy of five cars crammed with my mother's family, the Noonans. My cousins and I play all afternoon on the sand at Old Orchard or Rye. In the evenings when my father comes home from work he hoses the lawn and I run screaming through the spray. I eat bowls of blueberries with milk and sticks of raw rhubarb dipped in sugar. The front yard is a haze of bluettes, so small you can't see the single flowers unless you go down on your hands and knees. I bury my face in them. Their stems are fine as needles. I spend hours picking them one by one to make dolls' bouquets. In the fall I jump into heaps of leaves my mother has raked from the grass. I watch the ashes from a bonfire flutter in the air and slowly settle. Winter is the longest season. We have three to four feet of snow, though it melts more quickly here than inland. In the woods behind our house the sugar maples have tin pails hanging from their trunks. The icicles on their branches are full of sap and sweet to suck. Free popsicles dangling everywhere. When I am three I learn to skate.

My father straps a pair of double runners on me, plonks me on the ice, says, 'Here we go, kiddo', gives me a push and I am away, completely out of control, whizzing over the frozen waters of Black Pond, landing in a snowbank, a chubby astonished heap. At Long Swamp we can see the dead grasses and reeds in graceful tangles beneath the clear virgin ice. It is wonderful to be the first skater to criss-cross it with the marks of your blades. When it is very cold my mother Nora warms my underwear on the oven door and I dress in the kitchen. On snowy mornings she and I wait by the radio to hear what schools have been cancelled. When St Joseph's name comes up we smile at each other.

Downstairs in the cellar Foxie is a mother again. I have made a box for her and lined it with an old blanket. As she nurses her seven children she pants contentedly and gazes up at me with her great golden eyes. My mother says we are definitely not keeping all of the kittens. She expects me to reply or to make some sign of acknowledgement, but I refuse to say anything and pretend I haven't heard her.

In our den a record player is concealed in the large drawer of a console radio that is taller than I am. My parents have a collection of 78s which includes 'Tales From the Vienna Woods', all of the Ink Spots and Bob Crosby and the Bobcats. I hear the records playing late at night. The music mixes with the sound of rain and sometimes with the whistle of a train. I hear my parents laughing. They are dancing to 'If I Didn't Care'. Sometimes my father dances with me, holding my hand far out from our bodies, his other arm tucked under my bottom. He sways and turns and presses my cheek to his, shifting his weight on his long runner's legs. Then he spins me very fast and I have to hold tight, trying to focus on the picture of Roosevelt that hangs over the couch or on the small stone bulldog with a red collar that keeps ajar the door to the hall.

My father's name is Gabriel, but he is called Vincent, or rather, Vinnie. No one has ever told me that Vinnie Mullen is a star. But it is a certainty, and every day I am given new proofs. I catch them from the corner of my eye: the care my mother takes over the preparation and serving of his dinner and the ironing of his shirts, the way Aunt Bernie and Aunt Bea watch him with silent pride, as though they cannot get enough of looking, the way his friends Russ and Eddie address him with joking respect that really *is* respect; the comments everyone makes about his passing exams and getting promoted at the Navy Yard; his name in the paper in letters I cannot yet read; the photograph on the den wall of him accepting the prize for the 440-yard dash-back at Florence High. He is not so slender now because he loves fried clams with tartar sauce and drinks a lot of beer. He eats like I have seen him kiss my mother – eagerly, with his whole body, so that I feel embarrassed and excluded and have to look away. I myself do not like food all that much except for bread and butter sprinkled with sugar and rolled up into a soft white log, so my mother tempts me with eggnogs dyed blue or pink or green with food colouring – and usually this works. Because I am the child I am also given the chicken neck as a special delicacy. But best of all is a bit of marrowbone from which I scoop the sweet gelatinous contents with the point of a knife.

My father's lips remind me of a plum cut in two. There is a brown mark in the middle of his lower lip which I also have. Two deep lines enclose the corners of his mouth. He has a small nose about which my mother teases him in a way I can never understand. His skin is thick and smooth without very much hair. Its colour is even, as though the surface has the waxy coating of a leaf. Sometimes it bothers me because he seems more like a woman, made all of sugars and fats. His smile is celestial. But everyone, even his sisters, agrees that he ought to lose a little weight.

He laughs a lot, and sometimes his laughter gets out of control; the more he thinks about what is amusing him, the funnier it seems to get, so that tears begin to run from the corners of his screwed-up eyes and over the plains of his cheeks. Then, looking at him, everyone else loses control of their laughing too. My mother complains he is murder to sit next to at Mass.

'Well, you know,' he'll say about whatever it was that started him off, 'it just kinda struck me funny.'

He is the centre of all our attention which he simply accepts and takes more of like an extra helping at dinner. He makes me ache. I am afraid of him, of my need for him and of my mother's need. He cannot disgrace himself. Whatever he does we refuse to be disappointed. He is an only son and a youngest child, and his wife and two sisters and daughter and even his sisters-in-law are his harem. Aunt Bea, my mother says, only married because it was 'about time', and she has probably always loved Vinnie better than her husband Eugene, a night watchman who is very kind and has one leg shorter than the other so that he walks with a limp and has to wear a special black boot with a high-heel. Aunt Bernie, she explains, has kept herself for her brother, to be his agent and his goad, letting him drain away her love, all except that which she gave to God as an unofficial nun.

He is a child of glory. His sisters tell me how he was the first of the whole Mullen family to finish high school, to learn calculus, to have his picture in the paper, to own an automobile. And it is in the car that he and I have our best fun. For a while Vinnie has a part-time job collecting subscription money for *Collier's Magazine*. He makes his rounds two evenings a week and takes me with him for company. But really I am his audience on which he practises and rehearses his repertoire of stories, most of which I cannot understand at the time. Eventually, after listening for so many years, I memorize them.

I sit beside him in the front seat of our old black Ford – the danger seat, he calls it, because there is a hole in the floor which he covers with a rubber mat. If he is driving very fast through a deep puddle, not remembering, water gushes up through the floor like a geyser, drenching whoever is in the passenger seat, usually my mother, who screams in a way that scares me at first but later seems very funny. I am secretly hoping that I will get to scream too. One day it happens, just as we are passing the cemetery for dead countries. My father stops the car and dries me off with the dirty towel he keeps handy for these occasions, then we go to look at the gravestones. Each is marked with the name of a country in Eastern Europe (where is that?) which no longer exists because it has been killed by the Russians. My father reads the names to me: Romania, Poland, Czechoslovakia, Lithuania. What a strange thing to do. We speculate about who made it and why and who looks after it so beautifully.

My father tells me about his childhood, about his mother discovering that a sack of flour which was meant to last the family the winter had gone mouldy. She sat down on the floor beside the ruined flour and cried. 'And I sat down and cried with her.' He remembers how Mr Blaisdell who lived on a farm just outside of town would invite him in when he was doing his paper route and offer him a piece of his wife's apple pie, with milk straight from the cow.

He remembers, above all, the 1922 Strike, the meetings he attended with his father, the gatherings at the Florence Theatre and the Colonial Hall, the fierce speeches of Horace LaBranche who had been assigned to lead the strike. Florence had joined other textile workers throughout New Hampshire and southern Maine. The struggle achieved such national importance, my father says, that Thomas McMahon, president of the Textile Workers of America, made visits to support the workers in their opposition to the fifty-four-hour week. I picture my father, a boy among all those men, but accepted, encouraged. I see him moving through the crowds of desperate but determined workers in their drab winter clothing shouting their slogan 'Forty-eight hours, no cut!', a kind of mascot, slender, growing too fast, manoeuvring to get closer to his hero who is delivering a fiery address. It is so exciting. I don't really understand what a strike is.

He tells me how the priests sided with the management and tried to frighten the workers into betraying their brothers and sisters and surrendering to Wigram Boott's terms. He explains that this is why he has never liked the clergy. The police, the government and the newspapers were all against the strikers. Even now Vinnie gets angry about this, shouting about how 'state-aided monopoly capitalism' tried to destroy the Labour Unions. I have no idea what he means.

I can see how he loves to relive from a safe distance the hardships of that winter of 1922, the weeks and months of what he calls 'payless pay-days', the resentment and boredom and the anger, the card games at strike headquarters, the visits of the company agent who liked his employees and was scolded by Wigram Boott for fraternizing. He speaks of 'the grocer's bills that couldn't be paid, the sleepless nights', of the attempt by the company to break the strike and the unanimous refusal of the exhausted workers to return to the Mill under 'killing conditions'. He always pauses here. 'And then the end,' he goes on, 'with its sad compromise of a fifty-two-hour week with no increase in pay.' This is the part he likes best and he develops lots of variations around the closing scene. I can see the starved and beaten workers filing into the factory and it makes me want to cry, he is so good at describing it all. 'Those poor people,' I say.

'Labour history is a great adventure story, Frannie,' he says. 'Some people like Westerns, but me – I like labour history.'

He talks about Roosevelt, the greatest man who ever lived, greater than Jesus Christ, but I mustn't say that in front of my aunts. He assures me that the only thing we have to fear is fear itself and again I feel as if I might cry, even though I don't know what the New Deal was. He tells political stories about ward battles, caucuses, the Democratic City Committee, twelve-hour meetings. I am caught up in his contagious conviction, watching the movements of his beautiful mouth, not knowing what it means to pay a bill, to vote, to be on a committee. The words 'democracy' and 'economy' are huge and mysterious. They would also seem dull if it were not for the life with which my father infuses them.

He says he does not belong to a union now. 'But that doesn't stop me,' he chuckles. There are no unions at the Navy Yard. You can't strike on the government. The Navy Yard is a closed world of metal and mathematics where Vinnie goes every morning in his green-and-black plaid jacket and his visored cap to which his nametag is pinned. Carrying his lunchbox, he leaves me and my mother in the grey shingled house at the end of Black Water Road and drives to Portsmouth. My mother explains that they moved here from Florence because of his job.

Sometimes, when my mother needs the Ford, we drive Vinnie to work. When she is late or in a hurry, she throws her storm coat over her nightie and drives with her feet still in her slippers. I like it when she does this. So does my father. He teases her by threatening to tell the man at the tollbooth what she isn't wearing. Two guards with guns are stationed by the fence that surrounds the Navy Yard and the big ugly Naval prison that Vinnie says is famous. He shows them his picture and number and they admit him to the secret city and close the gates behind him. That is where he works and where he has taken the training courses for which he studied late into the night, and where he is given the promotions that get his name in the paper. He is listed as a master shipfitter although he doesn't like boats.

He reads newspapers and the life stories of important men. He loves to read, even books about nature. He never reads novels like Nora. He saves his money and buys himself a camera and starts to take photographs which, my mother complains, have no people in them – at least not people we know.

'You can't put these in an album, Vinnie. Photographs are to remember things by.'

'You're sentimental.'

'So are you. Only you're sentimental about dead trees and one-eyed cats and garbage cans and smelly rotten seaweed. You don't even take pictures of your own child.'

'She doesn't like having her picture taken, do you, Frannie? Anyway, when it's the right moment I'll take her picture. In a photograph you have to try to catch things as they really are.'

The right moment comes during a visit from my Aunt Bernie. She has brought me a present – a pink felt hat the shape of half a grapefruit with a narrow, turned-up brim and a horrible posy stuck on top. She takes the hat from its tissue-paper wrapping, baring her big teeth. She approaches me with the hat as my parents encourage me with their eyes. They want me to love her and to show my love. I stare at the hat. I hate it. I feel humiliated by it. I want to scream but I know I must not, so I run upstairs and hide under my bed, pursued by Aunt Bernie who's sure I'll come round in the end, and by my parents who are worried she'll find out I don't love her, at least not enough. My mother insists I come out from under the bed. I lie there looking at their legs and shoes, feeling

10

just so angry. My father takes an arm and my mother a leg and together they pull me from under the bed. I stand scowling before them. I know I am beaten. Aunt Bernie places the hat on my dishevelled head. My father produces the camera.

For supper that night we have hamburger soup with dumplings. I eat the dumplings and leave the soup.

'Cheer up, honey,' says Aunt Bernie.

We don't speak much because my father is listening to the six o'clock news, and we must be quiet to allow him to catch every word. His brow furrows as he strains to hear. I am alarmed by his complete seriousness.

I am in bed. I should be asleep, but it is impossible to tear my eyes from the mad abstractions that dance to no purpose on the wall before me – red and gold amoebas crowding upon an oily surface. The door opens and my father enters, his height dramatized by the hall lamp behind him. He carries something in his arms. He bends over and places Foxie, brought secretly up from the cellar, on my chest. He kisses me on the forehead.

'You're my sweetie – '

' – pie,' I respond, according to our ritual.

'And honey – '

' – bunny.'

He closes the door, leaving me in the dark with Foxie who kneads the blankets and purrs like mad. I close my eyes and cling to Foxie. I forgive my father.

A child of glory cannot disgrace himself. Aunt Bea says that even when he abandoned Florence and the Mill and the Union for the big money of the Navy Yard, no one was bitter about the loss to Ward Eight, Local Number Twenty-two, and the Democratic Party of Florence. No one begrudges him the committees and the meetings with which he is not now supposed to be involved, although they all worry in private. He does not run, he does not play baseball. He drives over to Dover Point and eats three lobster rolls and drinks three beers. He takes pictures of dead trees and derelict houses whose windows have a cross-eyed look. Not pictures to put in a family album. He reads books about men with unpronounceable names that Aunt Bernie is sure are on the Index. He listens to Jazz.

But whatever he does they turn it into pride and amazement, until one Sunday when he does not go to church. My mother and I sit alone in the pew. I stand and kneel and make the sign of the cross, and none of it means much beyond the comforting repetitions of children's stories

– once, twice, three times. There is a black crucifix on our kitchen wall, but I have not yet been told of Jesus's death. We do not say grace (though I say my prayers and am encouraged to ask for blessings for Aunt Bernie) but we would never miss Mass. No one, *no one* misses Mass. We go in blizzards and when we are running temperatures. We know everyone in the church and they know us. They would notice right away if we didn't come. So I am frightened by my father's absence.

For three Sundays in a row he stays at home to take photographs of the collapsed shed in the back yard. Nora calls Aunt Bea and speaks to her in whispers. They are reluctant to inform Aunt Bernie, but at last they tell her. It is unthinkable that Vinnie be scolded, so they say rosaries behind his back, and Aunt Bernie makes a Novena. Even the Noonans, not great prayers, are praying, or at least they say they are. Everyone is praying that Vinnie will come back to the Church. My mother visits Father Cullinane and Bernie visits Father Leahy, but no one says anything to my father because they don't dare approach his golden aura. But he gets wind of all the religion being directed at him and confronts Nora who remains calm. She tells him that there are rumours that he is simply too lazy to get up early on Sunday mornings. Vinnie is very angry, angrier than I have ever seen him.

We know he is planning something. He is waiting for the right Sunday. Late in November it comes.

A blizzard blankets the north-east. We don coats, boots and scarves and shovel out the driveway. To our surprise my father jumps into the car.

'I'm coming with you,' he says as my mother tries not to look too relieved. She is brilliant at pretending nothing abnormal is going on. I watch them from the back seat. Vinnie takes her hand and drives with one arm despite the condition of the roads.

'Vinnie,' she warns.

'Don't tear your shirt, Norrie. We got chains.'

We're early, and Vinnie parks the car right in front of the steps of St Joseph's.

'See you girls later,' he says, taking up a position to the left of the stairs. Already his overcoat is turning white.

'You're not coming,' Nora sighs.

'Nope.'

'You're going to stand out here in the snow.'

'Yep.'

'Until Mass is over.'

'Yep.'

She takes me by the hand and we go into the church. I turn to look at my father and he winks at me.

The next Sunday he stands outside the church during eight o'clock Mass. And the next and the next. My aunts say it is a scandal, though they don't scold him. Even Russ and Eddie wear worried expressions. But Vinnie wins. No one says ever again that he has lost his faith because he is lazy.

My uncles go hunting and fishing and invite my father, but he refuses to go with them, giving no reasons, smiling at them with what seems to be contempt. After a while they don't invite him. I beg Nora not to accept the deer meat they give us every November, and she says she can't refuse without offending them. They're her brothers after all, and she loves them. But we don't actually have to *eat* it. I must keep my mouth shut, though. She says she can't understand why men get pleasure out of shooting poor dumb animals, and I think how nice my parents are.

They agree about everything but religion and music. My father listens to Peggy Lee and Duke Ellington and Bennie Goodman. It's only when he plays the Gene Krupa version of 'Tuxedo Junction' over and over that she says, 'Oh Vinnie, *please!*' She prefers Doris Day and 'Tales From the Vienna Woods' which she plays on Tuesdays when she does the ironing. I love that she has a day for each thing, a time for each thing. Monday, washing; Saturday, baking; Wednesday, cleaning; Thursday, odds and ends; Friday, shopping; Sunday, reading – every day has its title like a chapter in a book. On Wednesdays she almost frightens me. My mother has a personal grudge against dirt, as though it had insulted her or injured someone she loved. She cleans with a ferocious energy, moving couches, chairs and beds unassisted, determined that not one 'kitty' will escape her. (She complains there are more 'kitties' under my bed than anywhere else in the house.) Sometimes I worry that she will lose her temper with the dust and stains. When I feel like this I hide in the attic. She beats the rugs as though she were punishing them. Yet I suspect she is really having a good time.

She feels the same way about bugs, except for bees. It is Vinnie who is afraid of bees. If a fly or a mosquito manages to sneak past our screens, she pursues it and does not stop until she has flattened it without mercy. If she sees an ant in the kitchen she is even more outraged and says, 'Oh, isn't that *awful!*' and searches for hours until she finds the crack or hole through which the enemy has invaded. During flying-ant season she is upset all the time. Then she says, 'Isn't that *just* awful!' which means that almost nothing worse could happen.

13

She has other funny expressions that are hers alone like 'Oh, dear me suds!' She says that when she is only pretending to be upset. I like this expression. It always makes me laugh. 'Say it again, Mummy,' I plead. 'Oh, dear me *suds*!' she answers and then we both laugh. When she is talking on the phone to her sisters she will say 'Eyah . . . Eyah . . .' which I know is an old-fashioned word for 'yes' that people use in Maine.

When I am not in school we are together all the time. I help her bake and rake up leaves. I go with her when she does the shopping. Sometimes I think Nora is more my friend than she is my mother.

In her way Nora is as famous as Vinnie. (I understand that women, unless they are like Peggy Lee or St Teresa or Betty Crocker, cannot be as famous as men.) People talk about how clean and bug-free our house is, of course, and how beautifully Nora sings and whistles, but her sense of smell is considered remarkable as well. She can detect all sorts of odours that other people can't. It is a strange personal talent, like her singing. Nora will come into a room and suddenly stop and sniff quite loudly and say, 'What's that *awful* smell?' then run around opening windows even in the middle of winter. She says she realizes this is annoying for other people, but she just can't help it, she's tried and you have no idea what an affliction a sensitive nose can be. And anyhow, sensitive noses run in the family, especially among the women. I will probably be the same, poor little girl. Then she always follows this remark with, 'But when it's time to smell the lilacs and appleblossom you'll get ten times more pleasure than anyone else. Then your nose will take you to heaven.'

Her packages are also a subject of conversation. Vinnie says they are real works of art. Nora spends hours with Scotch tape, scissors and stiff white twine. She wraps the peanut-butter cookies or the presents for far-away friends and relatives in layers of tissue paper then tapes the cover to the box on every side, then wraps that in sheets of newspaper. Then comes the heavy brown paper and the address and return address exactly centred in her beautiful handwriting. Not one cookie arrives broken. My father says she is a mailman's dream. At Christmas she is up all night. She says she really enjoys inventing new kinds of bows with the satiny ribbon, co-ordinating colours, writing nametags, all alone at the kitchen table in the quiet of the night, whistling and singing while her husband and daughter sleep upstairs. In the morning the stack of presents takes our breath away and we applaud and say how beautiful and she laughs and answers, 'Oh, don't be so silly.'

Nora is most famous for her letters of sympathy. No one else can write them like her. Vinnie jokes that people who know her actually look forward to a death in the family so that they too can receive one of these masterpieces. She writes the letter on a separate sheet of pale-blue paper, signs her full name, Nora Noonan Mullen, and slips it into the sympathy card, the verse of which never equals her own powers of expression. She can't explain why she's so good at it. 'I guess death brings out the best in me,' she says. 'Your mother has a knack for condolence,' Vinnie replies.

Her letters are filled with such lovely sentiments that their recipients phone her crying and thanking her. 'It's made us feel so much better,' they wail. 'Well, I'm glad,' says Nora modestly. Vinnie is proud of his wife's way with words and sometimes shows the letters to visitors (Nora always keeps a copy) and even to his best friends Russ and Eddie. Nora pretends to be embarrassed. 'Oh Vinnie, don't,' she pleads. But her eyes sparkle and she has trouble keeping the corners of her mouth straight. We know that people save these letters, putting them away in special drawers or cardboard files or fire-proof metal closets where their most precious possessions are kept. I imagine granddaughters and grandsons finding them many years after their parents are themselves dead. Will they throw them out during spring cleaning, send them to the dump with the rubbish to be burnt and disappear into the sky for ever like the autumn leaves? Or will they open them and read them and wonder who was Nora Noonan Mullen, the woman who wrote such wonderful letters of sympathy?

Nora is the best singer I know. I like her voice better than any of those on Vinnie's record. He says that I had the greatest lullabies of any kid in the State of Maine and I bet that's true. She always sings when she's working and I love to hear her.

It is a Tuesday afternoon and I sit watching our first television, with its twelve-inch screen, and making clothes for Foxie's children. I can hear the nice thump-thump of Nora's iron. She is a very energetic ironer – the whole board shakes. She is whistling along to the radio and sometimes singing:

> I'd love to get you
> On a slow boat to China . . .

I am waiting for *Kukla, Fran and Ollie* to come on, but today it doesn't. Instead, men with strange names, wearing suits and ties, sit together at a long curving desk. Before each one is a placecard with the name of a country I do not know. They speak in quiet voices, very serious. The programme has been running for hours. Nothing seems to happen. There are no women. The voice of an invisible man whose tone is calm and authoritative is using a word I have never heard before. He says it again and again in a way that makes my stomach tighten and my arms and legs grow weak. The house that holds me seems about to fly apart as if a giant magnet were pulling at every nail in its wooden frame. Where is my father? What will happen to Foxie and the kittens? The afternoon is suddenly dark. Someone has lowered the sky on a pulley and we will all be crushed. I go into the kitchen where Nora is singing 'My Secret Love', a pile of Vinnie's underwear beside her.

'Mummy, what's war?' I ask.

She looks at me, surprised, not wanting to frighten me more by explaining.

'Something that happens far away,' she says.

'Where the Thirty-ninth Parallel is?' The other words used by the invisible man.

'That's Korea, sweetie. That's not here. Daddy has a special job so he won't have to go. Don't worry. Daddy can stay here. The government says so.'

'What's the government?'

I realize that she is powerless to protect us from the threat I am sure I understand better than she does. The war is rumbling and rolling under the earth. Its blast-waves rise up from the cellar, its fire falls from the sky. Outdoors the trees wave their arms in panic as I stand on a green square of linoleum, unable to move, tears running down my face. Nora picks me up and holds me, bending me to an embrace I cannot return. She carries me to the den and turns off the television. She rocks me in her arms. She smells of the laundry she says she likes to do, and I cling to her wishing it were an hour ago before war was let out of the television and set free to poison the world for ever.

That night, and every night during the following year, I am allowed to sleep with the light on. When I wake up the next morning I look through the slats of the Venetian blinds. I see that the clothesline is still upright and rotating slowly in the breeze that blows in from the ocean. I see the hedge of bridal wreath that separates our yard from Millie Bison's, the fragile hammock still strung between two apple trees and Ginger our money cat balancing in the branches, not thinking about war. Our garbage can waits by the road for the truck's Wednesday visit. The collapsed shed decomposes just where it always has because my father cannot repair or replace anything. Insects collide with the screen, not thinking about the Thirty-ninth Parallel. Someone has raised the sky back to where it usually is, and nothing is special, only good. Nothing comes up too close or steps out of the background to frighten me. There is no rumble under the earth, no purpose lurking anywhere. Nothing is too new. It is a day without reason or intent when everything looks me in the face and tells me nothing. I go outdoors. I test the air to see if it is all right. It is. I want to wrap the day around me, to wear it like a costume of light.

At school I recite the catechism I have memorized, and it means nothing. I just like to memorize it. After supper we go to the Sunset Drive-In where we meet Uncle Harry and Aunt Lou and my three cousins, all in their pyjamas like me. We park the Ford next to theirs. The children take one car and the grown-ups the other. We bounce on the seats and squabble and giggle and throw popcorn and Uncle Harry shouts at us to keep quiet and watch the movie. My father brings us strawberry milkshakes. On the way home I fall asleep and do not remember being carried up to bed.

Sister Richard tells me I have reached the Age of Reason. I make my First Holy Communion along with thirty-two other seven year olds. We march in procession from the school to the church. Parents line the sidewalk, taking snapshots. I have never seen so many people all at once. I stand on the church steps in my short puff-sleeved white dress and my veil, waiting to march into the vestibule singing 'O Sacrum Convivium'. My father comes to church for the first time in over a year and my Aunt Bea cries. (I have never seen Aunt Bernie cry. She is only displeased or satisfied.) I'm glad Nora and Vinnie are there, but the taste of the wafer means nothing to me. It is so light, so neutral. The music and the Latin are beautiful. They mean nothing. It is June and the church is very warm. Up in the loft, where the flies hover, thousands of organ-notes echo and collide.

Late in the hot afternoon, my father disappears and my mother drives Aunt Bernie to the train station. She asks what Bea would never ask.

'Where's Vinnie?' Such a tone.

'He had a meeting.'

'On a *Sunday*?' Bernie is already unhappy because Nora is wearing shorts. My mother says she intends to wear shorts for ever, even when she's an old woman. To her mind, shorts are It.

'He said it was important,' she smiles.

Bernie sighs. 'Why does Vinnie have to go so far?'

I wonder whether she means far away or far extreme.

17

'And what do his bosses at the Yard think about these meetings?' She pronounces Yard 'Yahd'. I have never heard her criticize my father.

My mother says, 'Oh, it wasn't one of *those* meetings.'

When we have put Aunt Bernie on the train we both feel a lot happier, and on the way home we stop at the Big Dipper for a peppermint ice-cream. But I can still feel Aunt Bernie's displeasure all the way from Florence. I can feel it trying to penetrate the safety that holds us. Our life is a party for three to which not even God is invited.

The afternoon of the fire we visit Nora's best friend Marie McGowan, who lives in an isolated house near a crossroads. The house is large and exposed. It is at the top of a hill and you can see very far in every direction: the foothills of the White Mountains, the river with its elm trees and marshes below, and a tiny white church with green shutters, a doll's church, it looks like. The house has a big front porch with no screens. All the windows are open, and white curtains billow like sails. It is like being on a ship. There is no telephone.

The McGowan children won't play with me. I clutch my doll and refuse to leave my mother who sits at the kitchen table with Marie. The wind is so strong that Marie goes to the door and calls the children in.

'Dangerous time, end of August,' she says.

'So dry,' Nora answers. 'People throw cigarettes out of car windows.'

'Damned fools.'

At five we say goodbye. Marie kisses me, but the children keep back in the shadows, guarding their toys, not scolded for their hostility as my mother would have scolded me. We walk a little way along the verge and wait next to the crossroads with no shelter from the hot wind. My father is late and the light is going. Through a crack in the clouds we can see the zinnia-coloured sun. It fills the air with a thick orange light in which we look like strangers to each other. In its flash we see the smoke and the dust which are being carried on the wind that sweeps past us and makes our eyes smart. Then the sun vanishes and a premature night begins.

I hold tight to my mother's hand. She has stopped repeating that my father will be along any minute now and is silent like me. We cannot take our eyes from the horizon where we know that the fire is eating up the trees. A tall man comes walking along the road. He looks as if he has been walking all his life, as if his walking had taken him across the whole earth. Does he know my father? I wonder. Has he seen him? My mother says hello in that way she has of encouraging everyone to be polite and cheerful. He tips his hat and walks on towards East Rochester, pressing his body against the wind. We feel even lonelier when he has gone.

No cars pass. The thin dark road vanishes too soon in the smoky distance. I dangle my doll in the tall roadside grass, grass I would hardly notice if I were whizzing along with Vinnie, listening to his stories. And now here I am standing in it, its parched flowers tickling the backs of my knees. Then comes the sound of the Ford whose rattle is not mistakable and we let ourselves breathe again. My father opens the door with a smile, but I can see the worry in his eyes. He kisses my mother. I cannot control the urge to jump up and down on the back seat as we drive away from the smoke and the danger, back towards the sea.

That night I am allowed to come downstairs. It is three-thirty in the morning and Uncle Harry and Aunt Lou and my Grandmother Noonan and my three cousins and my Aunt Lil whose husband is away in the Army are coming through the kitchen door, frightened but laughing. Nora hugs and kisses them all. My grandmother is wrapped in a grey blanket the colour of her hair. They have fled the forest fire which they say is raging out of control and have come to stay with Nora and Vinnie and me. I imagine their small wooden houses on the outskirts of Sandford, abandoned by the side of the highway.

My mother tells them of our anxious moments at the crossroads. Everyone is speculating about the man we met.

'Tell you who that guy was,' says my uncle. 'Bet you anything it was Jim Hussey lives over by North Berwick. He still don't have a car. Walks everywhere.'

'Naw. Jim died last year. Polly went to the funeral.'

'You're thinking of the fella owns the gas station . . .'

'Why didn't you wait in the house?' my grandmother asks.

Nora smiles at me.

Now they are drinking coffee and discussing what you should do in case of a fire. Close all the doors, they say. You have to close the doors.

'Beat the damn thing with a wet sheet,' my uncle says and the children laugh. 'Hey, I'm serious,' he protests in mock offence.

I am carried up to bed and my cousin Janie is laid beside me. We are covered with a blue-and-white blanket that belonged to Grammy Mullen. Janie turns and pulls the covers with her, and with the last of my energy I pull back until we have settled our territory and our positions. I dream that we are rolled in sheets over and over, hundreds of yards of white cotton, wrapped in sheets, lapped in sheets, sheets that when wet can put out a fire.

The next morning we hear on the radio that the blaze is under control. The wind drops and my relatives return to their houses which must be glad to see them because it is terrible to be left behind. We get in the Ford and drive north to look at what the radio calls 'the devastation'. There are a lot of other cars because everyone wants to see the damage. A thin smoke still hovers over miles of black ground, and the charred trees stand against the sky like broken bones. My father says it will take thirty years to make a new forest. This reminds him that in South Africa there are flowers called fireball lilies whose bulbs will germinate only after they have been burned. Some must wait decades for the fire in whose ruins they flourish. But there are no fireball lilies in Maine, and until I am a grown woman I will see only dead trees every time I drive on this road.

2

Florence

In 1859 Wigram Boott travelled north from Boston to Florence, Maine where he was to assume control of the family textile company so successfully established and run by his father Wigram Boott I. His accession was to have great significance for me as I will explain. The Bootts were Yankees and Presbyterians, and though they did not believe that the meek would or should inherit the earth, they tried to ensure that they did not harbour an inconvenient resentment against those who did. Boott Senior built shops, a hotel and sturdy brick tenements for his operatives. He set up a company store, planted shade trees, and controlled the fire department. Through the medium of his watchful agents, he oversaw the workers' attendance both at the Mills and at church, their drinking habits and the limited education of their male children, all according to the tenets of his benign paternalism.

It was an era of great industrial advances. 'Solid prosperity and continuous progress', as Boott Senior put it: profits running to 40 per cent, cost of production declining, every spindle turning and double sets of hands working day and night. The number of unskilled foreign labourers had increased dramatically, and among them was my great-grandfather, Patsy Mullen, fresh from Sligo. His wages were a dollar a week. Of course Wigram Boott knew nothing of Patsy Mullen or of any of the weavers, loom fixers, dyers or spinners in his factory. Along with other manufacturers of his time he lived in Boston far from dreary Florence and its discontents. (It used to be said that the Boston aristocracy was founded on the profits of the New England textile mills.) Unlike most cotton kings, he did occasionally visit his holdings, but the actual management of the Mills, called Number One and Number Two respectively, he left to his agents.

From 1900 to World War I competition in the textile industry demanded a speeding up of both workers and machines. Weavers attended two looms instead of one. Mechanical advances steadily

21

increased the pace of the machines so that operatives were forced to keep up a killing pace. Life in the mills was an exhausting struggle.

My grandmother, for example, worked ten hours a day. She and the other women in the Number One Mill were employed on a piece-work basis and maintained this gruelling momentum against the nerve-shattering racket of grinding ply-frames, pounding thrashers, whizzing bobbins and the ferocious gnashing looms. She barely had time to stop for a sandwich and even then she could not escape the incessant clamour. Her hands would shake so badly she could barely get the food to her mouth.

When my aunts were small children she had to leave them with relatives or neighbours and sometimes on their own, locked in the apartment for safety's sake, until she was finally forced to stop working because of asthma caused by the cotton dust. Women worked through their pregnancies. There was no maternity leave, and there were also some very close calls. Many babies were born in the mill. My Aunt Bernadette claimed to have slid from my grandmother's womb straight on to the oil-soaked factory floor. The story may be apocryphal, but both my aunts, Bernie and Bea, swore it was true, and Bernie was very proud of her origins. Everyone in the family believed her, and I guess I do too. It is the most glamorous thing about her, and no one's life should be completely devoid of glamour.

The Red Scare scared Wigram Boott II. There were protests all over the country: marches, strikes and pitched battles with Pinkerton Men and the police. Like every other industrialist of the north-east, he dreaded a rehearsal of the Lawrence strikes in his own back yard, and decided to pre-empt rebellion by making an endowment to the people of Florence. Wigram's photographs show a tight-lipped mustachioed balding man with a slight mean body and a large head, and it is hard for me to imagine that his generosity was a manifestation of humanitarian impulses. Like his father, he wanted peaceful productivity. He also wanted to be, or at least appear to be, a good Christian. And so in March 1919, as one of his last proclamations before retiring and handing over the reins of power to his son Wigram III, he announced that half his stupendous World War I profits would be used to fund an institute of higher learning, the first of its kind in the state.

It came as no surprise that the new school was to be called Boott College. It would be set in planned parkland in the clean new northern end of the city, out of sight of the Mills which rose high and stark – red-bricked, four-towered, seven-storeyed – beside the Miomak River in the centre of the town which had grown up around them. (In the seventies there was talk of tearing them down, but they still stand, I am told. I haven't been to Florence in many years. Number One, the birthplace of my maiden aunt, was sold to an electronics firm and then abandoned, its machinery removed, its interior dark, its windows open to the dry cold wind of Florence.)

Wigram's gift to the employees who had made him rich was applauded by the city's leading lights whose children would be educated at Dartmouth and Tufts. My grandparents conceded that it was very decent of him, but they did not for a moment consider that it might one day ease the resentments of their children: Mary Helen, called Bea, Bernadette, and Gabriel, called Vinnie, or of their granddaughter Frances, known as Rose. Perhaps because they would all be obliged to contribute to the support of their family by going to work as soon as legally permissible, and secondary education would therefore be out of the question. Perhaps because my grandfather was then earning $6.43 for a fifty-four-hour week. The Bootts did not believe that money was good for the working classes. It only encouraged their natural sloth and viciousness. It was therefore a manufacturer's duty to protect them from themselves by paying out wages in meagre and strictly regulated amounts.

Some said Boott should have spent his money on improvements to the Number One which was showing its age and where working conditions had for some time been deplorable: the ventilation poor, the floors greasy, the carding machines packed dangerously close together and the walls not whitewashed in ten years. Some even dared to suggest that his profits should be shared outright with the workers. The college, they said, was only a monument to himself and would make no fundamental difference to a system that was stacked against them.

It must be admitted that, previous to the advent of the Bootts, there was nothing much to Florence. It was never one of those New England towns with a pure church white against the background of fiery foliage. It was never picturesque, but always seemed intent on becoming a small, grey-brown city, a 'company town', centre of a successful manufacturing complex.

During the Depression of 1922, Wigram Junior could not understand his workers' response to the proposed 20 per cent pay-cut. He must have been surprised when his entire work force walked out on him and went on strike for nine months. How shocked he must have been, how disappointed, how justifiably incensed. He detected the influence of the International Workers of the World. His sharp eyes saw its agents everywhere. Bravely he declared that he would make no compromises with Bolshevism. But he needn't have worried. Florence was firmly under the control of the Labour Right in the form of the Textile Workers of America. When, after nine months, the strikers, including my grandfather, returned to work, Wigram Boott forgave them as a father forgives his errant children and the construction of Boott College, my alma mater, was resumed.

The Boott Mills are so close to the river that if you stand on the bridge which is part of Central Avenue and look east, they seem almost to be the river's source, the brown water surging and gushing from the very foundations of the Boott Manufacturing Company. In fact, the river skirts the edge of the buildings, and there is a narrow greasy bank between them and the water where branches and bottles and paper accumulate, trailing slimy threads of algae along the foamy surface. Not a pretty spot, but potent. Easy to see why Wigram I chose it for his enterprise which he turned from a small rural saw mill like so many others, into an industrial fortress.

As the river approaches Florence from the north-west it picks up speed, as though wanting to hurry as quickly as possible through the drab landscape of south-central Maine and be on its way to the more romantic coast. Its haste is understandable. The interior of what we used to call the Neck of Maine is a melancholy place. But there is nothing sweetly reflective about it. Nor does its minimal landscape suggest an inner strength – nature austere and dangerous. With its sandy soil and its scrub pines, its homogeneous sky and featureless horizon, it is like a land under a curse. Only the poor live in this blighted area, many of them in trailer parks among the black woods. Most have lived in their trailers for many years, while along the coast millionaires, more of them per capita than in any other state, enjoy the short Maine summers. The country's desolation is broken only by the Maine Turnpike which stretches from below Portland to the Canadian border. The road is even more depressing than the landscape it transects. You pass maybe five cars in twenty miles. You wonder why it was built. It is beautiful for a week in November when the fields are like an old lion's hide and the sky hangs heavy with snow. I don't know why, perhaps it is the only time the light is interesting. Otherwise the sun is cheerless, making you feel exiled and exposed. You wonder why God put you here and you envy everyone who lives anywhere else.

When I was a child the toll was 10 cents, but I always felt I would pay any price to get off that road. When I travelled up from Kittery with my parents to visit Aunt Bernie it had only been completed as

far as Exit 9. The Florence exit was Number 6. I sat alone in the back
seat of our old black Ford as we turned right up a narrow ramp then
over a bridge with low iron railings which afforded a view of Florence
as dramatic as it was possible to get. Sometimes my father would slow
a little to take in the spectacle of his home town. And here my heart
would sink. I would turn my face from the square towers of the Mills,
the slate-coloured steeple of Holy Trinity and the neo-Gothic turrets
of St Blaise's. The former was my aunt's church, the Irish church, and
the latter the French, the façade of which she considered obscenely
ornate. Its architectural exuberance was made possible by the zeal
of the French Canadians, who not only outnumbered the Irish (who
in turn outnumbered the Yankees, the Greeks and the Poles in that
order) but who were inveterate card-players and earned thousands of
dollars for their parish by capacity-attendance whist drives. St Blaise's
was rich. There had always been a rivalry, not consistently friendly,
between the two ethnic groups that comprised the bulk of Wigram
Boott's workforce. The French antagonized the Irish and the Yankees
by continuing to speak their native language and to teach it to their
children in St Blaise's Grammar School.

Originally the operatives were not allowed to own property but lived
in the red-brick company houses near the factory, an area of what
was called in the sixties 'urban blight and decay'. Some houses were
demolished, the rest saved by an eleventh-hour realization of their
worth. An enlightened bureaucrat in Augusta discovered they were
of historic interest, and the city fathers saw them with new eyes. Now
they are clean but grim, a reminder of strictured lives. They are run as
public housing to accommodate the poorer families of Florence.

My Aunt Bea is proud of the fact that the Mullens escaped these
lodgings for their own house in Irish Town which they bought for
$350 in 1925. No one knows how they afforded the place on South
Street (Vinnie claimed my grandfather had a fluke win on the sulky
races at Rochester Fair), but they managed to live there until 1941 when
my grandparents were dead and Bea and Vinnie had married (late) and
only Bernadette was left.

She then sold up and moved into one of the newer clapboard
tenements with small bay windows in front, and porches, clotheslines
and outside stairways at the back. These structures are superior to the
older clapboard buildings, a few of which still remain, accommodating
bakeries, pizza shops, paint and appliance stores and a few families.
These are large buildings of five storeys with high, flat severe façades
under which the shops crouch low and dark. They seem to draw back

into themselves and hold themselves tight against the world. They are so inhospitable that the newer tenements seem almost welcoming with their bay windows making gestures of approach across the narrow streets.

How can I tell you about Florence? How can I make you understand what it was like, and anyway, do you really care about understanding? What is it to you, after all? A dull dream, the childhood memory of someone insignificant, a place without promise.

It seems to me now like a shallow pit that rimmed the lives of its inhabitants, keeping them tame and biased so that they worked well and were content with short-term improvements. Wigram Boott would have been pleased with his immigrants in the end. They were people for whom the colour of existence had shifted in one generation from black to grey, who were not destined to go forward but who would never slip again into complete darkness. I sensed their willed stasis in the midst of economic growth, their determination to remain exactly where they were, forever consuming more of the same, like invalids, needing decades to recover from past traumas, glad simply to be out of pain and danger, and superstitious lest a false move hurl them back into misery. Far enough, ran the general consensus; any farther would be tempting fate. They were only lately certain of their citizenship, working to maintain their modest but secure identity. They were still not sure how to behave, what was really expected of them, and so they trod cautiously, watching for mistakes, checking to see if they were doing OK. And I was like that too, I was one of them, self-doubting, trying to practise contentment, yet embarrassed to be who I was – a small citizen of a dreary town. One of many souls in this flat place with its cold light, harsh shadows, dull skies, bad snow. A place without promise. A place with just enough.

Irish Town is still standing, though it no longer bears that name. Until recently I possessed, as you know, a collection of old photographs showing its unsmiling occupants standing on its front steps: women with slipshod bouffants, men with caps and jackets too small for them, children in baggy cut-off trousers and bare feet. Strictured lives. I showed you these pictures, do you remember? You didn't seem impressed, but then why should you be?

There was Grammy Mullen, very serious, hair white at forty, who died on the kitchen table during an emergency appendicectomy. She'd been coming home on the tram when she collapsed. Three hours later she was gone. And Grampie Mullen with fellow members of the volunteer fire department. Always recognizable since he was the shortest (five feet-four – how did my father get to be six feet-two?), and the sweetest smile, a what-the-hell smile, and was missing the middle finger on his right hand – an accident in the carding room at the Mill. Then another picture of the three children in their twenties: my father handsome, rosy and self-possessed, the girls plain, and proud of their brother who had snapped up all the best genes.

My favourite photographs were taken in the Mills. There is one from about 1914 in the Cloth Hall, a long room with arched windows like a Romanesque church, low wooden ceilings and hanging gas lamps. Around a polished table stand men in white aprons and bow ties, women in high-collared white blouses, dressed up to have their picture taken. No one smiles. On the table and along the walls the white cloth is stacked, thousands of yards of fine cotton sheeting in rolls that are folded over and back, over and back, lapping endlessly upon themselves. They make me think of bandages and shrouds and altar cloths, of hospitals and nurseries, of tears and comfort and pain and sleep. At the end of the Hall is a french window, two arches with eight panes of glass each and contained in turn within a larger arch. The door is also white. Here is Wigram Boott's peaceful productivity.

Another picture was taken among the giant looms. Thirty-six operatives, mainly women, pose against a backdrop of pulleys and belts and wheels. A stocky overseer with slicked hair and large hands stands apart from the group. The men are in shirt-sleeves. No one smiles. They are sturdy and solemn. It is generations since they have worked the land. They are urban peasants, cut off from nature. A cross-eyed bobbin-boy with hair parted in the middle slumps on a stool. The girls in the front row sit with their arms linked or around each other's shoulders. One of them is my Aunt Bernie.

She was eighteen at the time but looks younger. Her hair is dark like mine, but severely controlled, the curls held back with a ribbon. She wears a plain cotton dress over black stockings. Her shoulders slump, and her full oval face, large eyes and expressionless mouth appear passive but reluctant. Yet the eyes look hard at the camera. They see through her prejudices, her resentments, her limitations. But they see *everything*. It isn't a face you love. My mother told me long ago that Aunt Bernie had a beau when she was in her late teens. He courted her for a year until the story got around that he had made another girl pregnant. He still insisted he wanted to marry Bernie, but she refused him and remained a spinster for the rest of her life.

I asked her once about her childhood and she told me that she remembered sitting in the cellar of the South Street house at the foot of the stairs by the open bulkhead. The floor was of earth, and it was where they kept the coal. In the summer she would set up a small blackboard on an easel in the one shaft of light.

'I'd sit there,' she said, 'and I'd draw and I'd draw and I'd draw.'

She never mentioned that, like most adolescents, she lied about her age and went to work in the Mill at thirteen. Nor did she make any comment on the service badges accummulated over forty years at Number Two, during which time she was not promoted once. She didn't say whether she found it hard being alone on Birch Street (where there was not a birch or any tree in sight) after so many years of crowded family living. She occupied one of the third-floor apartments with its bay window facing the street. There we would spend torpid Sunday afternoons in That Time when I lived with my parents. And there I ate supper with her at five every evening and did my homework in front of the television and slept in one of the twin beds in the room next to the parlour that was always called the guest-room, with Foxie beside me on her plaid blanket. It was there I nursed my aunt through her long recovery and where I came years after to see her again when it was almost too late.

Early suppers were customary in Maine. But they were also a necessity in Aunt Bernie's case since she rose at five-thirty to be at work by seven. She would leave on the table the ingredients for my breakfast which I would eat alone: a glass of sweetened grapefruit juice and a bowl for my Quaker Oats which I garnished with a slice of toast sunk in the middle. If there was extra condensed milk I would pour this over the top and sprinkle the whole with cinnamon. I made my own peanut-butter sandwiches and took them to school until the lunch programme became compulsory.

She was a terrible cook. And though I never complained I was happier when she was too tired to attempt anything more complicated than a cold baked-bean sandwich or a can of Habitant Pea Soup. Sometimes when her feet and ankles were swollen and she needed to lie down for an hour and say her rosary I would fix her favourite dish, fried cheese with black pepper. This I slid on to her plate straight from the pan.

'Delicious,' she would say with the look of satisfaction that she otherwise wore only after Holy Communion.

Once Daylight Saving Time began we could look out across the parking lot as we ate, usually in silence. The kitchen table stood next to the spotless rear window that framed a view of the backs of the big

stores on Central Avenue and the steeple of Holy Trinity. We felt safe
in its shadow. Unlike me, Aunt Bernie did not find it significant that
the front window was dominated by St Blaise's which had been raised
on the highest point in our otherwise flat town and whose two eastern
towers blocked out half our sky. To me it was a compelling structure,
and when I stood and looked at it for a long time I could almost imagine
myself in a European cathedral town.

But the French church, as we called it, was a place from which I
was as rigidly excluded as from the First Baptist. The Gospel and the
sermon were read in French, the altar was monstrous with brass, the
height of the ceilings dizzying. These pretensions were regarded by the
Irish as a confirmation of proverbial Kanuck vulgarity.

St Blaise was a real, if obscure, saint and not an abstraction like Holy
Trinity. He was the patron of wool combers and this connection to cloth
made him an appropriate guardian for a textile town. I read a story about
how his gentle nature, like St Francis of Assisi's, won him the trust and
companionship of wild animals and birds. Even at Holy Trinity we
celebrated his feast day with the blessing of the throats. Father Leahy
would hold two crossed candles tied with a red ribbon against our neck
and invoke the saint's protection against disease. (But I still had swollen
glands every spring.) I loved this sweet patron and his foreign tongue,
but I never spoke of my love and was loyal to Holy Trinity because it
was the Irish church to which my aunt gave 10 per cent of her yearly
income, and because she was devoted to Father Leahy and the Sisters
of Mercy who always said that she should have been a nun.

St Blaise's was our east, our sunrise and breakfast, I told Aunt Bernie,
and Holy Trinity was our west, our supper and sunset.

'St Blaise's isn't *ours*,' she corrected me and went on gobbling her
fried cheese.

Outside, the laundry we were always doing flapped in the breeze.
There were no pot plants on the landing or the stairs. Hardly anyone
had pot plants back in what you liked to call the Flat Decade.

'Do you think Holy Trinity is beautiful?' I asked.

'Very pretty, Honey.'

'But not St Blaise's?'

'Well . . .' She studied the gleaming linoleum.

'God is there, just like Holy Trinity.'

'Of course He is,' she snapped. 'Never said He wasn't. Do you
have any French friends?' She looked at me sharply. The evening
light reflected off her horn-rimmed glasses.

'Not any,' I replied honestly.

'Because there's no one like your own people.'

I knew my cue. 'Tell me about the card games and about Maime Doyle and how she cheated.'

'Cheat? Maime never cheated!' Her indignation relaxed and she smiled, exposing her large yellow teeth. I was embarrassed by Aunt Bernie's teeth and guilty at my embarrassment. But her figure was good and her hair thick and manageable, unlike mine.

'Every Wednesday we'd play at a different house. Sometimes me and your Aunt Bea would make sandwiches and a devil's-food cake and have all the girls over if your dad was out at a meeting. Or sometimes we'd go to your second cousin Marie's. One of us always got something up, you know. Maime was the great whist player and she usually won, that's why we'd make up little jokes about her cheating and all. But don't ever say that, honey. I mean, don't repeat it to your dad or your cousin Mikey, will you? We wouldn't want to hurt Kathleen's feelings.'

Kathleen was Maime's daughter, and Maime had been dead for fifteen years.

'Oh, they were grand times,' she sighed. 'Grand people.'

After supper we'd wash the dishes in silence, the long hours until ten still before us. Homework, television, prayers.

Foxie would come and rub at my ankles. Aunt Bernie would jump and give a little cry if she came near her. I would sit at the kitchen table and hold my cat while I pretended to be engrossed in my arithmetic work-book. Her tortoiseshell colours, her smell, the feel of her fur, always set me dreaming. She was the medium through which I could be again in That Time.

3

The Spy

'A father can't raise a daughter.'

'Well, Bernie, I don't know.'

'Not alone, he can't. Only rich men with servants do something like that. Men in the movies.'

'We'd help him. Anyhow, we shouldn't be talking like this yet.'

'What do you mean, *yet?*'

I stood next to the door, being careful not to let my shadow fall across the bed where my aunts sat, thinking they were alone, not knowing I'd come home from school. I couldn't understand their talk, but I knew I'd better listen because it involved me. I also knew Aunt Bernie could bend Aunt Bea and that in the end Bea would stop resisting and agree with her.

No one would tell me about my mother. During her time in the hospital Aunt Lil had come to stay with us. My father was good-natured at first, saying every night at supper what a treat it was to have her there, how it was like eating in a restaurant, like a picnic, like a vacation. Then he grew quiet, confided to me that he hated her cooking and took every opportunity for Knights of Columbus or Democratic City Committee meetings – that is, when we weren't visiting my mother. She said, everyone said, that she would be well in no time, and when she came back from the hospital I believed her, even though she was thin and lay down on the couch every afternoon between two and four with no energy to iron, or pursue ants.

Aunt Lil went back to my grandmother's, and the three of us were private again, not having to make up conversation as though we were actors. I nearly forgot the anxiety I felt when Nora was away, and the stomach cramps with which I awoke every morning had stopped. I played with my dolls while my mother rested on the couch, parading them up and down before her as they married, graduated, attended balls, went on world tours. Cradling Foxie in my arms, I watched

31

what television programmes I was allowed. They were strictly rationed since I had become hysterical over a science fiction film the previous Christmas. I could not bear to hear anything about the future.

On the Fourth of July the temperature was 102 degrees. After our supper of corn on the cob, tomatoes and cucumber with mayonnaise, and bread and butter, we sat on the porch and waited for a breeze. Mosquitoes clamouring for our blood battered the screens, and moths fluttered over the standard lamp. Out by the trees fireflies appeared. A baseball game broadcast from Boston could be heard from a house down the road. I wondered why my father, who was a Red Sox fan, wasn't listening. It was a holiday and there were no meetings. He could have spent the evening with a six-pack and half a gallon of ice-cream. But he sat with the *Boston Globe* unopened beside him, my mother's feet in his lap as he gently rocked the glider.

I asked if I could open the screen door for two of the cats who sat composed and waiting on the worn wooden steps, but as usual only Foxie was admitted to our company. Why wasn't Vinnie telling stories? I suddenly saw how big he'd grown in contrast to my mother's thinness. Beneath his second chin was an incipient third, at least in the slanted ray of the lamp. There was no trace of a beard, though it was past eight o'clock. The curve of his sweet mouth was enclosed by the parenthesis of two lines drawn deep in his flesh. His forearms were almost bare of hair. He was a man, strong, my father, yet disconcertingly like a woman. How clean you are, I thought, how big and round and clean. There is so much of you to love. Under my mother's nylon dressing gown her shoulders and elbows protruded, delicate as fishbones.

'Vinnie,' she said, 'I think I'm going to have to go to the hospital.'

She was still alive when I went back to school on the 6th of September. She would say she was getting better and ask me to rub her feet.

'You have a gentle touch, Frannie.'

I felt I must love her fast before she slipped away entirely.

One afternoon I opened the door to her darkened room and found Aunt Bernie and Aunt Bea and Aunt Bernie's friends Julia and Katie seated on stiff little chairs saying their rosaries. They looked at me but did not interrupt their mumbled prayers. Nora opened her eyes.

'Why are you praying?' she asked. 'Why are they praying like that? I'm not going to die. I'm not dying, am I?'

I hated my aunts and their friends. I wanted to call the police and have them put in jail for frightening my mother.

'They mean well,' my father said. 'They're good women.'

No one would tell me anything. Vinnie and I were in the same house, in our same beds, at the same dinner table, but he never discussed my mother's illness. Her sisters complained that the hospital was terrible and that Nora should be sent to Boston. But no one would tell me anything. I did not speak the words, I did not ask with my voice, but with my eyes, my hands, my whole body. They did not see or feel my question. Aunt Bernie said it was time to talk about heaven.

The next afternoon I stood and listened to her and Bea outside the bedroom door. And from then on I listened whenever I could, trying to find out what they meant, what they intended for me, what they really wanted.

And then Nora died and I knew that I was to be exiled to the Interior.

I had been to other wakes and seen other corpses. The coldness of my mother's forehead when I kissed it was not a surprise to me. My father picked me up and held me by the waist while I leaned over her. That was the end for me and for my friend Nora. There was no one left in the world to whistle like she did or to say 'Oh, dear me suds'. So many people were kneeling beside the shiny grey metal cabinet in which she was going to be locked away for good, so many packed into the undertaker's parlour that there was no time or space for us to be together ever again.

I was passed from one warm lap to another, embraced by arms both familiar and strange. I felt myself held by the crowd, as though I were melting into them, for once not expected to smile, even though it was not a solemn occasion. The women gossiped or talked about curtains and the men teased the women. My cousin Janie told me that some of my uncles were stepping outdoors to take their turns with a bottle of whisky. On the second evening when we had the most visitors I saw my father, standing next to the coffin with his best friend Russ, throw back his head and laugh as though he were watching Jackie Gleason. I wondered what had made him laugh like that, but I didn't ask him.

On the last day, just before we went to the funeral home for the church, all visitors were asked to leave so that the family could say their final farewells. After kissing Nora goodbye I waited by the door for everyone else to finish. In the crush of all those Noonans, Aunt Bernie was given the opportunity to entwine a crystal rosary around Nora's crossed hands. She knew she had to do it quickly, because it was something of which my father would definitely not approve. But his quick eye caught her and, without comment, he reached past her and removed the beads, pocketing them to return to her later along with a curt lecture. He may have been faster, but she was more determined. She made as if to leave with the others. Vinnie picked me up and carried me through the door. As he did so I saw my aunt hurry back to the coffin. Just as the undertaker was about to close the lid, she stepped right in front of him and wound her own pair of beads around my mother's hands. I did not see the lid close, but I knew she had won, and this was a very bad omen.

It wasn't until after the funeral that Vinnie cried. I had never seen him cry, and his sudden bare emotion frightened me as much as Nora's disappearance into death. He sat on the porch without a jacket in the chill evening while I watched from the kitchen, just able to see him in the dull light. He was perfectly still, his hands resting on his thighs as the tears ran in rivers over his large smooth cheeks and he gulped his silent sobs. Here was another person beneath the one I knew as my father; a presence I had suspected because he was sentimental, but had never seen without the protective clothing of his good humour. Where is my father? I thought. Where is Vinnie? He has to stop this crying and come back and love me. It was as if he'd gone away where I couldn't follow. I went down to the cellar to be with Foxie and the eleven cats. She'd had another litter of five and was absorbed in feeding them from the bottomless source of herself. Some of her children had stayed at home while others wandered off or appeared only sometimes for meals. She did not seem to miss them and was interested exclusively in the new ones, driving away ex-husbands and delinquent sons when they came too near. But she was always glad to see me, and I imagined she smiled as she butted her cold nose into my outstretched hand. I felt closer to Foxie than to my own father who had gone away into his grief. Her gaze was my gaze, and we saw the same world in the same way. We were so easily pleased and frightened and aroused. We were wary of whatever came up too close.

'Foxie,' I said to her, 'you're my mummy.'

She said she was quite prepared to take on another child. One more wouldn't make that much difference.

I missed Nora. No one else had so many special times for doing things. Only an event as important as death could have made her switch her ironing day from Tuesday. I wasn't sure whether she was watching over me, as Aunt Bernie insisted. I tended to put more faith in my guardian angel who was immortal and had never been alive and therefore could not be lost. And because he was invisible there was no memory of his presence to burn my heart away. Angels and animals, friends of children. I kept close to them during the months that followed while the secret debate was waged in voices never loud enough for me to hear unless I was presumed to be absent. Unless I spied.

He would have kept me if he could. I knew this from the telephone conversations with his sisters which I could hear late at night when I was supposed to be asleep.

'What makes you so sure what Norrie wanted? . . . Oh, I don't know yet . . . I'll get someone, I guess . . . What about that woman who took care of Olive Minnehan's kids . . . You know who I mean . . . Yes, you do . . . Well, I could get her, I guess . . . No, I haven't been to confession.'

I had never heard him bend to Aunt Bernie. It must have been because he had stopped going to Mass and now she had this power over him. Aunt Bea was also involved in the secret debate. One Saturday she and Uncle Eugene, who had the night off, drove over from Florence. I liked Aunt Bea. She was rosy as Vinnie and had a double chin like his. Her hair, like her mother's, was prematurely white and always beautifully dressed. She kept a vegetable garden which produced the best Swiss chard in the world. I was happy to see her, though disappointed they had not brought my cousin Bobby who played with me provided no other boys were around.

They often appeared without telephoning, but this time was different because I was sent out of the room. I crept down to the cellar and stood underneath the hot-air grate above the furnace. They were sitting at the kitchen table, and I could hear every word they said.

'How's the Yard, Vinnie? They workin' you hard?'

'Not bad, not bad.'

'Hear you'll be starting that new sub. How long you be building that, you think?'

'Five years, probably. Waste of thirty million. Oh, thanks, Bea.'

I was so close I could hear the rattling of cups and saucers as Aunt Bea came at him with the coffee. Her hands shook continually from drinking so much of it – and dead black, as Vinnie said. It was nerve-wracking to be served anything hot or spillable by her, and we all tensed instinctively at her hospitable approach. How she operated her machine at the Mill no one knew.

'You should be glad, Vinnie,' she said. 'God knows, we're all glad for you. They been layin' 'em off over at Clarostat.'

'Bea's right. That's five years of job for you, Vin, five years of pay-cheques for you and Frances.'

'You wouldn't make anywheres near that much at the Mill. In the end you was right to leave.'

'I wouldn't be making war machines either. I know what they're putting in this sub and so do you. It's damned dangerous.'

'Well, Vinnie, that ain't proved.' Uncle Eugene slurped his coffee.

They proceeded to have the argument which Vinnie always won, first by out-facting then by out-shouting them. Vinnie was not above a little table-thumping when he'd decided it was time to make his point once and for all and bring the current instalment to a close. They did this as part of a ritual which led inch by inch to the real business. There was more coffee, more rattling crockery.

'Well, you're entitled to your opinions, Vinnie, it's a free country.'

'You think so?'

'But if I was you I'd keep 'em to myself.'

'They know my opinions.'

'That's what I'm afraid of,' said Aunt Bea.

'You all believe whatever junk you're told. Why don't you ever read anything besides the *Florence Clarion*? You might learn some unpleasant truths.'

'Maybe so,' said Uncle Eugene. 'But it's jobs that count in the end.'

'And wars make jobs, huh?'

'I don't like that no more'n you.'

'I wonder why God made it this way,' Aunt Bea sighed.

'God's got nothing to do with it. It's men who're responsible. Men who see Reds under beds. And priests who twist people's minds.'

'Better not bring up religion, Vinnie.'

'Why? Bernie's not here. I suppose she sent you to find out if my wife's death has brought me back to the Church – if I'm finally good and scared.'

I knew just what they were thinking: 'Why does Vinnie have to go so far?'

'She only worries. She prays.'

'The hell . . . aw, I know she prays. Why, I don't understand. I'm all right.'

'Oh, we know that, Vinnie. Only there's Frances too . . .'

The real business.

I heard my father go to the refrigerator and open the door. I heard the scrape of the bottle on the metal rack, the drawer squeaking, the clatter of kitchen utensils, the snap of a metal cap, the hiss and foam of beer. They began to talk about me and I listened, perfectly still, taking shallow breaths. Foxie was out hunting. I could not go up to my room and get a doll without their hearing me. There was no one to hold, no arms in which to shelter. Then Vinnie summoned them into the den and out of earshot, so I was denied their conclusions, if they reached any.

More discussions followed, on the telephone and face to face, and, though I could not spy on them all, I heard enough to know for certain that I was in jeopardy, a word I had just learned. At first I prayed to the Virgin, Oh, please, Holy Mother, don't let them take me from here. Then it was: If I am taken from here please let me go with Aunt Bea and Uncle Eugene and Bobby. I believed for a while that this might happen, and I wouldn't let myself imagine the building on Birch Street with its dark hallway that smelled of the black rubber matting that covered the stairs, a smell that made me sick to my stomach. After all, it was not unusual for children in Irish families to spend long periods of time with relatives or friends. My Grandmother Noonan, with a family of seven, always had two or three of her sons' friends living with her and nobody thought anything of it. Perhaps it was going to be like that, and then one day I would just come back to Black Water Road. The Noonans were out, though. Too many children, every one of them, and the Mullens had so few. And then maybe there *was* something wrong with a father bringing up a daughter. No one we knew had ever done it. Bernie was right there. The custom was to shift the girl, setting Daddy free.

For a while Vinnie was stubborn and strong. For six months the woman who had taken care of Olive Minnehan's kids made our supper every night and cleaned the house once a week. But it was not enough. Vinnie was a disorderly person who'd always had women to clean up after him. He still photographed things nobody else wanted to look at and bought jazz records and listened to them late into the night even though he had to be up at six. When he danced with me, which he did less frequently now, I still watched the picture of Roosevelt whirl round and round, but I noticed too that the curls over Vinnie's forehead had begun to thin and that two Vs were making progress into the soft forest of his hair. His skull was being unveiled, pink and round above his creaseless forehead. His belly protruded. I rested on its tender bumpity-bump as we swayed and glided. He sweated easily, and the moisture smelled of pear and ammonia. After his meetings he would open three or four bottles of beer and watch the late news. If I were up I would bring him a plate of raspberry ripple ice-cream, pleading with my eyes: Don't send me to Florence. I heard Aunt Bernie tell Aunt Bea that he was drinking too much and that she would make a Novena to stop him.

Olive Minnehan's woman left and for three nights I heated up cans
of cream of mushroom soup and put more than half a loaf of bread in
the toaster. Vinnie's spirits were low. Years later I speculated about the
trouble he must have been in, about the Hatch Act which prevented
government employees from being actively involved in politics. Perhaps
he was afraid of being investigated. His views were not popular. You
were surprised when I told you that my father had not fought in a World
War, even though he had been too young for the First and too old for the
Second. 'If either had gone on for six months longer . . .' you said. You
didn't understand that he was a child of glory who just had so much
luck. And then of course he hated uniforms. He refused to take the
highest degree in the Knights of Columbus because formal dress was
obligatory. He said every uniform made him think of jackboots, even
the mailman's.

Christmas was always at Aunt Bea's. There were no lengths to which
she and Aunt Bernie would not go to feed and entertain us all. How,
I'm not sure, because they had very little money in those days. But there
were presents for everyone which must have stretched their Christmas
Clubs to the limits. (They began putting aside $5 a week on the 2nd of
January.) After the football game – during which the women washed the
dishes – and the demolishing of presents and stuffed dates, my father
rose from the heaps of crumpled wrapping paper and, swaying and
turning to some tune which played only in his own brain, decked his
head and shoulders with the pine wreaths on the mantel and door. The
children shrieked their delight as he picked them up and whirled them
around. They tore at his greenery and its big red ribbons. Pine cones
painted gold and silver were hurled among the presents, tree ornaments
were smashed, paper flew into the air like a popcorn machine. Then,
dizzy and drunk, he collapsed on the sofa. The children, greedy for
more, tried to rouse him as he lay there, crowned and festooned like
an Arctic Bacchus, his shirt unbuttoned over his bulging tummy, his
cherubic lips parted in a contented snore. Aunt Bernie and Aunt Bea
watched the scene with resigned disapproval. Even I threw papers into
the air and screamed and pushed and was pushed in return, despite my
aunts standing in the parlour doorway. Because that was a time when
I still had fits of joy, before life acquired a purpose; when I was still a
part of everything, whether it comforted or terrified me, before I was
exiled to the Interior.

The secret debate gathered new force from the Christmas incident.
Naturally no criticism was directed against Vinnie's behaviour, but

it was stressed once more that a father was ill-equipped to raise a daughter by himself. Especially once she'd reached adolescence. It was not natural, not healthy, not good, perhaps not even legal. And what if Vinnie married again? Vinnie had better have a rest anyway, at least for a while, just for Frannie's summer vacation. (And what would Frannie do alone in dismal Florence with no Black Pond, no wood next door, no cats, no bluettes in the grass, no Sunday convoys to Old Orchard Beach?) And what if he married a Protestant, that *would* be out of the question, or even an atheist, though no one had ever heard of a female atheist. And who's going to look after Frannie's religious education? He isn't exactly a sterling example in that department. And then his job. The bosses won't be nice for ever, if he doesn't give up these meetings and his complaining and his talking about those Rosenbergs at a time in America when nobody wants to hear things like that, and even if they're true (Vinnie *is* an ethical man) they are better not spoken about, Kittery just isn't the kind of place for that, but who can tell Vinnie Mullen anything, whether it's about his drinking or about his immortal soul? All you can do is ask in despair, Why why why does he have to go so far? Think what it'll cost him, it's bound to in the end, and the Yard bosses and the priests fit to be tied, and if he loses his job he can't raise that girl anyway and that's that, though we hope and pray it don't come to that.

'Don't bend, Daddy, oh, don't bend,' I prayed. 'Maybe to Aunt Bea, just to Aunt Bea for the summer and then back to Black Water Road for school in September. It won't be so bad. But bad enough. Bend a little if you have to, if they make you, but don't bend so much.'

He was out in the back yard, taking advantage of a fine Saturday morning to photograph the collapsed shed. He was escaping into his aperture, into shadows and shapes and rotting boards, yet he was also, I sensed, deciding. Since Christmas he had been deciding all the time.

What instinct made me ransack my cupboard in search of the hated pink hat? I'd worn it only twice, to coincide with Aunt Bernie's visits, but I had not been allowed to throw it out. It was too small for me now, but was held in place by the black elastic that stretched under my chin. On the way downstairs I turned away from every mirror. The spectacle was for his eyes alone. I stood behind him, barefoot, still in my nightie.

'Take my picture, Daddy,' I said.

The last time I visited Florence I saw that photo in the family album which Bobby inherited from Aunt Bea. I assume he has it still but I will never look again at the bitter memento of my first failed theatrical

gesture. It was shortly after I posed in the pink hat that I was sent away
to Aunt Bernie.

'Just for a while,' they soothed.

I behaved according to my character and complied. I was the sort of
child who, if she has a pain, does not tell her parents about it for fear
of punishment. Even though her parents are kind. So when I cried I
cried alone, because all my feelings were deaf mutes.

I asked about the cats.

'They'll be fine,' Vinnie assured me. 'They'll be right here.'

I was stubborn on only one point. 'I have to have Foxie,' I said.

'The landlady don't like cats in the building, honey,' Aunt Bernie
replied, as I knew she would. I also knew what was coming next because
I had heard it so many times before.

'You know, Sadie Delahandy was walking down South Street back
in 1941 and she saw this great big cat, and it was miaowing and playing
up to her, you know, like they do, and she stooped down to make a fuss
over it – Sadie was wild about cats – and it just suddenly *jumped* at her'
(here she always enacted the leap with her hands) 'and dug its claws
right into her neck and just hung there. Well, she nearly went crazy.'
Naturally Sadie still bore the scars from this encounter and naturally
she now avoided all cats, becoming hysterical at the very sight of one.
But I didn't care about Sadie's scars.

'Foxie's coming,' I said.

So I took Foxie with me and carried her up those stairs with their
sickening smell of rubber, and put a cardboard box for her next to one
of the single beds in the guest-room, which was to be my room. Foxie
hated the apartment, I could tell, and longed for our nice musty cellar
and her teenaged children, but she was brave. She knew she had to take
care of me because the Virgin had entrusted me to her. She thrived on
being a protectress. Her tortoiseshell coat grew even shinier, and her
golden eyes searched mine, asking questions not answerable with mere
human language. But this asking was my only comfort, and something
inside me, unknown, must have answered her.

Aunt Bernie shuddered whenever she saw Foxie, and would never
stop shuddering until the day Foxie was gone for good.

When we visited my father on the Fourth of July, only four of Foxie's
children waited on the porch steps to be admitted.

'Where've they gone?' I asked.

'Oh, they've gone off. Cats do, especially males.'

'But why?'

'I guess they missed you – like me. I miss my sweetie – '

' – pie.'

'And honey – '

' – bunny.'

As he held me on his comfortable knee, I imagined the souls of Foxie's children circulating in the air, searching for Foxie and me.

Here I am, I told them. You will come back and follow me. You will transmigrate.

Sister Henrietta had been telling us in catechism that the ancient people, people before Christ, believed that souls could travel after death and take up residence in another being, sort of move into them, like changing houses. It was a doctrine that we as Catholics were forbidden to believe.

When I visited at Thanksgiving only two cats waited on the steps.

'Where are the others?' I asked.

'They've gone to the farm.'

'But why?'

'They're happier on the farm, honey.'

I did not ask which farm, I was so eager to take his word. I went down to the cellar and spoke to all those who were no longer present.

You will change into someone else, I told them. You can come back because you are animals and powerful, not like humans all tied to themselves.

And so I was sent away from the coast with its wet air which flowers love, its salt-water inlets and little beaches and the wide anarchy of the sea to the east, and I was exiled to the Interior where the wind is hard and mean and dry and the snow is bad snow that isn't pretty and has a dirty frozen crust that never melts until April when you see nothing but ground you cannot believe will ever rise again from the dead. And there I went to Holy Trinity School and met Aunt Bernie outside the Number Two Mill and walked the dull streets of Florence, followed by the invisible procession of my guardian angel and the souls of Foxie's children.

4

The Ladies' Guild

I liked to make faces in front of the mirror. No. Like is not the word. I hated it really, but felt compelled to do it, to pull my features day after day into the most horrible contortions. Perhaps it was a kind of penance, volunteering to confront myself at my worst, to be repelled until the muscles of my mouth and cheeks ached with sufficient punishment. I would lock myself in the bathroom and frighten myself with my own face. During the first two years I lived with Aunt Bernie I made a regular practice of it until Rose emerged from my dark half and I began to think of my future.

It was the Church that gave me the idea. It was Sister Rosalie and Father Leahy and the Bishop. We were to take a new name for our Confirmation, a name by which we would be recognized as a Soldier of Christ. The Holy Ghost would descend upon us and, with his fire, brand this name upon our souls.

I saw my chance for a new identity and seized it. I developed a new bathroom ritual. I was in training for the person I was soon to become.

'I am Rose,' I would say, and study my reflection, not distorted this time, but serious and composed. 'I see that I still have Frances's dark hair and blue eyes, Frances's dimples that will one day turn into two creases like those of her father Vinnie. Frances's freckles decorate my nose, and there is a brown spot on my lower lip that belonged to Frances. I am bony and tall for my age as Frances was, but I am gaining weight, getting a figure. Frances has not got her period yet, but Rose is about to.

'Frances has gone away. She has gone inside and closed a door behind her, and Rose has come forward into the light, summoned by Sister Rosalie and Aunt Bernie and Aunt Bea and even Frances's father. Rose is not stupid. She answers questions. She is getting straight As. She does not cry alone at night like a retarded thing. She knows how

42

to be friendly and how to look on the bright side. She smiles and others return her smile. She looks them in the eye and is not embarrassed. For I have covered the face of Frances with a new expression which I wear like a Communion veil. And I know now. I can read the relief in people's eyes and already I know that it will be better being Rose.'

I called Rose to come to my assistance and help me do what was required of me, to give me the right clothing to put on, a magic garment to cover my sorrow. No one likes a sad child.

I was convinced by my bright idea, and I felt sure it would not be difficult to persuade everyone to collude with me. After all, Aunt Bea was baptized Mary Helen, Vinnie was really Gabriel and Bobby was Eugene like his father. I had been named for my paternal grandmother Frances, who was always called Minnie. In my family, as in many I knew, a child was named after a revered personage, usually a saint or a close relative. This formal name was a mark of respect and a sign of protection. The name of your soul, by which you would be summoned on Judgement Day. But for real life, which is so informal, the child would soon acquire a happenstance name, one that grew out of and suited its personality. Therefore, no one should be too surprised or upset by my decision. Especially since it would sanctioned by the Church. Still, I must introduce them cautiously to Rose. While awaiting Confirmation I would prepare and feed her like a young animal, make her ready to take the stage where the afflicted Frances could only cower.

Life with Aunt Bernie was hard. The thought of becoming Rose helped me to bear it. Gradually I discovered other things that helped. I began to perform small private rites and build small private shrines. During dull Sunday afternoons I would look through the *Webster's* my father had given me for my birthday, searching for words that would soften and blunt the pain of Nora's death. 'Melanosis', 'egrimony', 'deflagration'. I cherished these words. They raised my feelings to an exalted level, placed them upon an altar like a statue or a silver candlestick. I told no one about these words, only said them over and over to myself like I would say a rosary. They were like sheets that wrapped and lapped me, in whose folds I could be consoled and forgiven.

I would become lost in definitions. Sometimes I would read again and again the meanings of words I knew perfectly well. Often I discovered new implications for them. For instance the word 'character' which originally meant 'mark'. When I made faces or practised being Rose before the mirror, I would study the brown mark on my lower lip, the one that was just like Vinnie's. Was this mark our character? It didn't seem to be enough, somehow. What was implied, I decided, was that the bigger the mark, or the more *marked* we are, the stronger our character. That seemed to be the meaning.

From the time I decided to become Rose, I saw how the unpromising could be turned into a good thing if you used your mind to push it towards a happier future. If you believed it was already on its way. It was possible to invent another life for a poor loser if only you imagined hard enough and kept on imagining, pushing yourself towards the splendour your mind had constructed. Until this discovery, I had been creeping along like a worm, unable to look into anyone's eyes, failing to hide my grief and failing to express it.

I waited only for my father's visits. He came every other weekend, and Aunt Bernie and I took the train to Kittery for the Fourth of July and Labour Day. It was Aunt Bea's for Thanksgiving and Christmas. He was always jolly and made me forget my homesickness. When he was near by I was able to play with other children. Then he would go off in the Ford or we would climb aboard the dusty train and a curtain would come down over my life. What was to me a brutal uprooting was to everyone else a logical conclusion. Besides, it was not to be for ever. At some point in the future I would be returned to Black Water Road and to Vinnie. It was what they all hinted at, and it was what I prayed for.

Meanwhile I lived alongside Aunt Bernie and, most of the time, I did what she wanted. I went with her to confession once a week and to Mass, First Fridays, Benediction on Sunday evenings, and the Stations of the Cross during Lent (when we also gave up little pleasures like Hostess Cup Cakes and ate no meat on Wednesdays and Fridays). For church Aunt Bernie wore a brown felt hat with a short veil and a pheasant feather that stood straight up like an accusing finger. Before leaving for Holy Trinity she would remove her muskrat coat from the fireproof metal cabinet in her bedroom and daub herself with Emeraude. She was mad for Emeraude. The bathroom reeked of it, and for years I associated the smell with reflections of my contorted face. For Christmas, with the money I'd saved, I always bought her a boxed set of toilet water and bath powder.

Mass was the single occasion when Aunt Bernie could really dress up. Holy Trinity was the centre of her social and spiritual life, and I had the feeling that no matter where she might be, her heart was always before its tabernacle. In the glow of the sanctuary lamp that burned eternally under red glass, she would clasp the gloved hands of her best friends Katie or Julia or Margaret while they talked earnestly in low voices.

'Pray for me, Bernadette,' they would whisper.

'Pray for me, Julia,' she would say.

They treated each other with great respect, aware, probably, of the mutual regrets and anxieties which were voiced only in prayer. Most of these friends were, like the Byrne sisters, single; some, like Katie O'Connell, were widows. All supported themselves, either in the Boott Mills or teaching first or second grades or in the lower echelons of the civil service. They had good skin, plain, pleasant faces and a tendency to stoutness. It was difficult to imagine that the exhortations to prayer indicated some secret or incipient illness. They were not Noras, suddenly vacating the premises. They were built to last.

All of them belonged to the Holy Trinity Ladies' Auxiliary, otherwise known as the Ladies' Guild. They were active in its service (Julia and Katie had been secretary and treasurer) and never missed the meetings which took place on the second Tuesday of each month. They organized turkey raffles at Thanksgiving and whist drives in the teeth of fierce competition from the Filles de Marie, and, once a year, a late-summer carnival that was held in the school playground. I could sense, even then, how their financial independence, though modest, the fact that they were 'working girls', separated them from the other members who had the comfort and hardship of children. They were a band apart, regarded with a mixture of pity and esteem.

They created their own social life. They visited at weekends and occasionally during the week when they would play gin rummy or go to a movie if it was a musical. Katie, who was Aunt Bea's boss at the Number Two Mill, owned a car and might drive them once or twice a year to Portland for shopping and lunch; or, if it was someone's birthday, to Elmer's Chicken in a Basket. I saw how they made frames for each other, using dates and meetings and modest outings to set themselves in different contexts. Each saw in the rest her own potential desolation and so came willingly to the others' assistance, using frugal hospitalities and little private jokes devoid of malice to defend themselves from encroaching loneliness. They never complained of their lot, perhaps because they were blameless and had just expectations of paradise.

Aunt Bernie took me with her to the Byrnes' big house on Elm Street where I played dominoes with the eldest sister Mary who kept house for the other two; or looked through their books or stared dreaming at their rose-tinted sepia print of Sir Galahad. I tried out the right-hand parts of their sheet music. They favoured a series called *Programme Novelties for*

Proficient Pianists that included lots of Edward McDowell and titles such as 'The Old Scissors Grinder', 'Danse Orientale' by Gabriel Grovlez and 'In a Russian Cathedral', the latter being quite beyond me, though I did make some progress with 'The Happy Farmer'. Sometimes we went for a ride in Katie's Chevrolet, and I would sit in the back seat, not speaking, while Katie and Bernie gossiped respectfully about priests and nuns. Then we would end up at the North Star for an ice-cream.

I liked being the only child among these women, to whom I became a kind of mascot. They took great interest in my progress at school, speaking to their beloved nuns on my behalf, saying rosaries that I might pass my exams, convincing Aunt Bernie that I should and would go to college. Whenever I faced some test of courage or skill they would always give me the same advice. 'Be yourself.' They tried out their emotions on me, and I supplied them with expectations they could not have for themselves. They imagined me in grade schools and local libraries, standard fantasies of a class who wished their children to go so far and no farther. The fact that they imagined me into such jobs also meant that they imagined me a spinster.

Their concern was often oppressive, but I found myself wanting to please them. I was Vinnie's girl and therefore special, and I felt a glimmer of the golden light in which Vinnie had always basked, and was grateful to them. I did not have the opportunity to express my gratitude until years later, when I suppose I failed to show it.

I had no friends except Foxie, and apart from Bobby and my other cousins, no real playmates. I lived in Aunt Bernie's shadow.

Our extended family was huge, and everyone was Cousin Something – Third Cousin Kathleen, Second Cousin Brendan. Fourth Cousin Mikey was a monthly caller, as regular in his rounds as second Tuesdays and First Fridays. He spoke quietly, an exception in Florence. You could tell he had spruced himself up for the visit because his frayed cuffs were very white and his shiny trousers were sharply creased. I told Aunt Bernie I thought his trace of brogue was nice, but she pressed her lips together and made no comment. Something was not quite right between them. Still, she was always polite.

'Hello, Mikey. How you doing?'

'Not too bad, Bernadette.' Hat in hand. 'Not too bad. You?'

'Oh, grand. Just grand. Like a cup a coffee?'

'Oh, thanks, yes. Thank you, Bernie. Awful nice of you. And Frances, little Frances.' He extended his hand to me. 'You all right? And your dad? Saw his name in the *Portsmouth Herald*. Used to live in Portsmouth when I was in the Navy. Grand place. Always read the *Herald*.'

The limp in his left leg had come from his time in the Navy. I knew this but we never talked about it.

He had small Irish features and dull eyes that must once have been a beautiful pale-blue, and his skin was like mottled pink paper. He was very kind. I could not understand Aunt Bernie's suppressed impatience until I overheard her exacting promises from him. (I was still obliged to spy for my information.) This was after three cups of coffee followed by the usual invitation to stay and have Saturday night beans and franks and brown bread with us.

'Six weeks this time, Bernie,' I heard him say.

'Well, that's good, Mikey. You got that job still?'

'Eyah, eyah. But being a dish-washer don't pay much.'

'I know that, Mikey.'

'And now Mrs Hennessey's tearing her shirt about the rent.'

'Mrs Hennessey's a good woman. She only wants what's due her, no more.'

'Well, that's so, Bernie, that's so. Only this month – ' He hesitated.

'If it's been six weeks, Mikey, how come you haven't saved enough to pay the rent?'

'It's my leg, Bernie. Dr Toussaint's awful expensive.'

Sceptical silence broken by the thud of the bean pot being placed in the exact centre of the table.

'Supper's ready, Frances. Now you tell me just what the doctor said about that leg.'

She had demolished his story by the time he had finished the lump of salt pork which was his due as guest. He backed off and made polite enquiries about my progress at Holy Trinity. His gentleness, so unlike what I was used to from men of his age, made me pity him so that I was shyer than usual and miserable by the end of the meal, thinking how I must be hurting his feelings. But I could gauge no response in his filmy eyes. His effort at temporary self-control made him sweetly impenetrable. Without elaborating further on his dish-washing, his leg, his rent or what I eventually guessed was his drinking, he left at eight-thirty, refusing an invitation to watch Lawrence Welk but accepting the $5 Bernie pressed discreetly into his hand just as he was closing the door. She never refused him. And she never made any references to his visits.

Mikey, Kathleen (the great Maime's daughter) and other cousins at various removes would arrive unannounced because we had no telephone and nobody wrote notes or letters unless there was a funeral. Bea, Eugene and Bobby came on Thursday nights and on Sundays when Bobby and I would play games on the back stairs. These games were hard to get going. At first Bobby and I wouldn't speak. I'd hide in the guest-room to dress and undress my dolls and stuffed animals while Foxie watched me, purring away. Then I'd hear Aunt Bea giving instructions to her son (her very late son; the Mullens tended to have their children on the brink of middle age). Then he would appear in the bedroom, reluctant at first. But gradually I'd forget he was a boy and he'd forget I was a girl and pretty soon we were being raucous and silly. Chase, hide, stumble, giggle. I enjoyed myself with Bobby; he'd even condescend to play with my dolls. We were only children in families where there ought to have been many. When he left I would be sad and wonder again why Aunt Bea hadn't taken me.

We used the Coutures' telephone. Phyllis and Clovis Couture (pronounced 'Ku-cha') lived in the apartment opposite ours at the end of the hall which was saved from complete darkness by a glass door which opened on to the front balcony. No one ever sat on the balcony. It was bare and immaculate, without chairs, and afforded a view of an identical chairless balcony opposite and the towers of St Blaise's beyond.

The light in London often reminded me of the light in the third-floor hallway at 32 Birch Street. Sometimes the whole city was like the landing between apartments E and F. I didn't like crossing that hallway.

But Aunt Bernie and Phyllis seemed unaffected by the atmosphere and knocked on each other's doors whenever they felt the need for a cup of coffee – which was often in Phyllis's case since she had no job, no children and quickly ran out of domestic chores in a three-room apartment already antisceptically clean.

She did, however, have a devotion to the Infant of Prague, for whom she designed and made ensembles of nylon and lace in red, orchid, gold and white, colour-coded according to holy days and feasts. She had dressed dozens of little plaster statues of the crowned child who came golden-haired and garbed only in his white plaster tunic. Half the Catholic homes of Florence must have arrayed their sacred dolls in one of Phyllis Couture's creations, purchased at church fairs or given as birthday presents. The clothes came spread flat in a semi-circle beautifully ironed and boxed with tissue paper lining. They resembled tiny pinafores which tied at the back of the Infant's tender neck with two holds left for his hands, one of which was raised in benediction while the other held a pale-blue globe with its gold cross on top. Aunt Bernie's Infant had robes for Lent, Advent, Easter, and two holy days of obligation as well as the classic red and white ones. He stood on her dresser, his back reflected in the mirror, a fitting companion for the picture of the Sacred Heart on the wall, the statue of St Teresa, my aunt's Confirmation Saint, and the little holy water font (an angel holding a basin) which she hung between the bed and the door so that she might bless herself whenever she crossed the threshold. Phyllis, whose nervous hands sought constant occupation, turned out her Infant's wardrobes like other matrons did pot holders and toilet-roll covers. His clothes were washed and ironed with as much care as Nora had 'done' Vinnie's shirts.

I think Phyllis's jittery temperament sought refuge from the constant presence of her sickly husband in Bernie's stoical and rather tart personality. It seemed to set her anxieties temporarily at rest. Even when I was nine years old and not adept at uncovering motives, I could sense how she liked the *boredom* of Aunt Bernie's company. And I admit that their exchanges of platitudes at the kitchen table provided a kind of comfortable monotonous background against which I leant while I did my homework or played with my dolls.

Every Sunday night we watched *The Ed Sullivan Show* with the Coutures. I would sit silent while they commented on the performers, drank cup after cup of coffee and passed round the Candy Cupboard. Sometimes I wished myself elsewhere, out of earshot of all their predictable judgements, but then I would be lulled by the darkness of the room and the flickering screen and the voices with their flat Maine accents, and dread returning to five days of Sister Mildred's fusty classroom with its chalkdust that clogged my sinuses and the unpredictable, incomprehensible behaviour of thirty-one other children.

Downstairs, on the ground-floor back, was Irene Chabot. For reasons of her own she was devoted to the Ladies' Guild and Holy Trinity and contemptuous of the 'biddies' of St Blaise's. She preferred the Irish, she said. I loved Irene, though her deafness caused her to shout in an accent that made me wince. She was rosy and clean and plump like a pastry cook, and her hair was perpetually in pincurls. She was the only person I had ever met besides my Aunt Bea who had green fingers. African violets, wandering-Jew and prayer plants crowded her small apartment, and I liked to visit her just after she'd watered them and their rich damp smell reminded me of Black Water Road with the sea only a mile away. Unlike everyone else in the building, she was not afraid of the landlady and would allow my illicit Foxie to come in and sit on my lap or gnaw at the bones Irene always saved for her. I was not required to speak much as she could barely hear me, but she would give me weak tea, which I was not otherwise allowed, and tollhouse cookies which I would eat while she extolled the career prowess of her son, a manager at General Electric, and bewail the continual antagonism of the daughter-in-law who she was convinced was mentally unstable and determined to undermine the mother–son relationship. This constant threat of breach would cause Irene to weep unashamedly.

She had been left a little money by her husband Arthur with whom she had run a bleach business from the garage of their house. Now her stash was nearly gone, and she earned a small living looking after bed-ridden French matrons who were too exasperating for any private nurse to endure for more than a week and who could well have afforded to pay her twice what they did. Invariably they would die, and invariably Irene would be forgotten in their wills. 'Not even an *ashtray*!' she would wail. She'd swear never again to indenture herself to such monsters of ingratitude, but word of mouth was a powerful force in Florence, and after two or three months she would be summoned to another dim room, another linened and laced bedside, another tyrannical *memère*. She was worn out, she said, with the disappointment of it all. But despite her disillusionment and her anxiety over her son and the punishing diets to which she subjected herself, she could not lose weight. About this she lamented even more than the *memères*, and I knew, even in my ten-year-old ignorance, that her life was hard indeed. 'Poor Irene,' I would say, and Aunt Bernie would nod in agreement. *Memères*, she concurred, were a callous, avaricious lot.

Irene was to me the most vital of all the Birch Street residents. She was in there with life, inside it – fat, solitude, anxieties and all. Which was why she could make plants grow and why she was never afraid to admit Foxie to her kitchen, while Aunt Bernie hadn't a single plant in the apartment and grumbled about Foxie and shuddered whenever she came near.

'Hi, de-yah,' Irene would say to me, and 'Min, min, min, *tsi*-min,' to Foxie.

Every Christmas Irene presented Aunt Bernie with a pork pie. Aunt Bernie would say her thank yous, give Irene a cup of tea (she could not drink coffee) and present her with a small gift, usually Avon talcum powder, and they would part with a quick embrace. But in spite of my pleading, the pork pie would stay untouched in the refrigerator until Epiphany when it would be pronounced unfit for consumption and put, heavily camouflaged, into the garbage can. Its Pyrex dish would then be returned with further expressions of gratitude.

Aunt Bernie, I thought, you crud.

Further down the street at 96 were Mr and Mrs Grady, old friends of our family, who were deteriorating steadily in the house in which they'd raised five children, all but one of whom had migrated to Bangor or Dedham. Only Lizzie remained at home, the sacrificial daughter. Mrs Grady had the most enormous breasts I had ever seen, and always wore a man's sleeveless undershirt beneath her huge flowered dresses that zipped up the front. Her white hair still bore traces of its original corn-yellow, and her eyes, encased in folds of flesh, were a cheerful blue. She was truly hospitable, and had never been known to refuse a favour or turn anyone from her door, tramps and Fuller Brush men included. At one time or another, she had taken in most of the children of Irish Florence. Everyone of Aunt Bernie's generation adored her.

Jim Grady, a tall man of renowned physique, had been the pride of the Florence police force. Lately, however, he had turned peculiar. A dilated pathos replaced the piercing expression of his eyes. He could not remember what year it was and talked as if Toddy were still at home and playing short stop for Florence High. He would address at length his friend Brendan McGrael who had died of tuberculosis in 1921. He asked me a hundred times who I was and where I lived, that is, if he noticed me at all, though I always said a wary hello to him. Then the singing began. Not so much a tune as a motif, a four-note descending scale with which he regaled the street several times a day like a lugubrious town crier. No one knew what prompted these outbursts, delivered in what once had been a resonant bass. They seemed to be a keening at loss and decay, an accusation of a cruel God and a proclamation of Jim Grady's sorrow.

I could hear him through my open window in summer and even on winter afternoons as he stood in the snow, and my body would grow tense and I would pray for him to stop and not sing again his unvarying lament. But it went on for years, chilling us all who pretended to ignore it, until one day just after I turned thirteen there was silence on Birch Street. Bernie and Irene and Phyllis and Clovis whispered together about what I guessed was his abduction and incarceration. 'Gone to Augusta,' as we put it, meaning the state hospital for the mentally ill. How had they captured him, big as he was; with what low trick had they lured him into the trap? Was he singing still, or had they given him something to make him stop? It was not the sort of thing you discussed with children, and I knew better than to ask.

So we had visitors and relatives and neighbours. There were people in our life, but I remained a child alone among all of them. I was still Frances who walked to school by herself and was the last to be chosen for team games, and walked home with her classmates if and when they permitted because they considered her stuck up. I was mascot of the Bernadette Mullen faction of the Ladies' Guild, audience to their stories of ancestors and domesticity, object of their cautious designs. I waited for my aunt outside the Number Two Mill. I went with her to the shops, watching the people as she counted the change the assistant had given her. I was kept awake by her snoring. I listened to her singing as she prepared the Sunday lunch. When she didn't know the words she'd fill in the gaps with a refrain which went: 'Dye-de-dye-de-dye,' and so on. But mostly she sang the jingles she'd memorized from TV commercials. This made me nearly as crazy as the snoring.

My room continued to be called the guest-room, but I had made it my own with a few dolls and books and a shrine to the Virgin Mary beneath which Foxie slept. The plaster of Paris statue was like thousands of others. Mary was about three feet high and wore a blue mantle. She stood upon the golden-starred dome of heaven, crushing the serpent beneath her naked feet. I had placed her on a triangular shelf in the corner and made her a cardboard canopy to which I attached twisted streamers of blue-and-white crêpe paper. I surrounded her with my collection of holy cards, most of which had been given me by the nuns for the good marks I now was getting at school. Aunt Bea also sent me one every Christmas and birthday wrapped in a five-dollar bill. I kept a small vase of flowers before the Holy Mother – artificial, of course, since there was only one florist in Florence and he specialized in funerals and was so busy with them that he never had much besides wreaths. (People didn't put cut flowers in their parlours or on their tables unless they had a patch of zinnias out back. They filled Woolworth cut glass bowls with peanuts and M&M's, but bouquets were unheard of.)

The Virgin and the saints were real characters in my life, and they inhabited the atmosphere around me like the souls of Foxie's children. I prayed for all those souls and for Nora and Vinnie and Aunt Bea and even for Aunt Bernie, especially for her because my sense of obligation was strong. I sometimes felt almost sorry for her and for the way I had been given to her as a kind of booby prize. I prayed for Foxie and I prayed that Russia might be converted, as I had been instructed to do at school. I prayed to pass my weekly exams and to one day meet someone who would truly love me.

With Mary and Foxie I felt safe. When I closed the french windows between my room and the parlour every night and drew the thin nylon drapes and settled down in the dark – not to sleep but to read Nancy Drew by flashlight – I felt as close to pleasure as I could remember since

That Time. The street outside was quiet because the nearest bar was several blocks away and the neighbours went to bed early. I thought a lot about that bar and what went on there. It prompted fantasies about a looser kind of existence.

Except for the muffled racket of Aunt Bernie's snoring, I was undisturbed, close to all that was real to me. I would try to stretch out these nights, making them last and last until I could no longer keep my eyes open, so that when my alarm went off at seven I was bleary-eyed and queasy with insufficient sleep and wandered to school in a haze, always late for days that were always the same.

Two years passed this way. I did not give up hope that I would be returned to Vinnie who, miraculously assisted by my prayers to the Blessed Mother, would be able to take care of me in the way I was sure he really wanted to. He had stopped coming every other weekend and was not always in on the nights I called from Phyllis's apartment. He said he had a lot of meetings and I believed him. Aunt Bernie urged me to pray harder for my father. He now weighed two hundred pounds and I could understand why, because when he did come over it was with a six-pack and a bottle of Jim Beam. Aunt Bernie's mouth would not relax for a minute, but she didn't say anything about the liquor. She still could not bring herself to criticize her brother to his face.

The three of us would drive out to the cemetery where my grandparents were buried. Under the burnt grass a space was reserved for Bernie.

'And for Frances too,' said my aunt, as though it were a foregone conclusion. I felt as though I could never escape the dark chamber that had been prepared for me, that it would pull me back to itself no matter how far from it I might stray. The thought of it cramped my chest and made breathing difficult. Clearly Aunt Bernie conceived of no future for me other than one like her own.

As there was nothing interesting or beautiful in the immediate vicinity, our drives would be short and we would return all too soon to Birch Street. Vinnie always brought his electric razor and would shave the hairs on the back of Aunt Bernie's neck. He had done this for her ever since I could remember. She thought it looked 'neater' like that, but the hair would grow out bristly above the pale collar of her blouse, making me want to look away.

While she was cooking, Vinnie and I would go outside to the street or the parking lot, and he would take photographs of electric wires and television aerials and billboards. Sometimes he would take a picture of me. Once he surprised me by asking Aunt Bernie to photograph the two of us. The picture is gone now, lost along with all the others, but I remember it well: we are standing by the front steps, me in blue-and-white polka-dot shorts with straps that cross at the back and button in the front, Vinnie in wrinkled khaki trousers and a plaid shirt beneath which his stomach strains. With his big smooth forehead and receding curls, his *putti* lips and dimples not quite lost in the two creases on either side of his mouth, he looks like a giant baby and I his diminutive mother. It is a sad picture. Something was going on with Vinnie, something he would not talk about. I thought it might have to do with the meetings and the pass he had to show at the Navy Yard gates. But it was more than that, something we never suspected, not even Aunt Bernie. It was Denise Dubois. Pronounced 'Dew-boys'.

How long they had been 'going out' together we never discovered. But it must have started after I was exiled to the Interior.

'Which means Nora was less than a year dead,' said Aunt Bernie. And that he'd been hanging around Florence without telling us.

I would not answer. I would not criticize my father. He loved Nora, I was certain, but he could not live without women. Coddled by his mother and sisters, he had passed into Nora's consecrated care without an interval. He had never confronted unwashed sheets or an empty icebox. He would not teach himself to cook. So he had deteriorated, and I blamed my aunts for taking me away from him. If I had stayed he would be golden Vinnie still instead of a gross child looking for someone to mop up after him. He was marrying Denise because he needed care and feeding and I was not there to provide them.

He did not tell anyone, even me, that he intended to bring her to Aunt Bea's Labour Day. Everyone was nice to her because she was Vinnie's guest. Bernie and Bea were genuinely polite and kind in the homely way that always touched me. Only I was shy of her and stiffened at her attempt to kiss me, but she didn't seem to mind. She laughed loud and often and had the sort of confidence that comes from an unawareness of other people's reactions. A stupid impenetrability made her strong, and there seemed to me something lewd in her short stature, disproportionate breasts and large dark eyes. She was a compact five-foot-two machine, so unlike fine-boned Nora. She fitted comfortably under Vinnie's arm. I knew because I saw him draw her close to his big body as if this were the most ordinary thing in the world. And she was ten years younger than he.

They are like owner and pet, I thought, only I'm not sure which is which. They'd look terrible dancing to 'If I Didn't Care'.

I tried spying, but it was no use. Aunt Bernie and Aunt Bea did not exchange one word about Denise in my vicinity. Not until a month later did I overhear Bernie on the telephone during one of our Saturday-night visits with the Coutures.

'I don't know what makes you think he won't, Bea. You're a little soft in the head when it comes to your brother. He does what *he* likes, and what *she* is don't make no difference to him.'

What was she? She was French. One of a family of eight, a widow with a despotic *memère*, who hardly spoke English and shouted in a voice even louder than Irene's. I think my aunts would have been less pessimistic if Denise had been the daughter of an Orangeman. This was bad. This was the worst. They were openly criticizing Vinnie, and that could mean only one thing: he intended to marry Denise. His loneliness was that terrible. And it would seal my fate. I could not live with Vinnie now or ever. I could not be handed over to a dumb French girl with five rowdy brothers and a tyrannical mother, to pork pies and bad language. It was out of the question; it was not even open to discussion. It was a matter for rosaries and Masses and Novenas. If I had expressed my unhappiness I would have had the same response from Aunt Bernie as from Sister Mildred: 'Offer it up'. There was no point in expressing anything, so I offered it up, like a donation to a charity, not enquiring too closely how my gift would be disposed of.

I was eleven when Vinnie married Denise. The ceremony took place in St Blaise's on a March day when the ground was bare and frozen as a tundra. I sat next to Aunt Bernie grimly attired in her muskrat coat and pheasant-feather hat, enclosed in a cloud of Emeraude, as we listened to the priest address the newlyweds – in French. I stared at Denise's two bridesmaids, her sisters Peanut and Sue-Sue, dressed in yards of bright apricot organza, and at Madame Dubois whose gnarled fingers were crowded with rings and who wore an indecent amount of make-up and an excessive number of jangly bracelets. Her flashy style provoked a reluctant envy in me.

The occasion was worse than Nora's funeral, and not even dancing with my father at the reception could ease the anguish I was unable to show. I neither smiled nor cried. I behaved myself and prayed for my father to see the light.

An awful tension would grip me whenever I visited my father and Denise on Black Water Road, where she fed him all the fried clams and tartar sauce he wanted. To make conversation I asked him did he still go to the meetings.

'Not as many. Not any more,' he confessed as he pulled me on to his large solid thighs.

'How come?' I asked.

'Oh, they think your old man's a big-mouth,' he chuckled, pretending to be pleased with himself. 'Too outspoken in his opinions, too dangerous.' He opened his eyes wide and put his forehead next to mine so that I couldn't help laughing. But he was covering something up, I could tell.

'Aunt Bernie says you always go too far.' I wanted to be close to him so I tried to make us conspirators, which we were not.

He laughed. 'She thinks I'm going to get a telegram from old Joe McCarthy. She thinks I'm dangerous too. Because I have my own views and I express them. Because I've taken the trouble to find out what my rights are.'

'Mr McCarthy isn't going to bother you, is he?'

'Bother me? Fat chance, Frannie. In a way I almost wish he would.'

'Now I'm worried.'

'Then you'll just have to think of lots of good reasons not to be.'

'Sometimes praying makes me stop worrying.'

'Praying won't change anything, Honey. It's just a lot of priests' prattle. Like pledging allegiance to the flag. It's a way of hooking you. But don't you believe them.'

I was both shocked and excited when he talked this way, but his tone lacked something of the old bravado.

'Will you make another strike one day?' I was so glad to be close to him, to have him reveal himself even a little, that I simply wanted it to continue and didn't think too much about what I said as long as it kept to a subject he approved of.

'I never made a strike, Honey. I only watched and thought how terrific it all was, but then I was only a kid. Besides, you can't strike on the Navy.'

'I know that.'

He frowned. 'Then why ask me?' He pushed me gently off his lap and went to the icebox to get a beer.

Years later, you told me that my father was just a fantasizer; that he was soft, really, and selfish; that he had lost his direction. What he'd dreamed of achieving was beyond his brains and his will and he knew it, you said. But he liked to show off and to get everyone excited. He was limited by his background, a big frog in a small pond who had sabotaged his ideas and principles by working in the lucrative Navy Yard and marrying Denise. He had deliberately prevented himself from doing what he wanted to do. So he drank Black Label and Jim Beam and talked sedition to impress his friends and frighten his sisters. Maybe you were right, but I can't believe it was as neat as all that. I had come to see my father as a good but tragic person who had been transformed from star to burnt-out case, and that was not an easy fiction to surrender.

I asked Vinnie months in advance if he would be coming to my Confirmation. He seemed so slippery now that I was compelled to use every possible method to secure him, especially because I knew he had no interest in seeing me become a Soldier of Christ. He had acquired this talent for manoeuvring himself (while appearing not to do anything) into exactly the right position where it would be impossible for him to make a decision or even tell the truth. He always arranged for matters to be taken out of his hands.

For once Aunt Bernie was my ally, and brought the subject to his attention each Sunday evening during their telephone conversation. The Bishop came to Florence only once every three years, so Confirmation was a great occasion for Holy Trinity as well as for me, she insisted, though she must have known that the argument carried no weight with him. Still, she was always ready to make a stab at injecting guilt. People of all ages, she went on, would be confirmed together. I was officially entering adulthood, and I was his only child. The occasion was second only to reaching the Age of Reason and making my First Holy Communion. And all the time I thought: It's for me. Come for me. See me, look at me in my white gown and red beanie. I am becoming more, I am turning into someone else. You will hear the Bishop call me by my name, my new name which I have thought about for so long and been planning as a surprise for you and Aunt Bernie and Aunt Bea and Bobby and the Ladies' Guild. Come, please, Vinnie, and sanction my decision along with them and along with God.

He promised he would come, provided he didn't have a meeting, provided he was allowed to express his uncensored opinions of the proceedings, and provided all went well with Denise who was, to my horror, pregnant. That was it, I knew. That was his out. Not that I begrudged her the baby, only that he could now use it as an excuse, should he be feeling lazy or have had too much to drink the night before. Should he have a meeting.

Classes to prepare us for the Sacrament were held twice a week after school. This meant that I was late home on Tuesdays and Thursdays and therefore had the pleasure of eating supper alone with Foxie. She was old now, nearly fifteen, and sat panting on the floor beside me, searching my face when I looked down at her and questioning me with her golden eyes.

'What is it, Foxie, what? Magical Foxie. There is something you seem to want so badly and it is not my toasted cheese sandwich. Do you want to tell me or do you want me to tell you? But I can tell you nothing. You are the one who knows; you are my mother. You and the Blessed Virgin and my guardian angel keep watch over me in my separation.'

I lifted her in my arms and put her on my lap, though this was forbidden at the table, and the soft roar of her purr set my whole body vibrating. Magical Foxie. What did she make of my fierce love? A love not shared by Aunt Bernie, who had been critical lately of her little misdemeanours which, I had to admit, were growing more frequent. She predicted the landlady's retribution. I had encouraged Foxie to keep to our room by moving her box from the Virgin's shrine to the radiator, and she seemed content to spend most of the day reclining there while she meditated on her pantheon of children, one of whom was I.

I rushed to see her as soon as I came home from school, and stroked her and felt her nose which was still cold and wet. I was never more anxious to see her than after I had spent a rare weekend at Black Water Road. The worry was almost enough to extinguish the ambivalent pleasures of my father's company. In fact I was fearing for weeks the scene which met me one May evening after my return from Kittery.

'Don't call her,' said Aunt Bernie as I set down my suitcase. 'She's not here.'

I glanced at the balcony where the earth box had been, then ran to my room with a pounding in my ears. My hands shook as I turned over and over the pieces of sheeting and blanket on which Foxie had lain and which Aunt Bernie had washed and ironed and folded in a neat pile at the foot of my bed, so that I could find no trace of the precious fur.

'She was an old cat. You wouldn't want her to suffer.'

'She wasn't suffering.'

I sat down on the bed, and I thought Aunt Bernie would too, but she did not come near me.

'Why did she die?'

'God took her. He takes all his creatures back to Himself, honey. You know that.'

'No.' I could hardly hear my words above the buzzing in the room, or see Aunt Bernie for the glittering patterns before my eyes. 'Anyway, they can come back.'

'No, they can't. We have a soul and we can't even come back. Not till the Last Judgement.'

'They have souls. Animal comes from *anima* and *anima* means soul. I saw it in the dictionary, go look. It's in your Missal too.'

'It's only a word.'

'So is Bernadette.'

'Don't you sass me, Miss.'

'She was without sin. Even Father Leahy says they're without sin.'

'That's because they have no souls.'

Why was I engaging in this stupid argument with my stupid aunt?

'They do too have souls.'

'They do not.'

'Foxie does.'

'She does not.'

'So she's not gone?'

'Yes, she is, but you think that for now if it makes you feel better.'

Couldn't she even bring herself to say of course she lives on in your heart? She who spent her life with symbols could not manage the plainest metaphor. I wanted to kill my Aunt Bernie. I hoped she would die horribly. And I felt not the least bit guilty about it. In fact, if I'd had the will and the weapon I'd have done the job myself.

'What happened?' I asked.

'She just stopped breathing, honey. I found her this morning.'

'Where is she?'

'Phyllis and Clovis drove over to Clovis's mother's. She's got some land, and they'll bury her out there, don't you worry.'

'I want to see.'

'Well, maybe next time they go we can fix something up.'

That meant never. I clutched Foxie's blanket and curled up on the bed. I wished that I could be dead too, that we could all be dead. I blamed Aunt Bernie because she had wished Foxie gone, but then I thought: No. A devil has taken Foxie, that's all. But she will escape him somehow. I still told myself such stories.

For two days I would not go to school. Not even my aunt could make me. I wouldn't eat or dress or do anything inconsistent with my total mourning. I kept my vigil-light burning constantly before the Virgin, replacing the little candle as soon as the wick was drowned in its puddle of wax. I remember those days as a burrow into which I dug myself like a small animal, my nose pressed into the earth with no space even to turn around.

One night as I was washing the dishes I found Foxie's plate among them. I studied carefully what once had been touched by her teeth and tongue, looking for traces of her embedded in the hairline cracks. I spoke to Foxie inside myself. I sought her protection. I asked her for favours as I did Jesus and Mary and the Saints. If you feel alone you need someone to whom you can appeal. If no one exists they must be created. They can be created out of the dead and the lost who still live inside you; you can pray to them. They are the gods of your inner universe and their bright eyes shine in your galaxy's sky. How we love whoever is lost. The more completely they are lost, the more completely we love them, the sweeter becomes our love. It grows ripe in the luxuriant soil of grief.

Where to go to get away from Bernie, from myself? Into Rose. Way deep into Rose. Into a new story.

'It's in honour of my grandmother whose middle name was Rose,' I replied when Sister Rosalie asked us about our Confirmation names. 'And the Blessed Virgin because she is the rose without thorns.'

'All roses grew without thorns before the Fall of Man,' she explained. 'And there are other roses too: the red rose of Martyrdom, the white rose of Purity and the blue rose for the Impossible.'

'Like the colours of the American flag,' I offered and she seemed pleased with that.

'The rose is a symbol of the Beloved,' she concluded.

And who was the Beloved? Christ? The Virgin? Or simply that for which the soul cries? Sister Rosalie did not elaborate further.

I did not tell her that the real Rose was from all that long time ago. The real Rose was inside me. I was bringing her out under the guise of sainthood and religious imagery so that Frances could stay in her room, hide out in the dark and grieve undisturbed for Foxie and Nora and That Time.

Unlike Frances, Rose looked forward to her Confirmation, to the crowds of people, the hot church filled with flowers, the droning organ, the long ceremony. She wanted everyone watching as the Bishop anointed her with the chrism, placed his hands upon her head, pronounced her an adult and called her by her adult name for all to hear. After that, they too would call her by her adult name. She would insist on it. She had the right. She had the power. It would be easy to persuade them once the Bishop had made it official. It might take a while, a couple of years even, but they would do it. They would be pleased to do it because Rose could please them.

Vinnie was glad because I had begun to agree in secret with his opinions about religion. Perhaps it wasn't necessary, all that authority and rules and dead language, all that structure. I began to suspect the priests were lying, yet I could never be sure. Perhaps they were not qualified after all to tell us how to love God and the Saints in whom I still wanted to believe. My father viewed these doubts as progress, so he came to my Confirmation as an act of perverse approval. He came without Denise who rang early in the evening and made him leave the party at Aunt Bea's because she'd had a bad day, or maybe he'd told her to say that.

'You look good, Frances Rose,' he said, resting his hands on my shoulders. 'Let's have a smile.'

I obliged. His eyes glistened with easy tears.

'You're my sweetie – '

' – pie.'

'And honey – '

' – bunny.'

We laughed as I caught sight of our reflections in the living-room mirror.

Confirmation and a new name seemed to compound my religious doubts. I was no longer flirting with limited rebellion, and I was worried. So worried that I dared to broach the subject to Father Leahy.

'Father,' I whispered through the confessional screen, 'I'm having trouble believing in God. I think I don't love him enough. I – '

'That's just too bad,' was his immediate response. He sounded very angry. 'You know the First Commandment, young lady, so obey it. If you have trouble, pray. If you still have trouble, pray harder. Don't come running to me. I'm here to enforce the faith, not to persuade you to like it. Doubts are wicked. You have to drive them out. And you have no one to blame but yourself.'

'Yes, Father,' I answered and went off to say a stiff penance.

Now I see that the problem was not doubt but weariness and being fed up with guilt: the constant awareness that every little move you make could be the wrong one; becoming paralyzed by the fear of making those moves, always having to be watching yourself and the days and days of misery this entails. Feeling that you are unworthy to live, that you don't deserve the smallest pleasure or even the food on your plate, that you should rejoice in pain, in sadness, because you could 'offer them up'. I may have lost my faith simply because I couldn't bear the pressure and I wanted relief at any price. Maybe I was just weak and worn out. Rose did not think this was the way humanity was meant to live. She believed there was some hope for them and that they might not be cursed from the moment of their conception and had the right to expect some happiness in a world that was essentially beautiful. So she walked out on God and left Frances to do the penance.

Are you wondering where all this is leading, where it ends? I'll tell you. It ends with you.

5

Travis

I had one hour and twenty minutes to spend with Travis. All the way to Franklin Street I repeated his name to the rhythm of my footsteps: Travis, Travis, Travis. I did this all the time: at the North Star, at the college library, at night as I fell asleep in the guest-room.

Goldwater posters defaced some of the windows along the road. Northern Rednecks. How can they? I thought. What will he ever do for them but feed them into the war machine? Do they hate their children or what? But I was not too depressed. Johnson, a compromise devil, was sure to be elected. And I had Travis, Travis, Travis.

I took the stairs lightly, skipping over the broken slat which had gone unrepaired since Frank moved into the apartment two years ago. The smell of Mrs Mulvanity's lunch seeped from under the door. Travis had no telephone, but I knew he would be there, waiting for me. He was.

He chuckled in my ear as he hugged me. He never laughed out loud, but just about anything could make him chuckle. Often he seemed to do it for no reason at all. It was because he was from Carolina and therefore not dour and stiff like New Englanders. But sometimes it made me nervous.

'I've done a drawing for you, Rose,' he said, keeping his arm around me and guiding me towards the table that was covered with a printed oil-cloth and strewn with pads and inks and felt-tip pens and coloured pencils, the only art materials he could afford. The table stood in the larger of two rooms, the floor of which was covered with an edition of *The New York Times*, carefully tacked down and varnished. It still felt strange to be walking on newspaper, especially one with headlines a year old.

The drawing had been done in shocking-pink and bore the inscription 'Animal with Extrusion, for Rose'. I didn't know how to react to Travis's art. I'd never met anyone who could draw except Aunt Bernie. His accomplishment seemed to amuse him, as if he'd played a good joke on himself.

63

'Do you think they'd lock me up for this, Rosie? The university shrink said my drawings indicated narcissism and paranoia. Does this strike you as narcissism or paranoia or maybe both?'

The work was clever but combined mockery with eroticism in a way that some people might find perverse. I noticed Travis had also produced the sixth in a series of scatological pictures based on Caspar the Friendly Ghost. The caption for the most recent effort read 'I Am Dead'.

'I'm not bad, you know. I could have a show one day.'

I never knew whether I was supposed to take this seriously. The word 'show' thrilled me with intimations of a far-off glamour. The show was something we talked about as fruit to be gathered and eaten in our hazy future, like the trip to Greece, the banning of the bomb, my meeting his sister.

'Come on,' he smiled. 'I've made a potato salad. It's much better than the drawing.' In the here and now, and with limited resources, Travis was an excellent cook. I had never tasted anything as exotic as his black-eyed peas and pigs' knuckles. But Southern dishes were not his only speciality. He made salads, beautiful green salads unknown to me, with dressing that was his own invention and did not come out of a bottle. But potato salad was his staple since, as everyone knows, potatoes were once cheap and plentiful in Maine. These had been perfectly diced and piled high, glossy with Travis's mayonnaise, in an unworthy plastic bowl. I peered at the translucent slices of raw onion and the bright shreds of olive and pimento. Aunt Bernie would be certain to enquire about the smell of my breath, I thought, spearing a forkful of the delicious mess and eating it happily as I leaned against the scarred Formica counter.

'Let's sit on the bed,' said Travis. There was only one chair in the kitchen, so the bed, which sported an old American flag as a counterpane, was where we usually ate.

'Where'd you learn to make this, Travis?'

'A man in New York. He used to cook dinner for me once a week. He was a Southerner too. I met him at a bus stop. We'd go shopping together, then I'd watch him at the stove. He was very patient, and he liked to please.'

'It's so good – ' I gulped a mouthful – 'to be like that, I mean.'

'Yes, but it all became – ' he sighed – 'unbearable.'

It was a word Travis often used. I had never known anyone who did, and it made me anxious. Why were there so many things Travis could not bear, and why couldn't he bear them? They might be lurking anywhere, these unbearable things, appear at any time. He was so mysterious and, despite his build, so fragile. The first sensitive man I'd met.

'You stopped being friends?'

'Well, fall came and I went north to pick apples.'

And you met me, I thought, and smiled.

'It was a way of getting out. I felt badly, but I just couldn't call him again.'

'You disappeared out of his life? That's terrible.'

'Yes, it is terrible. I've done terrible things. Is it any wonder I'm tortured by guilt?'

'Oh, Travis.' I pressed his free hand. 'You can make up. You can always go and see him again. Why don't you? He'd be really glad, I'll bet.'

'Hmmm.' He squeezed my hand in return to show he appreciated my sympathy.

'You feel guilty because of your family.' This was a topic we discussed a lot. 'You're just including him in that guilt.'

'My mother . . .' Travis shook his head. 'My sister . . .' He looked away then back to me with a smile. 'I'm a vile wretch, Rosie.'

'Oh, Travis, no!'

As hard as I tried to encourage him to talk about his parents and siblings, I could never elicit more than dark hints, stories broken off with sighs or sobs, tragic scenes better not gone into – his father drinking a bottle of Clorox in the back seat of the car during a Sunday drive. How had that ended? Would I ever know? It was straight from Faulkner, as arcane and remote and literary. I loved Travis madly and I loved the literary doom that hung over him.

The radiators weren't working, and the apartment was cold and dark and smelt of rotting timber. Travis never opened the curtains (Franklin Street was unbearable) which were blood-red and splashed with huge white chrysanthemums and probably had not been laundered since they were hung ten years before. But hooks were missing and they did not quite meet in the middle, and so a patch of Florence light fell on to the floor, illuminating an ad for a Dionne Warwick concert.

I could just see the altar which had been constructed against the far wall and was the centre of this chaotic household. Every few days Travis and John would wreck it and make a new one out of the junk they'd gathered on the streets or at the Mills. They built altars from rocks and shells and comics, from beads, books, wrappers, cans and crackerjack prizes, any of which, they liked to pretend, might be the philosopher's stone. Their altars were made to be destroyed. They were homages to the transitory, the rejected, the despised, the unworthy; celebrations of everyone and everything that has no value. Travis and John loved to heap up urban detritus according to the non-rules of their peculiar aesthetic and their jokey mystical politics that were both animistic and anti-consumerist. Anyway, that was how they explained them to me. I found the matter mysterious, exciting. In the world I came from, everything had to be saved.

I was unused to domestic squalor and was only beginning to appreciate it. Today the apartment looked quite romantic, lit by the gas stove which was visible from where we lay on the bed. All four burners were blazing, not only warming the place but transforming it with an eerie blue light. We crawled into Travis's sleeping bag (the one he always took with him when he went apple picking) and made love in the cinematic glow. I was a novice still, and shy about my shortcomings, but Travis wasn't worried. He seemed to want to eat me alive in a way I could not comprehend and was only just starting to enjoy. My sexuality was retarded, but I could now imagine a future in which something more assertive and flamboyant would be added to the passivity he seemed to like so much.

I watched his face as he napped beside me, his hand still in my hair which I wore long despite complaints from Aunt Bernie who had always liked me best as a newly-shorn black sheep. I loved to look at Travis in repose, when he was not imagining himself a vile wretch. He was beautiful, at least I thought he was. Like my father Vinnie, he had an expanse of cheek where not very much happened and a small straight nose. His upper lip was not indented but followed a smooth curve that exactly matched that of the lower one. Porpoise-mouth, I called him, since the resulting expression could be construed as a constant enigmatic smile. He was very tall and his hair was thick and dirty-blond and fell over his eye. Travis was rare. Florence, probably all of Maine, held nothing like him. But the most remarkable thing about him, as far as I was concerned, was his resemblance to me.

'We could be related,' I said when I first knew him. And later, 'You could be my blond brother,' and he agreed with me. Now as I looked at him I thought: We could be twins.

Not everyone noticed, of course, not immediately. I was dark and he was fair, though my skin was pale. Our lower lips were similarly shaped, though I did not possess his distinctive upper. And he did not have my brown mark. I was and am a much more ordinary-looking person, but our cheekbones, our noses, the colour and expression of our eyes, the lines on either side of our mouths . . . Travis was what I had wanted all my life – someone so beautiful he would stop me dead, someone who'd 'send me', like Sam Cook says. I'd never had a teenage romance, but I was having it now.

'I'm going to fix *you* a cup of tea.' Travis was awake. 'And a plate of Oreos.'

He had this way of making every little event special, as it is when you are a child. Even going to the laundromat with Travis was a wonderful adventure.

I watched his long legs as he filled the kettle and felt reluctant to take up the rest of the day – Aunt Bernie, my English paper, the North Star. I sat naked in the sleeping bag as we talked and drank our tea. A year ago I would have been too shy to expose myself in this way, even in the flattering light of the gas burners. But now I was imagining myself through Travis's eyes, and what I saw was not too bad. Besides there was the silky logic of vanity which told me that if Travis could love me then I must indeed be lovable. And he paid the nicest, strangest compliments: 'You're my dream, Rosie, my fantasy.' I could not understand why and was in constant anxiety lest I betray the dream or the fantasy should end. 'I love your back. It's so expressive. I've never met anyone with such a sexy back. It's like Marilyn Monroe's.' Wow.

I finished the last Oreo. He insisted. 'You were sent to me, Travis,' I said.

'You think everything is providential. Why would I be sent to you?'

'To teach me not to despair.'

'A sin against the Holy Ghost.' Travis had been a Catholic too.

'I don't believe in the Holy Ghost.'

'Me neither.' We both glanced at the altar. There it was, gathering force, as Frank would say.

'Then who do you think wanted to teach you?'

'An Intelligence with a plan we can't understand.'

'To reward your virtue?'

'Oh no. It's got nothing to do with virtue. It's just that there are so many reasons, a million influences we can't understand, all mixed together, all swirling around. Impossible to disentangle. But someday, *someday* they'll be clear. Then we'll understand.'

He kissed me. 'I love you, Rosie. You're so precise. But why would this Intelligence want to send you a vile wretch?' He had this way of teasing himself through me. He was so complicated and I loved his complications.

He wanted to make love again, but it was four-thirty and time to go. He always understood when I had to leave like this.

'How is she today?' he asked as I dressed.

'Her knees were pretty swollen this morning. I left her on the couch with the game shows and the pills and her rosary, insisting she was going back to the Mill on Monday.'

We stood before the mirror that leaned against the wall. Travis held my raincoat for me, and when I slipped it on he lifted my hair from beneath the collar and arranged it over my shoulders. Where had he acquired such refinements?

'We're a handsome couple,' he smiled. No one, *no one* had ever called me handsome.

I hugged him hard. I wanted him to promise that he would stay in Florence and never leave until the day I could leave with him. Of course I didn't ask. As I went to the door, he caught my hand.

'Wait,' he said. 'I was going to do this with Frank, but – Do you think he'll mind if we start without him?'

'Oh no. Frank's very tolerant.'

'OK then. You go first.'

'No, you.'

Travis knelt down and with a flick of his hand toppled the carefully arranged junk, rescuing first the copy of *Molloy* and a gold plastic Buddha, the altar's only constants. He motioned to me. 'Now you.'

With the tip of my toe, I lifted the plasterboard platform and tipped the household gods all over *The New York Times*. We applauded politely.

'Leave it for Frank, won't you,' I said. 'He'll want to analyze the way everything fell.'

'I wouldn't dream of touching it.'

Rain had started to fall, heavy November rain that would last for two days at least. As usual I had no umbrella, so I took a scarf from my green book-bag and tied it around my head.

'Travis, Travis, Travis.' I kept up my mantra as I walked to the bus stop. (They had torn up the trolleycar tracks and soon they would stop the few bus services that remained and force everyone to own automobiles.) I must stop this chanting, I thought. It is a compulsion neurosis. I tried instead to plan my term paper, but it was impossible. At least think in sequence, I advised myself. And so I did. I thought of what I had already thought a thousand times: the story of me and Travis.

We were exactly the same age when we met. Well, almost. I was four months older. But he had seen the world, or at least America.

He had hitched all over the country during the school vacations and then after dropping out of the University of North Carolina where Thomas Wolfe had gone. I had never been further than the triangle of Boston, Montreal, Bar Harbor. He had a traveller's gentle cynicism, constantly curious and dissatisfied, but regarding himself as no better than the people and places he was always in such a hurry to leave. In fact, he seemed to consider himself less worthy than they. And though he wasn't vain about his good looks, he was alternately guilty and mistrustful about them. This bemused self-effacement was such a singular quality, especially in a place like Florence where irony of any kind meets with either suspicion or incomprehension, that he shone all the more brightly among the lesser mortals. There is no mistaking an elegant alien, even when he is dressed in jeans and a pea jacket and a moth-eaten grey turtleneck sweater.

That was what he wore the first day I saw him and what he continued to wear for the next three weeks. But he never acquired the wet-dog smell that hangs permanently around some men. He was always bathing, even when there was no hot water, and really I think he was obsessed with cleanliness. He had a well-scrubbed look, but it was a while before I learned the extent to which he fussed over himself. Shaving was his nemesis, and I have heard him crying with frustration as he repeatedly nicked his sensitive skin. He would curse under his breath, smash glasses, and emerge from the bathroom red-eyed and spotted with bits of blood-soaked Kleenex.

'Don't look at me!' he would plead, as I stood frozen with impotent concern.

The cuts would heal slowly and he would examine them under the glare of the bathroom strip-light, muttering his irritation. But on the afternoon I first met him, there were no cuts and no Kleenex, and he was sleek and intriguing, with his shabby clothes only enhancing his allure. I glanced up from my tuna sandwich and saw him across the cafeteria of the Student Union. He looked healthy all right, but a lazy dignified walk negated his wholesome bloom. It was a walk that was both sexy and a little unstable. You noticed the contradiction right away. I stared at him, my mouth open, my forgotten sandwich still in my hand. It took me a minute to realize he was following my friend Frank, and that Frank was coming towards me. I sat alone at the end of one of the long refectory tables. The chairs beside and opposite me were empty, so they took them.

'Rose, this is Travis Merriweather.' It was a principle of Frank's never to say hello or goodbye. He arrived and then he left.

'Oh, hi.' I put down my sandwich. Travis kissed my hand as I gaped at him, finding the gesture silly and theatrical, yet exciting. I suppressed an impulse to kiss his in return.

Never, I thought, have I seen anything like you. Not in church windows, not in art books not even in the movies. Not in all my Nancy Drew and Charlotte Brontë dreams.

'Travis has been picking apples,' Frank explained. He had a pock-marked face and slicked-back hair. He was too tall and too thin and had compensated by stooping to such an extent that he could almost have been a hunchback. When nervous, he was afflicted with an old stutter. But he rarely stuttered with me.

'Where?' I asked, trying to prevent my eyes straying to Travis.

He had been up north with a band of migrant workers, some of whom had travelled from as far away as Oklahoma. They came every year in October. Some would then move south to Florida for the orange crop or to California for the lemons.

Travis and Frank were an incongruous pair and came inevitably to be known as Beauty and the Beast. Frank feigned indifference, and perhaps it was true that he didn't mind because he loved Travis. We both loved Travis, we two drab friends who had found each other in high school, a lonely pair enduring teasing and neglect with hauteur in his case and good nature in mine. We read and the others didn't. We sometimes listened to music that wasn't rock and roll (although we were mad about it and loved to dance to it) and we talked about poetry and Dostoevsky and Marx and helping the wretched of this earth and living a free existence. And we went on talking about these things without being at all attracted to each other or even once holding hands. We were trapped together in our cultural heritage of the movie theatre, the bowling alley and the pizza parlour. Then we were trapped together at Boott, both of us the first person in either of our families to go to college and therefore chosen and special and different but not allowed off our very short reins. Anything further than Portland was neither thinkable nor affordable.

Early on we adopted distinct roles: he was the pessimist and I the optimist, he was the cynic and I the believer. We kept to these roles and maintained them in good repair for the sake of our friendship. Then Travis came and took up a third position somewhere between us. It was so interesting, the most interesting thing that had ever happened to me.

Travis said he would stay for a while, until Christmas, or perhaps he would get a job at the Mill. Or maybe he too would go to California for the lemons. My heart sank. I didn't want my sandwich. Stay, I thought. Please stay.

We sat for a couple of hours after the other students had left and my psychology class was long over. I never missed classes, but in this case I just let the spell of Travis carry me along. He had met Frank a few days ago with an apple-picking friend from New York who was acquainted with the few Boott radicals. Travis had a little money and he liked Frank so he attached himself temporarily to Frank's life. I later realized this was part of his roving pattern and that he could form strong attachments provided he knew they would shortly come to an end.

They invited me to see a movie with them, but Aunt Bernie was having a bad day, and I could not cut her as I had cut my psychology class. She was too strong a pull on my conscience.

'I can't,' I answered regretfully.

'Rose has an *aunt*,' Frank told Travis, and he seemed sympathetic and kissed my hand again when I left.

It nearly killed me, having to say no like that and go off to a duty that gave me no satisfaction. I did not wear my crown of virtue gladly. Offer it up, I'd have said to myself when I was a child, but now I thought: There is an end, only I can't yet see it. There is a purpose, only its components are too numerous for me to unravel. Someday it will be clear in a way I can't possibly imagine now. And for a while it was bearable because I had Travis.

A week after our meeting in the cafeteria Frank invited me over to Franklin Street and, as I had a precious night off from dishing out ice-cream at the North Star, I went. We talked for a while, but I was so nervous of Travis that eventually I lay down on the bed and pretended to fall asleep. It was the only way to prevent myself gaping at him and twisting the strands of my hair, feeling for split ends.

I turned towards the wall so that he could not see my face, only the hill of my hip and the tapering of my legs. I listened as he and Frank discussed the Draft and what they would do when the inevitable letter arrived. Frank was safe for another year, but Travis, having left school, was now vulnerable. They talked about going to Canada, about the Quakers, about disappearing into America. They speculated about who might hide them and about how long the war might go on, and what their chances as conscientious objectors might be. Travis knew of a group in Chicago. Frank thought it better to get out entirely and throw himself on the mercy of a more humane government.

I lay there studying a collage that Travis had made and pinned to the wall just above my nose. A celluloid medical illustration of the human internal organs overlay a colour reproduction of *The Mona Lisa*. Heart, lungs, and liver concealed the famous smile. I contemplated the disturbing effect as I listened to their now heated conversation. They were talking about killing and if it was ever justified and what constituted self-defence. Travis said that poverty was a form of violence. Frank said he thought torture a worse crime than murder, with which I wanted to agree but said nothing. Then they got very excited and the argument turned hot, considering they were pacifists. I wanted to tell them about Vinnie and his miraculous escape from two global conflicts, but I was too shy to intervene and went on pretending to sleep. Later, after he became my lover, Travis said he knew I'd been playing possum.

He was my first lover. That I was still a virgin at twenty is difficult to believe, I know. But Florence afforded very few opportunities for a Catholic girl guarded by her aunt and the Ladies' Guild. I 'went out' for several months with my fat third cousin Dennis, but physically it came to very little, and I don't think either of us cared. Obstacles relieved rather than inflamed us. And with our romance approved of but overseen as it was, there were plenty of obstacles. A ride or two on Denny's brother's motor scooter was as dashing as we ever got. (It was with Frank that I went cruising down the Maine Turnpike at a hundred miles an hour in a borrowed robin's egg-blue Oldsmobile convertible.) Denny and I went to some dances and we watched television on Sunday nights with Aunt Bernie and the Coutures. I was fond of Denny, and he saved me the humiliation of not having a date for the Senior Reception, but when I went to Boott and he went into the Mill that was that.

College brought no liberation since Boott was only two miles away and I had to live at Birch Street and study hard to keep the scholarship I'd managed to win. Wigram Boott controlled my life from beyond the grave.

How did I feel about my intact state? you asked me. Simply, I said, that though it was uncomfortable and embarrassing – acutely at times – there was no one with whom I cared to risk alteration. Besides I was convinced that one day I would be joyfully and beautifully relieved of it. You know me. But in this case my good sense paid off with the advent of Travis the beautiful. How typical, you scorned. The dam gives way at last and the arid plain of life is flooded with lapsed Catholic libido. Well, I replied, the wait was worth it. For a few months I was happier than I'd been since That Time. I rejoiced in my new condition, but even more in the tender adoration – yes, adoration, really – I got from Travis. 'You're my dream, Rosie, my fantasy.' And he was mine. You should have seen us, how alike we were. And I think we grew more so the longer we were together. Of course only I noticed it at first, but after a while Frank did too. But I felt superstitiously reluctant to discuss it with him, since I was worried about subjecting the magic to too close a scrutiny and, as in a fairy tale, breaking its spell.

This sense of dream was heightened by Travis's erratic, not to say surreal, behaviour. I mentioned the crying and the shaving and the morbid inspections before the mirror, and the laments over his Faulkneresque family. But these moods could give way to a sudden anarchic joy which was equally disturbing. Once he and Frank were walking me back to Birch Street on a winter night. The snow, which had been falling all day, was just beginning to taper off. The ploughs had not been able to keep pace with its accumulation, and so the roads were still a bright, new white with only a couple of tyre tracks. Under the street lights it glistened and winked. All sound was muffled by its insulation. Intoxicated by the spectacle, or in order to relieve some secret frustration, Travis began to strip off his clothes. Dancing ahead of us, he tossed first his scarf then his gloves then his pea jacket on to the snowbanks. Bewildered and alarmed, I scurried after him, collecting his garments. When I caught up with him he was naked to the waist and minus one boot and was about to unzip his fly. Snowflakes melted among the hairs on his chest.

'Travis,' I said, 'you'll catch pneumonia.' But he only chuckled as if that seemed to him a good idea and kicked off his other boot.

We were nearly at Birch Street, and I was beginning to panic. What if Phyllis should glance out of the window? Frank and I had to work hard to restrain him, and he finally agreed to put on his jacket and boots but insisted he didn't want the rest and that his clothes should be left on the street for the poor. I tried to make him understand that everyone on Birch Street was far too proud to accept anything for free. And even if they desperately needed his clothes, they'd never go out and collect them for fear someone else would see. It just wasn't the kind of poverty he had in mind.

Sometimes his attacks of euphoria manifested in elaborate meals, cleverly composed of the simplest ingredients, sometimes in bursts of affection that astonished me and left me breathless. And there were the small adventures – going to the movies or to the corner store for a jar of pickles – adventures which assumed such significance that they crowded out the rest of the world and pushed it to the furthest periphery.

It was not easy to find time to be alone with Travis. But in this case, obstacles were a spur, and when Aunt Bernie recovered and went back to the Mill, I could visit him at Frank's apartment in the afternoons. We'd drink lots of tea or beer and occasionally smoke grass and listen to Frank's records. His was the ipsissimus of 45 collections: 'Mocking Bird' and 'Baby, It's You', 'Love is Strange', 'Tears on my Pillow' and 'Why do Fools Fall in Love?'. Sometimes we'd dance, Travis and I, in a clutch if we were by ourselves, or the three of us free-form if Frank was there, bopping carelessly to 'Bye-Bye, Love' – such a happy song saying such terrible things. Frank was a wonderfully graceful dancer, his movements seemed to negate his stutter and his stooped back. Why does grace come to some people and not others? I wondered as I watched him. Perhaps physical grace *is* grace, the redemptive substance.

I had never been so self-expressive. I did not ask myself what I was doing or where all this was heading. I did not remind myself that I had a semi-dependent spinster aunt or that I was destined to take a mediocre degree from an insignificant college in an obscure Maine mill town and teach little children in that same mill town while probably remaining a spinster myself. I was on an exotic detour with a creature who, as far as I was concerned, might be supernatural.

I started to lie to my aunt. I invented extra hours to be worked at the North Star, went to collect non-existent books on hold for me at the library, and contrived new acquaintances to account for the hours I spent in the apartment on Franklin Street. I also relied on an old trick.

The diocese of Portland, like others throughout America, had followed the Vatican's advice that Roman Catholicism should become more accommodating and friendly and encourage strays to return to the Church by adopting a new flexibility about Masses and confessions. Holy Trinity now held a service on Saturday evenings as well as three on Sundays. Aunt Bernie, however, mistrusted these concessions to sloth and held to her old ten o'clock schedule. (We also continued to eat haddock on Fridays in what seemed to me a snooty contempt for the Dispensation.) I feigned attendance at these new services to keep dates with Travis.

Actually, I had begun to practise this trick four years earlier, pretending to be gripped by frantic energy at seven o'clock on Sunday mornings. These seizures, I maintained, made it impossible for me to stay in bed (though in fact I was exhausted from reading until after three) and compelled me to find an outlet for my enthusiasm in a walk to Holy Trinity. I knew nothing could make Aunt Bernie change her habits, and that I was free to leave the apartment at seven-forty-five and

74

be seen at Mass, though not taking Holy Communion – which was the object of the exercise since I had stopped receiving the Sacraments. Of course I couldn't tell Aunt Bernie because it would have upset her so badly that it might have brought on another attack of emphysema. The thought of her reaction to my lapse appalled me. I was convinced that my sins were my own business, but I also knew that I must protect her from my independence of mind. I did not have the *right* to cause her such distress. Tyrant she might be, but she had raised me. The least I could do was spare her the pain and confusion that knowledge of our irreparable differences would inflict on her. It was possible to think freely, I decided, without being a brute, and I kept a nice balance between the private revolt I shared only with Frank and my ritualized life with Aunt Bernie.

It had worked then, and it was working with Travis. But when my extra hours at the North Star produced no extra cash and when I returned at midnight from the library which closed at ten, I began to get suspicious looks. She wanted to ask me something, I could tell. She could not hold it back, and sooner or later she would catch me with the awful question. I would be forced to answer, and what would I say? We had hardly discussed boys, let alone someone like Travis. He would have shocked her more than my flight from orthodoxy. And so I prevaricated and postponed.

She guessed something was up, and it made her grumpy, and when she was grumpy she liked to beat me with an old stick: 'You're lucky you didn't have to go to work in the Mill,' she would scold; then alternately, 'It would have been better if you'd gone to work in the Mill,' implying that it was she who had saved me and that this was one of her few decisions that gave her cause for regret.

'Where've you been, honey? I was getting worried,' Aunt Bernie would call from her bedroom when I returned late at night.

'Just studying,' I'd say, 'with a friend.'

'Well, you better go to bed now. And no reading.'

'Yes. OK,' I would answer, standing rigid as beads of sweat accumulated on my nose and forehead.

There'd be a pause, then, 'Good-night, God bless you,' she'd call.

'God bless you too.'

Travis did not urge me to confess. I suppose he was not a great man for the truth, but he had other strengths. He could draw drama from just about anything, and that, after my prim upbringing, was like a transfusion. He would hold my hands and kiss my fingers.

'Your baby hands, Rosie. They make me feel so guilty.'

'But why, Travis?' He seemed much too young for this kind of talk, but nevertheless it thrilled me.

So I went on until March of my Junior year, thinking all the time that I must confess to Aunt Bernie.

One afternoon when I arrived at Franklin Street Travis was not at home. I waited and waited, nervous because I was sure to be late for the North Star. Was he working overtime at the Mill? Had he suddenly switched shifts? Anxiety poisoned every neuron and capillary in my body. Something I had held down and smothered for a long time was rising within me, a too familiar serpent preparing to strike, an old fit ready to seize and shake me. I felt an uncontrollable urge to urinate and barely made it to the bathroom. Something inside had to break and give or I could not continue to live sane.

I started walking around the apartment just to have something to do. Where was this fierce energy coming from? My mind ran mercilessly on: What has happened? Has his hand been mangled in a machine like my grandfather's? Has he met someone more beautiful who has made him forget me? Has he been hit by a car? Taken an overdose? Is he just late? His family has sent a message. Bad news combined with secret boredom has given him his excuse to flee and now he is gone. *Travis has gone.* I checked the closet. The old doctor's bag he used as a suitcase was missing. Travis had gone.

As there was no telephone I couldn't call anyone, and I was afraid to leave, even though I was overdue at the ice-cream counter. What would they say? Reliable Rose, letting them down. I lay on the bed, curled into a foetal position, intending to stay there and not move until something happened or Frank came back, to hang on, static and rigid, and pray with my whole rigid body, pray with my fierce energy to Mary, the clouds, the sky, the gods, the stars, to bring Travis back to me now, now, this very minute. The door opened and I sprang off the bed. It was Frank. He knew what had happened and what I wanted to hear.

'He got a letter from his s-s-s-sister. I thought something funny might h-h-happen.'

'Why do they have this power over him?' I could see them all, the whole depraved lot.

'She's a st-st-strange girl, I think.' Frank was not so good at showing emotion. His stutter showed it for him. But he was there and I trusted him, and at last I could cry.

He made me tea with a shot in it (I never drank spirits) and sat down beside me until I was quiet.

'I have to go to work,' I said. 'How can I do that?'

'Go. You just have to. I'll meet you tomorrow in the cafeteria at ten-thirty. Or I'll come over tonight if anything – '

Oh, he'll be back tomorrow, I almost said, prompted by my cultivated optimism. He's never coming back, said my despair. Frank pitied me, I knew, though he didn't express his thoughts. He would write a poem after I left but while I was present it was impossible for him to speak. I understood this about him. That's why we were friends.

But silent friendship did not ease my anxiety. As I walked back to Birch Street, it seemed to me that the colour had been drained from the world and I was looking at a banal programme on a small black-and-white television. I felt the low, closely packed buildings crash to the ground in my wake and a damp dead voice repeating: 'Who cares? who cares?' I stopped at a phone booth and made my excuses to the North Star. It was the first time I'd lied to them or played truant from work.

Aunt Bernie lay on the couch, saying her rosary and watching the game shows, her bottles of pills arrayed beside her. In the semi-darkness I was able to hide the twitching of my mouth, and to talk automatically, though the thickness of my speech made her turn from the television.

'You all right, honey?' Her large teeth flashed in the darkness.

'Yes.'

'You don't sound so good. Better take a couple aspirin.'

Her insistence on aspirin as a panacea always annoyed me, but I took some to keep her quiet and for an excuse to leave the parlour with its simpering china angels and the paint-by-numbers roses I had done when I was ten. I looked in the bathroom mirror and searched my face for Travis. Finding him there only made me more unhappy. For a moment I wanted to make faces. I cried into a towel instead and took a bath to delay bedtime and incarceration in my room with all its associations of Foxie. But in the end I went there, after telling my aunt some lies about the North Star.

A week later I received a tear-stained letter. He wanted to see me. He was guilty and sorry and could I forgive him and come somehow with Frank to meet him in the Christian Science Building in Boston at three o'clock next Tuesday. He realized what a terrible thing he'd done, it was the dark shadow that followed him around, he was a vile wretch, he loved me.

We borrowed a car. I invented a story. We left at seven in the morning, before which I was obliged to invent another story. Neither Frank nor I had had any breakfast and my stomach was in knots.

But I was going to find Travis; I was sure of finding him; I had his permission to find him. When I saw him in the reading room, my heart rose to the top of my head. He was so tall and splendid and radiant, glowing as if he had just spent two weeks in Miami Beach. I was more than ready to forget my ordeal and was certain I would understand its significance later.

Of course he had no money. But he knew a cheap restaurant on Boylston Street where we ate our first meal of the day before driving straight back to Florence. We didn't press Travis to tell us what had really happened. We just celebrated our reunion as a great occasion, which it was. Life had begun again, the world had colours once more and warmer wetter air. And for a while it went on that way.

I passed my exams and used them as an excuse to account to Aunt Bernie for my noticeable, alarming happiness. Telling her the truth seemed self-destructive. Summer was coming, and truth-telling could be postponed. I lived day to day and said to myself this is how one must live, this is the way it is meant to be – like when you were a child and even fear was exciting. There was not so much running around because I was juggling only three commitments instead of four. There were fewer lies, which relieved me, even though I had become an accomplished liar.

I had a good summer. I thought of it now as I walked the last block before turning into Birch Street. Travis and Frank and I borrowed the same car and drove to Ogunquit and walked along the Marginal Way. The next weekend we had a picnic at Goose Rocks Beach where, even on the hottest day, the water is too cold for swimming. We went to York Beach, ate salt-water taffy, rode on the Ferris wheel and swam in the freezing sea. I could feel its icy prickle now through my wet clothes. The bells of St Blaise's were ringing as I reached our building. They were followed by Holy Trinity's which always rang two minutes later. They made me feel as though I ought to beg forgiveness for all that fun. I stamped my feet to shake off the rain, opened the door and climbed the stairs.

6

Flight

In 1962 *Through A Glass Darkly* won the Academy Award for best foreign film. In 1964 it was shown in Florence and then only with the support of the Boott College Arts Club. Travis and Frank and I saw it twice during the week it was screened in a near-empty theatre. I had been to only a few foreign-language films (*Where the Hot Wind Blows* on one giggly occasion in high school) and never Bergman, so I was excited and receptive. Frank was too, though he always aimed for greater urbanity. Of course Travis was, by our standards, a film expert.

'In New York you can see just about any movie you want. There are so many it's almost unbearable.'

I was puzzled and disturbed by the film, but I wanted to see it again. What Harriet Anderson said about not being able to live in two worlds seemed uncomfortably relevant.

As it was May and finals were approaching and I was still working part-time at the North Star, I could manage the seven o'clock show without too much fuss from Aunt Bernie. I remember that night because my escape was easy, also because it was cold. Her favourite programme was on, and I cooked her fried cheese for her supper. She had been feeling better lately and her knees were nearly normal, so I left her content with no questions about my plans. I also remember that night because of a conversation sparked by the movie, the kind of exchange that flashes its fragments back at you years later, like the light of a star long after it has died.

We all loved the film, but Frank, who searched for quarrelsome basics, would not permit us simply to float in our adulation.

'I kept thinking about how they got the money to live that way,' he said. 'To have a house on an island and put on plays for each other and spend so much damn time over their own special pain.'

'Their individuality,' Travis corrected him.

79

'Same thing.'

'It's not only the middle class who worry about God and madness,' I answered, I thought, from experience. Travis agreed.

'They seemed cushioned from everything but themselves.'

'And each other.' Travis must have been thinking of his Gothic family. 'Bergman's just showing us how we need and torment each other. Everybody does that. Every one of us is a nightmare to the rest.'

My God. Was I a nightmare to Travis?

'Not always,' I suggested. 'Sometimes we're useful to each other. Sometimes we even help.'

'No,' Frank snapped. 'We have to *learn* to help. We have to learn how to be useful. By forgetting ourselves instead of analyzing ourselves. By breaking out of the prison built by Christianity.'

'The prison?' I asked.

'The guilt prison inside us.'

'It's the family that's made the guilt prison,' said Travis. 'Religion came later and developed a profitable idea.'

Frank considered it. 'Maybe. But the obsession with self-knowledge bothers me. Sure, it's interesting but it's still a luxury. It's selfish, like wanting to save your soul.'

'I keep trying to sell mine.' Travis sighed. 'But no one will make me an offer.'

'You're just a dandy.'

'I am. And feckless. And neurotic. A worthless piece of shit.'

'Don't p-p-p-pose.'

Frank enjoyed cutting Travis off whenever he began developing his favourite role. He turned the conversation back to the freedom which we talked about so optimistically, believing that one day it would emerge and flourish. As we walked we searched the streets for rubbish with which to construct a new altar. Travis found a real prize: a white, high-heeled woman's shoe.

Frank was still rattling on. 'We're encouraged by society to get what *we* want, to make money in *our* career.'

'That's right,' I said. 'You've got to give something to people that you don't get paid for and can't be paid for – something of yourself. Professional people, businessmen – they can never understand that.'

'I'm a worm,' Travis interrupted, determined to stay morose.

'Travis, what has that got to *do* with anything?'

'It doesn't even make sense.'

'Something doesn't have to make sense to be true.'

'Oh, sh-sh-shut up.'

We went back to Franklin Street and built an altar.

For weeks I was preoccupied with the film and what it said about living in two worlds. Failure to opt for one or the other seemed to result in terminal collapse. At least that is what happened to poor Harriet Anderson who was so beautiful and so sensitive. Was I risking a similar fate, heading for that same terrible room where the spider-god appears? My predicament was compounded by my approaching graduation. All conflicts converged around this point. My aunts, Irene, and the Ladies' Guild were very excited. They prayed for an A on my finals and pressed my hands encouragingly. Aunt Bernie had bought a new dress – synthethic raw silk in peacock-blue. She demonstrated to me how firmly attached its rhinestone buttons were, how neat the stitching on the hems, how smooth and perfectly matched the lining. Her obvious pride in me came as a relief, since she had been claiming once again that it would have been better for me to have been sent to work in the Mill and alternately that I should consider myself lucky this hadn't happened.

Everyone wanted tickets to the commencement exercises.

'It'll be a great occasion, Rose.' Katie's broad face beamed.

'Your aunts are so proud of you,' whispered Julia.

'Just remember we love you, darlin',' said Aunt Bea every other minute of my visit, punctuating her admonition with two smacking kisses and exclamations about how tall I was and how much I'd grown. Aunt Bea was sliding slowly and steadily off her rocker. Since Eugene had died of a heart attack three years ago, her natural dottiness had proceeded to the galloping stage. She had become unmanageable, wandering into the street in her slip and having two narrow escapes with the gas stove. 'Was the coffee done it,' everyone said. Bobby was off to Fort Dix and could not take care of her, and we all debated furiously about her future. Kellvale, a rest home for the elderly, had been proposed, but no one wanted to assume the responsibility of putting her there, though we all thought that was where she belonged. Eventually she went – just went, without a murmur, without a fuss. Poor Aunt Bea. She seemed content.

Even Cousin Mikey enquired about the possibility of an extra seat at my graduation. I was the only one who didn't want to go. The thought of the endless empty formalities made me cringe. How could I tell them that my cap and gown would be to me a comic anachronism and my diploma the symbol of a false sense of achievement? They would never understand my scruples or my explanations. They would be shocked by my cynicism. They would think me an ingrate and never say so. I was too guilty about them to run, too sorry for them to disappoint them. The only solution was to offer it up to the cause of some future enlightenment.

My unease was complicated by Frank. Brave Frank. Frank of unshakeable integrity. He was not bowing to family pressure. He was telling them flat out his opinion of the whole hypocritical business.

'God,' I said, 'aren't your parents having kittens?'

'They'll adjust. They know an iron w-w-w-will when they see one.'

Travis liked to fantasize about me in my cap and gown, and I was unable, as usual, to penetrate his irony.

'Promise me a photograph, Rosie. Save one for me. Are you sure you can't come here first and let me make love to you all dressed up?'

Of course Travis's attendance was out of the question. I could never have accounted for the extra ticket, not after Cousin Mikey had been refused. And what if this tall blond alien with a pony tail were to sit down next to Margaret or Katie or, God forbid, Aunt Bernie herself? You see, she was still unaware of his existence. I continued to protect her from the truth, although I occasionally received penetrating glances from members of the Ladies' Guild. But they couldn't possibly know.

There was only one reason for my conceding, yet again, to be their performing animal: the possibility that my father might show up. Aunt Bernie and I, in rare collusion, discussed whether it would be more effective to call him well in advance or to spring it on him at the very last minute. He might slither away in any case. We decided to prepare him gradually, to wear him down with polite persistent assaults. I rang him on the telephone that he had given us to compensate for his permanent absence after he had moved to Chesapeake Bay. I informed him, with simulated detachment, of the date, place and occasion. I did not express any wish that he be present. I hid my longing.

'Graduating, eh? Say . . . my little girl.' There was a pause in which I wondered if he were going to cry. 'Jeeze, honey, that's terrific.'

'Jeeze'?! He'd never used a word like 'jeeze'. Even his language had suffered under Denise's influence. He insisted, as he always did, that I speak to her.

'Hey, good goin', Rosie. We'll have to come up, huh? Real family reunion. Be a riot and a half.'

I handed the phone to Aunt Bernie.

'He won't come,' she said later.

'He didn't say he wouldn't.'

'He didn't need to say.'

They knew each other so well. Better than I knew either of them.

But I could not accept her verdict. If Vinnie failed to appear then my sacrifice would have no meaning. But then, I told myself, that's not true. Your participation in this empty rite will have a purpose. It will make them all happy. Not only for one morning in June, but for the years to come when they will remember it and refer to it with pride.

'I'll try again.' I could not help seeking assurance from her. 'You really don't think he'll come?'

'He likes where he is. He's got it easy now. He don't want to come back here and be reminded.'

'Of what?' I asked, though I knew the answer perfectly well.

'You know what.'

'I don't.' Things got so twisted sometimes between Aunt Bernie and me.

'Well, you just look, honey, and you'll see what he'll see.'

'But *what*?' I hesitated. 'There's Nora, I guess.'

'Nora's grave.'

'Yes, I suppose. And there's Aunt Bea.'

'Crazy as a bed bug, poor woman.'

'And his old job.'

'His old meetings, you mean, that nearly put him out of work for good.'

'A long time ago. That's all over.'

'He regrets it. He misses it.'

'That's true. And there's you.'

'What about me? I'm tip-top. But he's afraid I'll remind him he hasn't been to Mass or confession in thirteen years. And he'll see his daughter all grown-up without much help from him. He's a good man, really, and it bothers him. He'll be proud of you, but he'll feel guilty just as much as proud.'

'What do you mean?'

'He don't like the past. He's got a new family now.' The corners of her mouth drooped. 'He don't like the past.'

True enough, though I hated to admit it. My success, though modest, served only to remind him of his neglect, since I had done it 'without much help from him'. It was because of Aunt Bernie that I was going to college – even a third-rate organization like Boott. No one referred directly to my unique achievement, but its effects were always there, palpable among us. I was painfully conscious of my position, and I wanted to squirm away, to disappear with Travis into the margins of society where there was neither structure nor future, into the romantic chaos of an eternal present. I did not want to be defined by my unchosen profession. I did not want my life to be decided so soon, to be finished and put away when it was only just beginning. I did not want the narrow security so esteemed by Florentines, which would trap me for ever in repeated procedures. I did not want to be a lay teacher of third grade, at St Thomas's. I wanted to be something much more. Or much less.

'Next year,' Aunt Bernie would say (or Phyllis or Katie or Julia or Irene or Cousin Mikey), 'when you're at St Tom's.' And I would manage a weak smile.

Travis knew my ambivalence about what lay ahead of me. But as I faced my final exams, in which I was sure to do well and which would seal my fate, he seemed to have no alternative to offer me. Free himself, he could not understand how I had failed to be. Not that we were without fantasies of escape. We talked endlessly of Mexico, Turkey, Morocco, Greece, but we were incapable of getting there. I was not so blind as to believe that Travis wished to give the rest of his youth to the late shift at the Number One Mill. I told myself: He is hanging around for me, and that that is nice. But this was not a reliable source of consolation. I wanted to go forward with him down an unknown road towards wider horizons, but I was caught in the stasis of indecision while he joked and dreamed and wept before the mirror. Why wouldn't he say something?

I passed my exams with the grades I expected and a low Latin degree. On the 20th of June I went to my commencement exercises. They were reminiscent of my Confirmation, only this time the secret affirmation was absent. Wigram Boott, my family, all of Florence, were stamping me with their seal of approval. Rose Is Ready – not to live but to function. Of course Vinnie failed to show up. Kenny, my step-brother, had mumps and my father succumbed to the illness two days before his scheduled departure. His second chin was now so advanced that I wondered if the swelling would make any noticeable difference. Denise, though amused by his condition, was adamant that he remain in Maryland and in bed.

'See?' said Aunt Bernie, 'what did I tell you?'

Vinnie who had photographed electric wires and collapsed sheds, who had run the 440-yard dash, who had passed difficult exams and got his name in the *Portsmouth Herald*, Vinnie who had stood outside our church in the snow for a month of Sundays. Vinnie Mullen.

Afterwards Bernie had 'everybody' over. Sister Rosalie, Father Leahy, members of the Ladies' Guild in white cotton gloves though the temperature was 88 degrees; Phyllis and Clovis rubbing and wringing their hands, Irene jolly and loud, Cousin Mikey self-effacing, Aunt Bea, let out of the pen for the big event, remarking ceaselessly on how much I had grown. ('Isn't she big! Hasn't she got tall!') Legions of extended family.

Naturally the party was dry – tea, coffee, Kool-Aid, frozen orange juice, stuffed eggs, devilled ham sandwiches, Vienna rolls filled with tuna salad, more cakes and pie than we could ever eat. I was presented with dozens of Hallmark paper wallets containing a five- or ten-dollar bill, crisp and new. There was the obligatory Infant of Prague gown from Phyllis (to be worn during the Octave of the Nativity) and from Irene six washcloths with embroidered edges stitched by her dear self. I still have the tiny silver rosary in its silver-mail pouch which Aunt Bernie gave me, and I still sleep with it under my pillow when I am distressed or lonely or have seen a vampire movie.

I went through the day like a puppet, behaving automatically, behaving in the way I knew they liked, in the manner recognized and approved by them all, but thinking every minute of Travis and when I might escape to him; and somewhere further back in my mind, waiting for a phone call and the sound of Vinnie's voice. No one sensed my distraction. They saw only my surface which I was so practised in presenting to them, and my future as teacher, spinster, devoted niece. How could such a prospect excite them?

'It's a grand day, Rosie,' said Katie and kissed me. Then she whispered, 'Your aunt's so happy, dear. Never disappoint her.'

'I won't.'

'I know you won't,' she answered confidently and patted my cheek.

Bernie did look happy in her peacock-blue dress and white high-heeled sandals. I thought of that boy long ago and how she must sometimes grieve for him. How tough she was, how independent. She would never understand, let alone approve of, my obsession with Travis. She was used to going without; it was the norm. Though she did have her own apartment. 'There's nothing like your own little place,' she would say, 'no one like your own people.'

My own people. My own people made more sandwiches, started a game of gin, watched television, told the stories they always told, hung around until nine. They stood on the hot balcony, smoking and looking out at the parking lot towards the dark spire of Holy Trinity. My own people kept saying goodbye and not going, taking their leisurely Irish leaves. My heart was so tight and its beat so rapid I thought it would split with the strain. I wanted to race down the stairway and out the door to Franklin Street, but my own people kept me standing, talking, waiting, kissing me goodbye then hastening back to tell me some bit of news, some message unconveyed.

At ten I insisted that Aunt Bernie lie down. She resisted, but I was as firm as I ever dared be with her since I had the others to back me up in the matter of her health. She capitulated, even with some grace. In the warm darkness I helped her remove her dress and hung it in the closet. Within a minute she was asleep and snoring, her oxygen canister on the table beside her.

I was too impatient to change from my prim blouse and skirt into shorts and went out into the night as I was. I walked rapidly along Market Street past cars that, in the heat, smelt of metal and gas. There were thousands of stars. They made me think of Black Water Road and returning home on nights like this after a day at Rye Beach or Wallis Sands, and being carried up the front steps and into the house. I would die if Travis wasn't in.

I could hear them even before I reached the front porch. They were singing 'The Green Berets' and kept stopping to break up with laughter. An old black-and-white television flickered away with the sound off. Between them on the floor was a bottle of Cutty Sark and an overflowing ashtray which looked to me the epitome of freedom. On the bed was a book of Robert Motherwell's paintings. Where did they find such things in Florence? Travis kissed me, his blond hair sliding over one eye.

'How was it?' asked Frank.

'You were right not to go.'

'Where are the pictures, Rose? Didn't anyone have a Polaroid?'

Travis was disappointed when I told him there were no snapshots available just yet. I was still embarrassed by his eagerness to see me in commencement drag. I hated the idea of being captured for ever in that costume. As he turned to pour me a drink I was struck again by the similarity of our profiles. Of course his small nose was a little straighter than mine and did not turn up at the end in what Bobby called a ski-jump. ('Ski-jump nose, blueberry eyes,' he'd chant. Made me sound like Raggedy Ann.) But the cheekbones, the line of the jaw . . .

I took a sip of the whisky. Back then I didn't drink very much and never became intoxicated.

'Well, what would you like, Rose?' Travis tilted back his head, blew smoke high into the room and slung one leg over the arm of the chair. 'How will we celebrate your rite of passage?'

'Celebrations aren't really in order.' I watched the smoke rings issue in a steady stream from his lovely mouth.

'They're always in order,' said Frank. 'Shall we wr-wr-wreck an altar?'

'What am I going to do?' I burst out, suddenly impatient with them both. Perhaps the liquor had affected me after all. 'I don't want to be a teacher.' The late news flashed and jumped in the darkness.

'I've told you, you don't have to be. The ch-ch-choice is yours.'

'I know it is, only I – ' It was easy for him to say. His will was not dependent upon another's. He would work in the Mill for a while, save money, write poetry, move to Cambridge. If his name came up for the draft, he could emigrate to Canada. Not the greatest of futures, but one that was of his own choosing.

'Why don't we borrow a car and drive to Ogunquit?' said Travis. 'I've got enough money for gas. Do you have any cigarettes, Rosie?'

I smoked at Franklin Street though I never inhaled.

'I can't,' I answered dully. 'I start full-time at the North Star tomorrow. Until September. Remember?'

'Tell them you mixed up the dates.'

'Travis I can't *do* that!' I sat exasperated as he continued to blow perfect smoke rings, propelling the smaller through the larger, a mesmerizing trick.

'Wouldn't you love to be living in Morocco?' he sighed.

'I'd like to be gone from here.' I was trying not to sulk. 'I'd like to be free, even a little bit free.'

'You are free,' answered Frank. 'You're free right this minute.'

'Yes, of course, only – '

'You just don't behave as if you are.'

Was freedom, then, a matter of pretending, too?

'You're caught in the mainstream. You can't be free in the mainstream.'

'No,' Travis agreed. 'Only on the margins. You can only be free if you're obscure.'

'Marginal and obscure.'

'Wouldn't you love to be somewhere marginal?' Travis smiled at me.

'Don't tease me,' I said.

We went to bed in Frank's room. At 2 a.m. I made a move to rise and go, but he held me tight, and I could not disentangle myself from his legs and arms. The effort involved was made all the more strenuous by my reluctance to leave him. I was fighting myself as well as Travis.

'Eva,' he said, then opened his eyes. 'Don't go. It's not time yet.'

'You were calling for your sister.'

Travis moaned and I stroked his face. He had been dreaming of his Faulkneresque family and was trying to crawl out of his dreams.

'I'm sorry.'

'For what? We can't escape our relatives, especially in our unconscious. That's where they lie in wait for us.'

'There, especially. Oh, it's unbearable.' He rolled away then back to clasp me again. 'Stay here, Rose.'

'I can't. What if Aunt Bernie wakes up?'

'All right, sweetheart.' Poor Travis. He never argued, never forced me to skirt my obligations. It made me both relieved and sad. But it was better that everything go on for a while as it was. Peacefully. Until our wills asserted themselves and our course of action was revealed to us. We would know very soon what to do. I tore myself from Travis and walked back to Birch Street in the dark.

I worked the next few weeks with my mind in my right arm, which was growing noticeably larger than the left. I scooped ice-cream, stacked cones, dribbled sauces. It was a scorching summer and the place had never been so busy. The air was thick with the smell of French fries. I handed ice-cream cones and sundaes across the metal counter to hundreds of people a day – men in baseball caps, children with quarters clutched in their hot fists, a few barefoot students, women whose colliding thighs bulged from Madras Bermuda shorts and whose hair was done up in giant rollers covered with a triangle of scarf and tied at the nape of the neck. They all knew each other and they all knew me. I smiled at every one of them, my hair tucked up with bobby pins under my starched white cap. I could have passed for a nurse if my apron had not been smeared with chocolate mocha and butter pecan. Occasionally Travis and Frank stopped by to make faces at me from the back of the line, and I would slip them each a free double scoop. I was working too hard to think. My mind was a blank. So blank that when the call came I did not understand at first what I was being told or even that it was Katie who was speaking.

'But I can't leave the counter. I – '

'Are you OK, dear?'

'I'm fine. I'm sorry. What should I do?'

'Come right over to Boott Memorial,' she said with forced calm. 'Your aunt needs you.'

I replaced the receiver and took off my hat and apron. I found Cora, my boss, and said I had to leave because my aunt had collapsed and had been rushed to the hospital. She insisted on driving me herself. Everybody in Florence put family first.

We didn't say much in the car. My brain was beginning to discern the shape of coming events. There was a reason for this emergency. For a long time something had been trying to happen. Unknown to us it had been gathering force. The crisis would bring Vinnie back. Now, after everything else had failed to move him, he would come north again. We would be together, he and I, in the apartment. And Travis would come over and he would meet my father and would see at last where Foxie and I had lived and I had spent the past thirteen years of my life, and the place would be transformed by his presence, his and Vinnie's, and all its sad associations would dissolve and evaporate and fly out of the open windows. We would visit Aunt Bernie every day, but be together in the evenings. I would keep house for my father (of course I would receive a long leave of absence from work), maybe for both of them, who could tell, and Aunt Bernie would be sick for a long time, sick but not suffering. She would need her brother near by. Weeks would elapse, months. And then Aunt Bernie would grow weaker, become unconscious and finally comatose. Aunt Bernie would die.

I did not feel happy at the thought, only secure in the clarity of my vision.

She was in a semi-private room, an oxygen mask hanging on the wall beside her, and cylinders next to the bed. Her pills covered the bedside table. I hadn't realized how many she'd been taking. She looked at me, eyes wide and bloodshot.

'Come're till I see you,' she said.

'Don't be too long,' the nurse whispered, and I was glad.

I said everything I assumed I was expected to say: that it would be over soon, that she would be fine, that she shouldn't worry, that I would take care of her.

'The Marian Missal,' she croaked.

'I'll bring it. I'll bring whatever you want. Look, I'll make a list. You tell me and I'll write it all down, everything. See?' I fumbled in my bag for a notebook and pen and was surprised that I'd started to cry. The nurse patted my shoulder as I left, having received gasped instructions about the metal cabinet which I'd failed to note. At the door I met several members of the Ladies' Guild, brows furrowed, rosaries at the ready.

'Hard on you, Rose. Hard on you.'

'Anything we can do now, you just say.'

'We're so sorry, dear.'

'I'm sorry too,' I mumbled.

'We're praying for Bernadette and for you.'

I prepared for the arrival of the casseroles, the angel cakes and the green jell-os studded with miniature marshmallows. Frank and Travis would gladly take them off my hands tomorrow. Tonight I had the phone and the apartment to myself alone.

I kept postponing the call, out of nerves, I guess, and fear of the certain spoiling if I were to hear Denise's voice. Besides, after six the rates were cheaper. Finally I dialled his number. My hands were shaking and my stomach grumbling. I'd eaten nothing since the night before. Vinnie answered and I told him about his sister.

'Uh-huh. I was afraid of something like this.' Then he cried. I waited until he had stopped. 'Christ.' He gave a sigh that signalled the end of the seizure. 'Well, what are they saying?'

'It's serious.' I was very bold. 'She wants you. You ought to come.'

'Sure. Sure, I'll come. Sure, sweetheart.' Was it really going to be this easy?

'When, Daddy?'

'Soon as I can. What's the hospital number?'

I told him.

'How's your Aunt Bea?'

'Pretty weird.'

'Well, do your best, Rosie. I know you will. You need money?'

'It's all right.' I could barely control my voice. 'Love to Denise.' That's how glad I was.

He promised to phone the next day. I pictured him in his ranch-style house with the two cars in the garage and the two boys with catcher's mitts and the brace of beagles. Tyre marks on the front lawn and the ice-box crammed with giant economy everything. Beer, milk, soft-shell crabs. The television constantly on; Kenny and Greggy crawling all over him as he sat immobile watching the thirty-six-inch screen. Denise yelling in the kitchen, laughing on the telephone. He earned a good salary at the shipyard. He could buy fancy cameras and recordings of Heavy Metal rock to replace his collections of Dave Brubeck and Gerry Mulligan. But he was still Vinnie, crying like a big baby, golden still, and still loving his honeybunny.

He would not arrive on the first date set, or even the second, I knew that. (See how well I knew him.) But he would come. And I would wait for him, performing all my obligations, not getting anxious or upset. For two weeks I went to work, to the hospital, and to Travis. I nearly brought him to the apartment, but in the end I was too nervous to risk it. Phyllis and Clovis missed nothing. I deposited the money I earned along with my graduation loot in the Indian Head Bank and did not think about

St Tom's or the fall. I was very tired, but I worked almost cheerfully, intoxicated by the relative freedom of life without Aunt Bernie. Living alone, lying next to Travis into the early-morning hours, was luxurious. A delicious weight permeated my limbs, and a sweet fog filled my brain. I was not looking where I was going.

Every evening I spent two hours at the hospital. In the August nights that were cloudy and heavy and damp, I would sit beside Aunt Bernie saying nothing. I didn't even read. I knew I was supposed to just *be* with her, so I was. She mumbled her rosary, looked at the *Florence Tribune* and breathed more easily.

'I'm real glad to have you here, honey,' she said, as though I'd dropped by for coffee. I didn't know how to reply, so I squeezed her small shiny hand with its hardening fingertips and well-buffed nails painted with clear nail polish and ran my thumb over the onyx ring she'd worn ever since I could remember.

Father Leahy visited and prayed with her, as did Sister Mildred and Sister Rosalie and Sister Judith. She seemed happier to see them than to see anyone.

'Bernadette should have been a nun,' they concurred, as they always did. They praised my devotion, and I was both relieved and annoyed that everyone thought me so virtuous. I told Travis this.

'Do you want them to think you're bad?'

'Part of me does.'

He chuckled and exhaled an enormous cloud of smoke. Then he grew very quiet and abstracted which always made me anxious.

'Travis.' I touched him carefully. 'What is it? Please don't tell me you're a worm.'

'Look at my life,' he said at last in the tone I was most afraid of. 'I can't bear it.'

I didn't contradict. He had been like this a lot lately, and I had learned simply to wait for the black mood to pass. It was horrible for me, but I waited, thinking about his mystery and the exotic doom that hung over him. He threw tantrums over lost socks and often refused to get out of bed until four after watching late movies until dawn. He wore earplugs for a week – as an experiment, he said – and it was impossible to talk to him. He went for ten-mile walks into the tedious countryside or along the Turnpike. Later I found out he had not been going to work. No wonder he had started to borrow money from me. Now when I think back to that time, I can see these clear signs of the restless depression that was overtaking him. But then they were lost on me. I was being with my lover without limitations; I was waiting for my father; I was doing right by my aunt. I was so convinced that everything was in the process of working out for the best that I failed to see the obvious.

As I had predicted, Vinnie's scheduled arrival was postponed. He had stepped on a dead wasp while watering the back yard and the sting had produced an allergic reaction. His life-long fear of bees and their relatives was vindicated at last. I explained all this to Aunt Bernie who listened resignedly then turned her face away while I pretended not to hear her sniffles. It was now the 18th. I assured her that he would come on the 26th and made a special trip back to the hospital that evening with a butterscotch sundae which she ate greedily while Travis and Frank waited downstairs in the borrowed car.

We drove to Goose Rocks Beach to watch the sun come up then made a rapid return to Florence where I was in time for work at ten. I kept thinking of the beach and of how Travis and I had left Frank in his sleeping bag and wandered off by ourselves to make love. We'd talked about drowning and what a beautiful death it must be and how being buried alive must be the most gruesome. I remembered what Vinnie had said once about the submarine that went down off Block Island in 1923. Some of the men survived in the hold for several days. Radio contact was lost, but the divers attempting to rescue them could hear them tapping out Morse code on the walls with hammers. They all perished.

'But the sub was raised eventually, and you know what they did with it? Put it on display for one of the Navy Days. People could wander through it, even take a guided tour. My father saw the scratch marks on the walls where they'd been trying to get out, panicked from lack of oxygen.' I shuddered. It was the worst thing that could happen, being trapped in a room with no escape.

'Imagine, everybody looking at the scratch marks. Doesn't that seem obscene to you?'

'Yes.'

Then he told me about people he knew who had drowned, things he'd read, characters in novels and films.

I didn't know anyone who'd drowned or who'd even made a boat journey and I could not help reflecting – it's silly, I know – how pale my life was in comparison to his, how lacking in mystery and knowledge and experience. (See how I wasted my time thinking such things while precious moments were slipping away.) That evening when I knocked on the door at Franklin Street no one answered. And the door was locked.

I knew he had gone – like the last time, only worse. More dramatic and final. I should have been watching, paying closer attention. I had been too distracted and too content. I vowed that if he ever returned I would learn from my stupid carelessness. I would give him all of my life, not just a part of it. Aunt Bernie could go hang. Someone like Travis needed the entirety.

For a long time I just sat, paralyzed by the hopes I refused to bury and thereby free myself for action. Finally I did something very strange: I went to Frank's parents' house. It did not occur to me to leave him a note or take a bus or even a taxi. I walked all the way. The Hollands were amazed I'd come.

'Well, Rose, what you doing here? Haven't seen you in a whiles.'

'I know. I'm sorry. I'm looking for Frank.'

'He don't live here now. We thought you knew that.'

'I do, but I just wondered . . .'

Why had I come, seeking parents?

'He took that apartment with his friend.'

I listened to the story like a stranger whose life had been untouched by these events.

'You want a ginger ale? You don't look too good, dear.'

'No. I'll go now. Thank you.'

'We'll drive you,' they insisted. 'And we'll tell Frankie you come by. We'll tell him to phone you. How's your Aunt Bernadette?'

'She's better.' I realized with a shock that I was speaking the truth.

I searched Aunt Bernie's medicines for something tranquillizing. There was nothing, and so I lay awake all night in the empty apartment. Through the open window the street light illuminated the statue of the Virgin Mary, still in its niche but unadorned now. The ghosts of Foxie's children circled the room, watching me, concerned for my state of mind but unable to assist me.

Find Travis, I implored them. Find Travis and bring him back to me. I placed the little silver rosary under my pillow.

At six I rose, horribly energized. This time Frank was in. He was upset, for himself as well as for me.

'No note?' I asked.

'Nope.' He sat on the bed, his thin shoulders hunched. 'I think his sister must have turned up.'

'Why?'

'Yesterday morning he went to the window and opened the curtains and stood for a long time looking at the street. When he closed the curtains he seemed completely changed. It was like he'd received some

93

kind of signal. Then he said he was going out for a minute. Quarter of an hour later I heard a car drive off. He didn't come back. All his things are still here.'

The table was covered with Travis's drawings and collages.

'Do you want a cup of coffee?' I asked as I stacked and arranged the art works.

He watched me. 'We'll just have to wait to hear. It won't be too long.'

The next few days were prison, torture and sickness combined. I was aware of the advent of each moment because that moment might bring Travis or news of him. It brought neither, and left only the sense of its departure, another closed door. This terrible attention would not let me rest. I went to the North Star, visited Aunt Bernie, called on Frank, cleaned the apartment, phoned my father, constantly compelled to witness the ongoing murder and resurrection of hope that would have been otherwise merely the passage of time. Such was my condition that when the nurse called and told me that Aunt Bernie would be discharged in a matter of days I almost told Vinnie the truth. But I caught myself, and let him continue to regard her condition as critical. If it were to prove anything else, he would never come. And now his arrival was only three days away.

I hinted to the doctor that I was working overtime, that I was arranging leave so that I could look after my aunt at home. (Though she was better, she would require constant care and monitoring of her monstrous intake of medication.) I made no complaints. The Ladies' Guild continued to praise my devotion.

'We're so proud of our girl.'

'Heaven will reward you, honey.'

I was justifying their faith in me, and even at this point something perverse in me was warmed by their approval. Sister Mildred and Sister Rosalie gave me sympathetic smiles and encouraging words. Father Leahy assured me I was being prayed for. Why couldn't all these prayers deliver to me what I really wanted? I had learned patience without anyone's prayers. Now it served only to keep me alive and functioning in my misery. I seemed to be crawling along, groping my way towards Thursday when Vinnie's plane landed at Logan Airport and when – who knew? – Travis might come back to me.

At two in the morning the telephone rang. I fell over myself to get to it, certain, in my semi-conscious state, that it must be Travis. But instead I heard, 'Rosie, what's this about Bernie getting better? Don't the doctors tell you anything, honey?'

'She's not that better. How did you know?'

'Third Cousin Gerald ran into Denise's sister-in-law's mother in the Portland Mall.'

'Oh, that's nice. How's your foot?'

'Not too bad. Gives me some trouble now and then, but your old man's tough.' I could have predicted the next sentence word for word. 'The doctor says I should stay off it as much as possible for a while – it's the allergic reaction, you see. And if Bernie's on the mend there's no rush to get on a plane, and I can give it a few more days to recoup. You'll have lots of help with her anyway, family'll all pitch in and it'll put Denise's mind at rest if I'm in bed a little longer.'

'But what about *my* mind?' I couldn't help it, it just came out.

He went quiet, and I was immediately sorry.

'But, Rosie, you're my sweetiepie, you know that. My sweetiepie and – '

'Honeybunny,' I mumbled.

Vinnie was not going to help me. The curtain rose on my life as an unpaid nurse. I took the stage and the spotlight followed me towards the sick bed. Perhaps it would not be as bad as St Tom's.

'How's your Aunt Bea?'

'Forgetful. She forgets I'm twenty-two, that her husband's dead, that Bobby is her son. She says she intends to forget everything. I think she's happy.'

'Maybe.' Vinnie felt badly about Aunt Bea. 'It would be great for her and Bernie to be together.'

I began to consider the implications of this statement but pulled back, not daring, for the moment, to take it any further.

'They'd like to see you, you know.'

'And I'd like to see them, honey. And I will. I promise. Pretty soon now. You tell them that, OK?' I had to believe it.

'OK.'

'Goodnight, Rosie. My little girl. Sleep tight.'

'You too, Daddy.'

Some children love their father because he is firm and positive and makes them feel secure, or because he is severe and critical and this too gives them a kind of security. But my father was complex, both treacherous and vulnerable. It was for these weaknesses and these sins that I loved him. They exercised over me a seductive pull which was greater than that of conventional paternal integrity or the semblance of it.

I let all my sobs out of the cage I had built for them. When I was calmer I went to the front room. I sat on the couch, straight up with my hands on my knees. I could just make out the paint-by-numbers roses. Vinnie had taken such an interest in the work, inspecting my progress each evening, praising my neatness and my application, showing the finished picture to Russ and Eddie. I thought of Travis's macabre drawings and collages. His art and mine did not meet. Why had I ever thought we were related? Because our bone structure seemed to link us in some ancient way – a recognition that had excited and comforted me and continued to do so even now. I would be together again with Travis. The power that shaped our faces shaped our fates. This was a story, a mystery story, ours; the bones of our story. If I waited patiently, if I read on, I would be given a clue, a hint to the end and how I might find my way there, down the unknown road.

I was very tired. The heat plus the euphoria brought on by these consoling thoughts eased me into a kind of trance. The last thing I remembered as I leaned back against the rough green fabric of the couch was the bell at St Blaise's ringing four o'clock, followed two minutes later by the chimes at Holy Trinity. I slept very deeply, I guess, because Frank claimed he knocked several times before I finally opened the door. I must have looked disappointed. Everything – the telephone, the bells, the knocks – everything was not Travis.

'What time is it?' I let him in.

'It's ten. I thought you might have left for work.'

'Oh, my God!'

I turned towards the bathroom in a panic, but he caught my arm.

'Hang on. Look at this.' He handed me a postcard. It too is lost, but I remember what it said:

> New York unbearable. Will travel west. Or maybe not. Do you think Rose would speak to me? Tell her I beg her forgiveness and that I consider myself completely unworthy of her.

'But is he – does this mean – ' I spluttered, looking from the card to Frank and back again.

'We'll go and get him.'

'We don't know where he is.'

'He's in New York.'

'I know, but he says west – look, *west*.'

'He won't, he won't. He doesn't have any money.'

'How can you be sure? What about his sister?'

96

'We'll find her.'

'How?' I was in tears.

'We'll find the address. There are these things called phone books,' he soothed. 'I may even have it somewhere. I'll look, Rose.' He put his arms around me. 'She lives in New York, remember?'

'Yes, yes.'

'We'll find the address. We'll go there. I mean, I'll go with you.'

'You will? Really? He says would I speak to him. That must mean he wants to speak to me.'

''Course he wants to speak to you.'

The phone rang. We looked at each other, both thinking: It's him.

I picked up the receiver. 'Hello,' I said, my voice sounding like a child's.

'Miss Mullen?'

'Yes.'

'It's Doctor Toussaint. Good news for you, young lady. We're sending your aunt home day after tomorrow.'

7

Pursuit

I was thinking so hard I had to remind myself to breathe. I was trying
to make sense of what the doctor was telling me – that Aunt Bernie's
lungs plus the oedema on her knees would make it impossible, for
the foreseeable future, for her to go up and down stairs, that the
management of her medication would require strict surveillance, that
in effect she would be an invalid and a virtual prisoner in the apartment.
A prisoner who would need my constant attention. Did I understand
and was I prepared for that? He presumed I knew how expensive private
nurses were. What could I say? Yes, I understood.

'You're a sound human being, Miss Mullen.'

I put the phone down. 'We'll have to leave immediately,' I said.

'Who was that?' Frank asked.

'No one.'

'Do you want to borrow Roger's car?'

'Yes, please, yes. We'll have to leave immediately,' I repeated.

We said goodbye. I went to the bedroom to dress. Half-way there I
turned back to the bathroom. Before I reached it I went to the kitchen
and filled the kettle which I left beside the sink when I realized I had
not called the North Star. I dialled the number, having no idea what to
say. Cora answered and I hung up. I stood in my pyjamas, mumbling to
myself. Again I picked up the telephone. This time I dialled the hospital
and asked for Aunt Bernie's ward. Improved as she was, she had lost
her private room.

'Could I speak to the head nurse?'

'Just a minute.'

My throat was constricted. My voice was like water forcing itself
between two rocks.

'It's Rose Mullen, Nurse Cleary.'

'Eyah.'

'There's a problem?'

'Eyah.'

'I've promised to work overtime at the North Star and the apartment's a mess. I mean I don't think it would be a very nice place for my aunt to come back to.'

'Oh!'

'No, no, it's not that bad. It's just – well, you must know what she's like, and my boss is depending on me. Could you keep her for another day?'

'Keep who?'

'My aunt – Bernadette Mullen. I'm sorry. Is it too much trouble? I don't want to let anybody down. And you know she can't be alone.'

'*I* know that, Miss Mullen. But *she* thinks different.'

Despite the medical lectures, my aunt was determined to return to the Mill in two weeks.

'Two weeks! I'll tell ya something de-yah. She's nevah goin' back to that Mill. And even she'll admit it, first time she tries to climb a flight of stairs. Anyway, see what I can do for ya.'

'Thanks a million.'

If I had gained any grace I was at a loss to know how to use it. I was still trying to assimilate the contents of that postcard. I read it again and again. Only one thing was clear to me: my addiction to Travis. I could not live without Travis and the romance of Travis. I thought of my pre-Travis life and I knew I would die if forced to return to it. I had changed too much. But at the moment I was powerless. Aunt Bernie was coming home, I was due at work, I had no cash, no car and no New York address. So I tried to behave normally. I went to work.

I dressed, rang Cora and went out. *En route* I stopped at the Indian Head Bank and withdrew all but $10 from my account, withdrew the money that had filled all those paper wallets, the reward for my academic achievements. I scooped out the pistachio and the raspberry ripple. I spoke and moved mechanically. The robot I had become addressed customers in the pleasant vivacious manner they associated with Rose Mullen. I said something personal to each one of them, smiled, exchanged all the right greetings and goodbyes, aware as I always was that nobody likes a sourpuss. Inside I was mad, but they didn't notice. Smile and the world smiles with you, Rose. Occasionally I thought: This is a test. From this experience I will gain new knowledge of myself which will enable me to understand others better. Mainly, though, I was mad.

It had been a lie about the overtime. In fact I left early (using my aunt as an excuse) and went back to Birch Street, hoping for some news either from Frank or Nurse Cleary. Frank was sitting on the stoop, waiting for me, half-concealed by the late-afternoon shadows.

'No luck yet,' he said. 'Roger's brother needs the car to take the motorboat up to Lake Bawtucket.'

'Did you find the address?'

'No. I'll look again.'

I was going to cry, hard. I must get off the street and into the apartment.

'Come upstairs with me?'

'If you want me to, but I think you'd rather I got us a car.' He held out his hand which I took.

'You're really nice to me, Frank.'

'It's no t-t-trouble.'

As I walked up the stairs, I had a brainstorm. I thought, pathetically, that I had found a solution: Aunt Bea's home for the elderly. Kellvale. I ran the rest of the way to the top and called my father (who went to work at six and returned at three – the first shift).

'Well, well, Rosie. What a surprise.'

'I have to know what you think about something.' I'd never confronted him like this.

'Shoot.'

'I was thinking – I wondered if – say if this is horrible – but, maybe Aunt Bernie should go to Kellvale.'

Silence.

'You said it would be nice for Aunt Bernie and Aunt Bea to be together.'

'Yeah, but it's not exactly what I had in mind.'

I could sense him turning it over. I imagined him standing there like a giant puzzled teddy bear.

'She's so sick, Daddy,' I pressed. 'How can I take care of her, work, do everything? She needs a nurse, really, and she's so, so – '

'Stubborn. I know.'

'She'll never do what the doctor says and certainly not what I tell her. She'll never let herself be controlled. She'll fall down the stairs, she'll kill herself – '

'This isn't like you, Rosie. You're really upset.'

'Yes. I am.'

'Well, that's natural. 'Course you need some help. No one expects you to handle this alone. You seem to be forgetting,' he was very gentle, 'you've got a big family. They'll pitch in, all you have to do is ask. What

about your cousin, Mary Ellen? She doesn't have any children yet and
she lives three blocks away.'

'She won't speak to Aunt Bernie since she boycotted her wedding.'

'Why wouldn't Bernie go?'

'Mary Ellen married a Methodist. Don't you remember?'

He chuckled. 'What an old battleaxe your aunt is.' As though his
sister's bigotry were somehow endearing. Vinnie, who preached equal
rights and went to the Selma march, still liked a joke at a Protestant's
expense. I told myself that he was not perfect and that I must also get
him back on the track. He remained so adept at getting off it.

'Daddy, I'm really worried.'

'Well, sweetie, don't you be.'

'It's not going to work out.' I was beginning to panic.

'Sure, it will. Be more optimistic. Bernie's tough. She'll be on her
feet in no time. Outlive us all. Ask Third Cousin Bernard's wife to
come over.'

'She's pregnant. Besides, she wouldn't take care of her own mother.
What makes you think she'll help me with Aunt Bernie?'

'Well, shit, there's plenty of others. You've just got to calm down and
think it through. This won't be for ever.'

Oh yes, it will, I thought. I was so desperate I nearly told him about
Travis and hating teaching and Florence and everything.

'What's really on your mind?' he suddenly asked.

'What do you mean?'

'You're not acting like you. Something wrong?'

'Nothing.'

'You sure?'

'Yes.' Why didn't I tell him? Because it would have been like walking
into his bedroom naked.

'OK. But promise me you'll stop worrying. I'll think over what you
said about Kellvale. My mind isn't closed. It's only that – give me a
chance to get used to the idea.'

'All right.'

'That's my Sweetiepie. Got some great pictures for you. Denise'll
send them right along.'

'OK. Good.'

After we'd hung up, I realized I'd forgotten to ask when he was
coming.

My aunt was waiting for me, sitting in her wheelchair, alert and
furious.

101

'I had to unpack,' she announced.

I explained that she would be out in a couple of days.

'I want to be in my own place.' There was nothing pathetic about her. She was issuing commands.

'But it's only – '

'You get me outa here, Rose. I had enough.'

'Aunt Bernie.' I took her hand. 'You're not ready. You still need to be looked after.'

'I'll look after myself. I'll manage. I managed since I was thirteen.'

'I know. But you have had me.'

She looked at me, her eyes hard as jet. 'You! You just want to take off.' She missed nothing. Did she know? 'I wanna be *in my own place* where I can take care of myself like I always done. You. You don't care about your religion, so how can you care about me?'

'I do care about you.'

'Then take me home right now. Nurse!'

Her voice cracked. I saw how thin she'd grown, how her hands shook, how the fine hairs flourished on her cheeks. Her eyes were sunken, her face yellowish and drawn. But it was not the face of a dying woman. Behind those eyes that still saw everything there was rage. Indomitable rage, rage that could keep her alive indefinitely, rage that was also contagious.

'Aunt Bernie,' I said with a firmness that amazed me, 'I think you should go to Kellvale for a while.'

'Nurse!'

'I said,' I raised my voice, 'I think you should go to Kellvale for two weeks. I can't take care of you the way you are. You're too sick. You need rest.'

'I need to go home. Nurse!'

'I ain't deaf.' Margaret Cleary bustled up to the bed, checking charts and waving a thermometer. 'Time for your medication, Bernadette.'

'I don't want no more pills.' She turned her face away, suddenly tragic. 'I had enough pills. Where's my brother? Where's Vinnie?'

'He's coming,' I lied.

'Vinnie'll take me home.' There were tears in her eyes.

'Come on now, Bernadette, down the hatch.' Nurse Cleary pushed a cup of water under my aunt's nose. I had to look away.

'No,' she moaned, 'no.'

Nurse Cleary forced a green tablet into her mouth.

'There's a good girl.'

'I won't go to no Kellvale.' She swallowed two pink ones. 'They put my poor dumb sister in there and now they want to do the same thing to me.' She swallowed a blue-and-white capsule.

'It's not the same thing, Aunt Bernie. It's only for a little while.' I broke off, in tears myself.

'Kellvale,' she spat. 'Sounds like a washing machine.'

Nurse Cleary laughed as she fed her patient two green-and-black capsules. 'You're a real card, Bernadette. But think about it. There's worse places you could spend two weeks.'

'It's a prison. It's the end.' She glared at me, but already the anger in her eyes was beginning to dissolve. She was losing her focus, but not for long.

'Aunt Bernie,' I begged. 'Please. I want you to get well.' I meant it. 'And you need more care than I can give you.'

'You're a dirty liar, Rose Mullen.'

'Bernadette,' barked Nurse Cleary, 'you got a good niece. What's more, she's your only niece, so you be civil to her.' I motioned her to leave off the efforts on my behalf. 'Now it's time for her to go because you're a tired girl, but I'm gonna wheel you to the door so's you can give her a nice good-night kiss like I know you want to in your haht.'

Bernie stared straight before me, her jaw set like concrete. When we reached the door, I bent to kiss her. 'Happy dreams, Aunt Bernie,' I said miserably as she jerked her head away.

Margaret Cleary raised her eyes to heaven. 'Bernadette, *why* are you so difficult?'

Bernie waited as, despite ourselves, we hung on her words.

'*I'm me*,' she said, and her mouth snapped shut like a trap.

This is my most vivid memory of my aunt – grasping the arms of a wheelchair, deprived by the medical profession, her family and her own body of any power over her destiny. And yet we feared her. We drew back before this frail woman who had never risen more than five feet-one inches from the ground and submitted only one hundred and eight pounds to the pull of gravity. She had nothing with which to threaten us, but she held us all in her orbit like a planet its satellites.

'Can't you keep her a little longer?' I pleaded.

'There's people sicker'n her needs the beds. But we'll see.'

In my dazed state I walked straight past Julia who caught my arm in the entryway.

'Am I too late, Rose?'

I stared at her.

'I mean, is she still awake, dear?'

'Just. She'll be glad to see you.'

'Then I'll go right up. You're doing a wonderful job, Rose.'

On the way home I went to a liquor store and bought myself a fifth of Scotch. I mixed some with ginger ale and sat at the kitchen table, sipping it slowly. It seemed to steady my nerves. It was the first time I had ever drunk alone.

I felt Travis everywhere – in the still air, in the music that came from a car in the parking lot, in the earthy brown taste of the whisky itself. He seemed to permeate the world and to touch me across great distances. How was this possible? It couldn't just be the drink. He was trying to reach me, I knew, in his crazy Travis way that disdained the ordinary, more efficient methods. There could be no doubt; he was testing my capacity to hear him. I would pass the test. I would respond. Even now the message was coming clear. The message said: Hurry.

I was to find him before he went west, before he left the East Coast for ever and disappeared into America. (I had as little idea of what was really out there as I did of what lay beyond the Russian steppes.) I would lose my only treasure. Hurry, Rose. But how to hurry? There was till no message from Frank, my father would sweetly shilly-shally till doomsday and my family was clearly convinced that Bernie was my job, my privilege, almost. They would applaud and cheer and encourage and pray for me. But they would not help. There was Irene, but she was currently tending two *memères*. Besides, Bernie would pay no attention to Irene. The Byrnes already took care of their own mother. Phyllis and Clovis were nearly as crazy as Aunt Bea, though they had the iron constitutions of most hypochondriacs. Maybe Katie . . . but the moment the Ladies' Guild got wind of my true intention they would be outraged. They would remind me of my odious duties which, they were convinced, were my eternal lot. They would enlist the nuns, the priests, the full power of the Church against me and insist I remain in Florence. My aunt and her pious court would judge me. They would condemn me. Finally they would offer their forgiveness. And that forgiveness would bind me and hold me captive for good. No, I could not seek assistance from the Ladies' Guild. If only Frank would come, if only Travis would call. But he was waiting for me to find him. The onus was on me. Tomorrow, I encouraged myself, Frank would have the address and a car. Tomorrow Aunt Bernie would yield.

The next morning I went to the hospital but she would not speak to me. Sister Judith was distributing Communion, and the two of them were huddled together, heads bowed, eyes closed. My aunt's whole body was tensed and bent in prayer, and I felt an intruder as I watched them, my hands hypocritically folded. Then Bernie said she wanted to sleep and the nun gave a solemn nod of assent. I accosted her and explained what I could of my problem.

'But naturally, Rose, you'd worry all the time. We all would. You couldn't leave her alone for a minute.'

I thought I would faint with amazement. She was the first person to understand. I grasped her hand and she smiled at me. The smile cut crisp little lines into the skin around her eyes. Her gold-rimmed spectacles were immaculate.

'Would you like me to speak to your aunt?'

I nodded, not trusting my voice.

'Then I'll stay. You run along, and I'll stay.'

'Thank you, Sister.'

'That's what we're here for.'

I had an ally. My hopes were up and I went to Franklin Street almost lightheartedly.

'We've got a car,' Frank announced. 'Hank Lessard's brother's been drafted and he left him the Pontiac.'

'When can we go?'

'Well, today's Friday. How about tomorrow afternoon?'

'Yes. Somehow. Oh God, the address. Did you find it?'

'East 2nd Street.' He handed me a letter. 'There's no phone number.' There was no street number either. I scanned the letter.

'This is over a year ago.'

'I know.'

'What's her last name?'

'H-H-Hillier. She's married, I guess.'

I hadn't known. From all Travis's ominous hints I had learned nothing.

'Travis is very light and very dark,' Frank said, reading my thoughts and looking at me in that concentrated way he had.

'Like the moon,' I answered. 'Except everyone's always saying it's women who are like the moon.'

'Maybe Travis is part-woman.'

The idea intrigued and repelled me. I smiled in a way that I hoped was knowing. I still felt obliged to hide certain of my discomforts from Frank. Not that I fooled him.

The rest of the day was a sick grey chaos. I kept dropping my scoop to run to the bathroom. Nothing I ate would stay down or in, and so by three I was trembling with nervous exhaustion. My distress was so obvious that Cora ordered me home. Gratefully I surrendered my starched white cap and apron – as it turned out, for ever – and left.

After drinking a quarter bottle of Gelusil I lay down for half an hour, my hands clasped over my concave belly. I had read in a magazine about the effects of deep breathing on frayed nerves, and so I tried that with some success. I turned in order to be spared a view of St Blaise's spires. I thought of Travis and of his mystery and how the longing for someone can turn into the longing to *be* that someone, to become their secret. I wanted to be Travis, to disappear into him. To become his secret seemed the only way to ease the torment of wondering what that secret was.

Just as the bells rang five, Irene knocked.

'Hi, de-yah.' She waddled over and sat beside me, giving off a sweet-smelling heat. 'How is our poor Bernadette?'

She clicked her tongue and shook her head as I told her. I had no qualms about describing Aunt Bernie's behaviour of the previous evening. Irene patted my arm.

'Your aunt, she gets so upset, Rose. She tries alla time, alla time to hide it, you know, how mad she is at the world and everyone, but it don't always work. She tries not to do bad things when she's like that – so worked up and angry – but sometimes she just can't help it.'

'I know.'

'She was bad about your cat, and you was a good girl to forgive her.'

'What do you mean?'

'She was mad that weekend you was away. She couldn't take no more. I guess the cat made a mess or something, but that was no excuse and I told her. I told her she shouldn't have done what she did. I think she was sorry afterwards.'

'What did she do?'

'Why, she went right out and bought that chloroform – Oh, de-yah, I thought you knew!'

'Yes. Yes, of course I knew.' Only I'd known it unconsciously. Now the deed had come out of the dark half of my mind and into the light, an ugly piece of news, guided by kind Irene.

'I said Bernadette, you got no right to do that. She said no, I lost my temper. See, she agreed with me. But she *did not like* that I told her. I think she was sorry, though.'

'Maybe.' I kept very still. I hardly blinked.

'I don't like to say this, de-yah, but your aunt, she's very hard. She's good, but she's hard.'

'Yes.'

'So don't you mind what she says. You been nice to her, better than a daughter. It hasn't been easy, I know. Don't pay no attention when she gets nasty.'

'I won't. Thank you, Irene.' I kissed her. 'I have to go now.'

'OK, de-yah.' She gave me a hug. 'God bless you, now.'

From the entrance to the ward I could see a suitcase by my aunt's bed, packed, locked and ready to go. Nurse Cleary passed me at freeway velocity.

'We couldn't stop her,' she hissed. 'But I got you a day's grace.'

Bernie watched me walk towards her. She sat in the wheelchair, still in her nightie and bathrobe, but wearing her clip-on rhinestone bow earrings and clutching her brown handbag as if it were both a baby and a weapon.

'How are you today, Aunt Bernie?'

'Tip-top.'

'I brought you some ice-cream.'

'I don't want it.'

'OK, I'll give it to the nurses.'

'I want to go home.' She spoke with the same resolution as the day before. Obviously Sister Judith had not succeeded.

'Please, Aunt Bernie – ' The worst thing I could have said. But I hadn't the presence of mind for diplomacy nor the strength for bullying. I was coming apart before we had even begun. I am too rational a person for war, and I still had not learned that temperance is lost on a tyrant. (But you know my weaknesses all too well.)

'You call a taxi. Those nurses won't do it. I've got the money right here.' She patted her bag. No wonder everyone was avoiding us. I suddenly remembered that picture of her as a young girl in the Mill.

'I'm sorry. I can't do that.'

She sighed. 'Call a taxi. I'm getting out of this place.'

'Of course you are. But tomorrow.'

'Today. Now.'

'You're not even dressed.'

'You help me.'

'I'm sorry, but – oh, please!'

'You're not putting me into no home. I'm not crazy like my poor sister.'

I tried again. 'No. No. It's only for two weeks. Maybe only a week.'

'Once I'm in I'll never get out. I'm going home. It's my home, not yours, and you can't keep me out.'

'I don't want to keep you out. I just want you to go back in two weeks!'

'First two weeks, then two years. You just want to go chasing men.'

'I do not. I love someone.'

'You don't love nobody.'

'I do,' I shouted. Everyone turned to look at us. But I didn't care. I hated my aunt and I wanted to tell the world. 'I do. I do so. What do you know about love?'

'I know Jesus and Mary and they's the only love 'cept family. And you got neither of them. So what have you got? He don't love you, whoever he is. And you don't love him or your religion or your family, so what have you got?'

Had she really found out?

'You don't know anything about me. You think you do but you don't.'

'Call a taxi, Rose.' She placed her bag on the bed and began to remove her bathrobe. Nurse Cleary came towards us. 'Close those curtains.'

'I won't.' I stamped my foot. More nurses approached the periphery of our drama, but for the next minute I was conscious of nothing but the fury that was rising inside me, from a place I had not known existed or which I had forgotten after a visit paid there long ago. It pushed up like a geyser and flooded the space behind my eyes.

'Aunt Bernie, you're a stubborn old woman.'

'I know it.'

'You're a murderer, Aunt Bernie. You're going to Kellvale tomorrow. You deserve to go there. You deserve worse than that!'

'I won't go. You can't make me.'

'Listen to me, Aunt Bernie – ' I wagged my finger at her. Quick as a cat she reached for it, grabbed it and bit it through to the bone. To the bone. With her great yellow teeth, every one of which she still possessed. I screamed, not so much at the pain as in rage and loathing. I wanted to bash my aunt's head with a blunt instrument. I pictured her tiny brain splattered across the gleaming antiseptic hospital floor. I clutched my finger and went on screaming. I screamed until the hands of the nurses and their hurried whispered words calmed me and brought me from my furious trance. They led me away. I was very passive with them and, without a murmur, allowed them to apply disinfectant and bandages. One of them pressed a few painkillers on me and I accepted with a quiet thank you. Then I said I would go, and they nodded, their foreheads crumpled in concern. At the door, I glanced back at my aunt's bed, but it was shrouded in curtains. Was I coming tomorrow morning? they asked. I said yes, then left them.

On the way home I stopped on the Market Street bridge to watch the brown water rushing under the road and look at the Mill towers and feel the first real pain in my throbbing finger. If I had any thoughts I do not remember them. Someone tooted a horn and waved and I waved back and smiled without seeing or caring who it was. The evening was full of the pink light of late summer. It fell on the buildings and streets in a way that exaggerated the loneliness of the place. It made my whole body ache.

I was determined to leave the next afternoon for New York. Irene's disclosure had made me more determined than ever. I knew my rights now. When I arrived back at the apartment I double-locked the door in order to do what I had to do in peace. I telephoned Kellvale and enquired about vacancies for a patient needing a week or so to recover. They had one, in fact they had several since most elderly Florentines were cared for by their families. I began to pack, putting clothes in a suitcase then throwing them aside in an effort to keep luggage to a minimum. I thought of September and the cooler nights, but I took only one sweater. I could not project myself further forward in time. I would be gone for a couple of weeks, I told myself, a little longer, maybe. I had never faced such a hazy future. Then Frank called.

'I'm sorry,' he said. 'I c-c-c-can't get the car.'

'Why not?'

'Hank's father's decided to drive up to Nova Scotia at the last minute. Fishing. Do you want me to try Roger again? Perhaps my parents – '

'I don't think I can wait any longer. Besides, you have to be at work on Monday.'

'It doesn't matter.'

'Yes, it does.' I hesitated, waiting for the force that was carrying me along to switch into full throttle. 'I'll do something else. I'll go alone.'

'Rose, d-d-don't . . .'

'I'll call you when I get there. Bye, Frank.'

It was meant to be. It was. I still think so. And in that moment, I saw my situation clearly. I understood what had happened: Travis had disappeared in order to save me. He could not tell me outright, being the way he was, that I must leave Florence in order to save my soul. He could only show me. He was rescuing me by forcing me to follow him. He was throwing me a line. This time I would not hesitate to seize it.

I dialled the convent of the Sisters of Mercy. I thought of Sister Richard ringing her bell in the playground, calling us in from the cold and the sun and the rain, putting an end to our pursuit of Rose.

'Yes, Rose.'

'Sister Judith, did you speak to my aunt?'

'I did, dear. She's very upset.'

'I know. I'm giving up the idea of Kellvale. But listen, could you help me? I'm in trouble.'

'Of course.'

I told her that my father was in Boston for two days, that he had been ill for quite a while (which was why he had not come to see my aunt) and that he intended to consult a specialist at Mass. General. It would be my only opportunity to see him as he had to be back at work on Monday morning. Of course my aunt must know nothing of this. I had been deceiving her at my father's insistence. We had agreed that we did not have the right to upset her. (We were very close, my father and I.) She might even insist on going to Boston herself. No one in the family felt able to manage her. They were all afraid of her, I guessed she knew. But she would trust the nuns. She was practically one herself, they were always saying so. She would do what they suggested, provided it was only for a short time. Would they keep her for a few days so that I might visit my father and try to learn the truth about his sickness, which I hinted might be serious? Would they pick her up from Boott Memorial at nine tomorrow morning and take her to the convent for the weekend? She would regard it as a treat, now that the threat of Kellvale was past. And I would be eternally grateful. I would also, I swore, be back on Monday.

She did not answer immediately.

'Does Bernadette understand this arrangement?'

'Oh yes. She's really happy about it. That is, if it's OK with you, Sister.'

'Well, yes. I don't see why not. Should I call and reassure her?'

'Oh, please don't do that. They've only just quieted her down. She's had a tranquillizer and – '

'I understand perfectly. And you'd like us there at nine.'

'Please. If you can.'

'All right, Rose.'

'I don't know how to thank you,' I said sincerely.

'That's what we're here for.'

The Trailways bus to Boston left at eight-twenty-five, Saturday morning. I was on it with my one suitcase and the copy of *Lie Down In*

Darkness which Travis had given me. Inside was the last photograph taken of Foxie.

We passed the corner of Walnut Street where the convent was and where in less than an hour my aunt would struggle up the three front steps and along the narrow hallway; where she would be guided to the sitting-room with its pictures of St Teresa; where she would be placed carefully in a wooden chair and given a cup of tea and a Lorna Doone; and where she would receive the news that I had deserted her.

At Exit 6 we joined the Main Turnpike. I was tempted to look back one more time at the spires of St Blaise and Holy Trinity and the towers of the Mills, but instead I stared straight ahead at the grey road that did not curve and hardly dipped.

After all, I thought, you *are* the Sisters of Mercy.

8

Despair

I went without lunch then without supper. You said my loss of appetite was due to guilt, but this wasn't true. Excitement was the real cause. Not only at the certainty of seeing Travis, or at least finding some clue to his whereabouts, but the soaring sensation of being led on by powerful unknown forces. By destiny, I said, and you laughed at me.

You liked my description of the panic I felt when I walked into the heat and dirt and chaos of Port Authority bus terminal. I had forgotten about the Labour Day weekend and its attendant madness. I stood outside a phone booth for five minutes, intending to ring the convent of the Sisters of Mercy. Then I changed my mind. I found a seat and waited for my courage to come back. I gaped at the black people sweeping floors, selling grass, emptying rubbish, arriving from Mobile, Macon, Shreveport. Mothers with five children carrying cardboard boxes tied up with binder twine. I admired them and felt shy of them. I sensed in them a life undreamed of by me. There had been a few black people at the base in Kittery and one family in Florence who had stayed a year. None of them had looked like this. I knew I was staring, but I couldn't help it. I watched them and the Latin Americans I later found out were Puerto Ricans. They had a shabby defiant glamour that intrigued me. (I was a citizen of Florence where pastel neatness was the admired norm.) I thought that anyone who could wear colours like that could not be completely defeated.

I was too stunned and stupid to read the signs which everywhere directed me upstairs to the street. Without a thought, I left my suitcase unattended, drawn again to the telephone booths, this time in search of a Manhattan directory. There had been some, but now their plastic binders dangled from chains like sockets from which arms have been wrenched. I rushed back to my bag. A fat lady in flowered trousers had taken my seat and was reading a TV guide. She looked contemptuously at my white round-collared blouse and khaki skirt. I felt like a wren in a rainforest and resolved to acquire some protective clothing.

A notice pointed to a taxi rank, but that was out of the question. I intended to guard my stash. (For what? Until when?) I was attracted to a coffee shop ablaze with strip lights. Behind the counter was an elderly black man who took my order and smiled and presented me with toast and two fried eggs, hard and greasy and perfectly round. I ate the yolks and left the rest. It was nine-thirty when I asked him for a honey-dip doughnut. The couple beside me were accompanied by a stuffed four-foot rabbit. The woman's fingernails were painted gold and the man wore a narrow-brimmed straw hat with a sweat-stained band.

They were eating cheeseburgers and laughing hysterically, pretending to feed the rabbit. Now I would know their Bronx anywhere, but then I barely understood what they were saying. I wondered what the rabbit's origin and destination might be. I envied their crazy intimacy which made me miss Travis all the more.

No one noticed me. Everyone acted as though I didn't exist, though the pain in my finger and in my heart made me more certain then ever that I did. I paid and took the escalator to the street floor.

8th Avenue was raging. The heat, the music, the lights, the smells, made my head spin and my abused stomach heave. The air was so thick that the movement of the hundreds of other bodies seemed to push it up and over me in great nauseating waves. I was drowning in its density. The closer I came to 42nd Street the more overwhelmed I was by an atmosphere both wild and oppressive; an endless fascination and a hot steel trap. I turned and walked uptown, gaping at the buildings. Above 50th Street it was slightly cooler, but I still breathed with difficulty. I heard muted thunder above the traffic, and I longed for the ozone and the rain. But no deluge, it seemed, however prolonged, could have washed the city clean. It was like a gigantic soul stained with mortal sin. (How corny, I hear you say. What a pathetic cliché. But what did you expect? I was a little American smiler from the sticks.)

The man behind the reception desk at the Hotel Pearl did not make me feel welcome. He eyed me with suspicion as he showed me to the elevator. (What crime did he think I might commit? What possible trouble could I be?) I carried my own bag. At the third floor we stepped into a hallway that smelled like a men's room. I was sure I was the only woman in the place.

Number 32 was grey-green in the sticky glow of an overhead light. There was a single bed, a ragged brown armchair and some dismal curtains which concealed a view of a brick wall. Over the bed and next to the bathroom was some graffiti in Spanish. I was certain someone had committed suicide in that room.

'OK, miss?' he addressed me, and slammed the door before I could answer. My fear of sitting down was even greater than my exhaustion. Something vile would cling to me, something that could never be scrubbed away. The walls seemed about to cave in. When, after a few minutes, they were still upright, I decided to look for a telephone. I opened the door and squinted into the thick air. I saw a pay-phone at the end of the corridor but no directories. These too had been torn from their holders.

After several attempts to reach information, I was given a number for Eva Hillier. I could not believe my luck, and my hands shook with excitement as I dialled. I was told that the number was out of service at that time. I hung up. She was no better at paying her bills than her brother. But the operator had given me the street number.

I closed my door and turned back the limp yellowed sheets. Even in these circumstances, alone for the first time in my life in a strange and minatory room, I could not neglect my bedtime ritual. Assiduously I brushed my teeth and scrubbed my face before a mirror in which I appeared five years older than I had the day before. I put on a clean nightie and lay down, stiff and straight on my back, my ears pricked at the unmistakable sounds of scuttling in the dark. Simultaneously I thought: I cannot stay here and I am so glad I came.

I lay awake through the hot night, my finger throbbing and aching, listening to the roar of New York and sinister murmurings in the hall. I felt as though I were inside a gigantic animal, swallowed whole into the belly of the city. I made and abandoned a dozen plans. I had no idea where East 2nd Street was and I experienced the awful freedom of knowing nothing.

I left in the morning, intending to take the subway downtown, but when I came to the top of the stairs and looked into the stinking gloom my nerves failed me and I continued along 7th Avenue in a chemical haze still unrelieved by rain. I went into a coffee shop to study the map I had bought and to break my fast with two corn muffins and some tea. People at the counter talked as though in the early stages of a violent argument. I soon discovered that this was the normal New York mode of address and that here confrontation was sought to the same degree that it was avoided in Maine. Everyone was quick and jumpy and irritable as though operating on an excess of adrenalin. There seemed to be a stream of it running beneath the sidewalks, carrying us all along with more than enough to spare. It was probably this superfluous energy that made me feel what was happening to me was a drama, singular and important, yet part of a huge collective adventure.

I forced down half a muffin and most of the tea and was afraid I might have to run for the washroom. I must straighten out my diet, I thought. I must eat well and become healthy, clean and healthy. Travis and I will become healthy together.

Back on the street I waited twenty minutes for a downtown bus on which the driver shouted at me and the other passengers pressed me towards the back while trampling on my feet exposed in their white sandals. After 14th Street it was less crowded so I was able to make my way unsteadily forward to ask directions of the driver. He told me to get off at Houston Street and walk east. I didn't dare ask him more since, like everyone else, he seemed in a very bad mood.

Houston Street is stark and wide and rackety. Trucks thunder along it at top speed. Buildings are mainly from the thirties and forties and so there is an uninterrupted expanse of sky. It is a desolate road, impersonal, but one where you sense the power of the city in its primal form. For it marks the end of the numbered streets and of planned environment and the beginning of Lower Manhattan, an older New York that grew organically outwards from the docks – the area where Irish immigrants once kept pigs in the yards behind their tenements; where they then moved naturally into the garbage collection business; where the Jews later opened jewellery shops and pawn shops and pickle stores; where the Chinese ran restaurants and movie theatres and lived what everyone else regarded as a secret life. In the sixties Lower Manhattan was still a ghetto. It was also the warehouse and factory area that has since become glitzy Soho but was then grubby and interesting, in its own way beautiful and seldom visited by people who lived above 14th Street. In the winter Houston Street receives the full force of the wind off the East River. That morning in September it was hot, empty and grey. Labour Day traffic was thin and there were few pedestrians.

I turned into Avenue B and was amazed by the contrast. Here hundreds of people crowded the dirty sidewalks, many giving the impression that they spent most of their days outside in this teeming neighbourhood of bold shadows, makeshift shopfronts and crumbling brick. There were Puerto Ricans, Ukrainians, Hasidic Jews, hippies in beads and shawls. From every window and doorway came music I had never heard – brassy, full-blooded, flirty and insistent – impelled ceaselessly forward by the throb of bongos, some of which were set up next to the stoops and played by men with black moustaches, dark glasses and flowered shirts unbuttoned to the navel who shouted at me in Spanish. I was amazed by the general state of undress. Most women wore shorts and halters, many of the men were bare-chested and a few of both sexes were clearly in their underwear. It was like being on a cement beach. Every human shape and size was on view, some bizarrely compacted and distended, some beautiful.

The signs over the grocery stores, dry cleaners and drugstores were in Spanish, though the older ones were in Hebrew. I made my way through the hedges of garbage cans and past some storefront evangelical churches whose windows were crammed with a jumble of cheap religious memorabilia that was both scary and touching, a cross between a carnival stall and a black-magic altar. I felt drab, intoxicated, nervous and brave. I was among the exotic poor.

I was so distracted by the sight of a bearded man in sunglasses, flip-flops, a beard, hair to his shoulders and a dress like Nora wore in 1949 that I nearly missed Eva's building. The door was one of the few that was not wide open. I searched the names and rang the bell. I rang again and again but no reply. Why had I counted on an immediate response?

'But,' I encouraged myself, 'it's Sunday. She may have gone to see a friend, gone to church even.' I decided to sit down on the stoop like everyone else. I marvelled at the sight of so many people with seemingly nothing to do. What Frank would have called the sub-proletariat. My aunt, who assumed that society rested upon a bed-rock of working citizens who belonged to unions and voted Democrat and were continually employed, would have been astounded. It was nearly noon and the smell of frying food was everywhere. I rang again, this time without hope and just for something to do. The door opened.

'Whodjoo want?'

'Eva.' I answered the man in jeans and a black T-shirt who carried a bag of laundry.

'Eva who?'

'Eva Hillier. Lives in your building.'

'What's she look like?'

'I don't know. Tall, probably. Blonde.'

'No blondes here. She a friend of yours?'

'I don't really know her. I know her brother, though – '

'That's not much help.' He checked the bells.

'Oh-h-h, *Eva*. Here she is. 2C, at the back, dear. Just go in.'

'Do you know her?'

'Sure. Don't think she's been around lately. G'wan. Go wait.'

I was glad of shelter from the sun which was beating down on the even-numbered side of the street.

'Thank you,' I said as he let the door slam behind me. The light was so dim that I had to feel my way along the hall. The raised metallic pattern, in whose volutes dust congealed, slid beneath my fingers. I came to 2C and knocked, but there was no reply. I was discouraged and lightheaded from lack of food. I sat on the cool tiles, my back to Eva's door.

Throughout the afternoon tenants came and went, not noticing me, concealed as I was by the stairs. My eyes grew accustomed to the gloom, and I watched the ridges in the red door as they sharpened then blurred in the fading afternoon light. Behind that door lay all my clues, all my hope, and I could only sit before it like a paralytic. The romantic adventure was turning sour.

I was diverted by shouting and screaming coming from above and moving down the stairs. It was black T-shirt and a male friend. There must have been some unpleasantness about that laundry because clothes were raining down everywhere and covering the stairs and floor. Now both men were in the entryway, shrieking like banshees. I leaned forward from my hiding place for a better view.

'You bitch! You did that on purpose!' black T-shirt's friend screamed as he beat him determinedly with a pair of red underpants. Black T-shirt countered with a pair of lime-green ones. I think he was winning because his friend opened the door and ran into the street with black T-shirt hard on his heels. They didn't come back. I picked up the clothes, folded them and left them on the bottom step. It was something to do.

I was hot and badly wanted a drink. But if I left, how would I get back into the building? New Yorkers were suspicious and would not all be as obliging as black T-shirt, if he ever returned. Finally I had to go. I wrote a note to Eva saying that I would be back at seven if possible and giving her the number of the Hotel Pearl. As I pushed the note under the door, I heard a soft bumping followed by little pleading cries. A cat! Eva could not have gone far.

'Pussy, pussy,' I whispered and talked nonsense through the crack to my invisible friend. An orange paw tried to push its way under the door. When I touched it it immediately withdrew then reappeared. 'I have to go now,' I informed it. 'But I'll be back. Don't hide that letter, now, will you.'

I bought a Pepsi from the bodega next to Eva's building and returned to Houston Street with no intention but to wander until seven. At every corner I felt dizzy. The streets were narrow and dead straight, their vanishing points submerged in a jumble of signs and fire escapes. Looking north I could see the Empire State Building. I have still never been to the top.

A hawker with a pony-tail to his waist was selling copies of a paper called the *Great Eastern Zone*. It looked interesting but I didn't buy it. I was amazed to find everything open on a Sunday. I found myself back on Houston Street and stood there like a lost child or an alien being, not knowing what to do next. I noticed a small restaurant with a blue-and-white sign over the door that said 'Yona Shimmel's'. I peered through the window. The homely atmosphere and the delicious smell drew me to the place in spite of its shabby appearance. I was the only customer. A small man with a mournful expression stood behind the counter and asked me what I wanted. I read the menu: latkes, knishes, blintzes.

'I'm sorry, I don't know what these are,' I said. 'I'm from Maine.'

He looked at me in resigned disgust, his brown eyes sorrowful, his features shaped by experiences inconceivable to me. He sighed and walked off. I should leave, I thought. I've offended him. But I was too tired to get up. So I sat there until he returned with a glass full of thick white liquid and a plate on which was a square of soggy pastry.

'Eat,' he commanded, his patience obviously at an end. I didn't dare ask what the two items were, nor did I dare disobey his order. I alternated a bite of one with a sip of the other. In less than a minute I had consumed them both.

'Can I have one more of these?'

He had a way of nodding by moving his neck and head forward very slowly and to the right of his shoulder.

'What is it?' I asked.

He rapped a fingernail on the plate. 'Cherry knish.' Then on the glass. 'Yoghurt. We make it.' I nodded and smiled but he had no smile to return.

I had read about yoghurt but never tasted it. And the knish! As I bit into my second helping tears rolled down my cheeks. I just couldn't help it. The knish was sweet, soft, completely gratifying. It seemed to wrap up and console some part of me which had been raw and aching for so long I had almost got used to it. It was like a painkiller, like morphine. The yoghurt with its smooth texture and salty aftertaste was the perfect complement to the flour and fruit. They were an absolution in sugars and fats, the first good thing that had happened to me in many days. I wanted to tell the man behind the counter, to thank him. But I could see he had no interest in my gratitude.

'Very good,' I said, and he gave me his funny nod as I paid him. 'I'll come back.'

(I did go back many times, and I got to know Moishe and I learned that he came from Odessa and was related to the pickle man on Prince Street and had worked for Shimmel's for nearly twenty years. I went there when I was broke and when I needed comfort, which was often.)

Once again no one answered Eva's bell, but the food had given me new courage and I rang 1C. The crackle of static made it impossible to understand the reply. Whoever it was did not like the sound of my voice because I was not buzzed in. I tried 1B with the same results. Where was black T-shirt?

'Oh, come *on*,' I pleaded to the air and the wall and the door. Then I rang all the bells at once and the intercom vomited such abuses that I stepped backwards and nearly fell off the stoop. The men with the bongos shouted at me again. I decided to give up and go back to the hotel.

The Hotel Pearl was deserted. I opened the door to my room, afraid of what I might find. Help me, I prayed, and flipped the switch. Everything was as I had left it. I lay down for what I meant to be a minute, but when I woke up it was four-thirty in the morning. I had dreamt my mother gave me a package. 'Keep it,' she said. 'Take it 'cause I have to go now. Lots to do!' 'Wait,' I pleaded. 'Wait.' But she was already well along the path that led up into the rosy pink mountains with the white houses beyond. What were those mountains and who lived in the houses? Then I remembered everything that had happened in the past few days. I remembered that it was Labour Day morning and that I was in the Hotel Pearl waiting for Travis's sister who I didn't even know. I felt the pain in my finger and remembered that I was now alone in the world and that I was probably a fool.

I must have slept again because I did not hear the porter's first knock.

'Hayaguttacoll,' he repeated until I finally opened the door. I thought he was accusing me of something.

'I'm sorry.'

He thrust a slip of paper at me. 'She said to *coll*,' he said as though addressing a retarded child. 'Just coll uh.'

I shut the door in a hurry and read the note. There was a number – 628-9337 – and a name, Janice. This must be the link to Eva. Who else would telephone me at the Hotel Pearl? No one on earth knew where I was.

Even in my nightie I was sweating. I consulted my patch of sky for clouds, but all I could make out was a static poisonous grey with no promise of cleansing breezes. I was so distracted that I nearly went into the hall without putting on a bathrobe. I had 3 dimes. I prayed the phone would work. A woman answered.

'Janice?' Travis was coming closer every minute.

'Oh, you must be Rose.' I sensed a smile in her voice. 'Eva told me about you.' Really? 'I'm Eva's neighbour. I live downstairs, you know. I'm taking care of her cat while she's away.'

'Eva's away?'

'Out of town. You know – upstate. But she'll be back in a week.'

My disappointment must have been obvious.

'Don't worry,' said Janice. 'She has to come back 'cause she's got a doctor's appointment on the eighth.'

'It's just that I'm staying at a hotel and there's not much time. I'm trying to find her brother.'

'Which one?'

'Is he – I mean – '

'Are you all right, Rose?'

'I'm fine. Look, could I just see the apartment? I mean, I hope you don't think that's funny.'

'Oh no. In fact I spoke to Eva and she said if you didn't have a place to stay you could wait for her here.'

It was as though she had been expecting me.

'Only – ' Janice hesitated.

Yes?'

'Well, the place is a little crazy, know what I mean? The electricity's been turned off and there's no telephone. And Otis is sort of a problem.'

'Otis?'

'He's the cat. Cute cat. But a little schitzy. Eva's the only one who really understands him. They been together years.'

'You mean he bites?'

'Nooo. He – well, you'll see. When you want to come over?'

'Now?'

'Well, actually I'm doing some work, so how about twelve-thirty?'

'Fine.'

'OK, Rose, I'm sure looking forward – '

My dimes ran out. It was now nine-thirty. How to live through the next three hours? Eat, I told myself. You must have lost five pounds in the last week. If you don't eat and sleep you'll meet Travis looking just terrible. And then I thought: Travis is here. He's still here. I know it. Somewhere out in the city. Maybe even in that apartment, waiting for me to open the door. I only hope he knows I've understood the message, his running away and all it meant, and that I've done what he wanted me to do. He must realize I'd never let him down. Then anxiety spread through me like a dye, tinting everything with its sick colours.

'Hey, what happened to your finger?' Janice asked as soon as she'd opened the door.

'A dog. Thank you for doing this.' I couldn't be grateful enough.

'Oh, I got a dog. You like animals? I love them. That pure being, that innocence. So important for us twisted humans.'

Janice weighed two hundred and fifty pounds at least. I followed her as she puffed and panted down the stairs. The wobbling flesh on the backs of her arms reminded me of Mrs Grady, and her voluminous mu-mu could not conceal the terrible truth about her backside. Her round smiling face was flushed pink and perspiring when we reached her apartment. She insisted I come in to get the key, have a cup of Nescafé and meet Reese. Reese was a palsied Yorkie who resided in a white whicker minaret from which he tyrannized his mistress. The huge colourless eyes of this mini-pasha were those of a drugged mental patient, and at Janice's approach he made noises like a frantic sparrow.

'Oh no, oh never, never, never, never.' Janice cradled him in the enormous folds of her arm. 'I was *not* gone that long, I wasn't, was I Rose? This is Rose. Now you be nice to her my poor little tootsicroll.' She held out his paw for me to shake. I shrank from it, but performed my social duty, as always, with kissing noises and reassurances in what I hoped was appropriate doggie language.

'Why is he called Reese?'

Janice giggled. 'After Reese's Peanut Butter Cups. My favourite nosh. His too,' she confided. 'But don't tell anyone.'

'I won't.'

I sat on tenterhooks, sipping my Nescafé and burning to be upstairs in 2C. I had no time to discuss the terrier's pulmonary problems, but that is what I did. Reese obliged by staging a coughing fit during which Janice fussed and fretted and seemed about to burst into tears. But I remembered my own feelings for Foxie and I did not feel contempt.

The small crowded apartment was full of clay and wax sculptures of humans and animals, mainly heads and mainly dogs. Some appeared to be wounded, some forgiving. Others smiled beatifically or seemed to be undergoing a kind of transfiguration. There was a sheep in ecclesiastical robes, a cat with wings, a mouse which looked as if it was ascending into heaven. There was Reese in various hats – a jester's, a top hat, a baseball cap – all lined up on a plank. The human heads were more straightforward and realistic, though all were tinted with benign expression that I supposed was Janice's hallmark. Holy cards decked the mirror. On the walls were pictures of St Francis of Assisi with whom Janice obviously identified.

'You noticed my work,' she beamed.

'You're very talented.'

'Well, I try. I'm only an amateur, but I feel I participate in the Great Creative Force. In my own small way. Creativity is a divine gift.' She sighed and gazed at the collection of heads. 'I work nights mainly and at weekends. I don't get much time, you see, because of my job. I do the books for this little company that makes dancer's shoes. Funny, I got this weird head for figures even though I'm an artist. Now that's unusual, I think.'

'I'm very envious of artists.'

She studied me. 'But you – you have some hidden capacity. I can tell, you know, I'm never wrong.' She slapped her thigh. 'No doubt about it, you're a Sensitive.'

'I am?'

'Yip. Still unformed, of course, still questing . . .'

She was right on that score.

'Me and Eva, we talk about these things sometimes. We got a lot in common. You have a nice interesting face, Rose. Can I do you? Will you sit for me?'

'Sure.' I could feel my life beginning to change for the better. I was suddenly hopeful. I even gave the repulsive Reese a little squeeze.

'And you have a real connection with animals. You're a Sensitive, all right. More coffee?'

'No thanks. Actually I hardly drink coffee.' I did not say that I'd eaten nothing. Otherwise I was certain I'd be force fed the box of assorted cookies on the table beside her worn armchair.

'You're smart there. Coffee is garbage for your system. 'Course I'm an addict. Coffee and food – a real junkie, I guess you noticed. I've tried everything – diets, you name it. Even Novenas and First Fridays. No luck. Can't stop. I guess the Christ Child wanted me to be this way. I got a special devotion to the Christ Child. He chose to be born among the animals. He's the Light of the World.

He loves us just the way we are. Like animals do. Don't you think
so?'

'Oh yes.'

'He loves us all – the Puerto Ricans, too, and the Russians. Some
people, like my family (they live in Queens. I'm from Jamaica Plains,
true-blue New Yorker), my family say black people and Puerto Ricans,
they're lazy and they don't want to work. But I answer them – I do,
really, I'm not afraid – I say they're people whose time has not yet
come. But it will, it truly will. 'Course I don't know what'll happen to
this apartment when it does . . . but that's in God's hands, not mine.'

She went on and on. Finally I asked her for the key. She looked a
little offended at my haste. I apologized.

'Oh, that's OK.' She slipped straight back into good humour. 'Anything you need, you just call.'

With my heart in my throat and feeling a little like Nancy Drew I
turned the key in the lock of 2C. The blinds were drawn and I could
make out only a general tumult plus an underlying smell of cat pee and
vegetable decay. Neither Eva nor Janice were big on cleaning. The place
was stifling and I stumbled towards the large rear window, left slightly
open. I raised it with difficulty and looked out into a small yard full
of rubbish cans. I breathed in great gulps of stale air. I was afraid I
might faint and turned to look for the sink. The living-room (which
I soon discovered was the only room, this being a railroad apartment)
was piled with cardboard boxes, most of them open. Against the walls
stacks of books leaned precariously and scattered toys made walking
in the semi-darkness dangerous. The Castro Convertible was covered
with a tangle of dirty linen and clothes. Burnt-out candles sat on every
flat surface. It was impossble to tell whether someone was moving in
or leaving, but the apartment certainly reflected a life in flux.

I made it to the sink which was heaped with dirty dishes. Next to it a
bathtub held plastic pans and buckets and ducks. A blow-up swan, now
deflated, lay on the floor next to the reeking litter tray. Nowhere could I
find a clean cup, so I drank mouthfuls of water straight from the faucet.
How can anyone live here? I wondered. You'd go mad within a week.
Then I thought: Why am *I* here, why am I, Rose Mullen, gripping this
disgusting sink for dear life, afraid I'll fall on my face into this zoo of
an apartment and pass out and never be heard of again – serve me
right for abandoning my aunt and getting myself into this mess. But,
in my usual way, and according to the mental processes in which I
have trained myself and at which I have become so adept, I regained
my equilibrium.

'Rose,' I said to myself, 'you are here for a reason. You have promised Travis and you must keep your word. You love him and you must do everything you can to find him.'

I inspected the boxes. They held pots and pans and old kitchen utensils, greasy and broken; they held books and clothes and more toys. The books had titles like *Psychic Self Defence*, *Edgar Cayce, Prophet of the Unknown*, and *The Essential Book of Candle Burning*, and were written by people called Dion Fortune, Dane Rhudyar and Lobsang Rampa. The child's clothes were old, probably hand-me-downs, and were separated according to size – the only concession to organization – ending with some that appeared large enough for a four year old. The woman's clothes were mainly ordinary: T-shirts, shorts, denim skirts. Except for one box. I was attracted to a froth of black organza which peeped through the cover and, without shame, began to rifle its contents.

The organza proved to be the petticoat of a red satin strapless dress, much worn and trimmed with black velvet in a Spanish style. There were two pairs of stilettos, yellow and black, a pink satin costume which could have been a swimsuit had it not been boned and padded like a corset. This also had stilettos to match. There was a cat costume, very revealing, with a whiskered mask; there was a clingy, full-length gown, cut low in the back, with tarnished sequins and a rusted zipper; a blue feather boa; two pairs of gold lurex tights and, at the very bottom, a flattened blonde wig that had seen, I hoped, better days. I was intrigued. Eva was a secret glamour-puss, though not lately. She was a many-layered woman, a woman of mystery. I sensed the romance of a disastrous past.

But there was no trace of Travis. I searched for a letter, a postcard, an address book, but all I found was an appointment card for a Dr Gebb on Third Avenue. He and Eva had met every week in April, May and June, then twice in July. The most recent appointment was for the 30th of August. If what Janice said was true, she could not have kept it. But there was another for the second week in September.

I went on looking. I rifled drawers, suitcases, the cupboards under the sink. I forgot the heat and the smell and the pain in my finger. I was hot on Travis's trail, a heartbroken detective. What I first had thought was another room turned out to be a closet. I sensed weight behind the door and opened it very slowly. Papers, notebooks and old shoeboxes slithered on to the floor in a muffled landslide and lay around my feet. I hardly knew where to begin with such a trove. I found Eva's social security card, an expired medical insurance policy and some false fingernails. There was a birth certificate for Angela Iris Hillier which confirmed her age as four, a deck of playing cards and several back issues of the *Great Eastern Zone*, the paper being sold on the streets. In one of them was a picture of a thin girl with high cheekbones, a small nose, black hair and no indentation in her upper lip. She wore a mini skirt and a denim jacket and displayed a lot of leg. The caption read 'Slum Goddess Eva Hillier'. I stared at the picture. She was not as beautiful as Travis. I felt envious and alarmed at my envy. I went on, my assessment of Eva shifting and changing, sweat soaking my blouse and skirt, my hands and knees black from the dust.

I discovered family photographs, in none of which did I discern familiar features. They were an old brittle yellow and reminded me of pictures of my grandparents. There were several of Angela Iris as adorable baby and toddler, one of Eva and a bearded man with a handsome but rather sharp face, and then the one I had been hoping for: the Hilliers, mother and father and teenaged children, a girl and two boys. They posed in the yard next to a clothesline and a bird bath. Mrs Hillier had a round face and her eyes were myopic behind her glasses. Her husband was tall and melancholy and severe. The children seemed ordinary with undistinguished features, except for one who could only be Travis and who stood out instantly as a beautiful impossible original. I turned the picture over. 'Summer 1959', I read, then the names. 'The Hilliers: Desmond and Katherine, Oliver, Eva, Howard.' I looked again at the photo. Could that be some look-alike cousin of Travis? It must be. I searched some more and found a recent photograph of Oliver, the other brother who Travis had never mentioned, in a Marines' uniform. He looked callous and bloated, more a mystery than Eva. How could they have a sibling who seemed so brutal and why hadn't Travis told me about him? Then there was the problem of the last name. How was this to be explained?

Contrary to my theory that Eva had destroyed or hidden her personal papers, I discovered that she threw nothing away. I did not attribute this to sentiment but to alternating compulsion and amnesia. There were high school essays and Year Books, half-finished reports for a course on Egyptian art given at the New School, membership forms, not filled in, for the Theosophical Society, and the Society for Psychical Research, brochures for driving schools and tours of the Holy Land. Inspirations not followed up. And then I found it – a shoebox full of letters. Some of them dated back to 1952 and were from penpals and cousins and teenaged admirers. Some were from Travis. That is, they were in Travis's handwriting. The first was from Bard College:

. . . told myself I'll stay up until 1 a.m., just until one, then go to bed; then I stayed until two. I can still get five hours of sleep before the exam . . . Martha Hyer movie came on. Then it was four and I thought: Oh well, three hours' sleep isn't too bad, then started reading *Naked Lunch*, finally went to bed at 5.30, woke up at nine, missed the first hour of the exam so went back to sleep. Don't you wish we were living in Bali?

Then from Florida:

How is Angela? I think she's complicated like us. But tougher like Oliver . . . whatever you do please don't write to me at the above address . . . I can't bear for you to think of me here.

New York:

. . . if so I'll plead insanity or sexual perversion. Enclosed is a collage you're certain not to like. The little crab claw is from a beach on Long Island. Everything is crashing and crumbling around me. I hate New York. I am going to Maine. Miss you missyoumissyoumissyou. Love, H . . .

Don't tell mother where I am for Christ's sake. I love you.

This last one was from Florence and was signed 'Howard'.

I don't know how long I sat with the letter in my lap staring straight ahead of me. When I heard the knock at the door my whole body heaved as it does when I am drifting off to sleep and am suddenly snapped back into consciousness.

'Rose? Rose, it's Janice.'

'Hi, Janice.' I did not get up.

'Can I come in?'

'It's all right. I'm fine.'

'But – are you OK?'

'I'm resting.'

She waited. 'Well . . . I suppose . . . Has Otis come in?'

'I don't think so.'

126

'You want me to feed him?'

'No. I'll do it.'

'But I have the Little Friskies.'

I asked if I could go on resting and she went away, saying she'd come back in a couple of hours. I heard her put the can of cat food by the door.

I went over the letters again and again, I was so hungry for the sound of his voice, even out of the past, even if it was only in my mind, and even if he were not speaking to me, had not known me then, did not love me then. I read until the sun had moved beyond the building and it was too dark to see. Then I remembered that the electricity had been turned off. When I tried to stand I was so stiff that I cried out. I did not recognize the sound of my own voice. With difficulty I walked to the stove and tried the burners. The gas was still on so I ripped off a piece of old newspaper, lit it, and carried it to the bedside table where a dusty red candle had burned down nearly to the teak surface. The light from it and from another which I found on top of the empty refrigerator made the room almost bearable. The atmosphere suited me. I felt akin to my mad environment.

There was a soft thud on the windowsill. Against a backlighting of early evening stood Otis, the orange cat with problems. He was surprised to see me, I could tell, and doubtful about my credentials.

'Come on, Otis, it's all right.' I planned to win him with Little Friskies and slyly opened the door, careful not to let him out or to make any noise that might attract Janice. In a flash I grabbed the cat food and was back inside. He watched my every move. I put food on the plate and called again, and he came and ate with relish despite his mistrust of me. I tried to pat him, but he didn't like that.

I joined him by finishing off a package of stale Crax. I ate slowly and deliberately while Otis tore through his supper. He looked up at me, expectant and resentful, ready to flee. He was part of a family who fled.

'It's OK,' I told him. 'I've run away too. I guess I've earned the right to be here with you in this crazy place.'

Otis was unimpressed. He leapt into the crowded bathtub and quickly vomited before bolting for the open window. So that was his problem.

Cleaning up after him left me quite queasy. I lay on the bed intending to look through all the photographs again. But my head was bursting with what I had learned. What was I to do with my knowledge? Where should I put it and how would it help me? Travis seemed so distant, yet he might be staying around the corner. I had never encountered so many deceits. I kept returning to the central mystery. Why had he lied about his name? Was it as unbearable as all that or was he just nurturing some private fantasy? Oh, Travis, I prayed (for I could only think of him as Travis), come back.

I sat up. I got up. I pulled the pink satin costume out of the box. On the back of the closet door was a full-length mirror before which I undressed, not looking too closely at my thin white body. I stripped to my underpants and wriggled into the suit. The bust was too big, so I filled the gaps with the rolled-up lurex tights. I fished out the matching shoes and put them on. High-heels improved everything, and in the dim light I did not look too bad, except for my hair which I had not washed since the previous Wednesday and which was separating into greasy strands. I tried on the blonde wig which reminded me of my last doll, Cynthia. It was stiff, with a sticky surface that bore little relation to human hair. But when I studied my reflection I saw something amazing. The change of colouring had made my resemblance to Travis almost complete. (Eva was dark too. Was that why she had – ?) Of course the wig was too long. It fell past my shoulders, but if it were a bit shorter . . .

I searched the kitchen drawers, unsteady in the stilettos, nearly falling over with excitement. I found the shears and began hacking away at the wig. I could not see the back, no matter which way I turned, and so could not make it even with the front. (It never occurred to me to take the wig off.) But I persevered and the results were remarkable. From the neck down I was, despite my less exciting physique, Eva. From the neck up I was Travis.

I stood before the mirror a long time, staring into my own eyes as if I were a basilisk. When I grew tired of standing, I drew up a chair and sat crossing and uncrossing my legs, turning my head from right to left, studying every effect. How I wished that Vinnie were there to take my picture.

'Rose? It's Janice. You OK?'

'I'm fine.'

'Can I come in?'

'I've gone to bed. I was so tired.'

'What about Otis?' She sounded worried.

'I fed him. I'm sorry. I'd really like to talk to you but right now I just can't. Would tomorrow morning be OK?'

'But you don't have enough Little Friskies.'

'Yes, I do. Please, Janice. I just want to sleep.'

I realized that what I had said was true. At the same time, I did not want to stop being Travis. I was intoxicated with the image before me, drunk on the presence I had conjured. My eyelids were heavy. I could barely keep them open. I will put myself to bed, I thought. I will treat myself kindly.

I threw the boxes and clothing on to the floor, lay down in the shoes and the costume and the wig and covered myself with the sheets, in which I rolled over and over cocooning myself. 'Come, Sleep,' I whispered. 'Enough is enough.'

I woke up to the sound of thunder. The candles had burned themselves out. I could not determine where I was or why I was so uncomfortable. I could not move my legs, and the wig had slipped so that it was covering my eyes. I freed myself from the sheets, unzipped the costume and kicked off the shoes just as the rain began. It fell so hard and fast that it drowned even the noise of the bongos. There was another crack of thunder. I lay back on the bed and listened to the beating and rumbling of the storm, like nature having a heart attack. Something moved in the darkness and landed heavily beside me. I kept still as Otis began to purr and knead the covers. I made no move to touch him, but let him step gingerly on to my stomach where he made a few pirouettes before settling himself for the duration of the night.

9

Eva

I did not recognize her. As she turned her key in the lock, I stood tense, waiting to devour her. But when she walked in and set down her suitcase and looked up at me – no. I would have passed her on the street and not known her as Travis's sister. She was very thin. Her dark hair was dull, her eyes too bright, her bone structure disturbingly prominent. She was not the Slum Goddess now.

'Rose.' She held out her hand to me and smiled. 'I'm sorry about the telephone.'

'It's all right. I don't need it.'

'Do you have an orange?'

'What?'

'An orange. Or an apple. Oh, you do.' She helped herself from a bag on the counter and took an enormous bite. She smiled again when she had swallowed it. 'You cleaned up the apartment.'

'Yes. Do you mind that I stayed here?'

'Oh no. Have you been all right?'

'Yes. Janice helped. I've been feeding Otis.' I stopped, shy about my intrusion. 'The hotel was awful.'

She nodded. 'This is a terrible city. I want to leave. Don't you want to leave?' She took another bite, demolishing most of the apple, then finished off the core, seeds and even the stem.

'I just got here.'

'Of course. You want me to tell you about Howard. I don't know where he is. I'm very sorry for you.'

I sat down on the Castro Convertible, which now played its role of settee. Eva had begun to look more like Travis. Her blue-grey eyes were sympathetic like his, and her mouth was soft. She had his long limbs. If she'd been fleshier the resemblance would have been stronger. Still I did not feel free to give way to my feelings in front of her.

'I thought he might be with you,' I said.

'He isn't.' She came and sat beside me. She took my hand and held it in her lap while I stared miserably at the window. 'I'm sure he loves you, Rose.'

I shrugged. 'Then why did he leave?'

'It's my fault partly. I'll tell you about it if you want me to.'

'Please.'

'Well, I'd just been released from the hospital.' Janice hadn't mentioned this. 'I was in Bellevue for a while then in a place upstate. And when I got out I was, I don't know, I was just so sad. I wanted to see Howard.' I couldn't blame her. 'So I came and – took him away. I didn't mean it to be for so long.'

But how could he go? I wanted to ask. Why did he desert me? Instead I just said, 'Oh.'

'The i ching told me it was the right thing to do,' she went on. 'And then Laura – this very wise woman I met in the hospital – she told me once that I needed my brother and that my brother would heal me. She said my soul had cracked and that only he could mend it.'

'How did she know?'

'By the birds. She can read things in their flight patterns. Something about the way they swoop, especially at sunset. Isn't that beautiful?'

I stared at her, not understanding anything. She was so still, so earnest. She seemed backed up by something tremendous while I was frail, worn out by my efforts to find reasons and keep sane.

'You're very nice,' she suddenly said. 'I knew you would be. Do you know why? Because something amazing happened to me on the way from Grand Central. I passed this billboard and all the bottom of the sign was eggs.'

'Eggs?'

'Yes. You know. Like the Orphic egg?' She looked past me towards nothing in particular. Her eyes filled with tears. Then she readjusted her gaze. 'Are you religious, Rose?'

I wasn't sure how to answer. Cracked souls, Orphic eggs. I kept thinking of omelettes and custards. And we seemed an awfully long way from Travis. 'I used to be, but not any more.'

'Oh, I don't mean churches or organizations. I mean spiritual things.'

'I don't believe in God.'

She was silent, pitying me. 'Like Howard,' she sighed. 'He says it's my search for higher things that's made me ill. He thinks everything is political.'

'My father's like that too.' I don't know why I said it. Perhaps I didn't want her to think I was being contentious. Immediately she smiled.

131

'Men think spirituality is only for women. That it's weak. They feel obliged to reject it and be materialistic because it makes them seem independent. No one's independent.'

'My aunt is.'

'Does she believe in God?'

'She's a hardened Christian. That's what my father always says. But he loves her really.' And he loves me too, I wanted to add.

'I have an aunt,' she said. 'She's not very spiritual, but she's a good woman.'

'This is in Charleston?'

'No,' she answered, surprised. 'In Albany. My family's from Albany.'

'But I thought – Travis said – ' I was completely confused. So there was no Faulkneresque doom after all.

'He makes things up sometimes. Fantasy runs in the family. He's always been like that. But worse since Oliver was hurt in the war. My brother lost a leg, you see. Howard can't accept it, so he pretends Oliver doesn't exist. He can't see that it was meant to be and that it was just Oliver's destiny.'

That seemed to me a horrible dismissal, but I didn't say so. I only wanted to get back to Travis.

'But why does he do this?' I finally had to admit my ignorance and my shame at having been lied to.

'It's our fault,' she replied, meaning, I assumed, the Hilliers. 'We've caused him so much pain. He's the most sensitive of us and a very highly evolved person. But he wants to deny all that. Sometimes I think he despises himself on purpose.'

'That's true.'

'I think it gives him a kind of terrible pleasure. Would you like some tofu?' She removed a soggy packet from her bag and unwrapped a wet white cake. I was repelled and intrigued by the way it separated into neat firm chunks.

'No thanks.'

'You're thin like me. It would give you some high-calibre protein. I nearly starved in the hospital. It was all meat and grease and starch. I'm a vegetarian.'

'I've never met one.' And I had no idea what tofu was either. 'Are you – were you Catholic?'

She chewed rapidly. 'Well, sort of. But nothing really. Mixed up like everything else about us. One thing and another and all in conflict.'

'Did Travis ever mention me?'

'Oh yes.'

'And he called me by my name, Rose? He didn't – make somebody up?'

'No. He always said Rose.'

'What else did he say?'

'He said you were an angel.'

I burst into tears.

'Our parents hated each other,' she went on while I sobbed and sniffed. 'But they stayed together. Nobody got divorced then. Howard and I used to go and hide in the woodshed and hold each other while they fought. Oliver pretended not to care, but he did really. He wasn't so tough. My father was a handsome man but he got gloomy and withdrawn. Once he tried to kill himself in front of the whole family.'

'I know. The Clorox.'

'He told you that. Well, it's true. My mother was tyrannical. No one knew what made her so crazy. Finally my parents separated. He's somewhere in Texas and my mother just moves around. A lot of the time we don't know where she is. She disappears then she turns up. At the wrong moment. We're a family who's always losing and finding each other. I think that's very American, somehow. I've tried to make things better and to smooth it over between us. But Howard just runs. My mother is obsessed with him. She tracks him down. He yields and sees her, then there are a lot of accusations and tears. It's very bad. I tell him he should try to love her instead of hating her and feeling guilty, but he says loving her *is* the problem. Are you all right now?'

'Yes.'

'And listen, Rose. I don't know whether I should tell you this, but there was a letter – from the Draft Board. They'd sent it to my aunt's house because it was the only fixed address they had for Howard. My mother was there and found the letter. She sent me to tell him that if he didn't come to Albany and see her, she'd tell the Marines where he really was. I don't think she ever would have done it, it's just the kind of thing she says when she's desperate. She doesn't know how to express her emotions other than through negative actions. So I went to Florence, like I said, and I persuaded him to come back.'

My God, the Draft. Why hadn't I thought of it? There was a greater enemy involved here than Travis's family.

'Tell me more,' I said.

'Like what?'

'Like what really happened when he disappeared last year?'

'Last year? Let's see. I guess I wrote to him. It was just before my breakdown, and I'd left Angela with my aunt. (My mother won't take her. She still can't bear that my daughter's illegitimate.) I asked him to meet me at the Greyhound station in Boston. As usual my mother had discovered where he was.'

'Is that why he changed his name? To hide from her?'

'Maybe. I don't think there is any real reason. Like I said, he fantasizes. Well, I went to the station, not knowing if he'd come. I felt compelled to do a lot of strange things then. Finally it landed me in trouble. Anyway, he came. We spent two days together in an empty apartment in Cambridge and then I went back to Albany. That's when he told me about you.'

I was afraid to ask what he'd said. The vision of the two of them shut off from the world, absorbed only in each other for better or worse seemed so romantic. I felt envious, shy, greedy to know what had really happened in that room, wishing to be one of them or the other, eager for knowledge of their intimacy.

'He really cared for you,' she went on, 'but he felt guilty. How can I explain it? He locks himself into his love like a prison, then he blames himself for wanting to escape. And it is himself he blames, not you. He runs from me as well.'

'But he lets you find him.'

'He worries about me. He feels he ought to provide for me and Angela, but of course he can't. Why don't we light the candles? Would you do it?'

'All right.'

'He can't face the responsibilities no one's asking him to bear. What happened to your finger, Rose?'

'A dog.'

I lit the candles which were all white and new. I had made the apartment liveable, but I could not afford to pay the bills. Eva appeared to have no money at all. What were we going to do? I had to know more.

'Eva,' I asked again, 'why did you come to Florence?'

'I told you. To see him and to tell him he was in trouble. All the time when I was in the hospital he never wrote. It had been so long,' she sighed, 'that when I saw him again I just had to take him with me. I'm sorry, Rose. It's very hard. Sometimes I need to be with him all alone.'

'So do I.' I hesitated. 'Will he come back?'

'Yes. I'm not really sure. Probably.'

'You don't know where he went?'

'At Albany he stayed at my aunt's with all of us. Then he and my mother had an argument, and the next morning he was gone.'

'But what did she say?'

'She made him crazy as usual. They sat in the same room for hours not speaking to each other, just staring like cats. His hatred of her for what she'd threatened to do made him incapable of speech, I guess. Then he just erupted, accused her of wanting to send him off to be killed or maimed like Oliver. He called her a monster and an unnatural mother. And she kept sitting there, staring at him. It was horrible. Finally he said if she didn't leave him alone, he was going to disappear for ever.'

'Maybe he has.'

She looked at me. I was uncertain whether she wanted to help me or not.

'There'll be a sign,' she said at last, 'an omen, you'll see.'

Impatient as this made me, I had to admit that I knew what she meant. Yet I did not want to take this business quite as far as she did.

'Have you ever been in the hospital, Rose?'

'To have my tonsils out, but not like you mean.'

'It's like life in a coffin. It's death. You give up hope of resurrection. You can't even escape to your dreams because the doctors block the road to your unconscious. You think of oranges and plums. Not only because you have to chew on gristle to survive, but because you want to hang on to tangible memories, simple things, the way they look and taste. You imagine still lifes. That's all you can imagine. Your mind stops being a film and shows you only a once-in-a-while photograph – if you're lucky. Old faded photographs. You learn to be half-starved.'

'Why did you have to go there?'

She got up. 'I must see Janice – to tell her about the eggs. She'll want to know. And she's been good to poor Otis. Poor loony Otis.'

'He seems to get sick a lot.'

'Who wouldn't?'

I waited for her, sitting on the Castro Convertible and twisting strands of my hair. I was so uneasy. Something in Eva set me longing, not only because she was a living ghost of her brother, but because of the mixed pleasure and pain she aroused in me by her disarranged and over-lived life. How could I be so drawn to someone who had taken everything from me? It isn't her fault, I told myself. She needs Travis almost as much as I do. Who could blame her for stealing him? And now there was the Draft. It had to come, but I had hoped that when he ran he would ask me to run with him. It scared me to death because I figured it meant the end of the line for me and Travis. But in a strange and awful way it comforted me too, since it supplied a reason for his running. Perhaps I wasn't unbearable after all.

Eva smiled as she entered. 'Let's finish those apples,' she said. There was nothing else so we ate them. She lay back in the chair and looked at me like someone who had all the time in the world.

'Why did you have to go there?' I asked again.

'It was a mistake, really. I was walking down 10th Street. It was nearly two years ago. I came to a church and I was depressed, I suppose, so I went in. I sat in the back, looking at the altar and at the old women who came to pray. I saw some of them lighting candles in front of a statue of the Virgin, and all of a sudden I wanted to do it too. I lit one candle and dropped a quarter in the box. It looked so beautiful burning in its red glass that I couldn't help lighting another. I put in the last of my money, a few dimes and some pennies. I was really poor then.' She smiled as though that had been the least of her worries.

'Well, two was even better than one, so it seemed logical just to light them all. I didn't think the Virgin would mind that I couldn't pay for them, although the ladies probably minded. I didn't care, I was in such an exalted state. I felt it was possible to rise above my problems, to look down on them and see them for the ephemeral things they were. I wanted to be in the world of spirit, of magical ideas, and I suddenly knew I could be there, that if I simply wandered, not searching, I would discover the way.

'I walked around the church. I came to an arched door that opened on to a staircase. I went up, groping along in the dark, not able to see how high it was or where it led. I only knew I was going in the right direction, as though I were under a spell and could do no wrong. What I didn't know was that wrong could be done to me. I found another door with a latch. Behind the door was a ladder which I knew would be there. I went up the ladder and came to a sliding panel which was unlocked just like I knew it would be. A force was guiding me, you see; everything went along with me. It was a miracle.

'I crawled on to a flat roof. In front of me was a low parapet. I desperately wanted to look over, to look down and down and know I could never fall. Maybe I thought angels would catch me. It's what they said I said. But why would I tell that to people who weren't sympathetic?

'Someone on the street must have noticed me or maybe they found that the hatch was open because it didn't seem very long before the priest was standing behind me. I sensed his presence before I heard his footsteps, and when I turned and smiled at him he was obviously surprised. But I was too happy and too sad to pay much attention to his reactions. I should have, I suppose. But all I could say was, "It's beautiful up here." "Yes," he said. He kept clearing his throat. "But you ought to come away now. Come downstairs with me." He held out his hand. I'm sure he meant to be nice, but I just wasn't in the mood to go with him. I shook my head. "Not now." I turned away and went on staring at the clouds. There seemed to be faces in them, but just when I thought I recognized one it changed into someone else.

'I only wanted to remain in my blessed state, but he wouldn't let me. People don't like you remaining in blessed states, especially not priests. "Come with me," he repeated and took hold of my arm. I was glad not to be able to feel his skin through my jacket. "I'm praying," I said. "Then we'll pray together." "No thank you." He waited while I drank in the sky for as long as was left to me. "We pray in church here," he said, "not on roofs. And we don't light all our candles at once. Other people have devotions too. Don't you think what you did was selfish?" "I like it better here," I said. "Please." I tried to move my arm, but he held it tight. "Please," I begged. "I'm not doing anything wrong." "I'm worried about you," he answered. "Please don't be." Then, "Come along now." And, "No, thank you." '

I kept thinking of Father Leahy. The priest had his face.

'He began to tug at my arm, which I did not like. And I had been so polite to him. I tried to pull back, but I guess he assumed I wanted to throw myself into the street. He began dragging me away while I pulled in the opposite direction. He shouted and called someone's name. Oh, he shouted and shouted. It upset me so much I began to scream, at least they said I screamed. I can't remember. You see what a misunderstanding it was. Suddenly there was a second priest who grabbed my other arm. Then there was a woman. I lay down to stop them yanking at me, but as soon as I did this they decided I should be standing up. "Up, up," they said. That's when I heard the ambulance siren. A lot of men arrived and stuck a needle in my arm.'

'What a terrible story.'

'It was only the beginning. A month in Bellevue then transferred to the place upstate. At least it was in the country.'

'But no oranges.'

She smiled. 'No oranges.'

She went quiet, and I was reluctant to disturb her. I wanted to know still more – about the man in the photograph, the box of costumes.

'My mother never came to see me. Just couldn't bear it, I guess. But Howard came to Bellevue. I told him not to worry, that it was all

right, really. And it *was* all right. Sad, but all right. Do you know what
I mean?'

'Yes and no.' I wanted her to go on with the story because, as
stories do, even the most terrible, it distracted me from my own
unhappiness.

'What did you do before?'

She looked at me, not understanding. 'Oh, you mean before *that*?'

'Yes.'

'Things I'm ashamed of now. No, not ashamed. It's only that I see
what an illusion I was living, and it makes me sad that I ever let material
things matter so much.'

'You don't seem very materialistic to me.'

'I'm not. But I took an easy way because some people thought I was
pretty and I couldn't resist their admiration. I shouldn't be disgusted,
but I am. Still, it's the past. All that matters now is that I see what's
important, that I let myself be guided by spirit.'

'But what did you do that was so awful?'

'Oh, Rose.' She almost laughed, something she never did. 'If you
could have seen me. Prancing around in fishnet tights and stilettos
and skimpy costumes, stuffing the tops with tissues to make a better
cleavage. Wearing cat masks and rabbit ears and wigs, dressing up
as little animals to please men. God, what women do. What we let
ourselves be convinced of. And all for vanity and money. If you think
I'm a puritan I guess I am. After five years in bars and nightclubs
being yelled at by psychotic chefs and sadistic bartenders, pinched
and groped and insulted and propositioned by the customers – ugh!
I was even a go-go dancer, dancing in a cage, a golden cage. But I
made money. Money . . . I'm not very well educated and I've never
had much patience or concentration. Anyway, it all ended and I was
glad. The last club I worked in fired me for dating the customers. It
wasn't enough for me to work in those places, I had to be taken out
to them too. I'd go to bed at six in the morning, not ever seeing the
sun or the clouds. I looked well on it. Only underneath I was sick. I
don't mean ill. I mean spiritually sick.'

That explained the box. I wasn't brave enough to confess that I had
tried on those hated but kept clothes and pranced about to the tune of
my own dismal vanity. Or something worse.

'Anyway, Rose, please don't make me talk about it. I'd almost rather
talk about the hospital. At least it was real.'

'I understand.' I didn't. 'Tell me about Angela.'

'What can I say? She's my daughter. She's a miracle. Sort of a dazzler,

I think. Strong-willed. Too excited and too exciting. She mixes dark and light all at once. She frightens some people. My mother says I've spoiled her, but that's not true. She had a hard time and came through it and stayed her own self.'

'Who was her father? Do you mind my asking? Were you married?'

'Jake was already married.' Clearly she didn't want to say any more about him.

'Eva, I have to ask you, I can't help it. How have you lived?'

'I don't know what you mean.'

'Well, you don't work any more. How – '

'Oh, money!' She nearly laughed again. 'Rose, when I changed my life after Jake left and I knew I was pregnant, I stopped caring about it. You can see from this place I don't take much trouble any more.' She looked around. 'You've made it almost nice.'

'But you have to get by – day by day.' I was amazed at such insouciance. 'And there's Angela.'

'Jake gave me something for her. Then he went to South America and I stopped hearing from him. Of course that money's all gone now. I went on to Welfare and thought: Well, I'll just live on that, you know. I didn't want anything more. You see I'd realized at last – all money is tainted, *all* money, just covered in dirt. If you touch it, it dirties you, so it's better to touch as little of it as possible. I believe in what Christ said: "If thou wouldst be perfect, leave all thou hast and follow me. Blessed are the poor." '

I had been taught that too. We all had. Only no one I knew wanted to *be* poor.

She paused, as was her habit, and then went on. 'Howard was very good. He sent me money. For two years. Now it's stopped, of course.'

No wonder he'd had to borrow from me, even while he was earning a reasonable salary at the Mill. I told myself I must not begrudge it, and I did not.

'So what will you do, now that it's stopped?'

'I don't know. It doesn't matter. I have complete faith.'

'Phew!'

She looked at me as though she pitied me – something I resented since I wasn't exactly rolling in filthy lucre myself. Did I really seem money-tainted to her? Was I a camel stalled before the needle's eye? Then I reminded myself: She's tired, think what she's been through. Faith can be real, touching as well as absurd.

'You're kind, Rose,' she said. 'I'm sure Howard loves you.'

'I wish I were sure.'

'Don't give up.'

'It's not a choice that's open to me.'

'It's better not to make choices. Choosing means relying on our minds that are full of lies and confusion.'

'We can't not think.'

'But we can ignore our thoughts.'

How to do that? Withdraw, I guessed, withdraw from everything. Like Eva. Don't read newspapers or pay electricity bills. Believe in eggs. Follow dark passages up to the sky. Stand in forbidden places. Get caught and punished and say it doesn't matter. How terrifying. How awful.

'And what will you do, Rose?'

I hadn't thought. All my energies had been geared to my meeting with Eva. I'd had no future beyond that meeting.

'I'll wait for Travis. Try to find him. When my money runs out I'll get a job. If he turns up somewhere else I'll go there. I'll hide with him. I'll be like you a little and keep possessions to a minimum so I'll be unencumbered and light and can leave at any minute.'

'That's good. I have to meditate now.'

I'd heard about meditation, but I couldn't bring myself to ask what it entailed. 'Do you want me to leave?'

'No, stay. Or go to Janice if you feel like it. I won't be long.'

Two hours later I woke up in the armchair.

'Hello.' She was standing over me with a candle. It lit her face at an alarming angle, making her look like a benign version of Snow White's stepmother.

She touched my arm with her long fingers. 'I've just done the i ching. It's a miracle. Everything is so simple, and we always fail to see it. You know I'm leaving tomorrow,' she said.

'No, I don't.'

'I thought I told you.'

I hated the idea of being alone again. 'Where?'

'My aunt's. To get Angela. Then we'll see. I'll ask the Book. But I'll never come back to this city.'

'But you can't – '

'It's all right.' She shook me gently. 'You're keeping the apartment.'

In fact she left two days later. She stood in the doorway, handing me the key, wearing an old woollen coat though it was a hot afternoon. She said she would be in touch, that we were sure to meet again.

I nodded as if I shared her confidence. I was numb, incapable of putting to her the hundred new questions which bred in the mind I could not, like her, ignore. She closed the door, leaving me with Otis, the bills, the Castro and my ignorance. I knew nothing. Nothing at all.

10

The City

We comfort ourselves with invented certainties. That's what you told me; that's what you said I did. And you were right. If you could have seen me following all those men, if you could have seen me in my black leotard and saucy red apron, working in that bar; if you could have seen me then . . .

My money soon ran out, and it didn't seem worth sending for the $10 that was left in my account at the Indian Head Bank. I wanted no contact with Florence. For a long time my mind was closed to the place and to everyone in it. (I don't know how I managed such a complete cancellation. Anyway it didn't last. The past returns, we cannot escape. And that is one certainty that is *not* invented.) I thought only of finding Travis, or rather being there for him to find. Each day I rehearsed our meeting. It became more real than the music at night, the Puerto Ricans, the Ukrainians, the hippies on the street or the junkies on the doorstep, the Lower East Side itself. But I wasn't completely mad. I could not join Eva in being guided solely by spirit. I knew I had to live until that meeting occurred. And so I looked for a job.

I was diligent. I wanted to be of use and to serve mankind. In those days social work was considered a means to this end. I bought a small black notebook and made lists of all the orphanages, hostels and community centres in Manhattan. Throughout the fall and into the winter I walked the streets of Harlem, the East Village and Little Italy. I spent most mornings in the antique phone box in the back of my corner drugstore making appointments. I couldn't believe that no one wanted me. Most people wouldn't dream of offering their services, I told myself. Most people don't want to spend their working days with battered wives, disturbed adolescents, alcoholics and drug addicts. I did. What was the matter with me that I was considered unworthy to perform the tasks others disdained? It took me months

142

to realize that not just anyone could save the lost and shelter the homeless, and that to serve mankind you need credentials. But I kept crazily on, refusing to accept that I wasn't wanted or suited. I phoned and wrote and trudged. Sometimes I would get off the subway at Houston Street and walk exhausted to the apartment, pushing for five blocks against the freezing East River wind. My coat was inadequate, my head bare, my hands fisted in my pockets. I'll never make it, I would think. I'll die of the cold before I get home. I warmed myself with fantasies of turning the corner and finding Travis waiting for me on the stoop of my building. I would conjure him so completely that I really expected to see him there. I never did.

I'd arrive back, praying for heat, and find that the radiators were dead once again. I'd curl up under blankets and old clothes; there was nothing else to do until the boiler resumed operations. When I woke in the mornings dirty drifts of snow would be frozen on the floor beneath the window. Then I would make tea, walk to the drugstore and call more numbers. I seemed determined to go where I was not wanted.

It was just before Christmas that I saw the first man. I was in a shop on 3rd Avenue picking out a card for Aunt Bernie, having trouble finding an appropriate greeting. I was bored and anxious, not concentrating, my attention partly focused on the pedestrians outside. He was almost out of sight when I noticed him. I ran on to the slushy pavement, forgetting the card. I didn't chase or accost him. I was afraid to kill my hope. I followed discreetly, almost enjoying the agitation into which the slant of his shoulders had thrown me. Perhaps I knew I was wrong and wanted to postpone admission of my mistake.

He wore the same pea jacket, the same faded green corduroy jeans and cowboy boots. He was heavier and his dirty-blond hair was longer, but the walk had that same combination of uncertainty and sexiness. He stopped by a book store and I gained on him. He went in. I approached, pretended to scan the window display, looked up and saw a face that did not belong to Travis. No neat nose. No porpoise mouth. I returned to the Christmas cards.

Others appeared, more all the time. How could there have been so many tall, broad-shouldered dirty-blond men in New York, most of them in pea jackets? With each new sighting my expectations were reborn, the false alarms counted for nothing, and I was off. Always the trail ended the same way. With disappointment and tears and pretty soon retreat to a bar.

I would sit on a stool near the door and drink and contemplate my near-miss. 'God,' I thought once as I steadied my hands with bourbon. 'I'm behaving as if Travis were dead and I were being haunted by his ghost.'

Of course he was not dead. Eva wrote, saying that she'd had an enigmatic postcard from Wichita Falls. I was surprised to get the letter since I feared I might never hear from her again. She was still in Albany with her mother, her aunt and Angela. She was reading Edgar Cayce and *The Aquarian Gospels*. She must see Dr Gebb for her monthly appointment, could she stay with me.

For two days I left the welfare agencies in peace and devoted myself to Eva. She was even thinner, whereas I had grown plump on Yona Shimmel's knishes. She was restless too and hated the apartment, so we walked blocks to Midtown, huddled together and keeping to the sunny side of the street and out of the cold shadows, sharp as knives.

On the second afternoon we got as far as 56th Street. I suggested a visit to the Museum of Modern Art (it was free back then), and she agreed. But by the time we reached the second floor, her enthusiasm was cooling. I steered her towards Picasso's *Guernica*. Mistake. She stood absolutely still, looking hard at what was before her. Then she began to tremble and her eyes grew larger with dammed-up tears. She covered her mouth with her hand.

'Brutal,' I heard her mumble. 'Twisted . . . ugly . . .' Her lament gave way to convulsive sobs. I held her tight, but she was inconsolable. With difficulty I guided her towards the elevators. People stared at us. This was no place for emotion.

'Eva, Eva,' I whispered, 'it's only art.'

She insisted on returning to Albany that night.

She had forgotten to bring the postcard from which she had deduced that Travis was not only travelling west, but had joined some kind of political organization. It was impossible to tell if this was true without seeing for myself what he had written. You see, I did not trust Eva completely, though I loved her. Still it was a logical move if the Draft Board were pursuing him.

As I sat in the Treasure Chest Bar recovering from another rejection by the welfare agencies, I was all of a sudden stunned by my stupidity. Why hadn't I guessed what he was really up to? Political subversion explained everything. It was Travis's way of fighting the war. He was working in secret for the rights of man. He had pledged himself to some beneficent but dangerous cabal and outside contact might be a security risk, both for him and the organization. But why was I a security risk and Eva not? Clearly there was a point I was missing.

I was consoled. I ordered one more bourbon to help me face the winter night. I never got drunk. Only warmed. There were many times I wanted to be drunk, believe me, and I wondered why liquor didn't affect me in the way it did other people. I began to take in my surroundings. The bar was long and the café narrow and deep. The walls looked as though they'd been painted with a mixture of tobacco juice, beer and bacon fat. Otherwise the decor was red and black. The establishment was in transition. In a belated attempt to keep pace with the sexual revolution, waitresses, most of them middle aged, tottered about serving club sandwiches in high-heels and fishnet stockings, black leotards and red aprons. But the management was still old-fashioned enough to require that they wear hairnets.

I noticed a sign Scotch-taped to the mirror behind the bar: 'Part-time cocktail waitress required.' Why not? I thought, reviewing the recent rejections of my efforts to aid suffering humanity. Why not serve a lot of drunks instead? At least until I found a job I really wanted. I would go on waiting indefinitely for Travis, but meanwhile the weekly rent of $63.75 was overdue. Perhaps I was drunk after all. I certainly showed uncharacteristic bravado.

'Bartender,' I called, indicating the sign. 'Could you still use one of these?'

He looked me up and down with one bleary eye. The other was glass.

'Sure,' he said, polishing a tumbler with a dish towel. 'What makes you think you're her?'

He had me there. I smiled and shrugged.

'Hang on.' He disappeared through a small door I hadn't noticed and returned with a man in, yes, a shiny suit. This was Eddie Manilla, the manager, who was in a hurry and did not hide it.

'Any experience?'

'Plenty.' I was keeping it up, though all my experience had been with ice-cream cones.

He inspected me through narrowed eyes. 'Coulda fooled me.' Then he nudged the bartender and gave an unexpected grin.

'OK, Miss uh – '

'Mullen.'

'Mullen. Nice Jewish girl, huh. Stand up Miss Mullen. Remove the coat *por favor*. Turn around. Slow.'

145

I did what he asked as he exchanged glances with the bartender.
'Ever mixed drinks?'

'A little.' Vodka, beer and Gallo Red.

'OK. Mondays and Thursdays eight to two, more if you work out.
Tips in the kitty divided at shift change, leotard at your expense, no
fooling around with the clientele. Ray'll show you the ropes. I gotta
blow. See ya.'

I kind of liked Eddie Manilla.

As Ray was showing me the ropes I noticed a small glass of what
looked like whisky on a shelf just out of sight beneath the bar. He took
occasional sips from it and talked quietly. He was a quiet man.

With the last of my money, I purchased the leotard which didn't quite
fit because I couldn't afford the more expensive model. I pinned my hair
up in a bun which I dutifully enclosed in a brown hairnet. I appeared
on Monday at seven-forty-five and went to work, feeling exposed and
embarrassed.

'That leotard don't fit you right,' said Eddie. Too true. It flattened
my chest, chafed at the crotch and kept riding up over my backside. I
yanked it self-consciously down as though it were a girdle.

'Don't bother, Miss Mullen,' he sighed. 'Nothing you can do with
an ass like that.'

I blushed to the roots of my hair. I was slung a bit low, I knew. All
evening I felt assessing eyes upon me. But I took comfort from the fact
that among the four waitresses I was the thinnest, the most graceful and
by far the youngest. God, I felt stupid, though. Stupid and humiliated
and above all exposed.

The future was black, but at least there was a future, insofar as
I could pay the rent and keep Otis in Little Friskies. Eventually I
even managed to placate Con Ed. Hours at the Treasure Chest were
killing, but the tips weren't bad. I learned to balance heavy crowded
drinks trays on the tips of my fingers (it's actually easier that way) as
I weaved through legs slung across my path and perilously dangling
cigarettes. I stumbled and spilled a few Tom Collinses and Tequila
Sunrises but finally got the hang of it. The work was so demanding
that I forgot for a couple of hours my depressing circumstances,
and the ensuing pain in my muscles was a welcome relief from the
pain in my mind. I invested in Revlon and Max Factor and, for
the first time in my life, made up my face. I learned the social
advantages of wearing a mask. I learned that disguise can be a kind
of power, especially when you have no other power to wield. I became
a city girl.

Janice was still my only friend. I sat for her while we discussed the infirmities of Reese and the neuroses of Otis. I didn't mind. Her personality was so benign, despite the melancholy beneath her mountainous surface. I took shelter in her largeness and her largesse. There was always instant cocoa and cinnamon toast and the secret stash of Peanut Butter Cups. Her apartment was also several degrees warmer than mine.

She was very prolific. There was scarcely room in the place for her collection of metamorphosing animals. She did sell a few to a canine cemetery in Hartsdale, but I think her genius was lost on such patrons. And of course there were the heads, the ranks of which I was soon to join along with Eva who seemed to gaze at me, her brother's bitter-sweet *doppelgänger*. What would Janice ever do with us all? Apparently she wasn't worried and kept up her stream of animal chatter and speculations on the latest developments in psychic research. She believed in past existences, which gave me the creeps, though of course I was once convinced that loved animals could return to love us. She was particularly intrigued by what the Russians were up to, and hoped to God that their intentions in the field were pure.

'What if we end up being controlled from Moscow without even knowing it? It's possible, you know. Not that I hate the Russians, even though I'm Polish. I think the ideals of the Revolution are great, some of them. The Russian soul is a magnificent soul, no question. It's the scuzz-balls in the KGB that bother me. What's going on in those hospitals, I ask myself. I mean it's a good thing what they're doing, proving the power of the spirit in black and white and the force of the non-material powers on, well . . . on . . .'

Occasionally we saved a stray cat or a pigeon. We also lost a few.

Christmas was strange, my first ever alone. Janice went for three days to her family in Queens. Eva remained in Albany, boycotting New York. I got in a supply of vanilla yoghurts, frozen chicken and a bottle of Scotch. Even the Treasure Chest bar would not be open. Aunt Bernie relented with a card and a curt note, the first answer I received to the six letters I'd sent her:

Dear Rose,

I hate this place, but you don't want to hear that. Your father can't come up for Christmas because he says he has chicken pox. Can you imagine, a man of his age and brains. But I'm lucky, I guess, because I do know *some* very good people. The Byrnes have invited me to spend three days with them and I said yes. Anything to get out of here. Those women are saints. Bobby's home now and comes to see me and his mother a lot. He's going with a French girl. Your poor Aunt Bea is crazier than ever, and me, I'd wish I were dead if it wasn't a mortal sin. Thank you, I'm all right, and I don't need your money. You just lead your own life and don't bother about me. That's what you want. I'm real glad about your job. That's it, I guess.

Yours in Christ,

Bernadette Mullen

I had told her in my last letter – the one that produced the response – that I was working for a gallery uptown that dealt in Medieval art. I knew the vision of Madonnas and crucifixes would soften her. But as long as she remained at Kellvale she would never forgive me. My not notifying St Tom's hadn't helped. I'd meant to let them know my change of plans, only every time I sat down to write the letter, I became so depressed that I couldn't even begin. The Birch Street apartment was still hers. She insisted she would be returning there in the near future and we all humoured her and my father paid the rent. Whenever I thought of the place sitting empty and abandoned, I quickly shifted my mind to another topic.

I'd written to my father pretty quickly after I'd arrived in New York and eventually received a postcard from Dallas where he'd gone for a convention. He implied on the one hand that I had been hasty, not to say irresponsible, in my behaviour and on the other that Bernie was better off where she was and probably everyone else was better off too. Vinnie all over. But he did say he'd pay. Guilt money, I thought. You don't have to travel far to write a cheque. 'When will I see you?' I wrote back, but he hadn't answered yet.

I couldn't help it, I was preoccupied with them, my family. They and Travis and the bongos kept me awake at night, and I slept badly all summer. June was terrible, New York a kind of polluted tropics. Heavy curtains of heat hung in the avenues where air had been, and opening the window had no effect other than to increase the noise level. No one seemed ever to go to bed on the Lower East Side. They sat on the stoops and hung around bodegas and under the street lights talking and smoking and playing music, waiting to sell, waiting to bet, waiting to score, waiting for sex, for food, for a better life, waiting for the thunder storm that was three weeks in coming. Every day someone said, 'This is it.' Rain, the end, life bearable, well sort of, once more. Every afternoon the clouds gathered, purple-grey, pressing down on the city like a huge dirty quilt suffocating it, squeezing the life from it. Every evening they passed over to deposit their contents on the rich who lived further up the Hudson. A star or two was dispiritingly visible through the smog. Next morning in the bodega I would hear reports of murders, one of them on my street. I wasn't frightened or surprised. Sometimes I even forgot to lock my door.

Big bold rats patrolled the gutters. Giant waterbugs strutted in the light of day. Not one person in the neighbourhood could afford an exterminator, so the cockroaches were fruitful and multiplied, most of them beneath my kitchen sink. When I switched on the light over the bathtub I could hear hundreds of tiny feet scuttling away. Armies of the night, Janice called them. I fought them for the bar of soap. I lay awake in the darkness and feared them. (Nothing will murder sleep faster than finding a roach between your sheets.) I cleaned and sprayed and invested in Roach Motels. ('Mr Roach checks in, but he doesn't check out.') Nora would have been sick and Aunt Bernie would have died. Once I discovered an albino roach in the closet and shuddered until dawn. I asked Janice if such an insect existed or if she thought I had been hallucinating. She said oh yes she'd seen them. They were rare but they existed, no doubt about that, a hybrid strain, she'd heard, a landmark in roach evolution. But they were God's children too, let's remember, even the least of these, you know, serving a purpose in the great plan. (Yeah, to replace humans and just about every other species, come the final collapse.) I must open my heart and mind to them, they had a right to live just as much as I, none of which was deniable. Nevertheless, she sprayed.

Domestic rows, even violence, were commonplace in the summer, and it was not unusual for people to just stop dead in the middle of the street and start screaming, waving their arms and tearing off what little clothing they wore. No one paid much attention. After all, what could be done for them? On the most desperate evenings I would spend money I could ill afford at the air-conditioned movie theatre on 3rd Avenue. For two hours I'd be comfortable, even chilly, watching *Simon of the Desert* which I saw five times. I would return to East 2nd Street to soak in a cold bath, listening to the hideous comings and goings of the insect population. Then I caught a cold and sniffed miserably through marathon shifts at the Treasure Chest.

I was now working three to four nights a week and consequently had some money to spare. To complicate my disguise and prevent my being exposed as a little American smiler, I acquired a pair of false eyelashes and a set of false fingernails and spent hours learning to put them on. The latter looked quite impressive surrounding a Martini glass. Customers gaped at them. They were a very good set. From the head shop on 9th Street I purchased an Indian scarf and a set of wind chimes – my first timid venture into counter-culture consumerism. I also bought a print of Rama and Krishna in lurid blues, pinks and yellows and thumb-tacked it to the wall above the Castro Convertible. I liked such things for a while. They were the things to buy.

I felt drawn to the second-hand clothes shops which overflowed with beautiful rags. I observed the generation of both sexes who draped themselves in silks and velvets, whatever the weather, and painted their eyes with kohl. Intrigued but shy, I remained a spectator at the party that was going on all around me. I still wore cotton and khaki and denim and went soberly to work among the millions of metropolitan ciphers, while that other tribe flaunted their billowing finery and went laughing down the street, arms entwined, their shaggy heads thrown back, moving through clouds of marijuana. The freaks, they were known as, and called themselves freaks. Freak was not a derogatory word then. It was almost a term of endearment, tinged with humour and indulgent respect. It implied something like comrade or brother. It referred to those who inhabited the margins. The party was on the margins, though the margins were no longer narrow and were growing wider by the week.

I hadn't given up on social work. I continued to phone and write and be rejected. So much time had elapsed that I was able to go back to the beginning of my list and start all over again.

It was on the way to one of my ill-fated interviews that the real sighting occurred. After stopping off at the pickle man's for a breakfast of two of his round pale-green peppers, my favourites, I set off to keep an appointment at an uptown community centre. At 36th Street the bus stopped for a red light and I saw him. No illusions this time. It was a full-frontal Travis looking straight at the bus, looking almost but not quite into my eyes. For once I had managed to find a seat. This was unfortunate. In my excitement I rose and squeezed past the person beside me who was holding several parcels. The aisles were jammed. 'Let me out,' I yelled and pushed my way towards the door, all the time keeping my eye on Travis who stayed miraculously put. What or who was he staring at? Had he seen me too? If so, he gave no sign of recognition. God, I thought, this is just like the ending of *Doctor Zhivago*, only Lara is a man.

None of the passengers would or could move. The bus continued to idle. I reached the doors just as it pulled away from the lights. I did my best to hold back my tears while the other passengers ignored my distress. I got off at the next stop and ran back to the corner of 36th, but the pavement was a river of people, almost as unnavigable as the overcrowded bus. I scanned every face, every back, not one of which belonged to Travis. Of course I missed my interview.

For days I brooded over the incident. I wrote immediately to Eva, but there was no reply. Her aunt's telephone number was Ex-directory. He was in the city and he had not told me. How was I to interpret that? I began to wonder whether I had seen him at all, whether he was an apparition. Anything was possible. How could I tell what was real?

Three nights a week at the Treasure Chest were not enough to keep me without constant financial anxiety, so when I saw an advertisement in *The New York Times* for Christmas sales help at a Doubledays on 5th Avenue I went along and applied for the job. I got it. (America was rich, and it was easy to find employment. There was always a job – something, anything. Just never the one you really wanted.) I don't know why, I guess they liked me. It was hard work keeping the shelves in order, and we had to gift wrap the books as well as ring them up on the till and give advice to people who hardly ever read. Every shopping day of November and December brought a stampede of customers through the doors. The rest of the staff were men, out-of-work actors, mainly, who delighted in insult contests and rubber-band fights. Several times a day I would feel a smart sting on the back of my legs or neck and look up to see one of them grinning in triumph from his strategic position on the record mezzanine. Otherwise, they teased me about my bottom: 'Miss Mullen has a very nice ass, don't you think, Mr Metzler?' 'Indeed I do, Mr Lovell. Crackerjack.' I think they were genuinely fond of it, low-slung as it was.

Just before Christmas, the second I was to spend alone, two things happened which unnerved me terribly. A bomb went off and my father turned up. This is the beginning, I thought, really the beginning. But of what?

The building on West 12th Street was a distinguished brick edifice built in the mid-nineteenth century, well kept and well appointed. It blew up on Tuesday the 8th of December, 1967. I remember because it was the Feast of the Immaculate Conception. The fire department was called out and police cars and ambulances arrived in legions. But news of cause, deaths and survivors, if any, was withheld until the 14th of December when a piece appeared in *The Times*. One person, an unnamed woman, had been seriously injured. Everyone else (who? how many?) had escaped unharmed. Taut with a nagging certainty, I continued to scrutinize the dailies, fitting bits of information together. I tore myself up over what I assumed I had discovered. The house, it seemed, belonged to a wealthy stockbroker and his wife, now retired, and frequently away. Their brilliant daughter, a graduate of Radcliffe, had been using the place while they were in Tobago. Using it, in fact, to make bombs. The *Post* alluded to a 'small munitions factory', where, on the morning of the 8th, something had gone badly wrong. A mistake, they said, on the part of the chemist/manufacturer who worked for a small group of political extremists of which the daughter was the leader.

The Directory was based in Canada but worked out of Chicago. Their presence in New York was a surprise. No one, it seemed, had expected them to launch a campaign in the city. The brilliant daughter was now in jail. Her comrade-in-arms, the only other person in the house at the time of the explosion, was recovering in the hospital. Everyone else involved had disappeared, though promising leads and clever traps were hinted at. I knew of the Directory, their commitment and their daring. Their exploits horrified and impressed me. They went too far and yet, I thought, where else can they go? They blow up one house, one office, one monument, while America blows up an entire country. I was certain that Travis was among their numbers. Hadn't I seen him within a week of the explosion? No wonder I had heard nothing from him. He was in very deep. Now he had fled for sure. My mind followed him in all directions. Perhaps he had crossed the border into Canada or Mexico. Perhaps he could never write to me, never return. Perhaps at that very moment he was making his furtive way to my door.

The city leaned hard on me. The buildings seemed to bend and touch, blocking the sky. Windows were like eyes that watched me with jaded curiosity. Streets disappeared into infinity. I lived in tunnels and tubes with people who could not cope and who never looked up, all struggling with greater or less strength against a current that pulled us inexorably down the drain. Our best energies were spent in everyday aggressions. Only the people in kohl and velvet were carefree. Often they seemed to me to be merely blind and headed for the same dark drain as everyone else.

My state of mind was not improved by what I saw on the streets. On the Bowery bums died regularly of hypothermia. Meths drinkers huddled in groups around St Mark's place. None of my neighbours was adequately dressed for the cold, though they appeared more cheerful than the people uptown in fur coats. Once, as I was leaving the subway at 53rd Street and 6th, I came upon a heap of black rags. I was with another waitress from the Treasure Chest and we were on our way to a Jasper Johns exhibition before work. The heap lay on a landing where the concrete stairs turned upwards towards the half-dead daylight. We looked at each other then drew instantly back, sickened by the smell of advancing decay. I detected matted hair, abundant, coarse, red in parts, and two fingers crusted in filth. No face. The man, the woman, whatever it was, lay motionless. People passed without noticing, hurried on by. I felt compassionate, then sad, then disgusted, then afraid. We ran for the street like everybody else.

The next evening as I was restoring to order the wrecked shelves of the children's book department, tired after a day of the greedy and irritable New York public that always knows its rights, I heard a tapping on the window. There, standing in the snow, against the glamorous backdrop of 5th Avenue, an opalescent sky above him, was my father. Vinnie Mullen was smiling his most engaging smile, the one that registered to the full his intense pleasure in himself. He wore his zip-lined car coat wide open and his hat tipped back on his head like an overgrown cub reporter in a forties movie. He was delighted to have caught me unawares. I opened the door which was locked, it being after six.

'Well, well, surprised to see your old man?'

'How did you know I was here?' I kissed his cold rosy cheek.

'You told me.'

'I didn't. Did I? Oh, right, I wrote you. You never answered.'

'This *is* my answer, in person. Aren't you surprised?'

'Yes. It's all right, Mr Lovell. He's my father.'

Mr Lovell gave a mock salute and clicked his heels. 'As you wish, meine shöneführer.'

'They're all cards here,' I explained.

'Nice place, Rosie. Nice bookshop. You reading a lot?'

'A lot.' My appetite had been re-whetted after post-graduation fatigue. I chain-read, lighting one novel with the last. It helped me escape my life. 'You haven't told Aunt Bernie, have you?'

'Told her what?'

'That I'm really here and not – you know.'

'Oh yeah. The *gallery*.' He laughed. 'Now would I do that?'

'No.'

'You betcha. Got a good history department? Good biographies?'

'So-so. Revolution Books would be more your line.'

'Yeah.' He looked around and grinned. 'All hardened capitalists this neck of the woods. Can I take you to eat?'

'Sure.' I tried to hide my delight. I called the Treasure Chest and made the excuse that I was running a temperature. I had never called in sick before. Eddie was indulgent.

I telephoned well out of earshot. I did not want my father to know I was a cocktail waitress. There were reasons for this. Vinnie fancied himself enlightened. And in a funny way he was. But he was still a Catholic at heart and the father of a daughter. His lapse had not altered his small-town morals, and the fact that he had a new family and never saw me would be no argument against what he would regard as just indignation. Yet for all that he was not a prude. He still held to the conviction that life was to be enjoyed, that the pursuit of happiness was America's greatest invention and its number-one priority. But he also believed I could and should make more of myself.

I re-entered in my coat and scarf.

'Let's mosey,' said Vinnie.

I took him to a smörgasbord place on 61st called the Three Crowns where rollmop herrings and stuffed cabbage revolved slowly on an enormous lazy Susan, its arrayed delicacies reflected in an overhead mirror. For Vinnie this was the height of New York chic. For all his utopian fantasies, he was impressed by third-rate glitz. That's what I mean. A part of his brain was always in Florence.

He'd come to New York for a boat show and was in excellent spirits. He invited me to Maryland for Christmas.

'I don't know. I'll think about it.'

'What's to think about? Don't you want to see your brothers?'

'They're no brothers of mine,' I wanted to say, but of course I didn't. I didn't say that they and their mother were the reason I would not come.

'I promised Aunt Bernie.' I could revoke the lie at the last minute and he'd hardly notice. By that time he'd be once more in thrall to Denise.

'Atta girl. That's my good girl.' Jesus Christ, he was actually pleased. Even so, I could not be angry since he had never held my defection against me and never tried to extract from me the real reasons for my inexcusable behaviour. He'd figured I was fed up and he was right. For that I was grateful.

'I know how it is,' he'd said in our first telephone conversation after the event. 'I know how it is.'

Christmas dispensed with, we moved on to politics. He dished the President over shredded beetroot and tore at his cardamom bread as he castigated the villains at the Pentagon. Naturally the war came up. If this insanity was still going on when the boys were eighteen, why, he'd move the whole damned family to Canada. He poured himself another beer. Think of it, he said, ordinary parents were encouraging their kids to dodge the Draft. Didn't that tell those scum-bags in Washington something or were they deaf as well as stupid? Case of the inmates taking over the bin *there* all right. He raged against American foreign policy, predicted King Rat Nixon would win the next election anyway, then switched to the Navy Yard and why he'd left. He said he just couldn't go on making instruments of destruction and that the uranium scared him. That's why he went to Maryland to build plain ordinary boats. He'd told me all this before but I let him rave on. Then in the same breath he regaled me with tales of a Boston friend suspected of running guns for the IRA. There'd been a subpoena, the case was pending. Vinnie seemed to regard it all as a good adventure yarn and was smiling broadly. It struck me that he saw war not so much in terms of morality as of waste. Vinnie who'd never been drafted, who'd never known combat or the threat of combat, who'd never looked leering imminent death in the eye, and so, unlike other men his age, was fresh-faced and with the personality of an adolescent.

We adjourned to a bar where we talked more politics. Inevitably he worked his way round to the old stories, ending up where he always did, back in 1922 with the strikers, Thomas McMahon, Horace LaBranch, the entire cast and crew.

'You sure did enjoy that strike, didn't you?'

'You know, I did.' He leaned his chin on his hand and smiled to himself. 'I really did.'

He was weak-kneed and slurring his words when I took him, still talking, to a hotel in a taxi for which he forgot to give me the money. I paid the driver and caught a subway home.

In my box was a letter with an Albany postmark. I tore it open and read it under the dim entryhall light. Eva's aunt politely informed me that Eva and Angela had left. She'd had a postcard from Chicago then nothing. Chicago! I thought of the Directory, of a conversation years ago, 'some people in Chicago'. I saw stockyards, amber waves of grain and empty freeways, distant snow-capped mountains rising up out of the prairie. I pictured the three of them – brother, sister, child – wandering across America, travelling ever further from the East Coast into that, to me, unknown and alien territory so far from the sea.

11

Hadley

I had never made strong friendships. Friendship presumes equality, and I was conditioned for servility. There was Frank, who was still the most interesting person I knew. I wrote to him sometimes and he answered when he could in between his union work and his poetry writing. There was Travis who had been my great love and therefore probably not my friend. There was Eva, fleetingly, and there was Janice, very much on what she'd call a single plane. When I met Hadley I was unskilled in the social arts and, by her standards, practically a primitive.

Why she took to me and tolerated me I don't know. She was a little like you: not the sort to take pity on anyone. But she liked to be entertained, also like you. Perhaps I amused her. If so, I did it unconsciously. Which probably means that, also like you, she was laughing at me. Through her I acquired a higher sheen. Of course I could never match hers, but playing second fiddle doesn't bother me. I deliver my cues, a generous straight man. Aside from that, her befriending me may have had to do with the fact that we looked alike.

Not everybody noticed. And those who noticed usually didn't do so right away. Our looks seemed to grow towards each other the longer we were together. But I saw immediately. I saw, almost, without knowing that I saw.

In the spring of 1968 a huge anti-war demonstration was organized in New York. I went alone. I tried to persuade Janice to come, but she said her weight would not allow her to walk from East 79th Street to the Battery. She said she would stay at home and pray and that prayers would do just as much good as marching. I couldn't argue with her, and anyway, who knew? Frank intended to come but his car broke down and he did not have the money for the air fare. What does it matter? I thought. Is there that much difference between being alone in the

156

apartment and alone with one hundred and fifty thousand people? I was in a cynical phase. Besides, the protestors always talked to you at these affairs. The conversation would be very enthusiastic, then you'd lose them somewhere in the 40s or 50s and never see them again. I was used to this. I went to a lot of demos. They afforded me self-expression of a kind.

We started off from the Sheep's Meadow and turned into 5th Avenue. The column of marchers carrying banners and placards, chanting and playing instruments, was nearly two miles long. We marched past puzzled, cheering heckling spectators until we came to 58th Street. The demonstraters were rowdy but good-humoured. Suddenly a fight broke out between the police and a group of Puerto Rican boys who carried a banner which said something about our Vietnamese brothers. At first it seemed an ordinary scuffle of which there were always a few at every demo. But this one was different. I saw the crowds on both the street and the sidewalks draw back. I saw the looks in the policemen's eyes, and, within seconds, the lightning-quick aggression in the boys' movements. They were animated by a fury that made them oblivious to danger and pain. They were frightening but also beautiful in a way that stopped the heart. Sticks and rocks flew past my head. Smoke bombs exploded next to me. The policemen, each of them twice the size of one of the boys, wielded their truncheons with a clumsy malice. The march had come to a halt. I heard the thud of colliding bodies, a sound like the clash of two lines in a football game. The police were on the verge of being out-scrapped. Any moment now there would be knives and then, inevitably, guns. For minutes – I don't know how long, really – we all stood mesmerized as though watching a film or a dance.

People said:

'Let's go.'

'Yeah, we better go.'

'Right now. I mean this second.'

'It's turning nasty.'

'We should split.'

'Come on.'

'Yeah.'

We knew there'd be serious trouble, that we were all in danger. Yet we couldn't not watch. We couldn't leave and save ourselves even while wanting to run. It was just too exciting.

Finally some of the demonstrators ran back towards the Plaza. The side streets had been cordoned off, and thousands of people were backed up behind us. There were no margins, so we had little room to manoeuvre. We were trapped on the city's grid.

We began to push further and further away from the fight which in turn moved forwards towards us. Blood flowed. One of the boys lay on the pavement while the others attacked with renewed ferocity. They screamed and cursed while the police kept silent, hammering at them.

I panicked and forced my way back through the crowd, some of whom were now cheering on the boys. I was just far enough away from the scene to keep ahead of the stampede that followed the sound of the shot. I squeezed between two of the carriage horses, who stood with absurd placidity by the curb, and crossed the street to the park. Some of the marchers still pressed forward while others did as I did. Behind us I heard the clop-clop of mounted police approaching from 59th Street, and in the distance, the wail of a siren. It was then I caught sight of the dirty-blond hair and the dark-blue jacket. In my hysteria I failed to notice that the person to whom they belonged could not have been more than five foot-seven. Travis, was all my poor brain could inform me. It's Travis.

There had not been a sighting in six months, but it seemed natural that he should be there. I took off after the blue jacket, tears streaming down my face. The blue jacket slowed then stopped. I nearly collided with it and grabbed at it without preliminaries.

'Travis,' I cried.

'Nope.' She turned and looked at me, bright-eyed, smiling, then sobered when she saw my face.

'Come on.' She linked her arm through mine. 'I was scared too.' She hurried me across the brown grass.

'Been to many of these?'

'A few,' I said. 'But not as violent.'

'I got arrested on the last march to Washington,' one of the men told another. 'Fuzz broke my camera and I lost most of my footage.'

'Did you see the boy in the orange T-shirt? Wasn't he divine?'

'Shut up, this is serious.'

'It can't be serious *and* divine?'

I realized I was part of a group whose members I had not numbered nor faces taken in. One of them, a tall boy with straight hair in a grown-out Beatle cut, suddenly skipped in front of us, turned, produced an 8mm movie camera and, walking briskly backwards, began to film the retreating crowd whose numbers were now in the thousands. They were moving across the park like frightened sheep towards the safety of the West Side. It must have been difficult for him to keep pace without bumping into anyone, but he never faltered.

I didn't ask who they were. I let the girl lead me, her hand still grasping the crook of my arm. She had a rapid jaunty stride and I was panting to keep up. But I did not want her to stop or to let go of me. Once in a while she'd look at me and smile.

'How're you doing?'

'Better.' In no time we were standing on the brink of Columbus Circle with the tall boy still filming our progress and the traffic racing round and round the giant refrigerator of the Huntingford Hartford Museum.

'We're going to a coffee shop,' the blonde girl said. 'Why don't you come with us?'

I took them all in – one black girl, my new friend and three men, one of whom had grey hair and a grey beard and was clearly older than the rest. The third boy looked interesting with his blue-green eyes and tight black curls worn short. He has a regular job, I thought. They were all intent on each other and friendly to indifferent towards me. They took me for granted like a dog or a child who just tags along.

'Where?' I asked, not sure I'd heard her properly. But the light changed and I lost her answer in the sound of the traffic. The tall boy suddenly stopped in the middle of the road and turned his camera straight at the oncoming cars. We all screamed. Brakes screeched. Drivers cursed him. But he slipped out of their way.

We made it to a coffee shop on 7th where they threw themselves into a booth, slumping against each other and laughing with relief. They talked and lit cigarettes without stopping. There seemed to be no barriers, no formalities among them, although they leaned heavily on certain phrases. Their mockery was not malicious. Their teasing hid affection. Though their dress was raffish, they were not of the kohl and velvet brigade. They were slender without being emaciated. (It really was a time to be thin.) No one was particularly with anyone else; rather they were all friends together with a shared past and mutual assumptions. They'd had fun, I could tell, maybe quarrelled a little. Mainly had fun. Unused to groups and shy of them, I sat mute in the booth. Every so often the tall boy would take out his camera and film the others who paid no attention and behaved as if it were the most natural thing in the world.

The grey-haired man was telling them the story of an abortive movie production.

'Amazing, but Shavinsky gave Igor a hundred thousand dollars to shoot part of the film. I don't know how Igor convinced him, probably procured something Shavinsky couldn't resist. You know he's been sucking up to him for years. Shavinsky must have been out of his mind. Anyone who'd give Igor that much money is on an express train to the locked ward.'

'Igor thinks that if you just hand everyone a lot of drugs and switch the camera on and point it somewhere, doesn't matter where, you'll have an instant masterpiece.'

'There's something to be said for it . . .'

'That's a crock, he's read too much Breton.'

'Oh, he's just so last year.'

'What's he doing now?'

'Trying to raise money for a film version of *Maldoror.* I want to play the bull dog.'

He suddenly leaned across the table and spoke to me.

'May I stroke your cheek?' he asked, and gave me a charming smile.

What could I say?

He gently touched my skin with the tips of his stubby fingers. Then he stopped and began to sing an aria from *Traviata.* Everyone else carried on as if nothing were happening.

My heroine seemed to have forgotten all about me as she smoked and giggled with the others. Then she suddenly turned to me.

'What's your name?'

'Rose.'

'I'm Hadley. This is Steve, Jackson, Tony, Star. You new in New York?'

I shook my head. Did I still look so green? All attention shifted as Steve now turned the whirring camera on me. She asked me where I came from, where I lived, if I had any friends in the city, if I went to the bars, what I did. I didn't have to feign modesty. I told her the bare facts about myself. Even through my nervousness I could sense her taking me exactly as I was. There seemed to be no rules about privacy or discretion or what was suitable for discussion as there were in Maine. They told jokes against themselves, confessed to their venial sins in order to amuse the others. All they expected of me was to do more or less the same.

Jackson was singing a song called 'Peel Me a Grape.'

'Best way to cheer me, cashmere me.'

He waved his cigarette around with languid campy gestures.

'Never out-think me, just mink me.'

The other customers were watching us intently. Hadley told him enough, already. So he began to tickle Tony who was highly susceptible and quickly lost control of himself, just as I would have done had anyone been interested in teasing me in such an intimate way in a public place.

'Jackson, stop,' he gasped, throwing himself against Star who playfully pushed him back to Jackson. 'Oh my God, oh, stop. Please.'

Jackson relented and kissed Tony's springy curls.

'You're wonderful to tease,' he said. 'Mmm, Chuka, chuka, chuka.' He pinched Tony's chin. 'Well, my little mud larks, I must leave you.'

'Surely not.'

'My presence is required.'

'Where, the 42nd Street men's room?'

'I just think of myself as a public convenience.' He beamed and waved his fingers in the air.

The minute he was gone, they all began to talk about him.

'He's a little tiresome but he's a genius,' Hadley told me.

'He's very – playful.'

'For a forty-five year old I guess he is.'

Forty-five seemed to us a point so distant as to be extra-galactic.

'He likes to make fun of himself.'

'It's his greatest talent.'

'You should see his after-dinner ballets.'

Steve explained to me how Jackson and his boyfriend Harlan liked to stage impromptu dances and dramas. They sang, declaimed, leapt about with mock grace in denim and motor cycle boots, crashing on to the stripped pine floor of Jackson's apartment, draped in silk and beads and adorned with artificial flowers and ladies' millinery.

'They're great,' said Steve. 'Specially their Dance of the Hours.'

'Oh, I don't know,' grumbled Hadley. 'If I have to listen to one more rendition of "Surabaya Johnny" I'll scream.' She liked to criticize, I could tell, especially people she was fond of and places she frequented.

'Hey, what's the time?' Star interrupted.

Hadley consulted her watch. 'Got to split. We're on early tonight.' She addressed me, very serious. 'We're leaving, Rose. But they're going to a party later. You can go with them if you feel like it.'

Her spontaneous generosity kept amazing me.

'I have to get back.' It wasn't rue, but I didn't think I could handle being alone with the two men.

'Downtown?'

'Yes.'

'Then come with us. We can share a taxi as far as Union Square.'

I hadn't been in a taxi since the night I returned my drunken father to his hotel. Taxis were the ultimate luxury.

All the way downtown, Hadley bantered with the driver. She seemed so good-natured, so at home in the city. Star seemed equally at ease. She was not as extraverted as Hadley but had a sort of quiet charisma. She and Hadley pooled their resources to pay the fare. I tried to contribute but they shooed me off.

'You don't have a phone?' Star's forehead furrowed in disbelief.

I didn't, I said, I was sorry. I gave them my address. 'Will you come and visit me?'

'Sure.' Hadley smiled. Her dental work must have cost a fortune. 'I don't live far away. Maybe Star'll come too. Okay?' She glanced at her friend who nodded. 'See you later.'

They walked away. The taxi waited at the light. Suddenly she was back. I rolled down the window.

'I just had an idea,' she said. 'We're going to a film-showing on Monday. It's at a friend's place. Why don't you come?'

'Well, um, OK.'

'We'll pick you up.'

'What time?'

'I don't know, eight o'clock.'

I tried again to give her money for the taxi but she screwed up her face and made a dismissive gesture. I would have insisted had we been in Florence where it's *de rigueur* to battle over who pays. (Aunt Bernie and Bea had been known to slip cash into the pockets of hosts' and hostesses' coats when they weren't looking. No one in New England felt easy about accepting gifts. And in Irish families generosity is a contest.) The taxi lurched forward and left them behind. The driver was going so fast I had difficulty making him stop by the corner of 13th and 3rd where I got out, paid him what little was due and walked the rest of the way home.

My head was spinning. Life had not been this reckless since I abandoned my aunt to the Sisters of Mercy. I'm on the brink of a whole new adventure I thought.

I had the following Monday off. It was the sort of sunny winter day that in New York is bleakly bright. It depressed me, that northern light, when the sky is too high and objects too defined. So I stayed in bed reading *The Golden Bowl* with Otis on my lap and apples and a chocolate bar beside me. Such withdrawals, which I managed two or three times a month, were essential for preserving what was left of my health and sanity. The Treasure Chest and Doubleday's were taking their toll. I had now given up the idea of social work and was feeling, like I said, pretty cynical. If they didn't want me the hell with them.

I was so absorbed in the novel that I jumped when the buzzer rang and alarmed my highly-strung Otis so that he hurled himself from the Castro Convertible towards his beloved bathtub, vomiting as he went and depositing a stream of half-digested Little Friskies across the blanket and the floor. Should I clean up or answer the door? I gathered together the stinking blanket and tossed it into the tub where he lapped and quivered and purred. I pressed the entry button, forgetting that I was wearing only Travis's old T-shirt in which I always slept, on some occult principle, and a pair of knee socks. I opened the door to find Hadley, Star and Steve, camera in hand, coming down the hall. I remembered, too late, the way I looked. But they didn't notice or seem to care any more than they did about the trail of puke on the kitchen floor. I mopped it up as quickly as I could and put on a pair of jeans. (Those were the days when you had to lie down and hold your breath to zip yourself in.)

'Hi there.'

Hadley smiled at me. She could tell how desperate I was for them all to like me. But she understood and did not despise me for it. They told me about the films they had seen at the weekend, half a dozen, it seemed, none of which I knew. They talked all at once about wiping and panning and freeze frames, and it sounded so domestic that I thought I'd misheard them. I was surprised to find that they did not scorn Hollywood and that they talked about *Criss Cross* and *Out of the Past* with the same reverence they paid to Godard and Bresson. Mildred Pierce came up and I said that I used to watch it in Florence every time it was on *The Late Show*.

'I can just see you,' said Hadley.

'Curled up under a patchwork quilt,' added Steve.

'Not quite. I'm not that kind of New Englander.'

'I'm ignorant,' he apologized. 'I'm from Columbus.'

Despite his open rustic face, he was anything but ignorant. And he had been in New York a long time. First at the NYU film school, which he left before getting his degree, then working at the Film Makers' Co-operative which everyone called the Cinemateque, and making his own experimental films on a shoestring. He was accomplished and enthusiastic. He referred constantly to Jack Smith, Stan Brakhage,

Gregory Marcopolous and Kenneth Anger, heroes of the day. But, unlike most enthusiasts, his personality wasn't burdensome, and he was friendly in a boyish way. Hadley later confided to me that he was a little too wholesome for her tastes. Not twisted enough. 'You'd have loved Travis,' I said.

Star was an off-Broadway actress who was forced to take jobs in bars and restaurants when she was out of work, which was often. Hadley appeared to have no particular vocation, and no particular wish for one. We were alike in that way, you see.

'I'm a muse,' she would answer when questioned on the subject. She made it seem a good thing to be – a little money, lots of friends, no responsibilities, no guilt (apparently) and free as air. I later learned that her father was Richard Bell, the historian, who lived in a vast apartment on the Upper West Side when he was not in Nantucket with Hadley's stepmother and younger brother. Hadley was in open revolt against them and very proud of it.

'Stevie, get us a bottle of Southern Comfort, will you?' said Star, and flung $5 at him.

'Here,' I offered. 'Let me give you something for that.' But he wouldn't take the money. Just for a minute I resented being treated as a juvenile.

'Do you still want to come and see the rushes with us?' Hadley asked.

'OK. Should I change?'

She and Star laughed. They were wearing almost exactly what I was except that Hadley's black sweater was unbuttoned to expose an impressive cleavage, and her boots, I later discovered, were Charles Jourdan. She did that sort of thing, combining the elegant and the trashy. That's good, I thought. I like that. I should learn to do that. And I did learn, though I never quite matched her cachet.

'Come with us.' I turned the words over and over while I washed my face and brushed my teeth. But what were rushes? From behind the bathroom door, I heard Steve returning with the Southern Comfort.

We had a few drinks and smoked some grass. Normally weed didn't suit me, but the Southern Comfort lent it warmth and sparkle and made the occasion and even the room seem festive like Christmas. I didn't say much, only listened. My new friends appeared to have seizures which made them talk aggressively and inventively about subjects to which they were otherwise indifferent. Everyone fed the raconteur, cheering him on, encouraging him. The game involved adopting an attitude for the fun of it, in order to vent spleen or an unexpelled quantum of energy. Exaggeration and volume were essential.

We went out at nine. The cold bright weather had gone and it was snowing hard. The cityscape, so bare and dirty for the past two weeks, was being draped in white. From the hoods of automobiles that looked like giant sheep we scooped up the sticky snow and pelted each other. The storm had caused a traffic jam on Houston Street, but it was nothing to us, happy pedestrians. We laughed at commuters, trapped in their cars. Cars were the symbol of their smugness, their greed, their voluntary incarceration. Steve went up close to their windows with his Bolex and mischievously filmed their plight. He liked interfering with reality. It made him detached and powerful and everyone else either uncomfortable or a star, depending on their character.

Our destination was a loft in a large building on Broome Street. The façade had weathered to a sandy-browny rose, a colour I have never seen anywhere but New York, where a perfect balance of soot, damp, age and corrosive smog transformed every building below Houston Street into a work of art. The windows were high and arched and through them it was possible to watch the activities of all the inhabitants. I couldn't imagine a life so on display.

We walked four flights to the loft. The stairway was wide, drafty and not very clean. The first floor was occupied by a puppet-theatre company so famous that even I knew about it. The members lived communally and gave performances in the loft and in local schools and churches. The door on every landing bore an AIR sign. We opened the one on the fifth floor. Smoke billowed and eddied in the semi-darkness, occasionally lit up by a flash from the film which was being projected in the corner opposite – so far away I could barely make out the flickering images. I squinted through the haze at the silhouettes of about a hundred people, some of them seated on the floor in front of the screen, some standing in groups. It was like going into a cave inhabited, maybe, by some primitive tribe whose seemingly random movements were governed by a secret necessity which I, as an outsider, could not penetrate.

The loft belonged to a dark-haired woman named Nightshade to whom Hadley introduced me before vanishing among the guests. Nightshade pressed my hand between her long cold fingers. She was tall and beautiful in the Gothic style. Someone later told me that she was a bass viol player who gave concerts in the nude as well as a sought-after actress in experimental films. Her real name was Charlene Hoke.

'I'm so glad you came, Rose. You're just in time.' She had the voice

I expected her to have but was very kind and friendly. 'We're showing Jackson's film now. Please help yourself to whatever you like. And enjoy yourself, my dear.'

I made my way towards the projector, stopping to eat the last few potato chips in a glass bowl. I could hear Hadley's laughter but I couldn't see her. I felt out of place, nervous of everyone and glad of the dark. I sat on the floor with the audience, in front of the screen, more to be out of the way than to watch the film. But I was quickly drawn in.

A rocky and mountainous landscape tinted in pinks and ochres. In the foreground a ruined temple with a large tree to the left. On a distant hill a small white church. All around tall white flowers wave their leafless plumes. In the space before the ruin hermaphroditic creatures in scanty attire lounge and gambol amidst the scattered masonry. The director has shot them from every conceivable angle. Organs and facial expressions are tenderly examined. Colours are sumptuous and hazy, and the whole scene is lit by a scary sunset light. The actors' faces are painted and sad. They look like street urchins who have broken into a theatrical costumier's. All except one. The one without make-up. The one they all appear to be pursuing. He has a sharp nose, full mouth, fierce eyes and a graceful body. Though narrow in the chest, he appears strong, and his limbs have a wonderful delicacy. He is quite young. He is the only one who is not a helpless victim of his desires. The dream children fawn at his feet and attempt to caress him. But always he skirts their embraces and flits away laughing. The others, both men and women, run after him or weep or take consolation in each other.

'Where is this?' I asked the man beside me.

'Some Greek island,' he whispered. 'I think they were all thrown out or thrown in jail. Something.'

'Oh.'

At the film's climax the dancers or worshippers or whatever these strange being are, whirl madly, fly at each other as though to gouge, bite and scratch, waving their arms and uttering soundless cries, until suddenly they fall to their knees, and gaze enthralled at the sky. Here the director has done some clever time-lapsing: the clouds seem to converge into the features of the desired and elusive one. Has he fled to the Empyrean or have the others killed him, torn him to pieces? In either case, he is beyond their reach for good.

The lights went on. Exposed in this way the loft looked grim and cold. I was stiff from sitting cross-legged on the floor. When I looked around I realized that many of what I had taken to be human guests were in fact department-store dummies arranged in various poses and stages of undress, mostly in evening wear. They gave me the creeps. Even now my sense of humour does not extend to the bizarre in the home. Not after the Infant of Prague.

What now? I thought. Then I jumped up as I found myself the only person left seated. Since I wasn't smoking I had nothing to do with my hands. No one passed me the joint that was going around. I would have taken off my jacket only I was too cold. I continued to stand helpless until I was joined by Steve.

'Eee.' He shook his straight hair.

'Didn't you like that?' I asked.

'It was great. Great things always make me want to rattle my brains and grind my teeth. Know what I mean?'

'Yeah.' I did know. The desired and elusive one had made me want to do just that.

'I only liked the colours.' I heard Hadley adopting the aggressive tone she used when voicing her opinions, challenging the others to disagree, looking, it seemed, for a fight. Yet always smiling.

'Who made the film?'

'That guy over there. The one who was with us at the demo.' He pointed to a short man with a beard and a white sailor hat.

'Oh. Jackson.'

'He got a grant from the Ford Foundation. He took drugs and read books and travelled until the money ran out. Then he made the film.'

'Will there be more? I mean tonight?'

'Yeah. Mine.'

'Really?'

'Yeah. I'm next. You'll see yourself, Rose.'

'How come?'

'That stuff I shot at the march – you're in it.' He gave me a big smile. 'You look good.'

'I thought it was a fifth-rate *Inauguration of the Pleasure Dome.*' Hadley was still going on, not caring that Jackson was standing behind her.

'She doesn't seem to like the movie.'

'It's not very minimal. Hadley likes everyone to film white walls and shadows and bare beaches. That kind of thing.'

'She's like my father.'

'Your father was a film-maker?'

'No. But maybe he should have been. He takes photographs. Dead trees and garbage cans are his specialities.'

'Sounds great.' The lights went off again.

'Remember,' Steve whispered. 'They're rushes.'

'OK.'

The film began. Steve sat down beside me and passed me his can of beer. Behind us the projector went click-click-slap, click-click-slap.

The first roll is black-and-white. A man and a woman in a railroad apartment are preparing to make love. They're obviously in a hurry – a lunchtime tryst maybe. But whenever it seems as though they might actually get down to it, something unexpected happens. A gorilla jumps out of the icebox and begins to play a ukulele. An anaconda dangles from the fire escape. A Salvation Army band marches through, wanting contributions.

'This is all to the accompaniment of "The Anvil Chorus",' Steve announced.

Just when the couple have rid themselves of these pests and climbed back between the sheets, the fire brigade arrives and sprays them with confetti.

The reel came flapping to an end. The next was in colour.

I see the marchers in the Sheep's Meadow, placards, banners, police, horses. I see the buildings along 5th Avenue, the sky, the sun. I see the Puerto Rican boys, the fight. A thousand faces rush past, glimpses offering a spectrum of panic and hysteria. A collection of Munch paintings viewed at high speed. Cut to prancing police horses and their fat grim riders, the Puerto Rican boy wounded or dead on the pavement. (He did die.) No faces now. Legs. Hundreds of them, feet, running, churning up the grass, stepping on each other, stumbling. Bodies now, pushing, colliding, on the bare edge of control. Then a woman with a tear-stained face runs directly at the camera, not knowing that she does. A woman – Frances – coming so close that the frame blurs into her jacket. A confusion of hands, garments, more faces. Again the woman's face framed in brown hair, long and tangled, a small nose saddled with freckles. Frances.

It was many years since I'd seen her. Before I could catch and hold her she was gone and I was glad. Go away, Frances, why bother me now? It was disturbing to think she had just appeared like that, to other people, without my knowledge or permission.

Then comes an awkward jump. (I have figured out what rushes are.) Two women exchange looks, one concerned but cheerful, the other anxious and troubled. The viewer is struck by the similarity of their profiles. They walk on, arm in arm, one half-dragging, half-supporting the other, their legs now synchronized, now out of step. Another jump finds them with a girl and two men, one of whom carries a camera. The four stand poised on the brink of Columbus Circle. Just as they are about to step into the road, cars come screaming straight at them. The film ends.

The lights came on. Applause.

Steve grinned. I patted his arm.

'That was really good,' I said and he laughed.

Then Hadley was there with the dark, short-haired man, Tony Lasky.

'You were wonderful,' he said.

'Me?' I hadn't done anything. I'd cried but not even that very much. 'I'm not an actress,' I said.

'That's the point.'

'And the two of you.' He turned to Hadley. He had to get her attention by taking her arm. 'Did you see?' he asked Steve.

'Yeah. It's amazing.'

'What?' Hadley didn't seem to understand.

'The way you look. The two of you. You're just alike.'

'We are?'

'Well not perfectly.'

'Not exactly.'

'But the eyes. The jaw.' They studied us. Hadley was amused, liking it, ready to take them up on everything. 'The cheekbones, especially on film. Not so much in the flesh.'

'Somehow the camera –'

'Shows us what we always miss,' Tony said.

'Yeah.'

'Little things, vital details that get lost because we're always partially distracted.'

'I'd like to be fully distracted. All the time,' Hadley chirped. 'Well, well. Here's my distraction of the moment.' She took the hand of the man who'd just joined us.

'Hi, Kit,' they said. He nodded at everyone.

'Do you think Rose and I look alike?' she asked him. His eyebrows narrowed and he scrutinized us. She raised her chin slightly to give him a better view.

'A little,' he answered. 'I noticed it in the film.'

'See?' Tony was quite excited. He called to another friend, a woman named Aphrodite, and asked her what she thought about me and Hadley.

'Amazing,' she said with a foreign accent. 'Could be sisters.'

'Not sisters.' Tony still studied us. 'As much as long-lost relations.'

'Are we?' laughed Hadley. '*Are* we related, Rose?'

I shrugged. 'Maybe.'

'Then why haven't we seen it? Must be something the matter with us.'

'Must be.' I was not used to being the focus of so much attention. It was unnerving but pleasant. And it did not prevent my watching Hadley's boyfriend. He looked serious, quiet, patient. With Hadley he'd have to be. He seemed simply to be waiting for her, listening to us all while he waited, not wasting time that could be spent in observation. She told me he was a writer. I envied her. I envied them all. Artists were to me a kind of privileged, if poverty-stricken, aristocracy. A club whose membership-rules were revised for each new entry, so that you couldn't be too sure of getting in.

I was warm now. I was drinking a glass of mulled wine, and the blood throbbed in my hands. I stuck to Steve and Tony and let them introduce me to the others if and when they felt like it.

Then along came Jackson who was drunk and garrulous and expansively homosexual. He talked about his film, blowing smoke in all our faces as his wine sloshed dangerously in his glass. He had the habit of crooking his little finger and waving it while simultaneously scrunching up his lips as though trying to scratch his nose with his moustache. I could not stop giggling. He was talking about how he'd waltzed with the Pope at a gay ball on Capri. His eminence had not yet been made head of the One, Holy and Apostolic Church. Jackson claimed he was a mere bishop then, one of many in attendance that evening, all in drag like the dummies. Jackson hadn't realized his profession until they parted with a kiss at the edge of the ballroom floor and his holiness was whisked out to the balcony by another admirer.

'All I knew,' said Jackson, 'was that he danced divinely.' He flicked his Camel at ear-level and smiled.

I finally worked up the courage to ask him what his film was called. I'd missed the beginning, I said.

'*Vistas of the Heart Unveiled.* Everyone hates it, but I think it's perfection, don't you?'

'Oh yes. Where did you make it?'

'In Greece.'

'But where?'

'The Cyclades. An island. Excuse me, my dear, but who are you?'

He'd forgotten he'd stroked my cheek. I was just about to tell him when he was accosted by Aphrodite who led him away, whispering furiously.

Hadley danced up to us, singing along with The Doors. She made a tricky little turn and rubbed her shoulder against Steve who rubbed back.

'Hey, where you been?' The man next to Steve asked her, feigning lightness, but really wanting to know. 'You don't write, you don't call . . .'

'I've been very busy pursuing happiness.'

'Find any?'

'Not much. How can you smoke that stuff? It's absolutely disgusting. Give me some.'

'Maybe you haven't been going to the right places.'

'You're worried I've overlooked you?'

'There must be someone in New York you've overlooked.'

'If so, the reasons are obvious.'

'Help the needy.'

'I don't believe in charity. Get a government grant.' She went off with Kit.

The man pulled himself together, not unsuccessfully, I thought. Maybe he'd had a lot of practice. He looked at me and shrugged.

'She's one of those gals,' he said.

'I guess so.' She was. And I looked at her. But I was not 'one of those gals'.

Everyone was leaving. Steve and Tony were steering me towards the 'Exit' sign. I bumped into a dummy which tottered then righted itself.

'We're going.'

'Oh. I was just getting used to the dummies.'

We met Hadley, Kit and Star by the door.

'Come to Spring Street with us?' said Hadley.

All the way downstairs we could hear Jackson singing:

> I'm cooking his bacon,
> It's the bacon I'm makin',
> I'm cooking breakfast
> For the one I love.

I walked beside Tony. No one arranged it. It just happened that way.

'I'd like you to be in a film I'm making,' he said.

'Why?' I asked.

He explained at length. It was a little hard to concentrate with Jackson now behind us:

> He's takin' his shower,
> It's my happy hour,
> I'm cooking breakfast
> For the one I love.

171

I had forgotten about the storm, so when we reached the street I could hardly believe what I saw. There was no traffic. Cars were recognizable only as white humps along the sidewalks, which, like the roofs and windowsills, were covered to a depth of six inches. The result was something unprecedented in my three years in New York: complete quiet. Only a few human voices broke the silence, like the footprints in the snow, touching, magical. The city had fallen under a spell. The dirt, the ugliness and the art were submerged in an equalizing beauty. And the air – an air like I hadn't smelled in years. Wet and clean and sweet and sharp, like white laundry.

We went to a bar where everyone was drunk, celebrating the storm. Tony bought me a beer and we talked some more. He was easy to be with. He told me he'd been called up for the Draft and that he must report at six the next morning for his physical.

'Oh God, you poor thing.' Impulsively I hugged him.

This was the point of the evening, he said. They had all agreed to sit up with him, sleep being impossible and probably detrimental under the circumstances. They would wait at his apartment, wait until he came back and told them the good news. Or the bad.

'You'll get off,' I know it,' I said, sounding like Eva.

'Will you wait too?' he asked. 'You don't have to.'

'Of course I'll wait.' I'd call in sick, that's all. Or go to work anyway.

At about three we went back to Tony's, a first-floor front on Prince Street. He produced a bottle of Gallo and we drank that, lounging around the minimally furnished sitting-room (that was also the bed-room), some of us occasionally dozing. Just after five we sent him off. He'd probably have to walk all the way because of the snow. We each gave him a hug at the door. He was planning to plead homosexuality.

The others slept but I could not. I was anxious for Tony, though I hardly knew him. But I was also preoccupied with Jackson's film, specifically with the image of the boy, the Elusive One. He was striking, scary, unique. He seemed to care for nothing but his teasing liberty. I thought how I'd like to be that unencumbered, that hard to catch.

We woke to the sound of Tony's key in the lock. It was nine-thirty and he was smiling.

'The doctor asked me if I thought I could control myself in the Army. "Are you *kidding*?" I said. With all those handsome *men*? In *uniform*?"'

I did go to work that day. I was very happy, not tired at all. I didn't think about Aunt Bernie or Vinnie or even Travis. I had begun a new story.

12

Underground

The train was travelling so fast and the track was so bumpy that we were thrown about in our seats and knocked together. The racket of the wheels made talk impossible even for Hadley, and the Queens streets through which we were rushing were too boring to look at. I took the hand which lay in my lap and turned it over. I examined the heart line (very good), the fate line (a bit short) and traced with my finger the wonderful Uranus line. ('Technological genius. Extraordinary powers of invention.' I had not been able to resist Eva's palmistry book.) I felt each finger, so smooth and well-proportioned, without scars, blisters or callouses. A hand that had known neither field nor factory. A hand for pens, books, editing machines. A highly-developed human hand, not that much bigger than mine. Our fingers intertwined. I'd done my nails Cerise Verni and the fingers alternated red, white, painted, unpainted.

Tony's other hand rested on the Bolex. He studied it as though it were a precious jewel. I liked his profile when his head was inclined – the neat ears and slightly flattened nose, the crisp black curls and the dark eyelashes that brushed his cheek like a woman's. His blue-green eyes were his best feature, large and very sympathetic. He was a well-made, serious person. Sweet. Like blackberry jam.

In the seat ahead of us, Steve shot the scenery which interested no one but him. Unlike Tony who planned and deliberated and even had been known to use a script, Steve filmed incessantly and relied on miracles. He usually found a few and considered them well worth the hundreds of feet of film squandered in the process. He wasn't crazy about structure. He said he was more interested in force than form. He said there was no aesthetic absolute and that we had to destroy stereotypes and readjust our vision. He didn't want to be selective. He didn't want to make judgements based on outmoded criteria. He saw all human movement as beautiful, hated the ballet, for instance, said he

173

preferred to watch a fat woman waddle along with two shopping bags. He believed in chance. I told him about Frank and Travis's altar, and he liked that.

Beside Steve was Richard and opposite them Hadley and Maja. Hadley caught my eye and smiled. She was always ready to smile. Her good humour was broken only by arguments with taxi drivers or the customers at Cal's or what she considered to be the perverse conduct of Kit. She approved of my relationship with Tony and congratulated herself on having introduced us. She claimed we were perfect for each other and she was right. Everything would be fine, she said, as long as we did not live together. Hadley was for independence.

Independent but included, that's how I felt. They had taken me with them, first as mascot then as peer. I was part of a group. I no longer watched them like a fascinated outsider, through a pane of glass. I had a part in their game which I played well enough to take for granted, to forget about. It was the way childhood should have been and was not. I had broken free of the autism in which I had been trapped for the past three years and was becoming a good companion. I was being socialized – late, but I was learning.

My friends had also taught me about the movies and encouraged me to act. I had already played small parts in two films, one of them Tony's, and was now taking a leading role in his new film, part of which we were shooting today.

You said this was all rubbish. You said my friends had a playground mentality that brought out the worst in me, encouraging me in my old habit of imagining I was something I was not. But you didn't understand about my acting. I had no ambitions, no plans. I did not want it to lead to anything formal or defined or established. I was just there; acting came along; I did it.

None of us had a future. We did not think about making money. It didn't interest us, or we simply couldn't think that way. The moment a future occurred to me, my mind became a blank or it abruptly turned and went off sideways like a crab. I agreed with Janice that if you live for today you'll always be protected.

I was so inspired by my new friends that I had even tried to make a film of my own. I borrowed Tony's camera (the one he now held in his lap) and took it to the Etruscan Gallery at the Metropolitan Museum. There I filmed sarcophagi and funerary heads, using natural light and attempting to edit in the camera. It was all as basic as it could be. The movie was dedicated to my mother and was called *In Memory of Nora Noonan*. Tony and Hadley and I watched it at the Cinemateque. The images were a little fluttery and I still had a good deal to learn about the light meter. It didn't matter. What was important was the act of making the film, not how this one turned out or whether it led to another.

We were not afraid of failure. Movies were a game in which we, the makers, were at once divine and nothing special. When work is play – that is heaven on earth.

Steve was changing a roll. He had not stopped filming. Tony, who planned every frame, disapproved of his extravagance. But he loved him. We all loved him, *puer eternus* that he was. He was Tony's first assistant on this film. They performed such functions for each other, free of charge. We all worked for nothing. Tony had a job in the still department of 20th Century Fox and he saved what little he earned to make films. *Martyrs* would be his third. Steve worked on the docks in Brooklyn, where, because he was unionized, he made a good deal more than Tony, though he needed every bit of his salary to pay for the enormous amount of film he used. Both were saved by the free Cinemateque equipment.

The other actors in the film, Richard, Peter and Maja, were an out-of-work dancer, a social worker and a part-time cook respectively and lived in small apartments, the rent for which they could barely afford. Richard had even more trouble with his landlord because he dressed as a nun. Perhaps it wasn't so much the black robe, rosary and lace-up shoes (no wimple, it could have been worse) as the long curly hair and the beard. He insisted on being called Sister Richard and we indulged his little whim.

These three, like the rest of us, had been to college, and their horrified parents now wrung their hands over the money spent on expensive useless degrees. They could not understand why their children weren't ruthlessly pursuing careers. From their point of view, if you did not play to win you were simply not respectable.

I had left the Treasure Chest and joined Hadley and Star at the restaurant. They waited for an opening then hurried me in before anyone else seized the golden vacancy. Waitresses at Cal's earned large tips. The work was even more arduous than at the bar, and the hours were later – sometimes until four in the morning. The profits were gratifying, though I never saved much. Eddie said he was sorry to see me go and I believed him. I really liked Eddie, though I could not return his sentiments.

I was working hard, but I enjoyed it, and the rent was paid on time. In a way, Cal's was my real education, a very worldly college, unimaginable by Wigram Boott except as a vision of Sodom and Gomorrah. I had never enjoyed an atmosphere of such complete freedom, with straights and gays, blacks and whites and every shade between all together and nobody minding at all. This was due in part to Clyde, the owner/manager, who deeply loved artists and freaks and wanted his restaurant to cater exclusively for them. As far as he was concerned, once they had come into Cal's they could do anything they wanted – dance on the tables, take drugs, bring their Alsatians and St Bernards, arrive naked in a shopping cart (it happened), make love in the lavatories or under the tables, for all he cared. Anything.

The lavatories were notorious, especially the men's which must have been one of the most low-life in America. People screwed in the cubicles while others took drugs or conducted business meetings. The women's room was covered in famous graffiti. Those were racy, inventive girls.

The telephone booths were another curiosity. You could never make a phone call from Cal's. The booths were permanently occupied. They were the second-best location for intercourse, usually of the heterosexual variety. But they also served as offices. Customers who could not afford telephones or who were of no fixed address or who spent most of their waking lives at Cal's anyway would simply take over the booths and occupy them for two or three hours. Nothing could be done about it since Clyde didn't give a damn. They received all their calls at Cal's, their friends and business associates or dealers being instructed to ring them there at such and such a time. This policy provoked the largest number of fist fights at the restaurant.

Clyde's primary objective was to protect his clientele. You couldn't make a reservation at Cal's. He admitted only who he knew and liked, and if you looked too OB (other boroughs) you were not encouraged to frequent the place. Some would-be customers were indignant; others were plain scared and never returned. He didn't want any family types from New Jersey and Queens. He was a social purist. Those outsiders who did manage to get in were consigned to the upstairs where little happened except on Tuesday and Friday nights when it became a disco. Sometimes we'd go up there after work and just dance until five in the morning. But the truly great and historic raves went on in the back room which was reserved for the most erstwhile of the regulars.

Then there was the sexy staff, of which I was one. The busboys were especially famous. The customers all wanted to chase and grab us, and occasionally they'd succeed. It was an intoxicating place. It issued licences to be what ever you wanted to be. I'm told it's gone now and Clyde is dead.

I always arrived early in order to eat supper with Hadley and Star and

Hadley's friend Drexel, one of the busboys, at a table kept especially for us. When we had finished work at three we were often too up to go home and so sat around drinking and smoking and laughing or went for breakfast at the Great Jones Diner or the Pink Teacup. Steve or Kit often joined us. Tony had to be at work by nine. I woke up in the middle of the next afternoon with just enough time to take a bath and feed Otis and nip round to the bodega before meeting my colleagues for supper and a replay of the night before. On nights I didn't work I went to the movies with Tony, a double feature, usually. On Saturdays we'd go to a matinée and then to another film in the evening. By Monday Tony was usually broke and I'd have to lend him enough to get through the week. He repaid me on Friday afternoons, but by Monday or Tuesday at the latest, I'd have to make him another loan. He was saving for *Martyrs*. When we were really skint we'd visit his parents in Long Island to be fed, to come down in peace and to walk on the beach and take pictures. If we had to stay in the city with no money we'd just go for a long walk. The streets were our entertainment and they were completely free. The dramas and the antics one witnessed on a stroll between Thomkins Square Park and Canal, were as good as a film.

Hadley took me to parties, and though I was still far from being a flamboyant extravert, I got to know people. A lot recognized me from Cal's or from the dance pieces I'd been in with Hadley or Steve or Star, or even from the two films. I was regarded as Hadley's friend. In our way we were a famous duo, a class act. Hadley capitalized on the notoriety. It was just the sort of thing she knew how to do. And though I was always the other one, I didn't mind. (It did occur to me that I might be living in Hadley's shadow and that being her double was a way of appropriating an identity I was unable to muster for myself, and was there maybe something a little sinister about this? A little creepy? Sometimes I'd see the relationship as parasitical and wonder who was feeding off whom. I'd worry I was being smothered. But this never lasted long. So I was the Other One. So what. Why should I care when Hadley was like a free ticket to life?) Oh, I knew people, all right. It was the closest I ever came to being 'one of those gals'.

There's something I never told you about this part of my life. Ready? I had lovers. Besides Tony, I mean. Though the same word isn't applicable to both, since Tony was my friend as well as the person I went to bed with. Which certainly cannot be said of the others. The first two I met before I knew Tony. With the rest I was simply unfaithful to him. I adored Tony, but he was tame. Part of me was slightly bored with his domestication. I didn't tell him about the three small affairs, but then I didn't tell anyone. I liked my secret life. Everyone needs a few secrets. Perhaps to reassure themselves there is at least one part of their identity that isn't lost, strayed or stolen. I felt no need to justify myself, I was looking for something, that's all. I guess I was looking for you.

For a long time I was celibate. As I was intent on pursuing a phantom, I didn't think much about sex.

But there is such an excess of free-floating libido in New York, especially in the summer, that eventually you begin to imagine grasping some of those shoulders, stroking the fur on that flat naked abdomen. Impossible not to with everyone half-dressed. And the others think about you in the same way. It's in their eyes, in everyone's eyes.

I realized that my era of chastity was coming to an end as I was walking along Avenue C market one afternoon in July. I was barefoot, in shorts, carrying a brown paper bag full of peaches which I held against one breast. I passed some boys playing stick ball in the street. They must have been ten or eleven. One of them stopped playing and stared at me as I passed. He was quite beautiful, one of those racial mixes with fair hair and dark skin. Under his T-shirt and jeans his little body was strong and elegant. And he gave me such a *look*. A look like I've never had even from a grown man.

I realized that he would know exactly what to do with me, that he was already more experienced than I would ever be. I let him look, trying not to meet his gaze. He was exceptional, frightening. I hurried on, feeling his eyes on my back as I turned into 2nd Street.

A week later I met a handsome black man named Sonny, the friend of a retired boxer who lived across the street from me. He called me Springtime and Babycake. He'd turn up at odd hours and we'd go to bed. We'd do things you can't do any more, like drive up to Harlem in his white Mercury and cruise around with the top down, the object of every glance, and visit bars where he always had a little business to do, I never found out what. Then he disappeared, just vanished. A month later I started going out with a boy on 10th Street. He had wild hair, made tiny intricate drawings with a repitograph and worried a lot about animals.

Once, outside the New Yorker, I met a strange guy who I now realize must have been crazy. (I was incapable then of assessing the state of anyone's sanity. Not surprising, given the amount of time I spent at Cal's.) He was a drop-out from Columbia and obsessed with Leslie Fiedler. He lived in an awful apartment with orange walls just off Amsterdam Avenue. I went there with him, and he introduced me to his other obsession: Smokey Robinson and the Miracles. We'd play

'You Really Got a Hold On Me' over and over and dance to it. He could do a great Philadelphia Dip and was a wonderful sexy dancer. Great dancers are hard men to resist, even if they tell you that *you* dance like a sorority girl.

'It's about loosening up, not tightening up,' he'd shout. 'Let go of your *knees*.' He was a good teacher, firm but fair, and I improved under his instruction. We had so much fun dancing that I didn't mind his being weird to non-existent in bed. Rock and roll was a more than sufficient release for our libidos. It was when he tried to hypnotize me that I got nervous. I pretended to be in a deep trance and said what I thought I was expected to say: cave, father, whatever. I didn't want to hurt his feelings, you see. He was delighted with me and really pleased with himself, and beaming all over when, as he imagined, he returned me to consciousness. I said I was due at Cal's, ran down the four flights of stairs and never came back.

Last but not least, there was – you guessed it – the glass-eyed bartender Ray. He said he'd liked me right away, though it took him a while to make the first move. He was nice, though he lived in a really horrible apartment in Queens, all he could afford after his divorce settlement. Anyway I left him. Another one I never saw again.

Yes, I met a lot of people; I got an education. Hadley and Tony were my mentors. Between them they altered my taste, my appearance and my world view. Hadley worked on the exterior while Tony managed my inner life. Not that either of them consciously adopted their roles. It was just that I was so ripe for development, so ready to be directed. Tony took me towards the arts, but, unlike Travis whose aesthetic was idiosyncratic, even macabre, he did so in proper fashion, that is he went to the source. In music he began with the baroque, in literature with *Princesse des Clèves*, in painting with Duccio, in sculpture with Egypt, in film with Griffiths. We went not only to gallery openings but to every permanent exhibition in New York. Then we went again. We went to the library together. When I did not have the time, he chose books for me. I always loved them. He reserved tickets a month in advance for Sunday afternoon concerts at the Frick. The concerts were free on a first-come first-serve basis. We always got in. That's how organized he was. We heard Janis Joplin and Frank Zappa at the Filmore and went to the New Yorker twice a week. He introduced me to Alban Berg and Allen Ginsberg. We lay on the floor and smoked grass and listened to Maria Callas and Christa Ludwig, to Monteverdi's 'Vespers' and 'Song of the Earth'. I began to like them. I finally made it to the Met when he took me to see *The Magic Flute*. We agreed about everything. Our relationship was surreally harmonious. Consequently it was more like a friendship with sex. The latter has been slow in coming. He had been interested from the start, but I resisted. I think the refinement which drew me to him made me uneasy about physical contact. I could not imagine lying naked beside him, and imagination is everything. But he was patient. He never pressed me. I can't remember the first time we made love. All of a sudden we were lovers and it was as though we had been for ever. I do recall being pleasantly surprised. I liked the physical differences between us – his skin so dark and mine so pale, his hair so curly and mine so straight, his being rather short for a man, my being rather tall for a woman. Contrast was nice. The similarities were all mental. I felt as if we might go on indefinitely, making movies and ingesting culture and sleeping together almost without noticing it.

Even with the addition of sex, ours was still a Platonic relationship. Physical intimacy didn't seem to raise the usual demons. There were no tantrums, no jealousy, no regressive behaviour. We held on to our separate apartments. Yet we were quite domestic. We went to Fulton Street for fish and to Avenue C for fruit and vegetables. There were delis too numerous to count, each an Aladdin's cave of goodies, some of which even we could afford. Our cooking became more experimental. There was no question of restaurants. We needed all the money for films. We walked everywhere.

Living together was never discussed. I don't know if he even considered it. I know I didn't. I had still not abandoned the idea of giving my life to Travis, though I never said so and we never talked about him. I had mentioned him only to Hadley who was fascinated by the story. She was convinced Travis was in Chicago. Kit knew people who knew people in the Directory. She'd told him to make enquiries. I didn't prevent her, but I refused to get excited. I no longer lived in hope. I was happy with Tony. It was as though he'd slipped a fine mesh around my life, invisible but tough, which missiles from the outside world could not penetrate. He was like an anti-depressant, filtering out pain.

Perhaps we were happy because we were not isolated in our affection. We lived within a larger context. There was this third thing. There was the Group. We shared a productive anarchy. And did we produce. We had made three short films in the past seven months.

When I was acting, I tried not to act. I pulled no faces, made no attempt at timing. I looked straight at the camera. Tony told me to do these things, but he never said, Just be yourself. He knew that non-acting has nothing to do with naturalism.

'Unless something occurs to you, don't do anything. And even if something does occur to you, consider it before responding to the impulse. Do what I tell you; you're free within limits.' This made me feel very secure. No wonder I felt comfortable with him.

Such a partnership had been unimaginable. Travis had defined my emotional parameters, even before I met him, if you see what I mean. I had learned to equate love with anxiety. Love was a sandcastle, without foundations, washable-away at any moment. Tony made structure, in his art and in his life, and though it was not a confining structure, it had firm foundations. All he required was my agreement to live within that structure. Otherwise, I could do as I liked. He was the gentlest of stage-managers.

His films had stories of sorts, though not the beginning-middle-end variety. The one we had just finished was about a woman who hi-jacks a bus full of schoolboys. The film cost him everything. He'd borrowed from his father and his aunt and gone deeply into debt. But he won second prize at the Milwaukee Film Festival. The movie played to full houses in San Francisco. It was also shown in St Louis, Miami and Chicago and regularly at the New York art cinemas. I wondered if Travis might see it and what his reaction would be to my script-girl credit.

Steve's recent film had done almost as well, but it was wackier. He had devoted followers, and his work was screened at experimental film shows at universities, lofts and cinemateques. Reviews called them living collages. They disorientated on purpose. They made normality seem frighteningly abnormal and invited viewers to lightheartedly embrace insanity for the sake of their mental health. They used no actors. If you were around, you'd probably get filmed. They had no plot but came straight from grisly hilarious life.

Hadley had been really good as the hi-jacking housewife. She said the role satisfied a secret paedophilia, but it was hard to imagine her keeping anything a secret. She enjoyed making a point of her naughtiness, and kept reminding us all lest we forget. It was part of her fascination with her own character. Today she was playing my sister. We were the protagonists of one section of *Martyrs*, the first of its three stories of innocent victims. I was the victim. Hadley was the wicked sibling at whose hand I came to a sticky end. Well, sandy more than sticky, since I was to be buried alive on the beach. We were going to shoot the sequence this morning or this afternoon, depending on how late the truck arrived and the tide and how long it took to set up the mirrors. I'd had a cold for a week and was already snuffling and snivelling. Tony had suggested cancelling the shoot but I'd refused. The mirrors were hired and paid for. Everyone else had arranged their lives so as to leave this day free for Tony. There was no question of my letting them down. I insisted I would be fine. I would have a chilly time, though, for it was not the bright March day we'd hoped for. Long Island was overcast and windy, and I was to wear only a winding sheet. Sometimes making movies was like a risky play school.

Tony had been thinking about the story for years. He had a long gestation period. And my friendship with Hadley provided the opportunity he'd been waiting for. From the minute he'd seen the footage of the demo at Nightshade's loft and noticed our resemblance, he'd decided to make the picture with us.

The train arrived at Bayside. We alighted and struggled up the stairs with suitcases and equipment. Passers-by stared at us. We weren't your common or garden commuters. After waiting nearly half an hour we found three grumbling taxi drivers willing to drive us to Long Island Sound. They couldn't believe we wanted to be dropped by the side of the expressway next to an empty beach.

We stood and stared at it. Behind us were suburban houses with well-kept back yards of magnolia and lilac sloping down to the four-lane highway. Once in a golden Gatsby age those lawns extended all the way to the water. We climbed over the railing and trudged across the pebbly sands. To the left of the bay stood three giant water towers and some grim brick apartment buildings with the Whitestone Bridge beyond. Low clouds rolled in from the sea and over our heads towards Manhattan. A few seagulls patrolled the desolate shore.

Tony stopped and turned to me. 'Isn't it beautiful?' he said, his eyes shining. They were the eyes of someone about to make his dream come true.

'We'll have to build some sort of windbreak,' shouted Steve.

'Wait for the truck. They'll have screens as well.'

We began to set up the first shot, working against the weather. Tony stood apart, scanning the horizon with his Bolex. Maja held the blankets around us while Hadley and I undressed. I had dyed my hair almost to Hadley's shade of blonde so that, from a distance at least, our resemblance was even more striking. My nail polish must now come off. Maja produced some remover and Hadley a bottle of brandy, and we sat, me in my white sheet, she in her red jumpsuit, under the protection of the blanket while Steve, Richard and Peter tested light meters and marked out positions. Already I was shivering.

'How's Kit?' I asked.

'Mad at me.'

'Why?'

''Cause I spent last Sunday night at Mel's.' She tossed her head.

'Oh.' The way she flaunted her infidelities shocked and delighted me.

'What business is it of his? If the way I live upsets him that's his problem.'

'I guess it is.' I wanted to tell her that I too might be upset by her visits to old boyfriends, but felt obliged to feign indignation at Kit's regressive behaviour.

'What did he say?' I asked and took another swig from the bottle.

'Didn't say anything. Just sat across the table and stared into his beer like an old grunjy grump. I told him to sit up straight and pull his shoulders back. I hate people who slump.'

'It's because he's a writer, probably. Sits all day at his desk bent over his manuscript. Must be an unhealthy occupation.'

'You think so,' she snorted.

'Isn't he writing a novel?'

'*Supposed* to be writing a novel. He's at the desk all right. But nothing very much happens there, except when he rearranges his papers and thumb tacks and rubber bands and sharpens all his pencils. Boy, is that an orderly desk!'

'Does he have a block?'

'He's blocked himself, the dip-stick. He says he has to find the right word, by which he means the first word, and that he can't begin until this first word is revealed to him.'

'That's funny.'

'I mean I believe in integrity, but really! Six months he's been waiting for this fucking first word.' She flung a stone at the sea.

'I can imagine Travis doing something like that if he was a writer.'

'I said to him oh pick a word for Christ's sake, any word, go to the dictionary and stick your finger somewhere, at random, haven't you heard of chance, it's a very popular concept these days, influences quite a few people. I mean just *start*. But he's so stubborn. Too bad. He used to be nice.' She was secretly proud of him, I could tell. Why could she never admit it? 'I mean, what makes him think he's so special? Why doesn't he just get going and make art like everybody else?'

'We can't all work the same way at the same pace.'

'Oh, Rose, you're just so reasonable. Don't defend him. You're my friend, remember? So be on my side.' She'd get impatient with me sometimes, as though she resented my having thoughts and feelings of my own. She could be quite menacing.

I put my arm around her and shook her gently, as she pouted at the sea. Sometimes being with Hadley was like being back in fifth grade.

'He loves you.'

'That's not love, it's a man guarding his property.' She sighed. 'I just wish there were someone interesting to go to bed with.'

The truck arrived and everyone scrambled to help the driver and his mate unload it. This wasn't easy as the five mirrors were heavy and we had to manoeuvre them down the rocky slope and on to the shore. As I was immobile in my winding sheet, there was not much I could do to help, so I sat huddled under the blanket watching the others struggle with the mirrors and screens and thinking they looked like figures in a Fellini landscape. It was then I had the idea of making another movie, a film about Janice and her animals, through which I could both repay her kindness and somehow resurrect Foxie.

We had only three hours before they took the mirrors away, and rain was threatening. But Tony remained calm. The wind was so strong that Richard and Peter had to crouch behind the two outside mirrors in order to support them. Richard was having trouble with his skirts. Steve and Tony dug like mad as the sand flew in their faces. They were piling up my tumulus, which would be the focal point of the five mirrors.

Somehow we did it, and in under two hours.

Hadley appears in a red jumpsuit, leather flying helmet and goggles (from the shop in 8th Street). She ties my passive limbs with ropes and stands staring at me as I lie bound on the beach in my winding sheet. She produces a syringe and injects me with some sort of lethal drug, or maybe it only puts me to sleep. Then she dons a pair of black gauntlets and proceeds to bury me alive in the sand until only my head is left. She crowns me with a wreath of seaweed. All her actions are reflected in the mirrors as are the brick buildings and the water towers. Tony has to twist himself into impossible angles to stay out of frame, until the last shot in which his reflection appears holding the camera, an authorial signature. We proceed in an odd silence with the wind as our soundtrack. After a close-up of my face framed in black seaweed, Hadley walks away towards the water, her red suit reflected five times in the mirrors. I get to my feet with the help of Steve who unburies me. Maja rushes me into dry clothes. While I change, the others rebuild the mound and then film it again with me supposedly in it, now dead. I shiver as I look at my grave. My sinuses are so blocked I can hardly breathe. Then Tony shoots the waves breaking over flat sand. The tumulus has washed away leaving nothing to mark the spot where my body lies.

Now that I was dressed, I was able to help carry the screens to the truck. But I was shivering so badly I wasn't much use. I clamped my teeth shut to stop them from chattering. The driver and his assistant stared at us in disbelief as we gathered up props and equipment in the oncoming storm. Our timing had been perfect. But now we must pull a fast one. We were stranded, Hadley said. Could they give us a lift to the station?

'You mean you came all the way out here with this junk and didn't have no way back?'

'We didn't exactly plan it,' answered Hadley. 'That's just the way it worked out.'

The men exchanged disgusted glances. 'We'll take the girls and the bags,' they said.

There was no question of my not going in the truck since I was now alternately hot and cold and everyone was worried.

We made them take Tony as well, since he was exhausted. Hadley offered to go with the boys, but the driver wouldn't hear of it. So the boys set off, intending to cut through back yards and make their way to the station via the side streets. That's how we worked: we prepared as much as we could for eventualities then relied on luck. It was a good method.

Steve filmed us as we climbed into the back of the truck and drove off. Just as we pulled away from the shoulder, Hadley ripped open her jumpsuit and bared her breasts to the camera with a dazzling smile.

En route to the staion I told Tony about the Janice film.

'And you got the idea while dying in the film? Oh that's beautiful.'

I shivered and coughed all the way to the Penn station where we waited half an hour for the others. By that time my limbs were becoming uncontrollable and swallowing was painful.

I felt hazy and detached and didn't care. I would have surrendered to any force, allowed myself to be taken anywhere. We stood by the information booth surrounded by our gear. I leaned on Steve's arm and listened to the far-away voices of Tony and Hadley. They were talking about me. They seemed to be trying to reach some sort of decision. Bums and beggars wanted to carry our bags, moving in and out of focus in a kind of Brownian motion, not taking no for an answer. I suppose it didn't help that I kept smiling at them. Steve let go for a minute to fish some change from his jacket pocket. He gave it all to the beggar.

'You're crazy,' I heard Hadley say from far far away. 'We need it for a taxi.'

I wonder where we're going, I thought. Then I remembered a trip to Portland with Nora and Aunt Bernie. She saw a nun begging outside a department store and hastened to give her a few nickels. Nora admonished her. 'It can't be a real nun,' she said. 'They always go in twos.'

'Even so,' replied my aunt, 'there's merit in it.'

I tried to tell Steve that he had won merit, but the words wouldn't come out straight.

My friends pooled their resources so that Tony could take me in a car to Prince Street. We moved towards the door in slow motion. The station was cavernous and sinister, its ceilings so high and distant as to be lost in shadows like a Piranesi engraving. The doors opened on to the 34th Street-rush hour din and confusion. They pushed me into the taxi and all the bags after me. Then Tony got in and we were off.

When I woke up I did not know where or who I was. The room – pink walls, worn linoleum, a stereo and a single bed on which I lay – was familiar. I tried to fit it to places in the past: Black Water Road, Birch Street, Franklin Street, 2nd Street – but they didn't match. I struggled to bring myself into the present, wherever that might be. I groped for my short-term memory and managed to wrench out Tony and his apartment. His kitten, Miaow-Tse-Tung, slept at my feet. I called Tony and he came, wearing a dishcloth tied around his waist and carrying a coffee pot.

'I'm making you some chicken soup,' he said.

'That's what I smell. I didn't know you could make chicken soup.'

'I can't. I just went out to phone my mother and she gave me the recipe. She sends you love.'

I didn't really want chicken soup, but even in a febrile state I couldn't hurt Tony's feelings. I lay back on the pillow as the shakes began again, this time accompanied by aching in my limbs. After a while they stopped. I began to cough and to sweat. Then the shakes returned. There was no question of calling a doctor, since even if we could have paid one, none of them made house calls. ('In America you're on your own,' Steve had said once. 'That's why it's called the land of the free. Everything's a risk. It's kind of exciting.') The night passed in these dire alternations. Tony slept on the floor next to my bed and the untouched bowl of chicken soup.

I was in bed for a month, at the end of which a doctor on 16th Street whom I could not afford to see and who, to my shame, I never paid, informed me that I was recovering from walking pneumonia (walking?), and that I now had a scar on my lung. Oh well, at least it wasn't on my face.

During those weeks Tony was my nurse. No one except Nora has ever looked after me like that: giving me sponge baths, helping me to and from the bathroom, washing my hair, feeding me tiny spoonfuls of broth, running out to Yona Shimmel's for the yoghurt I craved, scoring Percodan from a dealer on Grand Street. When he was not at Fox he was in constant attendance, reading aloud to me (I got headaches when I tried myself, couldn't concentrate anyway) or just sitting on the bed holding my hand.

Janice visited in her best coat, with banana cake, and Reese on a leash. She reassured me about poor Otis whom she'd moved into the basement for convenience's sake.

'I'm working on a double life-size portrait bust of him,' she breathed, 'with a little ruff of feathers, like the Seraphim in Medieval paintings.'

Steve arrived and told us of a film he'd just seen about poisons in the environment, a documentary, but very aesthetic and scary, everything from polluted rivers to chemical warfare. A tainted world where nothing was safe from contagion. He was quite upset and said it had given him the creeps. Janice said she was sure Reese's lung condition was caused by the filthy New York air we were all forced to breathe and pay taxes for the privilege.

Hadley came most evenings before work (I think she missed her dinners in order to do so) with Star or Maja. They brought me a light-up Madonna with a brown face and brightly coloured robes which we placed in the cobwebby niche above the bed. They also brought a little ball of opium which had the most wonderful immediate effects on my ague. We thought drugs were the cure for everything. Can't sleep? Take heroin. No energy? Black bomber. Drugs were *good* for you.

We listened to Smokey Robinson and John Coltrane, playing the same tracks over and over again: 'Bad Girl', 'Tears of a Clown'. I thought about Franklin Street and dancing on the creaky wooden floor with Travis and Frank, and suddenly I wanted everyone to leave.

I'd been thinking about the past a lot, during those hours when I lay alone, waiting for the seizures and the chills to stop and the fever to start, watching the light fade and the room turn to darkness. I thought about Travis and Eva, about Vinnie and Denise and the stepbrothers I refused to see. I thought about Frank. I thought about Aunt Bernie.

She had now been four years in Kellvale, no longer near her sister, since Aunt Bea had been moved to what I guess would be called the psychiatric wing. She was mad but in perfect health, while Aunt Bernie wheezed and hobbled around on her swollen knees, her mercilessly lucid brain sorting through past wrongs. I sent her money sometimes. She had stopped returning my cheques and accepted them, along with Vinnie's, without comment or thanks. This change in behaviour did not, however, ease my conscience. I dreamt of my aunt all the time, and vowed that I would write her a letter as soon as I was well. I even fantasized about going to see her, but my courage was not equal to that confrontation. I planned a letter to my father. When I was better, perhaps, though I did not intend to tell him I was better. I wanted him to be worried enough to visit me. But I knew him too well. He would write immediately, say he was coming. He'd get the tickets, take a day off work and then at the last moment fall ill himself so that I would be forced to tell him the visit was out of the question, he must take care, I was miles better anyway, he was not to worry.

I had dramatic dreams drenched in atmosphere, delicious and scary. One in particular was not so nice. We were back on the beach. We hadn't filmed the *Martyrs* scenes at all. I had only dreamt we did. Or maybe the other time was a rehearsal and this was for real. Everything went exactly as before, down to each word and gesture and gust of wind. But this time the drug, whatever it was, was real, and I was dying. I didn't care. Because if I were dead it would explain a lot. Yes, Hadley had killed me. It occurred to me only as a small afterthought that Tony might have prevented it, but then he might have colluded, too. He was, after all, the director. She was only doing what he told her. But then Hadley never did anything she didn't want to do. It was her own idea, I knew it. Perhaps she was bored with our looking alike, and now I was dead, she could reign all alone. Well, let her. It's only right. To die by the hand of one's best friend is not such a bad fate.

There were other dreams in which a half-remembered face flashed like a stroboscope. A face so familiar – was it Travis? No, the eyes were too metallic, the hair less abundant, the bones sharper. I studied the face, fascinated. Just before I woke, I realized it was the boy in Jackson's film. The Elusive One. Him again.

When my temperature began to drop the dreams stopped and instead I lay on the bed, immobile but awake, playing games with my past life, following effects back to causes. Let me see, I would think, I'm in this apartment because I'm ill. I'm ill because I was filming. I was filming because I'm with Tony; I'm with Tony because I met Hadley; I met Hadley because I went to the demo alone because Reese was ill, because Janice is too fat to walk all the way to the Battery. No. I'm losing the main waterway and drifting off into inlets. But the sequence had an illness at both ends, and that is significant. Significant but negative. Is illness negative? Eva would say it was a kind of blessing, a signal from our soul that something was wrong and that we must stop and collect our wits (did Reese have wits to collect?) that we must turn our minds and hearts to God, that we had been ignoring something crucial to our development and must sort it out and therefore needed rest and quiet. She would say that anyway suffering was necessary.

Meanwhile Tony worked at the editing machine he'd borrowed from Jackson and for which he had to promise a tickling session in return. He wouldn't leave me to work at the Cinemateque. He had taken a week off from Fox to begin a rough edit on the footage he had, and he worked every evening and weekend. The film was nearly finished and he had an offer of a screening at the Electric Scorpion. I knew he needed me for a few more shots, but he never mentioned it. His patience made me feel guilty. Clyde had also been very understanding, but he couldn't hold my job for ever. Janice was supporting Otis, I knew. This couldn't go on. I had to get well.

13

Martyrs

It was a dark time, a dark spring. But we were snug in the darkness, Tony and Miaow and I. I liked the claustral atmosphere of the pink parlour, and as I fell asleep at night I actually looked forward to waking within its secure confines. The world was far away, and no one could reach me or find me unless they already knew my whereabouts or made a big effort. I had never, since I was a child, lived in such emotional proximity to someone. Aunt Bernie and I led parallel lives; we bore with each other, accomplished what was necessary for survival without ever sharing our secret selves. Domestically, Travis and I had barely touched. But Tony and I knew just about everything there was to know about each other. When we went into the bathroom, it never occurred to us to close the door.

It was nice to be babied by him and to baby him back, to regress together, to admit weaknesses and laugh at them, to make ourselves vulnerable on purpose. I hadn't experienced this before. Until recently, hiding had been the essence of my relationships, even with Travis. Now I sought for ways to reveal myself. This was because I felt completely protected. I loved it, and I almost feared the day I got better, because then I would be an individual again, walled up in myself. Life in the pink parlour seemed like an extension of movie-making.

I was sitting up in bed reading Djuna Barnes. The table lamp was on most of the time now, so Tony did not have to come home to a gloomy apartment. I heard him open the door and called hello to let him know he needn't tiptoe on my account.

'It's finished,' he said and smiled. He had a funny smile, almost a grimace. Lack of practice, probably.

I knew he meant the film and jumped out of bed to hug him.

'When?'

'This afternoon. Just now. Do we have anything to drink? I was pretty distracted. I forgot to pick up something on the way home.'

190

'Think so. Look in the kitchen cupboard.' I followed him in my bare feet. I wanted to be part of his happiness, and yet I did not want to come so close as to rob him of the solitary pleasure that was his right under the circumstances.

'Half a bottle of tequila. Any lemons?'

'Um, nope.'

'Salt?'

'Definitely. No clean glasses, though. Sorry, I'll do them now.' I hadn't been exactly busy in the kitchen.

He said he couldn't wait so we used teacups instead.

'Here's to *Martyrs*,' I said.

'And to freedom.' We drank again.

'And to love.'

'And to the imagination.' And so on until we had finished the bottle.

Then Tony found some whisky behind a rusting can of Ajax, so we finished that too. Afterwards I don't remember much except feeling very cold. Tony said he'd helped me back to bed where I'd shivered and muttered about being an Eskimo. How hard it was, I said, to be always cold and to have parents and grandparents and great-grandparents who were always cold, to be cold in one's genes . . .

'Perhaps we rushed things a little,' he said the next morning.

'No, I'm fine. I must have been remembering Florence in February. The drink has improved me, really. Celebration is good for you, whatever the consequences.' I wobbled towards the bathroom, a cold place behind the kitchen in which we spent as little time as possible.

'What's on today?' It was the first time since my illness began that I'd enquired about movies.

'Peter has a screening at the Bleeker Street this afternoon.'

'What is it?'

'Footage of his trip to Saskatchewan. More Scandinavian mysticism. He really has to free himself from Bergman's influence.'

'He's a Pisces. He becomes whoever he loves.'

A while after Tony left for the Bleeker Street Hadley arrived. I hadn't seen her for a week. And I was missing her badly. She'd brought me a giant Hershey Bar and sat fidgeting beside me on the bed. I handed her squares of chocolate as we talked.

'Tell me about Cal's.'

'Can't. I'm on probation again.' The second time in five months.

'What for?'

'Oh, I don't know.' She pouted. 'Someone complained about me,

191

I guess. Must have been one of the Saturday night creeps from Westchester.'

'You were working *upstairs?*'

'Drexel was doing a strip on a table in the back room, you know like he does when he's been emptying too many Martini glasses in the kitchen? The upstairs riff-raff had got wind of it and were salivating. Just what they were hoping for, right? Just what they'd come to see. I suppose they snicker about it in the office on Monday morning. Anyway, this guy made some stupid remarks about faggots and I got mad. Then he said a few things about me that I didn't like so I tipped his dinner into his lap. I guess it was him who complained.'

I could picture it. One deft movement and splot! She was such an expert.

'Careful, Had. Another time and you're out.'

'I could care.' I saw she was annoyed and I changed the subject. 'How's Kit?'

'Why are you always asking about Kit?'

'I just like him.'

There was a petulant little silence. 'He's started,' she said.

'He has?'

'Finally found his damned first word. Now I can't talk to him any more. He's locked in his room ten hours a day. Never wants to go out. God, it's just so boring.'

'But you wanted him to start.' It was a perverse game I played with Hadley, gently reminding her of her real wishes. I knew it made her angry to have her inconsistencies pointed out, but somehow I couldn't resist. Perhaps she even expected it of me. I provided her with opportunities to show off her brattiness.

'Did I know he'd turn into a Trappist? People who don't want to talk don't interest me. They're egotistical.' She looked around. 'How do you stand this colour?'

I shrugged.

'I mean, he used to be fun in a rainy-afternoon sort of way. Until he got serious.' She sighed. 'Introversion is selfish. I mean what good is this fucking book going to do anybody? Will it feed one mouth in Bangladesh?'

No, I thought, but it might feed yours.

'Can you imagine, he wants me to stay home and share the dungeon with him. I said listen, don't lay your gloom on me. I'm splitting. And here I am!' She gave me a radiant smile.

'I'm glad you came.'

'You're not thanking me, I hope.'

'Nope. You've cured me completely. I wouldn't dream of thinking a visit wasn't my due.'

'Glad to hear it. When are you going home?'

'Soon. After the opening of *Martyrs*.'

'Good.'

'I thought you wanted me to be with Tony?'

'I do. You're my creation, cookie. I think of you as my little golems. But you shouldn't live together. You're not planning to live together, are you?'

'Never crossed my mind.'

'Well, don't let it. None of us are meant to live together except as friends. Everything good comes out of friendship. Friendship is the transcendent aspect of the social function.'

'Phew!'

'OK, OK. Drexel said that. But I think it's true. Anyway, living together kills passion. Everyone knows that, but they go right on killing it. Don't they know things have changed? We're living in a completely different world. It's time for women to fight their domesticating natures. They also have to fight men encouraging them to be domesticated – you know, the little rewards for good behaviour, the make-believe appreciation and meanwhile they're chasing every skirt in sight. You have to refuse to be the Good Woman. Scream and yell till everyone gets the message.'

'I don't mind a little domesticity.'

'Oh, it's all right as a game. Playing house is fun sometimes, I know. But if you ever take it seriously you're dead.' She looked at me hard. 'Don't just slide into this because it's easy, Rose.'

'Don't *worry*.'

She patted my leg. 'Hurry up and get better because I want to take you to the new steam baths. Also an exhibition of Burmese fabrics at Asia House. Plus a new production of *Endgame* at the Cherry Lane and besides we all miss you at work.'

She checked her watch. 'I have to go, darling. I'm meeting Drexel for a drink and a party.'

'Have fun,' I said, smarting a little because I was not going with her.

When she left I fell asleep and dreamt I was in a tiny attic room with Travis. It was at the top of an old building looking out over the roofs of what I imagined must be London or Paris. We were in the midst of a subdued but painful scene, the cause of which was not clear. Suddenly the door flew open with a gust of wind, and a girl entered, dressed as a maid and very angry. She berated Travis for his many crimes then turned on me, holding up a mirror to my face, commanding me to look at my reflection. When I did I saw that I was wearing a necklace I did not recognize. It seemed to be choking me, or perhaps it was just the sight of it that choked me. I panicked and woke myself up. I was sweating. I must still be unwell. I lay in the dark wishing Tony would come home.

The 12th of April, the day of the premier, was my first out of door. It had been a month since I'd seen the sky. It was gloomy and overcast, but there was no East wind. *Martyrs* was to be screened at six before the feature film of the evening. Everyone we knew was coming.

I had never seen Tony so nervous. This was the longest, the most expensive, and the best film he had made. I was proud of him. When I considered the vicissitudes of the past months, how he had worked so hard while also going into Fox every day, the financial obstacles he'd overcome, I was amazed the film had ever been made. He was the most serious and dedicated of us all. (Which was why Hadley didn't completely love him.) I rubbed the sleeve of his blue duffel coat which he'd had since he was a freshman in university.

'Ready?' he asked.

'Ready when you are, CB.'

'I'm scared.'

'I'll bet.'

'I forgot to tell you, Rose. You were great. In the film, I mean. I mean you are great.'

'Stop. I'll think I'm Lana Turner.'

'In *The Bad and the Beautiful*?'

'Of course.'

Five o'clock and a fine drizzle. We set off under a big black umbrella, my arm through his. We intended to walk all the way to the Electric Scorpion which was on 2nd Avenue. We'd go slowly, taking into account my weakened state. We had forty minutes to do it. It was wonderful just to move, to breathe the cold damp air, even if it was polluted, to look at the people, no matter how bedraggled or bizarre, to lean against Tony's shoulder. I felt a rush of affection for the city. It seemed to double each delight, to continually up the emotional ante. It reflected your inner state back at you, and, provided that was good, you were in for a terrific time. If the reverse, then suicidal thoughts were imminent.

Even the bonfires on the corners were romantic until I realized what they were.

'What's that?' I asked, pointing to a studio couch that was being immolated atop what appeared to be a large heap of manure. It looked like a ritual furniture sacrifice, a tacky potlatch.

'Garbage. There's a strike. I did tell you.'

I saw another fire, then another by the corner of 4th and A. Children danced round them, hurling in whatever detritus they could find, and believe me there was a large selection. The fires were everywhere. So that was why the atmosphere was so thick and dreamy and why I had begun to cough again. Rats frisked in the gutters and paraded along the sidewalks until attacked by boys with pea shooters and sling shots. Bowery bums had drifted north to pick through the piles. An eerie dusk settled in. New York had become a medieval city.

'How long has this been going on?'

'Twenty-eight days and no sign of a settlement.'

The stench from an unburned heap was overpowering and we crossed the street to avoid both it and the rats who fed off it greedily. Field days for the vermin. Lights came on in stores and windows. Rain clouds lowered, enhancing the grim poetry of our surroundings. The children, the fire tenders, the bums who circled the stinking heaps were silhouetted against the electric background and the flames.

'It's beautiful,' said Tony, who saw everything in terms of lighting effects.

'I suppose it is.'

'Because it's the truth about itself that New York all of a sudden can't hide and has to face.'

'But it's scary too. It's decay.'

'Nietzsche said that decaying societies are the most interesting and the most creative.'

'Then I guess we're privileged.'

We were forced to cross the street again. I kept coughing.

'It's so dark,' I said. 'So early and so dark.'

'It's not, actually. It's getting lighter all the time. Three minutes more of light every day until the summer solstice.'

'How do you know these things?'

'I read,' he answered modestly.

I had imagined that watching the first section of *Martyrs* would be like watching one of my own dreams, and it was. But the experience was intriguing rather than pleasant. I could appreciate Tony's technical advances, his complex imagery, the fine photography. But it was too weird, at least the part with me and Hadley was. Frances kept making unnerving appearances. I would will her off the screen and she would

195

vanish only to turn up just when I felt certain she was gone for good.

The seaside burial was quite sinister. Rose suddenly seemed very fragile. On the one hand she was being absorbed into Hadley, on the other Frances waited, ever watchful for an opportunity to reclaim her lost territory, escape from the prison to which she had been confined like a mad relative and expose herself at the most embarrassing times. What would become of Rose if this were allowed to continue? What if she turned out to be a more unstable construction than I had imagined? I envied Tony. He was what he made, and so he didn't have to worry about phantom personalities. I envied Hadley. Phantom personalities had no power to frighten her. She would regard them as a welcome diversion. I was relieved when the second segment of the film began.

Richard's face fills the screen, dark, bearded, eyes large like a fish. The camera pulls back to show a mitre. From beneath it spreads his long hair, the same colour as his black beard. He is dressed in ecclesiastical robes. A mellow backlighting conceals their shabbiness. He holds two crossed white candles and a comb for carding wool. He is St Blaise whose gentleness won him the trust and companionship of animals and birds and whose story I had told to Tony when I first met him. He has treated the Bishop's miraculous affinity in a number of ways. By the clever use of montage, for instance, superimposing footage shot at the Bronx Zoo as well as nature documentaries.

Blaise is both shepherd and prelate. Six of us, dressed in black, kneel before him as he blesses our throats with the crossed candles.

(Drexel was particularly good in this scene in which he claimed to have experienced a miraculous regeneration of his vocal chords, so much so that he was now singing with the Big Bad Band on Saturday nights at the Dom.)

Blaise is tied to a pillar. His sad naked body is set upon by torturers with cruel metal combs in mocking resemblance to his wool carder. His tormentors are painted red and wear grotesque head-dresses of demonic animals. In the penultimate shot Blaise is covered by a network of tiny red lines, like a delicate scarlet web. He expires against a superimposition of circling diving swallows.

The third part was the longest and the best. Tony called it 'my melodrama'. It is about World War Two. Maja and Peter play the couple.

It begins with their parting. The man and the woman face each other. We see them separately then together, in Bergman close-ups.

There is smoke and lightning, fire; their faces with the fire superimposed.

Music. A soprano singing in the background. An exquisite German song – Schubert to the accompaniment of a piano.

Shots of Hasidic Jews in New York, one in his shop assisted by his sons with their payes. The pickle store on Prince Street.

The man is on a train now, his face at the window. Sounds of the train. The man's tired face intercut with mountains and forest.

A man drowning, we don't know who, maybe the man of the starring couple. He is gone, lost, swept away by terrible events no one can escape. He is swimming, struggling. His face is not visible. Has she lost him?

The soprano again. The woman is filling garbage cans with her jewellery. She tears rings from her fingers, bracelets from her arms, necklaces from her neck. She empties suitcases of jewellery into the bins. It is almost comic. Then she throws in fur coats, piles of paper money, bags of it.

She begins to smash mirrors and to throw these too into the garbage cans. Large mirrors, smash. Small mirrors, smash. Goodbye to her image and her vanity. Her broken face reflected in broken glass, the end of her old self.

The woman alone. No backdrop. She smears dirt on her face, arms and legs. It is a disguise, or a ritual mourning. She takes off her dress, shoes and stockings and dons a tattered soldier's uniform, from an old war. A war over and lost. She removes two sealed documents from a metal box and hides them in her shirt.

A city street. Suspicious eyes, faces. Eyes that follow her as she walks past, a sorry sight. But no one accosts her. She is magically protected because she has surrendered all earthly goods.

More fire, water, smoke. Everywhere houses burn and crumble. Fire is superimposed on Spring Street and Prince Street and Broome Street and Grand Street, Avenue A, 10th Street, 2nd Street and Canal Street. The Lower East Side in flames.

Money is falling through space, falling everywhere. Then the money too is burning. It turns to ashes in mid-air.

The woman walking through a forest. A hunter, cruel and clever, emerges from the trees with his big shiny gun. The woman runs, he follows her, stalking her like a deer.

The woman in the city. She has escaped the hunter. Again the hostile crowd. She walks among them, looking straight ahead. Again the evil eyes follow her. The same eyes as before. Without pity. No one accosts her. She has nothing they could want.

Hostile eyes and faces, intercut with the Hasidic Jews. The complete contrasts of their expressions.

Back to the forest. The forest is alight. It is burning. Trees crack and topple in a halo of flames.

A crowded street. Sunlight, busyness, happiness, towers, steeples, shops, ordinary freedom. Hundreds of people passing.

The man steps off a bus. He sees the woman. She is exhausted, in rags. She leans against a shop window. Inside the shop are a Hasidic Jew and his sons.

The woman takes the man's arm. They look at each other but do not speak, do not embrace. They are serious and satisfied. They walk together through the crowds, still not speaking. No music.

The man and the woman are in the forest. They are naked in the lights and shadows of the woods. Together they kneel and open a metal box, just like the first one. Inside are the documents. The woman hands one to the man and keeps one herself.

They stand and face each other. They break the seals, open the documents. What is written in them? Their names. Only their names which the woman has kept safe all this long time. Their hidden identities, their secret, their true selves which fire and war could not destroy.

Someone is crying. Is the crying on the soundtrack or in the theatre? I can't tell. Perhaps it is me crying. Me, Rose.

Martyrs did well, receiving good reviews in the *Village Voice* and later in most of the film magazines. Steve and Kit were ecstatic. Hadley was impressed but reserved. I think she wanted to act as a brake to what she saw as my adoration of Tony. She knew my weakness for mythologizing. If I ended up a handmaiden at someone's shrine it was not going to be through any fault of hers.

Kit had made a rare public appearance at the screening and Tony was touched.

'Well, that sure was worth coming out for,' he said. 'Beautiful. Great.'

Tony smiled and didn't say anything.

'Look. So modest. So reticent.' Drexel pointed at Tony. 'My God, immune to compliments. Remind me not to waste any of mine on you.'

Kit and Drexel's relationship was bristly. Drexel was always around, most of the time as Hadley's escort. Kit could not complain, but neither was he happy with the arrangement. My sympathies were with him because, in fact, Drexel frightened me. I was nervous he might turn his wicked tongue against me.

Two days after the screening I went home. I was sad to leave Tony and for a while felt lost without him. Breakfasts with Otis were not exactly lively, unless he suffered an attack. But I heeded Hadley's words. Living alone was more interesting, nobler even. Sort of.

I told Janice (who would not accept payment for the Little Friskies) that I wanted to make a short film about her and her work. I promised her – she had seen the Nora movie – that the technical level would be higher since Tony would oversee it. But she didn't seem worried about that. She was touched because I saw her as someone special, regarded her work as interesting and wished to pay her this tribute.

'I get it,' she said. 'You want to make me the subject of a *study*.'

'Sort of. I hadn't thought of it that way, but yes.'

'I'm gonna represent a world *view*.'

'Well . . .' Really, I wasn't sure what she represented. I just wanted to show her, put her on display, a living exhibition.

She began walking around the room – not easy given its size and hers – hands fluttering, eyes raised to the ceiling, imagining. She spoke of animal souls, metamorphoses, spirit guides and the sanctity of 'that pure being'. To all of which I nodded approval. Then she abruptly stopped, worn out by so much exercise, and proposed instant hot chocolate and cinnamon toast. Oh, I just loved Janice.

For the next three weeks or whenever they could, Tony and Hadley came to help me with the film. Tony had met Janice, but I had not introduced her to anyone else. She was my secret treasure.

I hadn't planned anything. There was no scenario. I shot whatever I felt like at the time, whatever seemed natural and right. Hadley helped in any way she could, sometimes only with comments, but they were always astute. I asked didn't she want to make a film or anything of her own.

'Oh, when I'm old, I'll teach myself tatting,' she said.

'And breed parakeets,' Drexel added.

'Somewhere on the Gulf coast of Florida.'

One day she brought him along to meet Janice. He adored her. My friendship with her was the only thing about me that seemed to impress him. He saw me, I could tell, in a new light. He was all gallantry, paying her compliments, asking questions, making her giggle and blush. At first I thought he was being ironic. Then I saw his interest was genuine. Janice was an original. He asked her to tell him about each of the sculptures, and she went on at great length.

'Now this here's called *And the Holy Ghost, the Paraclete* . . . You know what the Paraclete is?'

'That's what Hadley's going to breed when she's a faded beauty living in Tampa.'

Janice laughed and was not offended. 'There's worse fates. Anyway, you know perfectly well what it is.'

'I do, I do. But I'm a tease.'

'My mother always told me boys only tease you because they like you.'

'Your mother was so right.'

'Believe me, I've learned to take it.'

'I'd give anything to have a mother like you.' Drexel sighed and gazed at Janice.

'I know, dear. It's too bad. But it's my function to nurture art, not children. Don't know why God wanted it that way, but he did. Now this here's *The Wolf of Gubbio*. 'Course, he's really my brother's German police dog.'

It was May and I was still living in the dark, going from the gloom of the editing room to the gloom of Cal's; falling into bed just before sunrise, getting up at three in the gloom of my apartment. We all lived this upside-down life. But about this time of year we would grow restless, feel suffocated, dream of jet flights we could not afford and boat trips and endless unknown roads before us. We'd start to complain. But our only obeisance to the season was a walk through the West Village on *the* Saturday. *The* Saturday always came in May. The sun shone, the air was comparatively clean, and all the flowering trees were at their peak, graciously strewing the grimy pavements with confetti-petals so that it looked as if a wedding procession had passed. A day not to be missed.

As it happened, *the* Saturday in 1970 coincided with my completion of the Janice film. We had run it through the afternoon before, Tony and I alone in the cutting room, watching the closing flickers of Reese transcendent. It was all right. Better than all right, Tony assured me. We decided to celebrate both my film and the perfect afternoon. We set off at one, with the camera, of course.

Spring in the north-east lasts about ten days. The transition from winter to summer is almost immediate. Saturday must be grabbed and consumed because there would be no replay. The Village was out in force from West 12th to Canal and from 6th Avenue to the river. The gays from Christopher Street, tourists from New Jersey and Long Island, tripping hippies worshipping Flora, ageing beats from Bleeker Street, old-guard couples who had moved into the Village in the thirties when it was still cheap, raised families there and now sat upon real estate worth millions, and us. Shirts were off and chairs were on the sidewalks. Dogs yapped and chased each other as baby carriages collided. Lots of familiar faces, all in sunglasses. On the corner of Jane Street two people filmed each other from opposite sides of the road while their friends posed and cavorted.

On 4th Street we spotted Hadley and Kit, arm in arm, stopping to look in antique-shop windows, and smiling into each other's eyes. I didn't know why but it made me uneasy.

'They don't seem to be themselves,' Tony observed. It was true. They definitely weren't fighting.

'Hadley!' I called. They didn't turn around.

'Hadleee!' we yelled in unison. She saw us and immediately withdrew her arm from Kit's. She began waving and laughing. Kit looked at her and at us. Then he waved too.

'Well, how are ya?' He shifted his weight from foot to foot.

'We're pretending to shop,' Hadley announced. 'We don't want to completely forget what it's like. Got to keep in practice for better days.' She looked around. 'Isn't it pretty? It's just so pretty.' Nature had her approval. It had everyone's approval.

'Yep. Nature's the latest thing.'

'Definitely in – like the new night club.'

'Nature's the current exhibition.'

'Next week they'll take it down.'

'We'll all be inside again.'

'We're going to David's Potbelly for lunch,' said Hadley. 'Come with us.'

Five minutes later we were back in the dark. The restaurant was one of the oldest in the Village. There were no windows, and the only sources of light were the art deco table lamps whose amber glow was just sufficient to enable customers to read the menus. We ordered French toast and Constant Comment tea.

'We were visiting Peggy and the Clarisse last night?' Hadley liked turning declarative sentences into questions. Peggy and Clarisse were lesbians who ran a boutique on East 9th Street.

'I don't know how they live in that claustrophobic apartment. All that frou-frou. All that thirties junk.' Hadley made a face. 'If I see one more beaded bag slung over a mirror, I'll scream.'

We giggled over Peggy and Clarisse, over Drexel and Steve, then over Clyde and various busboys. We finished our French toast and ordered more Constant Comment.

'Well,' said Hadley. 'You two sure look fat and sassy.'

'We're celebrating.'

'Funny, so are we.'

'What?'

'You go first.'

'No you.'

'OK.' Hadley looked at Kit. 'Tell 'em, darlin'.'

'I finished.' He gave us a shy smile.

'He means the book.'

'My God. The book.'

'But it's been less than – '

'Two months. Just like *The Charterhouse of Parma*.' Tony had an artistic precedent ready for everything.

'Look.' Hadley pointed at Kit. 'He's trying not to smile too much. 'Oh, who's just so cool? Go on, Grump, don't smile, don't smile. I dare you not to smile.' At which Kit cracked up. She didn't wait for him to stop. 'Three publishers want it.'

Silence. This was a little too real. As if we were children and Kit had turned into a grown-up before our eyes. We congratulated him and ordered a bottle of house white.

Hadley craned her neck to see who else was in the restaurant. She was looking for someone to pay the bill, I knew.

'OK, now it's your turn,' said Kit who had been well brought up. A nice polite middle-class boy, trained to enquire after the well-being of those less fortunate than himself. Tony spoke for me, sensing I felt shy in the wake of such a triumph.

'Rose finished the Janice film last night.'

They behaved as if there was absolutely no difference in our accomplishments and shouted yeah Rosie, as if I had scored a touchdown, and kissed me. They made me feel as if I'd won the Palme d'Or. I loved them for it. Yet I felt as if something were slipping away from me, never to be reclaimed.

'Hey.' Hadley pointed. 'There's Ralphie.' She'd spied her sucker – the man who's accosted her after the screening in Nightshade's loft. She caught his eye and beckoned him excitedly, nodding and giggling. He joined us with a male friend, and in five minutes the Constant Comment had been cleared away, the house white cancelled and in its place two bottles of champagne put on the table.

'Never say,' she hissed at Kit, 'I don't take care of you. And sit up straight.'

I would not wish to be on the wrong side of Hadley.

Pretty soon we were quite drunk. The restaurant grew even darker. *The* Saturday was over. Ralph and Tony were arguing about Max Ophuls. Tony was winning, fired by his contempt for Ralph's dilettantism. Ralph had a job with an ad agency which was why he could afford the drink. He lived with an actress who had worked with Tony. It was his ticket to our company. Otherwise he would not have been admitted.

Hadley put her hand on my arm and leaned across the table. She had removed her sunglasses and I could see how tired she looked.

'Sorry about this.' She wasn't at all sorry. (And neither was I.) She was pleased to have lassoed Ralph. 'Come see us next week. Maybe Thursday. Are you working that night?'

It was unlike her to plan so far ahead. Normally she was a spur-of-the-moment girl.

'Come to Spring Street. That's where I'm staying now.'

'But that's Kit's – '

She waved her hand as though clearing away smoke. 'I know, I know. I had to do it. Can't pay my rent, so I've been staying with him.'

'You've moved in?'

'It's not like that,' she answered impatiently. 'Drexel's staying there too. His boyfriend threw him out, so I had to do this for him.'

'I'm – surprised.'

'I'll be out of there in a few weeks when Drexel and I get a place of our own.'

'You can always stay with me, you know.'

'Thanks. I can't wait to see the Janice film.'

'Oh . . .' I was a little dazed by her news.

'Drexel really liked Janice.'

She had given me no hint of the move. We told each other everything, and she must have known she was going to do it. Still, why should I feel so peculiar? I did feel peculiar, and left out. Hadley was forming her own family, one that didn't include me. She'd said she did not intend to stay, but I didn't believe that.

'Anyway, try to come Thursday. That's when the auction will be over.'

'Auction?'

'The book,' she said, as though I were retarded.

'Oh yes.'

She went on about someone named Robert whom she'd never mentioned before but assumed I must know all about. I finally twigged that he was Kit's agent. It was all so businesslike and structured. Kit was about to make money. And so, by extension, was Hadley and probably

203

Drexel too if Hadley had anything to say about it. I could just hear her arguing with Kit, making him feel selfish and guilty. You have a bank-manager mentality, she'd sneer, and he would write a cheque. She would invite us all to dinner and he would write a cheque. She would not have to scour the room for a Ralph ever again. But why was I pursuing this unworthy train of thought? I let her distract me with gossip, but the feeling of loss persisted. I had never been so grateful for Hadley's friendship, never wanted it so much, never been more afraid of losing it. Not since Travis had I experienced this anxiety. Why did I always love the one who left me, the one who fled?

'We're gonna go run around now,' she said. 'Wanna come?'

We did.

We had a good time, trailing after Ralph to a party on 11th Street, then to Cal's where the air hung heavy, there were lots of smart remarks and everyone looked like chic death.

Tony and I didn't wake up until three the next afternoon. He made *café au lait* with instant coffee which we drank in bed while scanning *The New York Times*. We debated in a leisurely way about which film we would see.

'There's *Across the Pacific* at the New Yorker.'

'Oh, I love Mary Astor.'

'Well, you can see her again at six in *Palm Beach Story*.'

'Oh, let's go.'

'OK. You know *Across the Pacific's* shot in sepia?'

'Sepia?'

'The colour. Comes from the ink sac of the cuttlefish.'

'Tony, how do you *know* these things?'

Of all the movie theatres in the city the New Yorker was our favourite. It was there I'd seen all the films that changed my life and altered my perceptions. *Rules of the Game* and *Citizen Kane* and *Lola Montez* and *Vivre Sa Vie* and *Eight and a Half* and my favourite of all favourites, *Vertigo*. The place was big, an old-fashioned cinema with great popcorn and the best repertoire in the world. It was completely comfortable. You could put your feet up on the seat in front of you and nobody cared, you could wear whatever you felt like, watch movies all day long. I felt happier on the way to the New Yorker than when I was going anywhere – the kind of pure, excited happiness you're supposed to feel as a child, only I hadn't.

As it turned out we stayed on for the evening show of *Les Enfants Terribles*, which disturbed me but which I also loved. See? That's how it was: Mary Astor for lunch, Jean Cocteau for supper.

Bleary-eyed as we were at the end of every weekend, we went to bed reasonably early, having eaten nothing but the New Yorker's delicious popcorn. Tony rose at eight and I slept on until mid-morning when I returned to 2nd Street, stopping on the way at Yona Shimmel's and the pickle man's.

There was a letter in my box. I threw it on the table where Otis began to sniff at it. I studied the penmanship while I took my coat off. It was New England writing, neat but fluid; childlike but correct. Not so different from my own but with an old-fashioned slant and propriety. Someone who had been taught by the nuns but who had acquired a little education. I opened the envelope and looked for the signature. It was from Julia Byrne, President of the Ladies' Guild.

> Dear Rose
>
> I apologize for intruding into your new life. Believe me, it is not my choice, and only an emergency would prompt me to remind you of what you obviously wish to forget. Your Aunt Bernadette is gravely ill. Let me hasten to say that this letter has not been written at her request. You know what she's like. She would never wish to upset you. If matters were left to her, she would die quietly without even notifying you. She's a saint.
>
> But I feel I would be neglecting my duty both to her and to you if I did not inform you of her present condition. You see, Rose, I give you – and have always given you – the benefit of the doubt. I think you *want* to know. I think you care about your aunt, whatever your past behaviour might indicate. You care about her and you want to show her you care. Well, here is your chance. Believe me, Rose, you will feel better for having made this sacrifice. You will have peace of mind. And you will bless her last days. Isn't that a wonderful thought? I feel sure – and to tell you the truth I am alone in this – that you will come. But come soon. There is very little time.
>
> God bless you,
>
> Julia Byrne

So there it was: redeem yourself now, Rose, or repent at leisure, pursued to the end of your days by the Irish Eumenides. Thanks a lot, Julia Byrne.

The trouble was that she was perfectly right. I couldn't not go. I knew myself well enough, and Julia did too, to see in advance how Aunt Bernie would haunt me. I must take the only action possible to prevent this future misery. I must make the voluntary sacrifice. That way something positive might be salvaged from the awful few weeks that lay ahead. I would be cheered about them and see them as attrition. They might even be interesting, who knew? One thing was certain: this was my fate, my karmic, pre-determined, chromosomal, astrological, synchronistic destiny. Shit.

Janice concurred with all the above, though she would never have used bad language. Janice was a lady. Have a light heart, she advised. Be grateful to Miss Julia Byrne. What's happening is proof of God's love. (Why, I wondered, were horrors always the proof rather than plain old good luck in all its fatness and sassiness?) But I couldn't say this to Janice who never complained of anything. Sunny Janice. Adiposity and pop metaphysics had not made scrambled Orphic eggs of *her* brain.

'When things get bad, think of St Rose of Lima, your saint,' she said. 'Think of a rose – it's your flower, after all. It's impossible to be depressed if you visualize a rose and concentrate on it.'

The red rose of Martyrdom, the white rose of Purity, the blue rose of the Impossible – which should I choose?

Tony was sad, resigned, determined to support me. Being close to his own family, he understood why I had to go. Stoically he prepared for my departure. He made everything easy for me, even offering me his own 8mm camera to 'film my ghosts'.

'When things get bad, think of *The Marriage of Figaro*,' he said. 'Make your mind a stereo and play the arias over and over.'

Hadley's advice was, as usual, to the point. 'It's a trap,' she told me. 'Don't you dare let them do this to you.' I overheard her grumbling to Drexel about grown-up people 'running off to their mummies and daddies,' which was unfair, but that was Hadley.

Steve made only one comment, but it was the best of all. 'Don't lose your sense of humour.'

Tony, Hadley, Star and Kit accompanied me to Port Authority where I was to catch a bus for Boston, where I would transfer to one for Portland, there to wait for an hour, maybe two, for my connection to Florence. Their presence confirmed the transformation my life had undergone since I had last been in the place four years before.

They stood on the greasy tarmac smiling and waving, Hadley with her hand secretly in Kit's. I looked away. But when the bus pulled out I turned to them again, just in case. There were Steve and Tony, cameras to their eyes, filming my departure.

I still see them like that. I hold that shot in my mind. But where, I wonder, is that final flickering image of my face framed by the window of the bus? The last moving picture of Rose.

14
Summoned

Rose is going home. Like Gloria Swanson in *Sunset Boulevard*, she is making a Return. The journey already embarked upon, she sits lethargic, unable to turn the pages of *Last Exit to Brooklyn*, watching the shabby streets of Harlem and the Bronx, their bleak avenues running from the despair of the West Side to the futility of the East. For as long as she can she turns round for another glimpse of the Manhattan skyline. Another and then another. Oh well, that's it, that's the last one, she thinks, then on instinct, turns again to find it still there, its glamour and malevolence visible from a whole new angle. The most beautiful city. Then it is gone, really gone, and there is nothing before her but provincial America, which is lustreless and populated by philistines nurturing fantasies of traditional values and where seldom is heard a smart remark. Where sex and cynicism are punishable by law, where deer (and not a few people) are slaughtered in hundreds every November; where air bases and 4H Clubs abound; where Elks and Moose and American Legions flourish; where woods and farmland are ploughed up to build shopping malls; where there is no racism because blacks are confined to said air bases; where church attendance is always high; where withered Yankees restore historic red barns and the great beast, the Northern Redneck, holds secret sway.

Of course I was hoping for a glimpse of my father, a moment alone, even. If Bernie was dying there would be a wake, and Vinnie was not a man to miss a wake. I imagined the scene as we rumbled past Plainville, site of Holy Land, USA, with its grim factories and its huge cross (lit up at night) on a hill high above the town. By the time we reached Boston, I had convinced myself all over again that good would come from bad and that my sacrifice would be rewarded. This visit would enable me to reassess my life, and what I learned would, I felt sure, allow me to face the future with new understanding. Pathetic, wasn't it?

SUMMONED

As I sat waiting in the Boston Greyhound station my confidence waned. The only way to hold on to my seat was to keep dropping quarters into the meter which fed the six-inch television screen on the edge of the armrest. Vagrants hustled me for those same quarters. I couldn't help thinking of Eva waiting years ago in this very terminal waiting for Travis and not in vain. What must it have been like to catch sight of that walk, that blond wave flopping over the right eye and know for certain that both were his? I began to scan the crowd for pea jackets. Old habits dies hard.

Outside Portland I finally faced what lay before me. It would be like looking at my own cells under a microscope. The past is a dream, an interesting game until it comes up too close and turns us all to cowards. My unhappy body resumed its old shrinking posture. It shrank from a drab cityscape lit by a hard northern sun that flattered neither buildings nor people, a place without terror or charm.

The bus idled by the toll booth. It was the end of the day, and the light was dim, but, even blind, I would have known where I was. The atmosphere of the Maine Turnpike permeates every sense, every nerve. The illuminated letters above the entrance should have read 'Abandon Hope'.

I told myself: I will not lose my sense of humour; I will think of roses and *Figaro*; I will not allow them to do this to me.

I cannot sustain anger. With me anxiety is the only constant. And so when I took my suitcase from the driver and carried it into the Florence bus station which is really Nadeau's drugstore, my hands were shaking. There was Bobby, right on time. He had gained about twenty pounds – another good-looking boy run to fat on fried clams and lobster rolls and six-packs of Moose Head Beer. He wore Bermuda shorts and horn-rimmed glasses through which he stared at me, recognizing me and refusing to recognize me.

'Hi, Rose.' His voice had the dull crackle of stale potato chips. 'How'yadoin'? Gee, you sure look different.'

I was a blonde, and with black roots too. I had completely forgotten. My hair had grown quite a lot since we'd filmed *Martyrs*, and because of the heat I had pinned it hastily up at the back so that it now fell in limp strands around my face. My shadowed, lined and mascaraed eyes were concealed as usual behind sunglasses. I wore tight jeans and sandals and a red cotton blouse which must have been damp with the heat because Bobby kept staring at my tits. Or maybe it was the peace button on my lapel. My lips and nails were highly visible in my favourite Cerise Verni. I spent money on make-up, occasionally on clothes, never on roots. What a naughty girl I must have appeared to him, and how funny he looked in his shocked surprise. Nevertheless, he hugged and kissed me. We were cousins, after all, and Bobby always was a good egg.

'Solange has got your bed all ready.' He had married Solange Lambert.

'My old one?'

'I guess so. You're sleeping with Kevin, hope you don't mind.'

'Nope.' I was doing my best to appear jaunty, but I wanted to weep, to wail in private long and loud, to just give up. Clearly that wasn't going to be possible.

'Your room's the nursery now. Kevin's two. Guess you forgot, huh.'

'Sorry, Bobby. Aunt Bernie did tell me. Congratulations.' I had never sent a present or a card on the birth of my first cousin, once removed. 'I'm happy for you.'

'So. They keepin' you busy at that art gallery?'

Something else I'd forgotten – my ancient lie, alive in innocent Bobby. What else had I told Aunt Bernie? He'd know better than I.

'Yes. I'm learning to make films.' I said it more to get him off the subject than because I thought it would mean anything to him.

'No kiddin'. What kinda films?'

What kinda, what kinda. Would he know about the Underground? How about Experimental? 'Just what's around me. I film what I see.'

'You mean like documentaries?'

'Sort of.'

'Well, it must be real interestin', huh? New York. Fun, huh? Fun City.' He laughed.

'That's what they call it.' I tried a laugh as well.

'Yup. That's what they say.'

We were driving up Market Street, passing one tower then another: Holy Trinity, St Blaise, the Number Two Mill. I couldn't concentrate on what Bobby was saying.

'Pretty different from Florence, I'll bet.'

'Not much comparison.'

'Well, well. So little Rose found herself excitement.' He shook his head in amazement that such a thing was possible then looked at me and winked. 'Has she found romance too?' Completely out of character. It must have been my black roots. Was this the boy who'd called me Blueberry Eyes and Skijump Nose and Strawberry Mouth?

'I have a boyfriend, if that's what you mean.'

'No offence, Rosie.'

'I know.'

'Solange'll be glad to see you. You'll get on like a house on fire.'

I saw my grandmother shivering in our kitchen, wrapped in a grey blanket, hugged by Nora. This is how it would be from now on. Memories conjured by trifles. There was nowhere to hide from them. Nowhere was safe. Of course, it wouldn't last long.

'How's Aunt Bernie?'

'Well, she didn't want you to know. She raised Cain when we told her you was coming.'

'She still mad at me?'

'No-o. She just didn't want you to be – inconvenienced.' He shook his head and chuckled. What a riot Aunt Bernie was, what a great old gal. She'd never stretched *his* good egg's patience to the breaking point.

'What's the prognosis?'

'Not too good, Rose.'

'How long's she got?'

'I guess that depends. Lungs are shot, but her heart's pretty strong. You wanna see her tomorrow? I'll run you over on the way to work.'

'Sure, thanks. Where is she?'

'She's been goin' back and forth between Boott Memorial and Kellvale. Right now she's in the hospital. Semi-private room. Could be worse.'

'How's your Mom?'

'Health-wise she's OK. But she sorta mixes people up, you know. Like she used to, only worse. One day she's knows I'm Bobby, the next she's talking a blue streak to me like I'm Cousin Mikey aged twelve. Or Vinnie aged six. People slip in and out of each other, know what I mean? She kinda time-travels. Must be fun in a way. She seems all right.'

I wondered if the stairway would still smell of rubber. It did.

That night I lay awake listening to Kevin's adenoidal breathing. The 'guest-room', 'my' room, was no longer recognizable. It was now known as the transport room because it had been papered with a design featuring whizzing cars and chugging trains and swooping planes. A K-Mart Special. The every-which-way movements of these frenetic machines were guaranteed to murder sleep even if I had not already been a nervous wreck in anticipation of tomorrow's visit. Think of roses, think of *Figaro*, don't lose your sense of humour. Solange and

211

Bobby were being nice. I detected no resentment. To them old people were funny or boring, something to be cheerfully endured (though not abandoned). They could obviously imagine just how hard it must be for me to come back. Besides, they were completely wrapped up in Kevin. But members of the Ladies' Guild had all the time in the world for disapproval.

They were waiting for me. Katie, Margaret and Mary sat on orange plastic chairs beside the door to my aunt's room. Rosary beads dangled between their worn but immaculate fingers. They looked me up and down, recognition darkening their faces. I looked straight back at them. I was scared enough to have worn a skirt instead of jeans.

'Hello, Rose. Hello, dear.' They were a little strained.

'They're changing the bed. You can't go in just yet.'

'She's so excited you're here.'

'This is a happy day for Bernadette.'

'A blessed day.'

I kept smiling. It's something I really know how to do. The door opened and the nurse beckoned. I removed my sunglasses when I saw the darkened room. I felt a hand on my arm.

'Don't you think it would be more appropriate,' Katie whispered, 'if you took off some of that eye make-up?'

'I'm afraid it's too late,' I said stupidly. She nodded. She did not expect the impossible.

I went in. It took a moment for my eyes to adjust to the dim interior. I saw the bedside table with its array of medicine bottles, its prayer books, bobby pins, orange juice and statue of the Sacred Heart. On the bed was a tiny shrivelled woman clutching a rosary. The bed seemed far too big for her. She looked breakable, insignificant.

'Well,' she said. 'You came.'

I kissed her forehead. 'Of course I came.'

'What's the matter with your eyes?'

'It's only make-up. How are you feeling?'

'Terrible.' She sighed. 'Just pray this don't ever happen to you.'

No use my being encouraging. She was beyond lies.

'I hate this place. I wanna go home.' Nothing had changed. 'Bobby and Solange said they're gonna take care of me.' Easy to say when she was nearly dead. But I was being cynical. 'They been real good to me.' Evidently Bobby had redeemed himself. 'Real good.' She sighed again. 'I'm gonna go back.' She turned away suddenly so I wouldn't see her tears. 'Back to Birch Street and my own little place.'

'Soon as you're better, Aunt Bernie.'

'Fat chance.'

And so it went. Every day twice a day for three weeks. Three weeks with no improvement and no deterioration. I arrived with ice-cream, apple sauce, canned peaches. A light would flicker across her face. 'Well, maybe. Just a dite,' she'd say. The nurse and I would ease her forward then gradually into an upright position. I would sit on the bed and we would watch hopefully as I lifted the plastic spoon to her mouth. She would make a few satisfied noises then suddenly push my encouraging hand away.

'No more right now, honey. Maybe later.' Our faces would fall. The ice-cream would melt on the bedside table, waiting for Later.

'How come your boss give you so much time off?'

'He's very understanding.'

'He must be!' She took a dim view of such lenience.

'They get a temp in?'

'I guess so.'

'You wanna watch out she don't replace you, Rose.'

'She won't.' I felt obliged to go on at length about the affection and esteem in which I was held by my employer. She was unconvinced. Had I ever really convinced her?

'They never kept my job for me.'

'But you passed retirement age, remember?' I patted her hand. 'You don't have to work any more.'

'Am I supposed to be glad about that?' She turned away. 'But it don't matter now. They're closing the Mills anyway.'

I'd heard that. It was hard to imagine those vast structures empty, but already contractors were stripping the fixtures and selling off the machinery.

The first crisis came that Wednesday morning. Her pain was bad, and morphine was reluctantly administered. Bobby and I were summoned, but when we arrived she was sleeping peacefully. Julia and Katie, up since six, met us at the hospital door. The day was so warm that even they were hatless and gloveless and their softly crinkled skin was pink with the muggy heat. But they still wore nylons and white high-heeled sandals. I stared at the stockings stretched tight over their protruding toes.

'What happened?'

'It's all right. She's sleeping.'

'Thank God,' they exclaimed in unison and crossed themselves.

'You heard from your father, Rose?' Julia peered at me.

213

'He's coming.' Vinnie had gone all Vinnie and was simultaneously making and unmaking arrangements.

'Well, that's good to hear. Bernadette needs her brother now. Poor Bea's not much use.' Didn't my presence count for anything? 'She sure is proud of your father.'

'He still taking pictures?' They stood firmly, their crossed forearms resting on their pocket books which in turn rested on their soft respectable stomachs. I said I thought so.

'It's a relief to hear she's not in pain.'

'This must be terrible for you, Rose.'

'It's terrible for us all.'

'Didn't see you at Mass, dear. Were you at the eight o'clock?'

'Yes.'

'Well, God bless you, dear. We're praying for you.'

We left them debating whether to say their rosaries in the cool nave of Holy Trinity or in my aunt's darkened room. Aunt Bernie inspired devotion as well as fear.

I slept through the oppressive noon then rang the hospital at four. A posse of third cousins had arrived from Portland, and Bernie was now exhausted. The ward nurse suggested I too get some rest.

Phyllis and Clovis were thinner and even more wired up, bickering hypochondriacs of whom I was very fond and who would outlive all the other inhabitants of 49 Birch Street. In contrast, Irene continued to swell like one of her succulents in the ground-floor heat. She still wore the cotton print work-dresses that exposed her bare arms. Her cheeks were red and shiny and her eyes were bright. Her hair still spent half its time in pincurls and a hairnet. I was beginning to wonder when it was she combed it out.

'Merry Christmas, deyah.'

She handed me three packages, wrapped in red-and-green paper patterned with reindeer and stars of Bethlehem and fastened with gleaming elaborate bows and tags with my name written in red ball pen.

'I been keeping them for you. We was expecting you last year then the year before that and the year before that too.' She said this without a trace of resentment and watched me while I opened my presents.

The first contained a red apron, handmade, in the shape of a heart and trimmed with white lace. The second was a set of washcloths with her characteristic embroidered edging. The third was a Santa Claus pot holder, also handmade. I kissed her, holding all three against my chest. I carefully folded up the wrapping paper like I knew she expected me to do. I didn't know what to say. I wanted at once to cry and to wriggle away. But she was in a hurry to get on to the topic nearest her heart.

'Come with me, deyah.' She led me into the dim crowded bedroom where a candle in a red glass burned before a statue of St Joseph. She had, she explained, a special devotion to him now (St Teresa having proved a disappointment) and was praying that he might soften the heart of her cruel and possibly psychotic daughter-in-law.

'She don't let Albert come at all,' she whispered, clutching my arm. 'He has to sneak over to see me. Ain't that something? His own mother.' She blessed herself and mumbled a short prayer before the little shrine. Then she gave me a glass of iced tea and some low-cal cookies and told me how she could not lose weight. She should have a garden, I thought, friends, unlimited access to a dozen grandchildren. It was a cruel injustice that she did not.

Solange came to fetch me upstairs. I had a telephone call. She remained behind with Irene, giving her an opportunity to repeat everything she had just said to me.

I took the stairs in twos. 'Tony?' I panted. It was the first time we'd spoken since I'd left New York. No one else had called me.

'Rose, are you all right? You never answered my letter.'

'I'm OK. I'm sorry. Irene just gave me an apron.'

Tony was silent. He didn't understand.

'I'm calling from the office. Everyone's left, so I thought I'd chance it. How are you, Rose?'

'Like I said, I'm fine.'

'I really miss you.'

'What have you been doing?' I felt detached. I could not make my two worlds merge.

'There's a Bresson festival at the Thalia. Steve and I went to see *Au Hazard, Balthazar.*' *Balthazar* was his favourite film. He'd seen it at least eight times. 'Then we went to meet Hadley and Kit and Drexel.'

'At Cal's?'

'Yes. Horowitz is playing at Carnegie Hall. Will you be back in time?'

'Of course.'

'Are you feeling peculiar?'

'A little. I'm sorry. I thought when I spoke to you you'd be near but somehow you're very far away.'

'I understand. Do you love me, Rose?'

'Yes.'

'How long will this go on?'

'I can't say. No one can, not even the doctors. That's what cancer is like. Keeps you waiting.'

'Well, I might go to California.'

'What!'

'To UCLA. Jackson was going to teach a film course there in the fall, but he decided to go to Europe instead. He wants to shoot another film in Greece. Anyway, he suggested me for the job.'

'*California?*'

'I know it's awful, but it's better than Fox and I could meet some people out there and the money is very good. Rose, will you come too? When this is over?'

'If it's ever over. I don't know. Yes. Maybe. California . . .'

Hadley had said it was awful. She'd gone out there the previous summer to visit an old boyfriend. 'I thought if I saw one more perfect body I'd throw up all over it,' she said. What would cultured, sensitive Tony do among all those people who had no sense of irony and had never read Stendhal?

'How's Hadley?'

Everything he said made me feel jealous and excluded. Kit had received the first instalment of his advance, and they had been on a week-long celebration. They looked like hell and were madly in love. Drexel, naturally, was always in tow. And I, without eye make-up, sharing a room with my two-year-old cousin once removed and waiting for my poor aunt to die in a hospital which, as far as I could tell, had neither the means nor inclination to help her do this. A hospital that relied on prayers.

'Steve's off work. There's a strike.'

'Oh.'

'What about California? Do you want to think about it and I'll call you back?'

'Yes.'

'I'd have to be there the first week in September.'

'OK. Call me.'

Immediately I replaced the receiver, my brain did a wipe out. I could not, would not consider the prospect. I had never been further west than New York, and the idea of crossing the continent was akin to a lunar landing. I threw the whole scenario into the lap of the gods. Then I rang Frank. We'd spoken twice since my arrival but had been unable to meet because of hospital visits and overtime. Frank was saving for a trip to Latin America. His numerous allergies had saved him from the Draft. He had risen in the ranks of his union and was now a shop steward, single, working lucrative overtimes, living at home, writing poetry, some of which was about to be published, and raking in the money.

'Frank, gemme outa heah.'

'Wh-wh-where to?'

'Dunno. Around. Show me all the sights I haven't been longing to see.'

'OK. When?'

'Sunday. That's when the Bangor Mullens arrive. Come at ten if you can.'

'And m-m-m-miss, *M-m-m-mass?*'

'Oh, shut up.'

'Well, see you shotly.'

'Shotly. Bye.'

'Wait. What about Mary Lou?' His girlfriend.

'Please don't bring her.'

The next morning I found Aunt Bernie alone, moaning in the shadowy room which she continued to have to herself. I noticed someone had hung a cloth over the mirror. A mercy and a curt reminder. She would never see her own face again.

She lay quietly then suddenly mumbled, and thrashed about. She didn't seem to recognize me. I ran for the nurse.

'We know all about your aunt.' Miss Bison took everything in her stride.

'She's due for an injection in,' she consulted her watch, 'an hour and fifteen minutes.'

'But she's in pain now.'

'An hour and fifteen minutes. You can sit with her if you want to.'

'Where's the doctor?'

'It's Saturday. Doctor McKee isn't in.'

I went back to my aunt's room and sat by the bed, hoping, for a change, that the Ladies' Guild would turn up. Her pain was so threatening. I felt as if I were alone with a dangerous animal. I grew weary from not being able to take my eyes off it, not being able for one second to drop my guard. I needed someone else to share the vigil. She wouldn't let me hold her hand. Sometimes she called for her mother, for Bea or Vinnie.

'He's coming, Aunt Bernie,' I whispered over and over. She'd calm down then start to moan again. She asked for water. I held the glass and straw for her, my hands shaking with fear. I was afraid of Aunt Bernie. I've always been afraid of her. I still am.

217

At twelve-thirty precisely the nurse arrived to administer another injection. By the time Mary and Sadie arrived my aunt was quiet and managed a little smile for their benefit.

'You're doing a wonderful job, Rose.' They were amazed I hadn't bolted, unstable and ungrateful as I was.

At two o'clock peace ended. She began to moan again, to mumble and thrash. Again I rang for the nurse.

'Four-thirty,' she said.

'Why isn't the morphine working?'

'Because it isn't mawphine.'

'What is it?'

'Pentazocine.'

'But that's what they were giving her last week.'

'That's right.'

'But now she's had the morphine the pentazocine won't be as effective.'

She shot me a sharp glance, obviously wondering how I had acquired such information. 'That's the point, Miss Mullen. We don't want her building up a mawphine tolerance.'

'Why not?'

'Mawphine, as you may know – ' another sharp glance – 'affects the lungs.'

'It also affects the pain. I thought that was the point.'

'Look, you discuss this with the doctor. I'm only following orders.'

It sounded like 'awdas', and it made me think of Auschwitz.

I was very angry, but this was Aunt Bernie's nurse and I needed her on my side and must not alienate her with a display of what she would regard as Irish temper. I sat out the two and a half hours. When Aunt Bernie was at last asleep I went downstairs for a tuna melt and a Marlboro in the hospital cafeteria. I caught sight of my pale face and black roots in a mirror. I looked a tired tart.

Throughout the evening the cycle was repeated. My aunt was being ground down to nothing in order that in the course of her last days on earth she might not become a junkie. What they were giving her would not have kept Drexel high for five minutes.

'They're mouse doses,' I told Frank the next morning after the Bangor Mullens had paid their respects at Birch Street and left for the hospital.

'Can't you slip her something?'

I'd considered it, but my desperation had yet to peak. I hesitated, the morality of ordinary people in ordinary predicaments still holding me on its leash. I had yet to find out what death does to you, the way it takes you beyond good and bad, makes morality seem fatuous and wholly inadequate.

We were standing on Market Street bridge. The yellow-brown water surged beneath our feet, seeming, as always, to issue straight from the womb of the Number Two Mill, a gigantic, dirty afterbirth.

'Aunt Bernie said it was going to close.'

'Well, her memory's shot. It closed six months ago.'

Already the windows were broken and it had that haunted look that made you want to turn away.

'What will everybody do?'

'Go on to welfare. Not many of them were skilled.'

'Old Wigram must be turning in his grave.'

'Who c-c-cares about him?'

'The whole town looks seedy.'

'It's been seedy for a while. But it's up for some urban renewal. Lots of government money around. L.B.J.'s good for something. But if that happens the old Number One might come down and the Number Two with it.'

'Impossible.'

'Very possible. Unless they turn it into housing.'

'I can't imagine living in a factory. All that oil and grease in the floors, all the drudgery lived out in the place . . .'

'If you'd been in a trailer for ten years it might not seem so bad. You might not think too much about the past.'

'Everything's dying.'

'That's just your point of view and fortunately your point of view is very limited.'

'I'm glad to hear it.'

'Good. Let's b-b-blow this pop stand.'

I slipped my arm around his skinny hips and hugged him. I loved Frank. He was one of my own ones.

His 1960 Pontiac convertible waited at the end of the bridge, illegally parked. It had a few dents and could have done with a visit to the car wash, but under its hood it was, Frank said, the equal of any hick hot rod. Frank didn't care much about appearances, and in many ways the car was like him. Seeing it there, I suddenly wanted to fly, to race, to be pinned against the seat as a male foot lowered upon the accelerator. Like those few precious times in high school when we rode on summer nights in a robin's egg-blue Oldsmobile with the top down and the fox tail on the aerial flapping in the wind.

'Let's go out to the Turnpike, Frank,' I said, 'and really floor it. Let's drive south. Let's go to Black Water Road.'

'As your ladyship desires.'

The view from the Kittery Bridge is spectacular, especially on a sunny day, the water of Portsmouth Harbour gleaming under a royal-blue sky. White houses with black shutters nestle among the crowding green, squawking gulls career past the overhead girders. To the north are the foothills of the White Mountains. The air is salty, fresh and lazy, and the scene is spoiled only by the Navy Yard and the prison, a grey sprawl at the mouth of Piscataqua. I remembered the times we took Vinnie to work, watching him approach the wire fence, show his pass at the gate, not thinking at all about the significance of the ritual because of being so intent on another: his turn, his smile, the tipping of his visored cap, his final jaunty wave.

'The prison's closed,' he said.

'What?'

'Yup.'

'How come?'

'No one knows. But something's going on there, something.'

We stared at the building, incongruous on the edge of the sparkling sea. We pictured locked rooms never opened to the sunlight of scrutiny. We imagined horrors behind those doors, experiments, secret, unnamable, an evil technology.

'Remember Navy Days?' Frank asked.

'Sure do. It always seemed such an innocent celebration. At the time, I mean. A happy day out for all the family. Nobody thinking about the things those nice white-uniformed boys were trained to do.'

'And the submarines were just – interesting.'

'Yes. Interesting.' We were quiet for a few minutes, looking.

I asked Frank what went on in the Yard now.

'Busy. Plenty of jobs. Plenty of money. There's a war on, you know.'

'Of course I know. I'm not living an art-for-art's-sake existence, Frank. I am aware of what's happening in the world.'

He turned to me. 'Are you sure you want to see Sea Point?'

'Of course. Why shouldn't I? Frank, what's happened?'

'I was coming to this, but sometimes – well, you can't get in.'

'What do you mean? They can't close Sea Point like the prison.'

'Sometimes they have to. It may be polluted.'

'Oh no.'

'Radioactive effluent from the Yard.'

'I don't believe it.'

'They've tried to keep it quiet. One article in the *Portsmouth Herald* then zilch. But dead fish keep being washed up on to the beach. The water's too warm. People have stopped collecting seaweed for their gardens. They don't dig for clams any more.'

This was too much. 'I can't bear it. Let's go to Ogunquit instead.'

'What about Black Water Road?'

'Save it for another time, another life, the way things are going.'

'OK. Don't be depressed.' He swung the car into a driveway, backed it out and headed north.

'Sorry, kiddo. They're planning to build a reactor further down the New Hampshire coast.' Now he was into it he couldn't stop.

'Don't tell me about it. Where?'

'At Seaford. Top secret, except everybody knows. There've been protests already. But nothing will have any effect.'

That mist, cool and consoling, that rises off the water. That poisoned mist. Everything dying, contracting; everything tainted. Strange to think Maine was still safe. For how long no one could tell. But they all knew Bath Iron Works was a euphemism.

We stopped at York Beach and pushed our way through the crowds to buy salt-water taffy and watch the famous window where long gooey ropes of the stuff poured out of a machine the size of a cement mixer like pink, green and yellow snakes. We unwrapped two pieces, sucked on them, let them lock our jaws, then felt too queasy to go on the Ferris wheel so drove on to Ogunquit. Absurdly, I took a box of taffy for Aunt Bernie, so she'd know I'd been thinking of her.

Along the Marginal Way, at least, surroundings were unchanged: the rocky coast, the sea that battered it and, small concession to man, this vertiginous little path. I resolved to go only north from now on. North was still unsullied. The lobster rolls were glorious as they had always been. On the way back to Florence we put the top down and turned the radio up so high that it was impossible to talk.

We turned off at the usual exit. Frank decided to end the day on a light note by taking me on a tour of illuminated Virgin Marys.

'The new craze,' he said, 'is bathtubs.'

We wove in and out of the suburban streets to the north of Florence. The front lawn of nearly every fourth house boasted an enormous bathtub, upended and decked with fairy lights, its interior painted blue to serve as a fitting halo cum niche for the merciful Mother of God. The better constructions were floodlit, making Mary appear to float against an undifferentiated celestial background.

I told Frank about Nightshade's dummies, and we agreed they weren't a patch on these creations. True madness, we concurred, is to be found in the sticks.

I opened the apartment door to the anxious faces of Bobby and Solange.

'We'd better go to the hospital, Rose. She's real bad, I guess.'

We left immediately and I stayed with my aunt until six the next morning. She was ferociously awake and commented upon every detail of my appearance, every action and gesture of the nurses, every change in the feeble light. Her senses had perversely heightened to complement her lowered threshold of pain. Grimly the nurses adminstered the prescribed dose of her usual drug, no more, no less. They arrived on the minute, needles at the ready, jaws firmly set. I knew it was pointless to argue with them, and when they came I sat, silent and tense, refusing to answer their questions or make any comment on what was to me their indefensible behaviour.

At seven-thirty I telephoned Dr McKee. He had not yet left for the office.

'Doctor, I need to talk to you.' I was very calm.

'Yes, Miss Mullen.' Phlegmatic as ever.

'I'd like you to put my aunt back on the morphine and increase her doses when necessary.'

'It's not time for that yet.'

'Yes, it is.'

'I'll be the judge of that, Miss Mullen.'

'No, you won't. I'm her next of kin. It's my decision and I say do it now, please.'

'I'm sorry. I appreciate your feelings.'

'No, you don't. You're a Catholic and you don't appreciate anything but fear for your immortal soul.'

'It's my business to keep your aunt alive.'

'Medicine isn't a business. You're worried about the Last Judgement.'

'Really, Miss Mullen.'

'You're worried God will punish you for murdering my aunt. God and the AMA.'

'I am not!'

'And therefore you're willing to condemn her to a prolonged and agonizing death.'

'Are you accusing me of malpractice?'

'I'm accusing you of caring more about your own salvation than the sufferings of your patient.'

'Miss Mullen, if you continue to be abusive – '

'Don't you dare tell me you'll put the phone down.' I was seeing black now, but my voice was still steady. I was determined not to blow my Irish stack entirely. 'Don't you dare do it. You just get in your expensive car which you paid for with your patients' blood and you just get right over here to the hospital and you just give Bernadette Mullen a great big syringe full of morphine. And do it now.'

'I will not.'

'Oh yes you will, because if you don't I swear to God I will personally come over and kill you.'

He arrived at eight-thirty, nervous and vexed and not meeting my eyes. He himself administered the dose to my aunt who looked upon him as a god. If he had told her it was necessary for her to live in agony for the next ten years, she would have accepted his verdict with a grateful smile.

This was the beginning of my life-long aversion to doctors. How ironic that you should have been in the medical profession.

When she was finally asleep I left the hospital. In the corridor I passed a flock of nuns casting their cool shadow on the bright June day. They made the sign of the cross at me. I wanted to wipe off their blessing like a child does an unwanted kiss. When I went out into the hot morning I found I didn't have my sunglasses. A headache began that went on for the next two days. I boarded a bus that took me to the top of Birch Street.

Bobby and Solange looked at me, wide-eyed. Someone had telephoned them. They certainly knew. I smiled and went to my room. My hands were trembling as I unbuttoned my shirt.

I did not go back to the hospital that day. In the evening I rang my father.

'Hear you been giving the doctors hell, Rosie.'

'Christ, how did you know that?'

'That's my girl. Don't let them bully you. Stand up to the AMA.'

'When are you coming?' It almost didn't matter what he said. I was just curious.

'Well, right away, if you want me to.'

'I do want you to.' Reckless of me to be so direct with him. Desperation emboldens me. Perhaps I would have made a good revolutionary.

'OK,' he said. 'I'll fix it up.'

'*Please*.'

'OK. OK.'

Later that night Tony rang. I sat, stupefied, with a whisky, in front of the television, while Bobby and Solange whispered in the kitchen. Maybe they thought I'd come completely unstrung. I didn't care what they thought. I was marginal, you see, and I didn't care.

'Rose, what's happening?'

'She's still with us.'

'Oh, I'm sorry. I meant California.'

I had forgotten all about California.

'Can you come, Rose?'

'I really have no idea.'

'Rose, what's wrong?'

'I'm drunk. Be glad you're not here.'

'I have to leave in three weeks. There's been a change in plans.' I could hear the desperation in his voice but it failed to move me. I was now in the realm of death. I moved within its darkly charmed circle, from which nothing can pass in or out.

'Leave, then. There are telephones in California too, you know. I'm sorry. I can't make a decision.'

'I understand.'

'No, you don't.'

Why was I being surly with the only person who was truly kind to me and understood me? 'I'm sorry, Tony. I didn't mean it to be like this.'

'That's all right. Do you want me to come up there?'

'No.' I did, but I said no anyway. In the realm of the dead one does not act rationally. It does not occur to one to satisfy desires.

'I'm angry. I'm angry with everything in the universe. I'm so angry I don't want to stop being angry. That's how angry I am.'

He was tolerant and soothing. I guess he knew how drunk I was. He said he would call me before he left and that we would sort it out later, any time I wanted. Why wasn't I grateful to him? I suppose because people who are always good to you don't ever teach you anything. That is why they end up boring you. Only the ones who hurt you and run away and don't explain force you to find out who you are and who they are and what you're both made of. Maybe I had done that for Aunt Bernie. Now *there* was a roseate thought.

At nine the next morning I was back at my aunt's bedside. Two days of calm followed during which I talked and moved like a zombie in daylight and hit the whisky at night. I used it as a kind of expensive tranquillizer. Otherwise I would not have been able to sleep, haunted as I was by a grey cancer face and luminous cancer eyes.

Mainly she slept, but sometimes we talked, her mind becoming increasingly centred on the past. The closer she came to death the harder she strained towards childhood. She repeated the story about sitting at the entrance to the cellar and drawing on a slate. She told me of my grandmother's death on the kitchen table during that extemporaneous operation for a burst appendix. How Aunt Bea had fainted and my father wept on his knees while she was left to manage everything. I waited for her to tell me at last about the boy she had refused to marry but she never mentioned him. Then began the incomprehensible Beckett monologues that went on for hours, punctuated by cries for her mother or Vinnie. I sat helpless as these loop casettes rolled horribly on. The Ladies' Guild, the nuns, the priests, the second cousins came and prayed and went, but I stayed, unable to do anything other than ensure and monitor the morphine injections. It was as though my other life, the life in New York, which I had loved and believed to be the only reality, had never existed. What use was it to me now? What had I learned from it that I could apply to my current predicament? I didn't yet know that one is always unprepared for death. My state of mind must have been plain to Hadley when she called.

'I hear you're really angry. That's good.' There was laughter in her voice as usual. Laughter and mockery. She still disapproved of my submitting to all this. 'Are you shaking your fists at heaven?'

I sighed. Anger wasn't mentioned again. I was impenetrable.

'I'm tired. How are you?'

She told me about three parties, one involving a swimming pool, one a llama and one the police. She said she had purchased a pink feather boa but that nothing especially interesting had happened except for the usual dance pieces, boutiques and demos. Kit wasn't very interesting either since he had started another book. They were going to Greece.

'Why don't you come?' she said.

'Can't. No money.'

'Don't be crazy. I'll lend you money. You can meet us in Athens in August and we can go to the island. Your aunt will be dead by then. Jackson made a movie there, remember? We might meet up with him.'

'I don't know. I can't make decisions.'

'Well, I can. You're coming. Drexel's going off with his new lover and I don't want to be bored alone with Kit.'

'I've never been out of America. I've never left the eastern sea-board.'

'There's sea everywhere as well as east, you know.'

That afternoon I had another fight with the doctor. This time he was adamant about the morphine dose. I lost my temper, and Sister Rosalie caught me at it. She warned me about my 'provocative behaviour' while members of the Ladies' Guild looked on. I had to take it. Duly chastened. Only the whisky kept my spirits up. Whisky and cigarettes. Disgusting. But I was unable to comfort myself with the idea that I was doing my duty.

At last Denise called to say that Vinnie had left for the airport. I told Bobby that I would believe this when my father walked through the hospital doors, tipped his baseball cap at us and proceeded to charm everyone, including the priests. And the priests were gathering. You'd have thought that a sure-bet soul like Aunt Bernie's would have made them lighten up a little, but no. They hovered outside the door and around the bed, each one, it seemed, hoping to capture the prize of her death. Even Mr Kinsman, the Baptist minister, came by on the off-chance. But he got short shrift from Father Leahy who regarded my aunt's salvation as his personal patch. I guess after all those years he was entitled to it. On the 2nd of July he pipped them all at the post by administering to her the last rites which she welcomed like a lost love, surrendering to them as once I would have surrendered to Travis had he ever appeared at my door.

'Your aunt is well prepared for death,' was Leahy's consoling remark.

But he was wrong. They were all wrong, and that evening the Beckett monologues began all over again, dragging on into the next morning when Dr McKee at last raised the morphine dose. And Vinnie? My father had missed his plane and gone home to give it another whirl the next day.

About 4 a.m. she became lucid. We were alone. She opened her eyes and looked straight at me.

'No skating,' she said.

'What?' I went to her side.

'No skating till you've done your homework.'

'I've done it, Aunt Bernie.'

'Done what?'

'My homework.'

'Rose, have you gone crazy? You're twenty-seven years old.'

She closed her eyes. Her face wore that old expression of savage satisfaction. A few minutes later she called out.

'Bea!'

I went back to the bedside. 'Yes, Bernie.'

'Did you see that girl, Bea? That poor little girl?'

'No.'

She looked at me hard. Lucid again, she knew who I was.

'I told you about her. No bigger'n me. That afternoon – it was raining. Oh my, did it rain.'

'When, Aunt Bernie?'

'Mary Donovan, that was her name. You remember Mary? Her ma was second cousin to Sadie's ma. No, no. You wouldn't remember. They took her away to the hospital, and we never heard a word. Never a word.'

'What happened to Mary?'

'She was working the machine, and she'd been there quite a while, ten hours, maybe. I guess she got tired. Doing all that overtime. We all did too much overtime. She was so young, like me. Well, poor Mary Donovan, she leaned over too far to pull the lever, or something went wrong with the machine, they never said. Not a word. Just took her away and never said nothing. Well the machine caught her, caught in her hair, you know, and she couldn't get out and it pulled her scalp clean off. Happened so fast. Pulled her whole scalp right off. Only fourteen years old, same as me. I was January and she was April. Oh my, but she screamed.'

'And you saw this?'

'Happened right beside me. I was at the next machine . . .'

'Aunt Bernie?'

She was gone again. I'd never know what happened to Mary Donovan. What do you do without a scalp?

On the morning of the Fourth of July my father's plane was delayed and he waited two hours at Washington Airport. Bobby drove him all the way from Boston, the car windows open to the scorching wind. His sister called for him all day, alternating cries and whispers. He and Bobby were held up again by traffic on the outskirts of Florence. Everyone had come to see the parade which itself delayed them by another hour. It was evening when he finally arrived, by which time his sister had been dead for one hour. She lay in perfect repose, her workworn hands suddenly and completely white and crossed upon her breast. Father Leahy had been right after all, because she did not look in the least surprised by whatever it was that had just happened to her. She looked almost well, her tiny desiccated body laid out on sheets she had probably helped to make.

My father threw himself upon the bed, weeping openly and loudly.

I sat limp in a blue plastic chair and watched as the others consoled him. But Vinnie Mullen went too far as always and carried on until it suited him to stop.

I was thinking about what Eva had told me of *The Tibetan Book of the Dead* and all the bardo states the soul must pass through after death. She once said that since there is a nine-month gestation period, there must be an equal and opposite time for the soul to hang around, accustoming itself to death, growing into it as a foetus grows into life. In which case Aunt Bernie might be with us for a while. I hoped it wasn't true.

When we left the hospital at eight the fireworks were just beginning. We all stood in the parking lot and watched them explode against a sky that turned from opaline to indigo to black. Everyone agreed the display wasn't as good as last year's.

15

Waking

Vinnie promised me dinner if I would go with him to choose the casket. I was the one, he said, with the cultivated eye. I think I would have chosen my own coffin for dinner alone with my father. As the undertaker hovered solicitously I decided on a steel-grey number with baby-blue quilted velvet interior which he assured me looked stunning with grey hair. It was one of his most popular items, he said, and at $2,300 the second most expensive. Vinnie accepted the bill without a murmur. That was Saturday.

We drove up to Wiscasset and stopped at Kinnear's which was crowded even at two-thirty in a part of the country where people eat promptly at seven, twelve and five-thirty. The annual invasion from Massachusetts and New York was well underway.

'You can't beat Maine,' said Vinnie, looking around with an expression reminiscent of his sister's after Holy Communion.

'Why don't you come back?'

'Naw.' He shook his head and gazed at the pile of empty clam shells and solidifying drawn butter before him. 'Denise likes Maryland. Likes the climate. Winters are better.'

'So that's it, then – whatever Denise likes.'

'Your old man's a slave to the whims of women.' He winked. Then in the space of a breath his eyes filled with tears. He looked out the window to where the ocean lapped against huge rotting hulls of ships and the ancient wooden pylons that still supported the jetty. Beyond were the rocks where harbour seals liked to lounge and flirt with the tourists. And beyond them, tucked neatly away, the brand-new nuclear-power station.

'Poor Bernadette. Poor Bea.' He rested his forehead in his hands while tears clinked on to his plate.

'Don't, Daddy.' I shook his arm gently. 'It's very sad. But talk to me. I'm alive and well.'

229

'Too depressed, Rosie. You talk to me, how about it. Talk to your old man.' He glanced up. 'Tell me about New York.'

I told him about everything but Cal's. I mentioned Tony and Hadley (I took pride in my friends) and about the Nora film which provoked another fit of weeping. This time we had to leave, and I led him from the restaurant with all eyes upon us.

'You drive, Rosie,' he said, collapsing into the passenger seat.

'You know I don't have a licence.' I'd let it lapse in New York.

'So what?' The flood of emotion abruptly ceased and he looked at me as though I'd lost my reason. 'It's an emergency. We're bereaved! If we're stopped, just tell them that. They'll have to accept it. They'll understand. Everybody's got family.' He waved his hand in a grand gesture of police dismissal. 'Anyway, no one will stop us. You'll see, honey. Just drive like a good girl.'

'OK.' I started Bobby's car, uninsured for third party, and nervously backed it out of the parking lot. I hadn't driven in years and not even then very much. I'd been saving for a car when I was overtaken by events. And in New York automobiles were simply an impediment.

Of course Vinnie was right. No one stopped us. He snored beside me as we sailed past the State Troopers who were out in force. I had the same feeling I'd had as a child whenever we'd gone on drives together, that we were under a divine dispensation and might break all rules with impunity.

Tony had rung me from his parents in Long Island, but when I called back he'd left. I intended to try him again at work, but the next few days were full of the commotion that death rituals are there to create, so I was unable to think of anything but the faces before me and had no time to consider my future, if I had one. Each night after three or four hours at the funeral parlour, during which I slipped off to the ladies' room at regular intervals to sip from a small bottle of Jameson's, I would return to the apartment, drink some more with Vinnie, Bobby and Solange, and go to bed, sleeping until ten or eleven the next morning and returning to the funeral parlour for the lunchtime session.

Hundreds of people came to the wake, some of them on all three days. There were faces I hadn't seen for ten years. (I was filming my ghosts all right, if only in my mind.) They came to keep us company, and did not do much praying aside from the compulsory genuflection by the corpse on arrival. Like the many wakes we had all been to, it was an occasion for good humour, more like an ordinary party, but with a touch of hysteria. No dancing with the corpse as in the bad old days, of course, but lots of ribald family in-jokes, most of them instigated by or directed at Vinnie, and discreet slipping outside by uncles and male cousins to share a bottle behind the garage where the hearses were parked.

On the second night, as I stood shaking hands beside the coffin, overcome with the heat and the stifling scent of dyed-green carnations, I saw an elderly man hovering by the door. He was thin but erect, and his manner was nervous and self-effacing. By the coffin he made a hasty genuflection as though it were difficult for him to bend his knee, and stood gazing at my aunt's waxy puffed-out face and her white hands around which Julia Byrne had entwined some crystal rosary beads. When he greeted me there were tears in his hazy blue eyes, eyes that looked like mismatched marbles. I was glad to find Fourth Cousin Mikey still among the living.

'Evening, Rose.' He shook my hand lightly, formally, the shabby gentleman still, with his fragile dignity. 'I'm awful sorry about your Aunt Bernadette. Awful sorry.' He shook his head, making no effort to hide his tears. He'd been drinking but not immoderately.

'She was real good to me.'

'How are you these days, Mikey?'

'Can't complain, Rose.' His voice trailed off. He looked back at the coffin.

'Bernadette was a fine woman. A real lady. Glad you was here. Meant a lot to her, I know. Well, I won't keep you, Rose. Lot of people want to pay their respects. Don't want to hold you up. I see your dad's here. I'm awful glad. God bless you, Rose.'

'Bless you too, Mikey.'

He made his way unsteadily to an empty chair and sat holding his hat on his knees. My father joined him. They talked for a while and I saw Vinnie slip a few bills into his hand before he left him.

The nuns and the Ladies' Guild were present at every session. Their attitude to me was cool, and I was the target of many a sidelong glance from narrowed eyes. I had stuck it out, all right. They had not expected that, and they were impressed. But I had taken the matter of the morphine too far. Not only did they disapprove of my behaviour, they were shocked by the way I had hastened Aunt Bernie's demise. Deaths were not to be hastened, however much one might deplore the victim's suffering. Suffering was expiation, there was a good reason for it. Otherwise God wouldn't have inflicted it. Moreover, it gave everyone else a chance to practise two or three of the Corporal Works of Mercy. Spiritual merit to be gained all round. I had deprived my aunt and them of some of this merit – that was the way they were thinking, I was sure. I was trained to read their minds. I knew them as I would never know another group of humans in my life. A depressing thought. And in a funny way they knew me. They knew in particular my weaknesses. If I had not been in such a state of indifference I would have told myself: Let them show you yourself in all your limitations. Benefit from it. It's a good thing to know, the only way to become strong.

My father, however, was under no such interdict, and they clustered around him as though he were a shy young curate instead of an overweight atheist of nearly sixty.

By Wednesday morning our throats were sore from talking and laughing and our heads dull from drink. Vinnie had been the naughtiest and made more than his fair share of trips to the garage. We had been living on fried clams and cheeseburgers plus the steady stream of tuna casseroles and green-frosted devil's-food cakes. I felt queasy and I dreaded the church ritual and my father's return to Maryland. In my strange out-of-time condition, I had been happy with him, my whole being concentrated on his huge presence.

The morning of the funeral I received a postcard from Tony with a poem:

> Rose. Open Rose.
> Giving away
> Your sweetest scents
> For free.

I put it aside and never found it again.

We assembled in the parlour at eight. The room was still in shadows as Vinnie had not opened the drapes or made up his bed. He was used to being looked after by women, and Solange and I were just too busy to oblige. The air was already warm and damp. It clung to our sober clothing. Vinnie wore a dark-blue suit which made him look marginally slimmer. His cheeks were pink and his thinning curls without a trace of grey. I wore the black dress he had insisted on buying for me, and its synthetic fabric stuck to my waist and back. I had pleaded that it was summer and besides, no one wore black to funerals any more. But sometimes he was a stickler for old-fashioned formalities, usually when I least expected it.

'Ready?' He reviewed his troops right down to Kevin, dressed like a little man in a suit, tie and brown straw hat. I thought him grotesque, but to everyone else he was the height of baby chic. He seemed to be working himself up, gathering his energies for an extended whine.

'OK,' said Bobby, 'let's hit the goddamn road.'

Solange's four-inch heels clacked behind me on the rubber matting. She was followed by Phyllis and Clovis. Irene waited on the steps, already mopping her brow and dabbing her eyes with a lace-trimmed handkerchief. It was eight-thirty and the streets were blazing. I put on my sunglasses and took hold of Vinnie's arm.

'You'll take those off for the service, won't you, honey,' he whispered. I nodded like the good little girl I was. At least I wasn't being forced to wear a hat and would probably be the only woman without one. I kept my hand in his arm as we walked the five blocks to the funeral parlour where a limousine would drive us four blocks to Holy Trinity.

Faces peeped between Venetian blinds and curtains as we passed. Everyone likes a good funeral. Some of the neighbours stood on the doorsteps to wave us off. Some fell in behind us. Mrs Grady was out on the street in her wheelchair, attended by Lizzie the faithful. My father brought the procession to a halt and made us wait while he kissed her and teased her and told her she was the best-looking woman on the street and how as a boy he'd cried when she married Jim Grady. (Now deceased. No more singing.) Lizzie looked on, smiling bravely. The sacrificial daughter. No one ever teased her. Morris and May had driven up from Dedham for the funeral. My father was touched. Everyone treated him like a returning hero. You'd have thought he was the mayor. Of course he had not chosen to stand outside *their* church in the snow. Nevertheless I could not help feeling proud to be the daughter of such a splendid smiling lion of a man, albeit with clipped claws and filed fangs.

Just before we reached the funeral parlour I turned and saw the full length of our sedate procession. For the first time since Aunt Bernie's death, I wanted to cry.

In the cool dim room we performed the ritual of kissing the corpse goodbye. Each of us was given a moment alone to kneel and contemplate the remains of Bernadette Mullen and the state to which we would one day be reduced. In case, perhaps, there were any little last-minute messages we'd neglected to deliver. Then we kissed her stony brow. She wore her horn-rimmed glasses and a pink dress which I'd chosen. My favourite, the old peacock-blue, would have clashed with the casket's pastel interior.

'Goodbye, Aunt Bernie,' I whispered. 'I am very grateful to you. Please do not hold your hastened death against me. I couldn't bear to see you suffer, and anyway I assumed you were in a hurry to get to heaven. I hope I was right.'

The cortège was twenty minutes late in setting off because my father was once again overcome by emotion and had to be removed by the undertaker who administered a shot of brandy. That seemed to do the trick. But he gave way again at the church and, as everyone now expected, at the graveside. I sat rigid and, I suppose, grim-faced, through the Mass for the Dead, Vinnie's hand in mine.

I had not set foot in Holy Trinity in nearly five years. For my father it must have been three times as long. Whatever his grief, Vinnie was sticking to his guns as far as the Sacraments were concerned, and sat resolutely in his seat when the time came for Holy Communion. I had told him already that I would be receiving. He failed to understand my wish to do so, but said if that was what I wanted, well, go right ahead and don't mind him. I gave my reasons as communal and sentimental rather than religious. I concealed my perverse curiosity as to whether the Deity would strike me dead for such an offence, being in a state of mortal sin several times over. Part of me wished to pile up yet another offence. Silly, I know. There were some raised eyebrows when I approached the Communion rail, Father Leahy's among them. But all I felt was the pleasant familiar tasteless taste of the wafer which I had to work my tongue around to pry loose from the roof of my mouth. They still stuck. No new improved variety. Afterwards I did not sit with my head in my hands like everybody else. I was relieved. It had been nice to share this sacrificial act with the others. Nice, but that was all. Religion in its cultural social aspect was not too bad, and the play-acting made it almost fun. It was sensual, visual, not unlike the opera. I didn't dislike these people at all. It was only their orthodoxy that threatened me.

Aunt Bernie was lowered into the Mullen family plot. In the midday sun banks of garish flowers with satin bows and gold lettering began to wilt on the parched grass. Irene and my father sobbed audibly, and there were sniffs and snuffles and fluttering tissues throughout the crowd of mourners. Only my eyes were dry, a fact which was sure to be remarked on later.

So now it was over, and what would I do? Again I postponed decisions. There was still the reception to get through; more relatives and Cliquot Club ginger ale and Vienna rolls. The party was spread between our apartment and the Coutures' with the opposing doors open wide and a breeze blowing in from the balcony. It was like a replay of my graduation party, only the hostess was now the absent guest of honour and the guest of honour was now, in a funny way, the hostess. The role did not suit me, and I resented sharing my father on what would be our last day together, especially when I was made to give a guided tour of the many sympathy cards on display. The women read all the signatures as well as every word of every verse, exclaiming over the touching sentiments.

'Nora would have done it much better,' whispered my Aunt Lou who was representing the Noonans.

Among the remembrances was a card from Janice with an attached photo of Reese and Otis asleep in the minaret.

Throughout the afternoon, Vinnie was the centre of a changing circle of guests. They all wanted to be near him and to claim, even briefly, his wandering attention. (He had been hitting the Moose Head Beer since we returned from the cemetery.) I was jealous, even though I myself was swamped with kinfolk eager to tell me how good I had been to my aunt *in the end*. They were pleased to see me, I knew. They cared about me since I was one of them. Someone mentioned the story of Bernie's birth on the factory floor. Vinnie swore all over again that it was true.

'Ma went to work one morning and came home with a baby that night,' Vinnie recalled. 'Bea thought she'd picked it up at the five and dime.'

No one had told Bea about Bernie's death. She would forget it within half an hour and it would have to be explained all over again, and we saw no point in that.

At eight the last of the Bangor Mullens departed, and Solange and I put Vinnie and Bobby and Kevin to bed and wrapped up the remaining Vienna rolls and put clingfilm over the bowl of potato salad and threw out the paper plates and washed the cups and saucers which Phyllis and Irene helped dry.

That night I slept on the couch. Towards morning I had a dream about Foxie and the souls of Foxie's children who fluttered behind me as I walked the streets of Florence in bad snow.

When we returned from Portland where Bobby and I had put Vinnie on a plane to Boston, Solange told me that Tony had called and left a number where I could reach him at nine. Tony! I hadn't thought about him in four days. I was guilty and wanted to make it up to him, to give him my entire attention. I didn't wait, but called at eight-thirty just in case, and keeping one eye on the clock. Bobby and Solange weren't exactly rich.

The number was Hadley's and he'd already arrived. I apologized for not calling and he was very understanding. He had to leave sooner than he'd planned for the coast. There were complications. He was subletting his apartment. What was I going to do? He was sorry, he had to know.

'I'll follow you.' There, I'd done it.

'When?'

'When everything's settled.'

'You mean in Florence?'

'Well, Florence and New York. There's the apartment. There's Otis.'

'You can bring Otis.'

'He might prefer to stay with Janice. I don't know how his stomach would react to the Californian climate. Oh, all right.'

'In August, maybe, or September.'

'August or September.'

He gave me an address and telephone number in Los Angeles.

'I love you, Tony, I really do, and I've missed you.' There, I'd said it. He was happy now, I could tell.

'Hadley wants to speak to you. Don't hang up without saying goodbye.'

'I won't. I promise.' He was insecure, like me. Hansel and Gretel trying to feel safe together in the big forest.

'Well, hi there.'

'Oh Hadley, thank God it's over.'

'I'm really glad, Rose. We've just been to a dance piece and Star and Steve were in it? In a loft on 13th Street?' As usual, nothing was real outside New York. 'Drexel's not going off with his boyfriend after all, so that's a relief. We went to a party in Easthampton. It was awful but De Kooning was there.' More boutiques, dances and demos. She was in excellent humour. Suddenly her voice dropped.

'Rose, I've got something to tell you. I was waiting until Tony left the room because I don't want anyone to know just yet.'

'Know what?'

'Kit and I are getting married.'

'Get serious,' I laughed.

'I am serious, although I realize it's out of character. We're keeping it secret for a little while. I don't want our parents to find out.'

'Why not?'

'Don't you think,' her voice rose, 'I want my wedding to be fun? Oh-oh, did they hear me? No, I don't think so. Never mind. So we've decided to do it fast and get it out of the way. I guess you're surprised, huh?'

'A little.'

'It won't change anything, it won't make any difference. My life will be exactly the same, I'm keeping my maiden name. Anyway, you know me – even if I'm married I can't be married.'

'Who decided?'

'Does it matter? *Him*, naturally. Just an old-fashioned boy.' She giggled. 'Can you be bridesmaid?'

'What? Sure. When?'

'Next Saturday. I told you we were doing it quick. We're having it in Nightshade's loft.

'But that's like – soon.'

'So? It only takes an hour to get from Boston to New York. Just hop on a plane. She must have left you some money. We'll meet you and you can stay with us. We want to cheer you up, Rose.' It was what she was best at, after all. Commiseration wasn't one of her strong points.

'Thanks. But I'm not sure . . .'

'Then we'll go to Greece and you can stay in the apartment for the rest of the summer. It'll be cooler than your place.'

She went on mapping out my life.

'There is California,' I managed to interject.

'Oh, you don't want to go there before October. It's awful in the summer, I mean it's awful anyway. Actually, why don't you meet us in Greece instead, like I said before? It'd be great, the two of us and you and Drexel. You can go out to the Coast any time. We'll lend you the money for planc fare and you can stay with us at Aphrodite's house on the island. It's time you did Europe. But first you have to get out of Maine.'

I said I was too tired to talk any more and could she ring me back in the morning.

'Perfect. Bye, darlin'. Oh, Kit sends love. Bye.'

I went to the transport room, being careful not to wake Kevin who was like an enraged hornet when disturbed. I lay down, too tired to remove my clothes. I had been knocked over by giant waves from my other life, washing all this way from a distant shore with me in mind. Tony and California, Hadley and secret matrimony. Was I being forced to choose between them? Was that what was really happening? The thought depressed me badly.

I woke at five, remembering that I had not said goodbye to Tony as I had promised. And he had not rung back. Perhaps he was becoming fed up with my neglect. I pictured him, loved him, missed him. I felt no desire for him. My libido had dwindled to nothing. A month in Florence had returned me to an almost virginal state.

Aunt Bernie left me the muskrat coat, also the onyx ring which I put carefully away in the box in which it was originally purchased. I would keep it but not wear it. Onyx was too saturnine for me. The apartment rightly went to Bobby and Solange, and the remaining money in Bernie's account was to buy a few savings bonds for Kevin. That left the contents of the metal cabinet to be sorted out and disposed of. I knew it contained a box of stamps purchased in the Second World War and now worth a couple of hundred dollars. Otherwise the cabinet probably held what were no doubt treasures to her but fit only for the Salvation Army.

I knew where the key to the cabinet was. She had told me, in her harsh whisper, often enough during those last weeks. But I did not let on. I knew Solange was anxious to get her hands on the stamps, but I was not ready to face confrontation with its contents. Apparently I was not intending to be Hadley's bridesmaid either. (She hadn't telephoned.) Instead I spent two days writing thank-you notes at the kitchen table. I probably wasted hours staring out at the parking lot towards the spire of Holy Trinity, hoping Tony wouldn't call and wondering what I would say if he did.

I could no longer postpone thinking about California. I would have to give him a better answer than I had and, if I did not want to hurt him, the answer would have to be yes. But what about my apartment and Otis and Cal's? What about money? What little I'd saved I'd taken with me to Florence, and that was now running low. I'd left $35 in the apartment, but it would go to pay Janice for Otis's Little Friskies. I wasn't sure whether Cal's would have me back. They'd given me bereavement leave of sorts, but I hadn't called or written to say when I'd be returning. I was probably in a mess there. But I just kept on staring at the parking lot, ball pen poised above the black-edged notelets. I missed New York and I did not want to leave it. I didn't want to go to California and was probably going there. I hated Florence yet I could not uproot myself and go. Vinnie, down on Chesapeake Bay, Travis and Eva in Chicago or God knew where, Hadley leaving for Europe, Tony for the coast. America was all departures then: farewell dinners and scattered lives. A place in which not even my own family stayed put any more.

By the weekend we were prostrate with the continuing heat wave. Mosquitoes hurled themselves all night against the screens as, sweating, we threw aside the sheets. Early Sunday morning it rained, and we all slept through our alarms and no one made it to Mass. After lunch, Solange and I resolved to tackle the metal cabinet. Its ancient odours hit me as soon as I turned the key in the lock: metal and mothballs, dry-cleaned fabrics, fur and Emeraude. It was a potent familiar preserve, an Egyptian tomb sealed up by Aunt Bernie the day she went into hospital all those years ago. I handed the stamps over to Bobby who protested but took them without much of a struggle. I found the deed to the apartment; Vinnie's graduation photo; a pressed rose from the corsage Aunt Bernie had worn on the day of my graduation; an old stock cube; some Canadian coins from a pilgrimage with Sadie and Margaret to Saint Ann de Beaupré in 1941; a picture of me and Aunt Bea on my First Holy Communion; three pairs of brown gloves; the hat with the pheasant feather which I playfully placed on Kevin's head and made him scream; my freshman-reception dress and four costumes for the Infant of Prague who had mysteriously disappeared; Aunt Bernie's ten- and twenty-year service pins from the Number Two Mill; a rosary, a Marian Missal, brand-new; an Imitation of Christ, and *The Official Ritual Manual of the Ladies' Auxiliary of the Ancient Order of Hibernians, Organized 1895*, and inscribed with my grandmother's name and a picture of Our Lady of Limerick on the frontispiece. There were the Mill photographs, which I kept; newspaper clippings of Vinnie's prize-winning exam results and of Father Happny's farewell party; eighty-four holy cards, many from the jubilee years of various nuns. Seven dresses; two suits; a pair of black overshoes and the muskrat coat. On the floor in a box of shoes which must have been purchased in the early fifties, I found three sepia photographs framed in warped grey cardboard, wrapped in newspaper and fastened with elastics. One was of my father's first-grade class, one of barefoot Mill workers, none of them over fifteen, one of my grandfather with the Florence fire department, and one of Aunt Bernie with an overseer and fellow operatives. There were a couple of Vinnie's rare family snaps and even a few bare trees, telegraph poles and trash cans. Maybe she valued them after all.

I spread the pictures on the bed and looked at them for a long time. I felt helpless, useless, paralyzed. I stretched out beside them and stared at the ceiling. When Solange woke me with a cup of black coffee and a Hostess Twinkie she said I had been crying, but I denied this.

'It's turned cooler,' she said. 'Hurricane season'll be here 'fore you know it. It was terrible two years ago. Bobby show you the pictures?'

'Yes.' They'd reminded me of the devastation caused by Hurricane Carol when I was a child. Nora and I standing by the kitchen window, holding each other and crying as we watched the maples, elms and black pines crashing to the ground. The atmosphere that afternoon had the same sinister quiet.

'I'm going to change all the beds.'

'OK.' I collected the photographs. 'I'll give you a hand.'

'That's all right, Rose. Well, maybe you could make your bed.'

'No, no. I'll strip this one if you'll get the sheets.'

I put the photos aside and began to peel back the bedclothes. Solange left and came back.

'Wouldn't you know it. Not enough clean sheets.'

'Oh hell. Want me to go to the laundromat?'

'Maa-yy-bee. Hey, wait a minute. There's a big package on the top shelf of the cabinet. Looks like linen.'

I'd missed it completely. We removed the sheets from their multiple coverings of plastic.

'Jeeze, some of these have never been opened. Look at that. Brand-new.'

'Christmas presents from Wigram Boott.'

'Hey, Rosie, don't use them old ones. They look all yellowed.'

'No, I like them. I remember them.'

'Sure you don't want me to wash 'em? Easy as pie, you know.'

'Thanks, Solange. It's all right.'

'Okie-doke.'

I carried the sheets to the transport room. I was glad to get away from the metal cabinet which reminded me of an upright coffin. I stripped the bed, being careful not to wake Kevin who was having his nap. I unfolded a sheet with a scalloped edge, embroidered with an M. My grandmother's handiwork, or even Aunt Bernie's. She'd been a whizz with the needle once. I smoothed out the ivory-coloured fabric which would turn blue-white when it was laundered. I made hospital corners the way Nora had taught me. I opened the second sheet and unfurled it high into the air like a sail. As I did so, dozens of ten- and twenty-dollar bills floated over the bed and around my ears. Some whirled like maple seeds. Others performed the slow dance of milkweed and settled softly by my feet. I picked one up. I picked up another and another. One was a fifty. She'd stashed the money in the sheet and forgotten all about it. Or maybe she intended things to end this way.

Quietly I collected the money from the floor, the dresser, the windowsill, and the sleeping body of my first cousin once removed.

PART II

PART II

16

This Time

The path dips sharply at the approach to the sacred grove. The rocks are like steps. It is difficult to tell if they are natural or man-made, holy antiquities or merely rocks.

What building blocks remain are covered, like everything else, with a fine ochre dust. As the sun sets and the shadows lengthen they will turn to orange and finally, in the witchy twilight, to pink. I know because I came here yesterday evening. But now it is afternoon and lizards frisk among the ruins, if they are ruins. The lizards I recognize. They are like the ones that live in the bamboo ceiling of Aphrodite's house.

I kick aside charred sticks with my foot. Someone made a fire last night. Many fires have been made here. Five years ago a crew from Athens found bones on this site. Human bones. They took them away to be analyzed and never came back.

I climb to the top of the low wall which continues a few hundred yards to the left then crumbles away into the dry yellow gravel which miraculously supports the sage and wild thyme that perfume the air.

Behind me is a mulberry tree. The ground beneath it is stained red with the fallen fruit, as if there have been hundreds of tiny murders. No rain has come to wash the stains away. Eva said once that if you sleep beneath a mulberry tree you will have beautiful dreams, premonitory dreams, even.

Over the hill straight ahead of me is the sea: translucent aquamarine along the white sand shore, then shadowed black by the underwater rocks where octopuses hide and urchins cluster, then sapphire just beyond the two small peninsulas where all day the kaikis come and go, then indigo flecked white to the edge of the flawless horizon. To the south is a large island, Naxos, maybe, its highest peak just visible above the heat haze which perpetually surrounds it.

On either side of the bay the mountains rise, jagged, irregular, bare. They are at once protective and oppressive. They call and then forbid.

243

They are like a warm body whose scent mingles with that of the scorched thyme. Across the valley is a little white church with a red roof. Near by is a single palm tree. I can see them both from Aphrodite's patio.

The hills are covered with tall white flowers whose elegant spikes are tossed in the constant wind. They have no leaves, no companions but each other. They rise up out of the rocks and the cracked soil and the ochre dust, viviparous, eternal. Later I will gather armsful of them and carry them back to the house where I will study their self-sufficiency.

But now I will spread my towel and lie down under the mulberry tree in hopes of beautiful dreams.

Something is missing here. What is it? Memories of this bleached landscape scramble my reasoning processes. I long to surrender to it, but am made self-conscious by its beauty. I am unworthy of such loveliness. I spoil the sensuous perfection of the environment. I am an irritant, unsightly. It would like to be rid of me. Already the old gods plan my eviction.

I wait for sleep. In the branches above my head the cicadas make wild atonal music. It is mad but restful. At the house next to Aphrodite's, cockerels join in an antiphonal chorus with friends and enemies across the valley. Dogs bark. Music comes from the direction of the beach. The island is never quiet.

I move my sunburned legs into the shadows. The afternoon seems endless, though I know that night comes quickly here. Suddenly a blue curtain will fall, tinting the world with its arcane light.

I realize now what is missing. There were columns once, there where the rocks divide and the path continues down to the beach. What happened to the columns?

I am disturbed by voices, but I do not open my eyes. I hear footsteps, sandals slipping and stumbling on the rocks, a man and a woman speaking French and moving in the direction of the beach and the taverna. Again I sleep, but like an animal, not completely. Some inner guard keeps watch. The heat covers me like a blanket. I am a child in a cradle of heat.

The tumble of loose rocks seems part of the dream I am having. Bare feet are almost silent, especially if their soles are hardened by the terrain in which they are at home and their step is as sure as the long-haired goats I have seen on the mountain.

'We'll have to do something about that sunburn, dear.'

I open my eyes and there you are.

'I guess I should have worn a hat.' Instantly I am the friendly American, despite the aching in my head and limbs.

'You should have worn a kaftan too. Why didn't you borrow Aphrodite's? It's hanging behind the curtain in the bedroom.'

You squat beside me in the dust, arms resting on your knees, legs drawn up under a green sarong. I would rise if I could, throw aside this heat blanket that has grown so heavy.

'How do you know where Aphrodite's kaftan is?'

'Because I live in Aphrodite's house.'

'I didn't know – '

'Well, now you do. You're not alone.'

Smile at me. Please smile at me like that again.

'I've seen you before.'

No response. 'Don't worry, you can keep the big bed. I prefer the floor. Can you stand?'

'You know something, I'm not really sure.'

'Let's see.' You extend your hand, the nails of which are beautifully manicured like a woman's. I stare at it, probably with a stupid expression.

'C'mon, up you get. Hup!'

I am yanked to my feet. The rocks begin to rotate. I am steadied by the grip on my forearm, so tight it hurts.

'All right?'

I don't say anything. I am looking at the deep lines on either side of a mouth marred only by the sardonic expression on the full lips. I want to ask a question, but I'm taking too long to frame it. I'm distracted by the nose with its suggestion of a hook, the saurian bone structure beneath the thin tight skin, lank hair bleached by the sun, copper-coloured eyes which are all the more interesting for not being blue. Blue, I am thinking, would have been just too much.

'Hey!' You give me a little shake.

'You're an actor, aren't you?'

'Never mind that. Just come along, there's a good girl.'

'Where are we going?'

'Aphrodite's house. Can you make it?'

'Yes. What's wrong with me?'

'Sunstroke probably. You'll have a bad night then everything'll be fine.'

'My dark glasses – '

'Got 'em.' You put your arm around my waist.

'I'm Rose.'

'I realize that.'

*

245

'Don't eye that Scrabble game. I'm not fond of it, and you're in no condition to play, anyway.'

'I just wondered what it was doing here.'

'Arrived *au bateau* like the rest of us, I expect.'

'It's in English.'

'Aphrodite is an American, like your dear self. Are you drinking your infusion?'

'Yes. What is it?'

'We're very inquisitive.'

'I want to learn.'

'Very well, it's called dichtoma. Common as dirt in all of Greece, though each area has its own particular variety. Ace for the blood and bladder. Here is madam's toast.'

'What's this?'

'Tahini. And that is honey.'

'I know what that is.'

'Good. I will now withdraw to the other room to meditate.'

'Wait!'

'Yeeesss?' You pirouette and abruptly stop.

'How did you make the toast? There's no electricity.'

'No, but there is *gas*. If you look out of the kitchen window you will see one of the *tanks* which are delivered to our resourceful Aphrodite every month. The tank is connected by means of a *tube* to the gas ring. Ah, you haven't noticed the gas ring. Try opening your *eyes*, Rose, instead of asking busy people a lot of irritating questions. See ya.'

'Are we refreshed after our little snooze?'

'What are you doing?'

'I'm preparing to rub your skin with aloe.'

'But that's a cactus.'

'No, it is a succulent, used for millennia for healing the skin.'

'What are you doing now?'

'I am removing the sheet. Please don't feign modesty. Your health is at stake.'

'Ooh, it's nice.'

'Yes, dear. Now roll over. And don't look at me like an affronted rabbit. I'm trying to help you.'

'Thank you. I know.'

'I've seen you before.'

'Anything is possible.'

'You were in a movie.'

'Poor girl's hallucinating.' Delivered in an aside to an imaginary audience. A favoured mannerism. 'I prescribe French bread and a little pigeon.'

'I did see you.'

'Just rest. You'll recover in time.'

'The film was shot down there, wasn't it – where I met you? Everyone was chasing you around in a kind of dance.'

'Her condition is worse than I suspected.' Another aside. 'We'll have to amputate.'

'But there were columns in the film – like a ruined temple.'

'Made out of plasterboard. All fake. Built by Georgios next door. Georgios is the garbage man.'

'I had a friend once who was always finding treasures in the garbage.'

'Were you one of them?'

'In a way. Isn't the sacred grove real?'

'Oh, it's real, all right. It's just not sacred and never has been. Of course Jackson and Aphrodite thought it was. They would, wouldn't they? Divine manifestations, Bacchic rites, you name it. The Naxians and the Parians and a few gods over from Delos for a weekend break – all venting their libidos and blood-lust. That's why she gave him money to make the movie. They thought they were re-creating some pagan religious ceremony.'

'So you *were* in the film. What's your name?'

'Call me Miles.'

'How did you know I was Rose?'

'I read the note your friend left for you. I'm not above that sort of thing, so consider yourself warned.'

'You know Hadley?'

'Haven't had the pleasure, though the lady's reputation precedes her.'

'So it does.' You seemed to find it cheeky and fun to adopt an unearned superiority over your fellow men. 'You're English.'

'Yes, God help me.' Eyes raised to heaven. Profile shown to great advantage.

This is the evening's entertainment: we take mats out on to the walled and whitewashed patio where we lie and smoke grass and stare at the roof of our world-tent. The sky is so crowded with stars I doubt the gods could squeeze in another. We can make our way along the footpath by their light alone. You show me Arcturus which I've never seen before. It is low in the south-west, its elegant point cut off by the horizon. Overhead the Milky Way spans half the sky. For the first time I see that it is truly milk. Fiery milk. A celestial pathway whose radiance makes it impossible to stay vertical. The only way to bear such a vision is in a position of complete surrender.

You tell me how these distant fires – a hundred thousand million galaxies each with a hundred thousand million stars – are flying away from each other at the rate of millions of miles per second, dying sparks from the primal explosion, cooling and spreading, a universe rushing apart, fleeing itself, fleeing to no end, falling, and falling nowhere, never landing, nowhere to land. A terrible immensity, yet I am not terrified.

'Even in the Sahara the stars aren't this good. Not as close, not as intense.'

'You've travelled a lot?'

'Yes.'

'Every continent?'

'Haven't seen Antarctica. That's next.'

'I never left the East Coast of America. Until now.'

'Don't think it doesn't show.'

Basouki music comes from Georgios's house where every window is alight.

'There's a radio reprieve at weekends. They can play them as loud as they like – and as late.'

'Well, why not? They seem to work very hard. They should enjoy themselves.'

'Don't worry, they do.'

'There are guns in the morning.'

'Hunting season.'

'That's much worse than the radios.'

'You disapprove of firearms?'

'I'm a pacifist.'

'You're silly.'

'Miles, let's not argue.'

'Take a look at your teeth, Roseate. You're an omnivore, not a frugarian. You kill to live, only you pay someone else to do the killing for you. Americans are good at pretending they're not killers. You pay someone to do your killing like you wage your wars in other people's countries. Neat. Of course the Vietcong will win. They're Buddhists. Their brains aren't muddled by worrying about their killer image. They know they can baffle the giant.'

'Are you a Buddhist?'

'In my way.'

'Is that why you wear that little skull around your neck?'

'No. I just like being reminded of death. It warms my heart, gets me through many a bad night.'

'Your own death or other people's?'

'That depends. Rose, do you want this joint or not?'

The house is very old. Hundreds of layers of whitewash have rounded and softened the angles and corners so that from the outside parts of it look like an Arp sculpture. The inside is a white womb. Its three rooms are each at slightly different levels and have no connecting doors. It is necessary to go outside to pass from the big bedroom to the kitchen or from the kitchen to the small guest-room. There is no plumbing. We defecate in the open behind the bamboo grove, and the sun dries our faeces like it does an animal's. Water must be carried from the well. There is an outdoor sink by the side of the house, and a shower fed by a tank on the roof. The red doors are never locked. There is no telephone. Two small fireplaces are tucked into the wall at chest-level. If one works the other doesn't. No one knows why. The place is lit by candles and oil lamps which must be filled every three days. The ceiling is made of bamboo which is supported by worm-eaten wooden beams and stuffed with seaweed for insulation.

'I've never seen such a *particular* house.'

'Clarify, please.'

We eat breakfast under the eucalyptus tree. I am still recovering, allowing myself to be waited on.

'Every object seems to be chosen and placed with great care. Sometimes I'm afraid to touch anything.'

'Aphrodite is an artist. She has what's called an aesthetic sense, perhaps you've heard of that. Oh, excuse me, I forgot you number cineastes among your acquaintances.'

'It's almost like a temple.'

'She has a strong personal vision.'

'You mean she hasn't let herself be influenced?'

'Oh, she's been influenced – and by some pretty appalling types.'

'You take a very dim view of most people.'

'You've noticed.'

'Are you a misanthrope?'

'Mmm – fifty-five per cent, I'd say. More Lapsang Souchong?'

Long silence.

'Speaking of particular, have you seen the Papadopolus hoard?'

'No.'

'Then come with me.' You seize my hand, I feel a hot shock of contact. But you don't seem to notice it. I do not affect you the way you affect me.

'Here.' You part the bedroom curtains I wouldn't dare touch. Clearly you are at home here. You open a trunk covered by some fabric embroidered in bright circles enclosing tiny mirrors. Inside are more fabrics, beautiful and exotic, from all over the Balkans and the Far East. Submerged in the fragrant heap is a silver box, very old, which you remove and carry to the window. You lift its ornately worked cover to show me jewels tangled and gleaming – rings, earrings, bracelets, brooches, necklaces.

'Where did she *get* these?'

'Quite a little collector is our Aph. Some were her grandmother's. Look at this.'

You lift a black necklace from the box and dangle it in the sunlight like a glossy wriggling snake.

'What is it?'

'Jet. Very old. *Very*. Want to try it on?'

'No.' I back away.

'Go on, it won't bite.' You hold it closer to my face, ensnaring me with the shining facets of its beads. For some reason I don't understand you really want me to wear the thing.

'I can't.' I shake my head. 'It's too special.'

'You're right. It is too special, for you.'

When I see the ocean through a diving mask it is as though someone has shown me a world in which I could be content for ever. I float, mesmerized. Across the dappled rocks and sand the marine life slowly glides. The seaweed throws its dark-green hair from side to side, while schools of bright fish – plaid, polka-dotted, pin-striped – flick in syncopation to the flickering light. The rhythm is so entirely new, so entirely old. It induces a kind of amniotic trance. This is the first time I have seen the sea bed. I hold your hand and let you guide me towards the glittering reef.

You squeeze my fingers and point to a tangerine starfish, an anemone waving its tiny red arms, amorphous black sponges that cling to the rocks, heaps of abandoned urchin shells in mauve and green which are octopuses' gardens and which, when scattered, expose the shy, sad-eyed resident in his lair.

We have reached the point where the bay meets the open sea. Suddenly the fish are gone. There are no rocks, no dancing light, only deep-blue nothingness. It frightens me. I am too scared to go on and swim back towards the populated world. But you continue. Further out into the undifferentiated blue. This is the part you like best.

'I'm going to teach you about urchins. Are you listening? First of all, don't tread on them.'

We stand dripping and shiny on the shore. The masks have left deep red circles on our faces.

'Got it.'

'So pay close attention. This chap here with the long spikes, he's a boy. He tastes revolting. Yukko. So back you go, old sport.' The urchin traces a high arc and lands in the sea. 'And this one with the shorter spikes is a girl. But it's very difficult to tell them apart under water. Water magnifies. You may have noticed. So look carefully before you scoop them up. I · will now demonstrate to you how to pry them loose with a flat knife. Observe . . .'

'Do you like them?'

'So-so.'

'Eat them anyway. They're good for you. You look peaky to me still, in spite of the suntan.'

'I'm a victim of urban blight and decay.'

'You certainly are a dummy when it comes to nature.'

'You're not. What do you do, anyway?'

'I run a mime academy.'

'Please be serious.'

'Why?'

'Then be a sport.'

'All right, I'm a psychiatrist.'

'You're too young.'

'I'm a prodigy. You have very long legs.'

'I'm an American. They're my right. Come on, Miles, tell me.'

'OK, if it will shut you up. I'm a medical student.'

'You don't seem like one.'

'Tell me, from your vast experience of medical students, why I don't.'

'Well, you're not a square. And you're very negative.'

251

'Merely objective.'

'Are you "objective" about me?'

'Listen, Rose, I'm going to tell you something because I'm a nice guy. You don't have the least idea how to live, or how to look after yourself. You're sloppy, you just let things happen. Oh, don't give me that wounded look. Eat your urchins.'

You got up at dawn. I heard you. You left the house to go swimming. When I am brushing my teeth at the sink I find your sponge bag. Unusual. You always put it carefully away and rinse the sink, leaving not a trace of your presence. But today here it is and you are absent and I cannot resist unzipping the smart leather case and looking inside. Everything is in miniature: shampoo bottle, half full; soap case, rinsed, pristine, unencrusted; a tiny razor in its disguised container, an orange stick, an emery board, an expensive set of nail clippers with multiple extensions; a pumice stone, a brown bottle containing scented oil, a white toothbrush that looks like ivory and has real hair bristles, a round box of black tooth powder, an expensive after-shave that smells of limes. Aha, you indulge yourself. But how organized you are, how well yet minimally equipped, how experienced a traveller. I sniff the inside of the bag. I hesitate then zip it up. I replace it exactly where you left it.

'Miles, how old are you?'

'Twenty-two. You should do something about those cuticles, dear.'

'You're very critical of me.'

'Be glad. You could do with some improvement. Clearly no one's ever cared enough about you to suggest this before. By the way, why are *you* here?'

'I'm on vacation. My aunt died. She left me a little money, and I'm squandering it.'

'Really? Then where are my silk ties and balls of opium and gold cigarette cases?'

'You don't smoke.'

'More than I can say for you. Put that nasty thing out. Now what about my pressies?'

'I'll get you some worry beads.'

'But I never worry.'

'It can be arranged.'

'You don't have the equipment. Give us a kiss.'

'No.'

252

'Oh, pretty please, just a little one so Milesie knows you're not angry
with him.'

'Oh well, all right.'

'Stop! I said a little one. How old are you?'

'Twenty-eight.'

'Liar. How do you know Aphrodite?'

'I don't, although I met her once a long time ago. In fact, I came here
looking for Hadley. We were supposed to meet.'

'Ah yes, your closest friend. Who ran out on you.'

'She is on her honeymoon.'

'And do you intend to follow her and hubby?'

'I don't know. I haven't given any thought to my future.'

'You should. At thirty there can't be much left of it. Kiss me again.
Harder, for God's sake.'

The mountains rise straight out of the sand. The sea is so dazzling
that not even sunglasses can protect the eyes from its razory sparkle.
At the far end of the beach and half-way up the hill, a taverna is built
into the rock. Across its foundations the word 'TABEPVA' is scrawled
in red like a revolutionary slogan. Its large verandah faces west, and
a crude path winds steeply to its entrance. Although it is lunchtime,
there is not a sign of life there, save for the cats who lounge on
the terrace wall. There are few people on the beach. They are all
naked.

'Miles, Miles, stop, please!'

'Stop what?'

'The paraplegic imitations.'

'OK, how about this?'

'No, no. Cut the orangutan.'

'Can't Junior have any fun? How am I supposed to pass the time?
I'm so easily bored.'

'Please, it's horrible.'

'Then why are you laughing?'

'Miles, everyone is staring.'

'I enjoy making a spectacle of myself. It's one of my few little
pleasures.'

'Walk on your hands, then.'

'The thought of my willie dangling upside down depresses me,
somehow.'

'Then do your karate or your ballet.'

Several jetés, followed by kicks and abrupt turns.

'It's no good, you can't bounce in sand. I'll have to go back to the paraplegic.'

'Miles, don't. It's cruel.'

'What's cruel? It's cathartic. In fact, it's kind. I'm a very kind person, one of the few who dares to be kind. To be really kind you have to break taboos. You're too conventional to be really kind.'

'That's very twisted logic, Miles.'

'Unlike yours, of course, Rose Reason – all sanity and grace, mistress of linear and lateral thinking.'

'How come you want to be a doctor when you're so misanthropic?'

'Only fifty-five per cent, remember? Besides, I'm curious. It's my one failing.'

'You seem to despise everyone.'

'I'm always looking for reasons not to. It's not my fault if they can't be found. Let's have lunch, sweetiepie.'

'I don't want to be a doctor.' Glum expression. Toys with octopus tentacles.

'So what *do* you want to do?'

'Research. Disease is much more interesting than health.'

'Nothing to do with helping mankind, of course.'

'It would only get in the way of observation.'

'That doesn't mean you'll do experiments on animals, does it?'

'What a petal it is. No, dear. Even Miles would prefer to avoid vivisection. However, it is unavoidable.'

'What makes you so sure?'

'Listen, toots. You'd like a cure for inherited cancer, right?'

'Of course.'

'Well, it is my unpleasant duty to inform you that without vivisection the oncogene would never have been discovered.'

'The oncogene?'

'Christ, the ignorance of people. And you dare get on your high horse. The oncogene is the cancer gene. It was discovered in the twenties through experiments on mice. This led ultimately to the discovery that DNA was the basic genetic material. Then came Watson and Crick. Even you must know who they are. Eventually the scientific ogres found that the oncogenes in chickens and mice are the same as those in human tumours. This is hardly trivial. They're now working on localizing the genes for a bowel cancer which kills nineteen thousand people a year in Britain alone. Like I said, not trivial.'

'OK, but what about dioxin – agent orange – right? You've heard of that? Well, it was developed and tested on laboratory animals before it was used on the Vietnamese. If it's animals today, it'll be people tomorrow.'

'Civilization is founded on cruelty. All progress demands sacrifice, usually of the weakest.'

'I don't believe that. Scientists are whores.'

'They're certainly peculiar people.'

'They sell themselves to drug companies and chemical companies and to the nuclear industry and the military. The collusion of science with capitalism is the cause of everything that's wrong with the planet.'

'Sorry, but you'll have to face it: there are certain poisons we simply can't do without any more. For example, PCBs – one of the most toxic substances ever made and one of the most stable compounds known. Stays in the environment for years. Doesn't break down. (Not unlike me, come to think of it.) Anyway, it's in all electrical wiring, every appliance, every fluorescent light fixture. This society would grind to a halt without it. And one more item. Let me remind you that it's the scientists who've enabled women – for the first time ever – to take control of their own lives. The Pill has liberated them more than the feminists have.'

'You're armed to the teeth, aren't you, Miles?'

'An arsenal of information. I've read and studied, hard subjects, understand, *hard*. I've applied myself. Consequently I've learned a thing or two. Which can hardly be said of you. Of course I understand you went to a fifth-rate school.'

'I'm going.'

'Sit down! I haven't finished. What about record players? Bet you like those. Vinyl! Poison! What about the colour of your nice red shirt? Dyes! Poison! Without the science whores you probably wouldn't be alive to plague me with your pastel waffle. You'd have died at two of some minor infection.'

'Miles, I'm getting tired of this abuse.'

'And I'm tired of abusing you. Let's shut up and look at the view.'

At night the house is like a church. After the climb up the rocky path, we light the candles and the oil lamps and burn incense from Tinos where there is a famous statue of the Black Virgin covered in diamonds. The incense looks like pale-brown pebbles and emits a sizzling smoke that smells of allspice, lemons and wood. Tonight it is too windy to lie on the patio. We sit at the rickety kitchen table and eat a stew of chickpeas and aubergines followed by slices of watermelon.

'You're a good cook, Miles.'

'Thank you. The weather's going to change.'

'How can you tell?'

'It was hot and damp today. Then the wind came up. Now it's dying down. Did you see those clouds in the north?'

'Yes. But you know I don't attach any interpretation to things like clouds – unless I see faces in them. I've lived too long with brick and concrete. I'm out of touch.'

'We'll have to remedy that.'

'I'll do the dishes.'

'Sit! You're not a well woman. We'll just leave them outside in the rain.'

'Is it raining?'

'Listen.'

'You're awfully grown-up for twenty-two.'

'I told you. I'm a prodigy.'

'You certainly are when it comes to checkers. That's the fourth time in a row you've beaten me.'

'All I can say to console you is that I was taught by the best. By the way, we call it draughts.'

'Who was that?'

'Mrs Vera Zahl.'

'I'm jealous.'

'Don't be. She's seventy-three. We play every Thursday afternoon – chess, cribbage, backgammon, gin, bezique, you name it. We eat chocolates and drink port and listen to Schubert – her late husband's favourite.'

'How did you meet her?'

'She's my landlady. I call her Madam Zed. She likes that.'

'Where is she?'

'London. Her husband died years ago and left her with a Victorian pile near the Cromwell Road. She couldn't afford to run it, so she turned it into a boarding house. Men Only.'

'Really? Why?'

'She doesn't like women. Thinks they're devious.'

'And what do you think of that?'

'Pass.'

'How do you manage without them?'

'I don't have to manage. My mistresses all have flats of their own. Besides, there are times when I like being unavailable.'

'And do you cook dinners for these mistresses and empty their rubbish and bring them tea and toast in bed?'

'Naturally. They deserve it.'

'Then you run and hide.'

'Now, now . . . whoops! Won again. You're improving, though.'

'Miles, what are you doing here?'

'Playing draughts with you.' You blow me a kiss.

'Miles, you know what I mean. How do you know Aphrodite?'

'I met her when we made that silly film. She asked me back. I visit once or twice a year. We went to Athens together. She stayed for another week and I returned. I thought I'd explained all this. Heavens, you're slow.'

'Then how do you know Jackson?'

'Jackson, hmm . . .' Exaggerated clearing of throat and looking as if to offer an aside to the invisible audience. Empty theatre, however.

'Didn't you like the film?'

'I have no patience with amateurism. There's far too much of it where I come from.'

'I thought it was beautiful.'

'I suppose it kept Jackson off the streets and out of the lavatories.'

'You're very fond of him.'

'What gives you that idea?'

'I'm getting to know you. Anyway, I like him too.'

'He's a dreadful monster.'

The rain taps at the roof like a thousand tiny fingers, wanting to tell us something, to remind us – of what? One of the orange lizards scampers up the wall to its ceiling nest. The candles gutter.

'Pour me another glass of that wine, Miles.'

'There you are, my darling. Aphrodite gets it from the farmer over the hill. It's his own brew. He won't sell any but he gives some away.'

'That's how life should be. Mmm, it's so good. And no hangover.'

'Put this shawl around you. It's turned a bit nippy.'

'That's nice. Now kiss me good-night, Miles.'

'There we are.'

'I'm going to bed.'

'I'm coming with you.'

'This is strange, Miles.'

'Not at all. People do it every day.'

'It feels incestuous.'

'Why?'

'Don't make fun of me, but you're like my brother. I hardly know you and you're a very peculiar person who I don't understand at all, but I feel very close to you.'

'Ditto.'

'The candle's gone.'

'Turn over, Rose.'

The little church with the red roof stands beside the dirt road that leads down to the beach. It is just wide enough for two motor scooters or the odd jeep. A donkey is tethered by the church wall, the shady side. He is there every afternoon. We seldom take this road because we prefer the shortcut to the sea via the sacred grove – which you insist is not sacred.

'There are so many churches here. Look, you can see seven from this hill alone.'

'They're private chapels. This one belongs to Georgios's family.'

'It's locked. How do we get in?'

'Yours truly knows where the key is hidden.' You put your finger to your lips.

'How did you find out?'

'Not telling. Let's see, third wall-stone from the right, two down. Like a safe. Aha, here it is.'

'Will they mind?'

'Trust me. I'm a doctor.'

Inside it's cool with grey light, and I can smell the incense we burn at the house. There is one main room with an altar, candles, an icon black with smoke and age, and a small space behind a drawn curtain which is a changing room for the priest. Everything is simple, humble not very clean. On a low table are tapers and some matches. A flame burns in a red glass lamp. Four wooden chairs are lined up before the altar. You lock the door, straddle one of the chairs and fix me with a look. I feel nervous, as though I'm about to be interrogated by the secret police.

'Now, Rose, you're going to tell me everything.'

'Why should I?'

'Because I love you and I want to know. It will be good for you to confess. You'll thank me. You should never have left the Catholic Church. However, I'll try to repair what damage I can.'

'But why must I tell you all at once? Shouldn't these things emerge gradually, over time, as we get to know each other?'

'Life is short, Rose. You'll never amount to anything until you gaze into your dark half and invite your shadow to tea.'

'Miles, you're not talking like you at all. And what does that mean – "amount to anything"? You know I'm not ambitious.'

'I'm referring to your soul.'

'You don't believe in souls.'

'No, but *you* do.'

'I do not – well, not in a religious sense.'

'Once a soul, always a soul.'

'Oh, please!'

'Think of me as your confessor, as this Father Leahy you mentioned. It'll be fun. Think of it as fun.'

'I don't like talking about myself. I feel shy.'

'Nonsense. Everyone likes to talk about themselves. Now be a sport, Rose, and spill the beans to Father Leahy. Don't you want to please me?'

'I thought I did please you.'

'No resting on laurels. Confess, there's a good girl.'

'Help me. Ask questions.'

'What is the most reprehensible thing you've done in your life?'

'I abandoned my aunt.'

'Explain.'

'She'd been good to me in her way. I deserted her when she needed me most.' I cannot tell you about Foxie. I cannot say that I thought Aunt Bernie deserved to be abandoned.'

'Ingrate. Why did you do that?'

'I did it for love.'

'*Father.*'

'I did it for love, *Father.*'

'Happens to the best of us. However, this is a very big blot on your copy book. Now, was he worth it?'

'I guess he was. He was interesting, a good person, really, but a little confused.'

'In other words, a pillock. Oops, sorry. That could be a description of yourself. Perhaps you're projecting.'

'I thought you were a priest, Miles. Not a shrink.'

'Priests – the good ones like Father Leahy – are doctors of the soul.'

'You'll be pleased to hear I lost him in the process. Perhaps that constitutes sufficient punishment.'

'That's what you think.'

259

'I was with my aunt in the end, though. I came back, for her death, I mean. I think she was glad.'

'And . . .'

'I was accused of hastening her death.'

'To get the money for this holiday?'

'Miles, please.'

'*Father*.'

'*Father* – oh, *stop* it, Miles. The money was an accident, a fluke. There wasn't much of it anyway, about seven hundred dollars. I only tried to spare her more suffering.'

'Always a mistake.'

'I forced the doctor to increase her morphine dose. I refuse to believe that was wrong of me.'

'Hubris, hubris. Another black mark. They're adding up fast.'

'She was terminal. She was going to die anyway.'

'That's what they all say. Especially when they see an easy way to bag two weeks in Greece and probably a bit of nooky as well. Are those tears I see? I told you this would be fun.'

'Fun for you.'

'Not only me. In the end you'll be happy, much happier than I'll ever be. You'll thank me for bullying you. Now carry on.'

'I never told her about the boy, although she guessed. Not much escaped Aunt Bernie. I don't think she ever believed my story about working in an art gallery either. She knew all the time I was something like a waitress.'

'More lies. Are you even sure you're who you say you are?'

'Actually, I changed my name.'

'Aha, an imposter!' Extravagant aside. 'I thought as much. So come on, who are you really? How did you come by this wild Irish name?'

I hesitate. I cannot get the words out. 'It was all to do with Confirmation. I didn't want to be confirmed. I didn't feel anything like a Soldier of Christ. I was a pacifist even then. But you can take a new name at Confirmation, so I thought: I'll take this opportunity and use it to my own advantage. I'll become another person. You see, I never liked my name.'

'Oh, get on with it.'

I take a deep breath. Even now I can't bear to tell you the whole truth about the real Rose. I promise myself I'll tell you later. Some day. Just not right now.

The little church is in shadows. The tapers have burned to puddles.

'Excuses, excuses, Frances Mullen, aka Rose. You don't learn from your mistakes, do you? A common failing. Your sins demand the ultimate penalty. Take off your clothes.'

'Here?'

'Where better? Do as I say. I have your best interests at heart.'

'I'm beginning to wonder.'

'Nonsense. No one's ever paid as much attention to you as I have and you know it.'

'It's too weird.'

'That's the point. Look, I'll spread the sarong. The floor's cold. Always thinking of you. Now come and lie down with me, sinner.'

Arcturus is sinking further into the south-west, though its tail is still visible. The wind has dropped, the clouds have vanished. There is no moon. The passage of the night is lit only by the Milky Way. Without the moon it is more than ever a veil of fire and milk: hot, cold, dense, thin, wide, shallow and deep.

'Don't sulk, darling. It was only a game.'

'You're good at games. I'm not.'

'That's true. Perhaps we should play one I can lose. Would that satisfy the female lust for revenge you've been trying so unsuccessfully to suppress?'

'You're on – and I'm not sulking. And I'm not vengeful, either.'

'All right, you're not. See how amenable I am?'

'OK, let's play. A game you can lose, remember.'

'I'm afraid there's only one game like that. The one we played this afternoon. No one can face up to their own past. Makes us all look a twit.'

'Give me your hand, Miles. You're always so warm, like you have extra blood. Tell me what you've done that's really bad.'

'I hardly know where to begin.'

'Begin with last spring and work backwards.'

'Last spring. Last spring. I had a part-time job in the hospital office. I was processing breast scans and was bored to death. One afternoon I was typing up a report when – how shall I put it? – the devil got into me. I can't explain; you know what I'm like when I'm bored. I took every tenth card and reversed the results. Got the idea from Caesar. I admit it's not very original.'

'Miles, what are you saying?'

'You wanted to know. You insisted. Look, here I am, losing. Aren't you glad?'

'Please don't tease.'

'I assure you I'm not teasing. This is for real, and I make no excuses, in which respect I have more integrity than you do. Yup, I sent off twenty falsified reports. Then I left the job.'

'I don't believe you.'

'All right, don't. But you certainly are hard to please. I had no idea you could be so difficult. Here was I thinking you were malleable, tender, responsive . . .'

'Miles, if you really did that, it means that there are – '

'Ten.'

'Ten woman who may have cancer and don't know it. And – '

'Ten.'

'Ten who were terrified for nothing.'

'Dawn breaks over Marblehead. Don't you love that expression?'

'I've never heard anything so awful. I know you're lying.'

'Think what you like.'

'It's not right to upset me with a story like that. It's unfair.'

'Darling, in the country I come from everything is unfair. Our way of life was founded on unfairness. You ought to visit sometime.'

'I'm going inside.'

'Rose! Stop. Come back. I'm sorry. I'm a brute.'

'Then you were making it up?'

'I was only attempting to purge you of pity and fear. That's very Greek, you know.'

'Don't do it again, Miles. If you do, I'll be really angry. It's too perverse.'

'OK. I promise. To tell the truth. It wasn't one of my better lies. I based it on a story I read in the *Evening Standard*. Would you like a substitute sin?'

'No. I don't like this game, if you really want to know.'

'What can I do, didums, to make it up to you?'

'Tell me about yourself. Your real self. What your childhood was like, what schools you went to, brothers and sisters, that kind of thing.'

'I was a foundling. Consequently my childhood was appalling and I have nothing more to say about it.'

'Oh Miles, that's terrible.'

'Slap in the gob with a wet kipper, you might say. I graduated from maladjusted child to disturbed adolescent. As for schools, I've seen a few. Fortunately I was quite cute, so eventually the right person ran after me.'

'Who was that?'

'No one interesting. But he was helpful. He saw I was intelligent and got me a decent education.'

'I should have realized you came from a deprived background.'

'Not deprived, dear. Twisted. Bent. Way outta shape.'

'No wonder you're misanthropic. It explains everything. Please tell me more.'

'Not now.'

'I understand, Miles. It's too painful. You will tell me, won't you?'

'At some point. Perhaps.'

'Yes. I see. It's all right. Whenever you feel ready.'

'God, what a sweet, sympathetic creature you are. I can see why you'd make a weaker man feel guilty. He wouldn't be able to bear it. He'd have to run away.'

'Perhaps you were better off without parents and siblings. Look at it that way. The family is the root of all fascism.'

You laugh out loud. 'Who taught you to say that?'

'No one taught me.'

'Rose, I adore you.'

For a long time now I have been unwell. Stricken with a mysterious and debilitating malady that overcomes me without warning, draining my limbs of energy, freezing my brain like an anaesthetic, covering my body like an insidious blanket being drawn over me. It starts at my feet and creeps up to my mouth, nose, eyes, the roots of my hair, until I am smothered alive.

I am in a foreign capital – Paris or London or Prague. I wander into the centre of the city and come to a large open square, somewhere grand and official and public, bearing the hallmarks of empire. Suddenly my strength leaves me. I fall down. I lie helpless on the pavement among the passers-by. No one helps me or even notices me. They hurry past intent on their private destinations, their secret plans. But none of this matters. I know my end is near. I try to take in every detail of what is around me. I am seeing it all for the last time. I look up at the sky where the clouds gather, group, and disperse. Slowly they mass in the south-west. They form themselves into a human face: sharp nose, celestial smile, coppery eyes. The vision grows and spreads until it encompasses the entire sky. I lie, straining to absorb every detail of the impassive expression. Straining, with near-sightless eyes . . .

'Wake up, please, immediately. Who are you?'

'What? I'm Rose.'

'Yes. Well, who is Rose?'

'I'm sorry. I feel very weak . . .'

'No excuse. Out of my bed, please. This minute.'

'Aphrodite!'

'That's me, all right. What are you doing here? Answer.'

'I'm Rose Mullen. I'm a friend of Hadley's. She told me – '

'Hadley's gone. Who said you could stay here, sleep in my bed? Ugh! Get out! Now! Where is my necklace? Tell me!'

'What? I'm very confused. Yes, yes, I'm out of the bed. Look. Completely out. I was having a dream.'

'Dream? I could care about your damn dreams. My money is gone, my necklace – the only thing I care about that was my great-grandmother's. What have you done with it?'

'I don't know. I mean, it can't be. Where is Miles?'

'Miles?'

'Miles. I don't know his last name. He's a friend of yours. He told me. He invited me, he said it would be all right. I was going to leave, but he said you wouldn't mind, that you were in Athens and that you wouldn't mind. Hadley had left. I didn't know what to do. I'd never been out of America. He must have gone swimming. He'll be back. We can discuss everything. We've taken good care of the house, see, it's nice and clean. We swept the floors and the patio every day. We bought you new oil for the lamps – '

'Fuck the oil! My necklace and money are gone. Get that through your head. The Greeks could not have done it. It's impossible. They are honest people. I haven't locked the door in twenty years. Nothing was ever taken, do you hear? Until *you*. You disgusting American girls who come here to screw Greek boys and in my bed. It's revolting. Now get out! No, don't you dare move. I will call the police. I'll have you put in jail. You come here, you foreigners, and you ruin this beautiful island. You pollute it, you grab everything you can. Nothing was ever taken before. Nothing!'

'Please don't yell.'

'Yell! I will yell. This is my house and I *will* scream. E-E-E-Y-A-A-A! Get out! Where is my necklace, my money? This person, this – '

'Miles.' I was trembling.

'*Miles? Miles?* You must explain, and pretty fast. What does he look like, this *Miles?*'

'He – looks – like – me.'

17

Florence

I never imagined that a boat trip on the Mediterranean could turn into an Arctic voyage. So I was unprepared for a night on the *Aegina*. I pictured deckchairs and copious blankets under which those without cabins could huddle while gazing at a panoply of stars. The daytime, I assumed, would be spent lounging in the sun while the Gulf of Corinth slid majestically past. Instead I found yellow and orange plastic chairs which cut into bare flesh and, when unoccupied, slid about the drenched surfaces colliding like dodgem cars.

I laid a towel and jacket on the cold metal floor amongst the other raggedy passengers, and, having failed to find a sheltered corner, tried to make myself as comfortable as I could. But after the first big gust met the first big wave I was wet and shivering. It was impossible to stay where I was. I found a dry sweater, gathered up my belongings and stuffed them into my suitcase. At least I was travelling light. I joined the other bedraggled wanderers of the ferry's inner passages, bars and washrooms, in search of somewhere I might sit until my coffee or Coca-Cola had been nursed to its last drop. Since I didn't bear the least resemblance to a first- or even second-class passenger, I could only sit in their privileged lounges until the staff began giving me hostile looks and asking with greater frequency if I wanted another drink.

After a sojourn indoors, I would take heart and venture on deck. Immediately I was sprayed and blown by a wind that would have done credit to the coast of Maine in February, and I would be forced back inside in search of a new bar.

What the hell, I thought, it's only one night. Brindisi will be warm, something will happen. Meanwhile I sat, damp and shivering, trying to read by the overhead lighting in the passageway. Why had I thought boats were romantic? I knew now why my father would not set foot on one unless he was building it, safe in dry dock. The blank restive hours were filled with waking dreams, not the sort you invoke but the kind that inflict themselves on you. There I was, passive victim. Every sort of free-range succubus and larva invaded my helpless brain.

I remembered, of all things, a sermon of Father Leahy's. 'We live,' he said, 'as though we thought we would never die.' But isn't that the point? I mean, how else can we live? It's that or be paralyzed by the spectre of our own corpse. I guess the latter was exactly what Father Leahy had in mind. Keep 'em good and scared. Consider me, for instance. If I had allowed myself full cognisance of my uncertain future, into what sort of spiritual abyss would I have fallen? The outlook was bleak, I knew. I assessed the probabilities and purposely ignored them. I was marginal again – and really, this time. It wasn't nice being broke and alone. It wasn't good without a friend. But there was also the elation that attends freedom. I proceeded on blind faith, straight into the gale of an anarchistic existence, trusting in my God-given right to ignore the facts and go by my roseate reason if it suited me.

I thought of those days on the island and felt I would never recover. Then the same events would be re-cast in a pink Aegean mode. Even the humiliation of being banished by Aphrodite to the smelly cement rooms behind the taverna acquired the dignity of high drama. But only after the fact. On the day itself, and all through the following night, I lay on my unmade cot and cried. I tormented myself with questions and puzzles, teasing out motives and explanations that only left me craving for more, like slaking a thirst with salt water. My initial feelings of rejection by the island now seemed horribly justified. I had been cast out. I lay on the shore with nothing but the sea before me. The islands were invisible behind a mantle of haze, deliberately hiding their grandeur, which was not for the likes of me.

The following morning, very early, there was a knock at the door. I could hear the usual sound of rifle fire in the distance. I sat up, certain that the owners of the taverna who rented these hovels had also come to evict me. But it was Aphrodite. She walked in after the second knock. Her greying hair was dishevelled. She wore a white antique nightie and a pair of glasses that magnified her black pupils and all the crinkly lines around her eyes. She was hasty and abrasive, but essentially kind. Like most Greeks, she said, she operated on a short fuse. She gushed apologies, wrung her hands and ran them through her cloud of hair while sitting on my bed, nervously arranging the covers. She had read the note from Hadley.

Was it really true that most of my money had also been stolen? It was terrible, unbelievable. I must forgive her bad manners. Money meant nothing to her, she was an artist. But she was upset about the necklace, she was sure I understood that. I did understand. How else, I asked, could she have been expected to react?

I must return with her, she said, to the house. There we would decide what to do, that is, if anything could be done. But first we would go for breakfast, for which she insisted she would pay. We were the only customers in the taverna, the change in the weather having driven away all the holiday-makers. There was a breeze, and the air was so clear that you could make out some of the mountain roads on Naxos. We took a table next to the wall and nearest the sea.

Aphrodite ordered coffee and yoghurt and a plate of the last figs, saying with a smile that this was what James Bond had for breakfast in *From Russia with Love*. She encouraged me to eat.

'I remember Miles,' she confessed. 'We all worked with Jackson on a movie. We made it just up there where the grove is.'

'I know. I recognized you. We met once in New York.'

'We did? You see, I don't remember these things. Miles arrived with Jackson and another American man. He was very noticeable, this Miles. You do look a little alike. Just a little. His face is much more predatory than yours. There is no predator in you.'

'I guess not.'

'Well, I'm a victim too. We are victims together. Don't frown, Rose Mullen, don't worry. You're in a mess, but I'll help you out.'

Again she invited me to return with her to the house. At first I hesitated, worried that I would find the sight of the well and the eucalyptus tree and those white rooms too painful. But neither could I face solitary confinement in a concrete cell, and so I said yes and thanked her, I hope graciously.

I spent three nights in the little room, lying on the floor, woken continually by cockerels, dogs, and the morning gunfire. During the day I went swimming in a sea that was suddenly cold. I visited the grove, but I could not remain. The movie mixed with my own memories of the place, and made me run as from a hail of poisoned arrows. Yet I was unable simply to pick myself up and leave the island.

'How much money do you have?' Aphrodite asked me.

'About thirty dollars and a return ticket to Boston.'

'You could almost do it for that – get home, I mean. But I said I'd help you. Here's the address of a decent cheap hotel in Athens, and here's a cheque for a hundred dollars. Please take it. I can afford it, provided you pay me back when you get to New York. I trust you. I think you've had a bad time. Please don't be stupid and refuse. You're also welcome to stay longer if you want.'

I didn't deserve this. I was an intruder in Aphrodite's house, and she treated me like a life-long friend. She even came with me to the boat.

'I have business in the port. I'm not doing you a favour really.'

For a long time after we left port the boat slid slowly past the island's east coast, most of which was uninhabited. There was the odd shepherd's hut, a couple of little churches and a network of paths leading down to the sea.

A short stocky woman in a black kerchief leaned over the rail beside me. She shouted and waved as tears streamed over her weathered cheeks. Her theatrical farewells continued long after we were out of sight of the town. I saw that no one was with her. Why did she go on waving and calling at the barren landscape? Then I understood. She was saying goodbye, not to anyone in particular, but to the island itself, bit by bit of it: to each promontory, each cove, each hamlet. She could not have been going far, as she carried only an old shopping basket. She did not stop waving and crying and shouting until land was out of sight entirely. Then she turned to me and smiled.

The next morning I made the decision I knew all along I would make, and sold my return ticket. With the money I booked into the hotel in Plaka which Hadley had suggested and bought a ticket for the boat to Italy. Then I walked up to the Acropolis and sat and looked at it, eating Greek pastries that were like Shredded Wheat soaked in sweetened motor oil.

There were several good reasons for my following you to London. I rehearsed them over the course of that night on the *Aegina*.

One: Miles's recent behaviour confirms a malice which I sensed but chose to ignore. That story about the faked test results might be true. It might also be a lie, but I cannot allow myself to behave as though it were. What if he is up to new mischief in some other hospital office? Perhaps he's psychotic and compelled, from time to time, to commit such crimes. Perhaps he's been warped by his early life but is nevertheless treatable. In that case he needs my help. Perhaps he is a pathological liar and enjoys deception for its own sake. If any of the above is true, it is my duty to find him and somehow, I don't know how, prevent his causing further damage.

Two: Frankly, I am attracted by his wickedness. He is a really interesting piece of exotica. If he is bad I want to know how bad. I want to satisfy the curiosity which is its own excuse for being. I want to go further into the shadows of his personality and let them menace me. Whether he turns out to be sick, dangerous or merely perverse, I can't let the idea of him alone. It is exciting to uncover a demon.

Three: This is a life-lesson. Miles is a means. Whether he is conscious of it or not, he is the instrument by which I have been punished for abandoning my aunt and hastening her death. Perhaps I myself have invoked him for the purpose. I wanted to suffer in reparation and didn't know it. Or something, someone wanted me to suffer – for my own good. In order that I might become whole, conscious, enlightened, grown-up. A part of me obviously feels I deserve Miles the way I used to feel I deserved Aunt Bernie.

Four: I want my money back. My money that flew like little green birds from the white nest of Grammy Mullen's sheets. Even with the addition of what I got in exchange for my ticket, finances were going to be tight. But something would happen, I was certain. I even felt good. When you surrender your fate to the gods, refusing to battle against circumstance, you become strangely light-hearted. It struck me that the way to respond to this disaster was not to close up protectively but to open myself even wider to random influences.

Therefore I was not particularly surprised when I saw a sign at Brindisi station for a train to Florence. Without thinking twice, I bought a ticket and sat on the platform to wait, shedding clothes as the morning advanced.

The real Florence. As I boarded the train I felt I was rising towards what Eva called the higher octave of my life. The fact is I was beginning to see what she meant about a lot of things. She wasn't all that crazy. She had simply chosen a crazy way of life, a way which now seemed as exhilarating as it was perilous. The trick was to close your mind and listen to your inner reason which was older and smarter than the newer addition upstairs. Clues were everywhere, signs abundant. Life itself would tell you what to do.

I sank into hebetude and stayed there as far as the hot Florence train station. Again I was not particularly surprised when I was met at the exit by the Fantoni twins. As I stood, rumpled and groggy and disorientated, I felt the pressure of eyes upon me. I turned and looked into those eyes, four of them, serious and concerned, behind two pairs of horn-rimmed glasses. They didn't approach me immediately but waited while I shifted jacket, tickets and suitcase and walked towards the street. Then they stepped apologetically into my path.

'*Inglese?*'

'American.'

'Lost? Dinner? We are happy.'

I shook my head no. They looked at me sorrowfully as though I had deprived them of a long-awaited pleasure.

'You understand Florence?'

Again I shook my head, but this time I smiled at them.

'Please.' One of them tugged at my suitcase. 'Too heavy for you.'

They were thirty, maybe thirty-five, and they were identical: both over six feet, large-boned, awkward, not at all as I'd imagined Italian men, and nothing like the ones I'd known in New York. They were shy, kind, if a little oppressive in their kindness. I was exhausted, wide open, and I was saying no to nothing. I surrendered my suitcase which they accepted with relief, pleased that I had at last seen the light.

'Do you know a cheap place to stay?' I asked.

'Yes, yes. We take. We eat.'

They'd got my number, all right, like beggars in reverse. I followed them obediently through the back streets of the city until we came to a new but modest apartment block.

'*Casa*,' they announced.

'*Casa*,' I nodded. If I had not been so tired I would have asked them the names for everything. I knew no Italian, and my French was undistinguished. I had been so badly educated. All I could say in their language was Pasolini, Rossellini and Fellini.

They led me up the bare cement staircase to the door of their flat. Inside, the walls and carpets were bright and new while the furniture dated from the early part of the century; it was well worn and comfy. The walls were covered with pictures of saints. They had moved in, they said, six months ago. Their old building had been demolished to make way for a shopping centre. I was surprised. I thought Europe preserved its ancient architecture. But I did not know how to tell them this.

One of them pointed to a dark-green door at the end of the corridor.

'Mama,' he said, and put his finger to his lips.

At first I thought they wanted to keep my presence a secret. But it turned out that Paulo and Roberto looked after their mother who was aged and infirm. I would be fortunate enough to meet her later when she ate supper. Now she was having her nap. But she would be delighted to see me, I was assured. I said I would be honoured to make her acquaintance.

Meanwhile, they urged, I must remove my jacket, I must take off my shoes, I must sit on the brown couch which engulfed me like a big friendly bear. I must drink a glass of red wine, presented to me with a plate of almond biscuits. When I had eaten these which were very dry and clearly from a packet, I was encouraged to stretch out and rest before dinner. I could not remember having agreed to dinner, but this didn't seem important. As I could barely hold my head up or keep my eyes from drooping, I accepted their invitation and lay down. I fell asleep immediately.

I was awakened by a gentle tapping on my arm. Paulo, or maybe it was Roberto, was telling me to sit up and eat what had been placed before me on a metal tray which sported the image of two pink-bowed Yorkies in a basket. On it was a steaming bowl of Campbell's tomato soup, slices of what looked like the equivalent of Wonder Bread and some salami. On a plate by itself, unadorned, was a round lump of pure-white cheese. They pointed at it, beaming.

'Try.'

Unlike the bread, the soup, and the salami, it was delicious.

'Good,' I nodded enthusiastically.

'Ours,' they proclaimed and watched me while I ate.

It was not until next morning that I discovered that Roberto and Paulo ran a mozzarella factory. After devouring the contents of the tray, it did not take much persuading to make me lie down again and go back to sleep, this time under a plaid blanket with which they ceremoniously covered me. I felt very safe.

I woke the next morning in a panic, not knowing where I was. Paulo or Roberto rushed in wearing an apron, as if realizing instinctively that I was conscious.

'Break-fast!'

'Yes, please.'

He had a serious smile, if such a thing is possible.

I was introduced to the delights of *Café latte fredo* with hard white rolls, followed by little chocolates wrapped in foil. I ate several of them, drank another *café latte* and felt quite energetic. Again they sat and watched me eat. I didn't mind at all. Their watching was consistent with the rest of their odd, intense domesticity.

'Thank you,' I said. 'That was so good. You've been really nice to me, but now I have to go.' I thought of offering them something for the food, which is what Aunts Bernie and Bea would have done, but realized in time what an outrage this would be. You were right; Americans are insensitive.

They were alarmed. '*Non possible.*'

For one second I was afraid.

'*Fattoria*, Mama.' It appeared I could not leave without seeing both. I agreed. Well, it wasn't like I was pressed for time, was it?

I had an awful shock when I switched on the bathroom light. No wonder the twins thought I needed help. I had hardly looked in a mirror during the days in Greece. My skin was dry and freckled, my nose was peeling, and my roots had grown to the point where I was more brunette than blonde. My nails were broken and dirty, my clothes wrinkled and equally dirty, and there were dark rings under my eyes. But this was not the half of it.

Behind the freckles, right out in the open and, as always, without permission, was Frances. 'What are you doing here?' I shouted inside, furious that she had pursued me across an ocean and a continent. I switched off the light. When I turned it on again she had gone.

Once more I followed the twins through the winding streets, stopping at stands to sample wines the colour of stained-glass windows. By the time we reached the factory I was tipsy. It was a Sunday and the only employee present was a caretaker. Normally there were three or four girls to watch over the little fat cheeses as they daily grew in their milk bath. The factory itself was a large stone room, serenely cool. Hundreds of mozzarellas were lined up on a series of shallow wooden troughs which were gently tilted at a hundred and twenty degrees to each other. From a source behind the wall, milk was sluiced through these troughs, washing the cheeses in a mild continuous flow. The dairy smell was sweet and consoling. The apparatus made me think of the great band of stars across the night sky above the island. The Milky Way as universal mozzarella factory.

'This is very nice,' I said. 'I like it here.'

'You want job?'

'Doing what?'

Paulo (I could now tell them apart) demonstrated by rolling a cheese with the tips of his fingers.

'Ah! Baby-sit the cheeses!' They laughed. We all laughed, including the watchman. And that was how I became a mozzarella nurse.

I wore a white dress, white cap and apron. I looked as if I belonged in a hospital rather than a factory. The two other girls were similarly attired. (The third was on maternity leave, which is why I got the job.) I worked happily, my mind a blank, tending the cheeses with affection and care. To me they were touching, helpless, like foetuses in their white amniotic fluid. I did well by them. I was at peace. You see, this white world was another North Star. I found it satisfying to deal once more with the transmutations of milk. It was the best possible omen. A return, a symmetry, an advancement.

The factory was ferociously cleaned and scrubbed. There was never

that sour stench of near-curdling. Often the twins would undertake
the task themselves, so devoted were they to their enterprise. When
the cheeses were ready they were taken to the room next door to be
packaged. I was asked if I would like to move in there, but I said no.
I preferred to be where I was – in the nursery, bathing the children.
I could not explain to them why I was so fascinated by the fatalistic
overtones of my occupation.

I worked at the factory for a month, during which time I lived with
the twins. They continued to treat me like a visiting princess and were
horrified when I offered to pay them board. I thought they were going
to cry, and hastened to assure them that I would never again press
money on them. I did not meet Mama. I heard her talking to her
sons or to herself behind the green door and sometimes at night in
the bathroom. But if she otherwise came out of the room she must
have done so when I was out. Three times a day she sent me greetings
and enquired after my health and happiness. I returned the salutations.
Paulo and Roberto continued to express their regrets over her failure to
materialize, and I continued to express my disappointment. She wasn't
well, they explained, she was having a bad time, conversation was a
strain, they must protect her. I said many times how sorry I was.

When I was not at the factory I was at the Uffizi or the Pitti Palace. I
learned my way around Florence. I even learned some Italian. I floated,
cheerful and detached, thinking of little more than paintings and food. I
ate lots of ice-cream and mozzarella. I gained weight. One day I walked
into a hairdresser's and had my blonde ends cut off.

At the end of the month I had earned about a hundred dollars which
the twins presented to me *in toto* and in cash. Since it was now October
and I was heading north, I would use part of the money for a winter
coat which I intended to buy in Rome. (My other coat was in the
cupboard on East 2nd Street along with the rest of my possessions.
Whoever took over the apartment would now have to deal with two
discarded lives. Perhaps the place attracted migrants.) It seemed like
a treat I owed myself as a reward for keeping my chin up. I bought a
large reproduction of *The Pietà* to give to Mama, which I knew would
please the twins more than any gift for themselves.

I was so sad to leave my little cheeses and my big twins and the
comfort and shelter of the brown couch, but it was time to continue
my journey, and suddenly I was anxious to be off. I had to find you
even though I feared what I might find.

The train to Rome was packed to capacity, and I would have had
to stand for the entire journey if Roberto had not rushed ahead and

staked a claim on a window seat in a second-class compartment. When we said goodbye we all cried. Waving and smiling, the twins waited on the platform until the train pulled out. I waved back, holding in my lap the lunch basket they had prepared for me. Why don't I stay here? I thought, knowing such a thing was impossible. I waved until the train was out of the station, craning my neck to see them until the very last moment. Saintly people do exist. There are more of them in heaven and earth than are dreamt of in the Ladies' Guild philosophy.

In Rome I found a room in an old *pensione*. There was no hot water, but I did have a rusted wrought-iron balcony which hung over a viney courtyard where dozens of skinny cats led a raucous existence and vied for territorial supremacy.

I spent three days looking at ruins and eating the best and least expensive food I'd ever tasted. I discovered the delights of cheap luxury, and again it occurred to me that I'd never learned to just live, that nothing in my life had prepared me to just live. I bought a coat in a little shop not far from the Spanish Steps. My hair was brown and soft and shiny again. Very simple. When I wore the coat and covered my tatty clothes I almost looked good. (I had given up nail polish, mascara, foundation, everything. I met the world bare-faced and that felt right.)

I sat in a café and wrote postcards:

Dear Tony,

I haven't forgotten. Please forgive me, but I needed to get away. I took my chance for the vacation I never had. Well, it was better and worse than I'd imagined. I'm in a mess, and I'm going to London for a couple of weeks. I'll write to you from there. I will try to join you as soon as this phase comes to an end. Please believe me, it is necessary. I know you understand that. I hope you like your job and that you're happy. I promise I won't take a month to write next time. Love, Rose. P.S. I worked in a really interesting place that would make a great setting for a film.

Dear Hadley,

I suppose by now you are back in New York. It was weird missing you like that. I'm not sure when I'm coming back. I've had a strange experience and as a result I feel pretty mixed up. Write to me at American Express in London where I have some unfinished business. Love to you, Kit and Drexel, Rose.

FLORENCE

Dear Daddy,

I'm in Italy! Decided to see more of Europe while I was
here. Please don't worry about me. I'm having a fantastic
time. You'd hate the churches. But there are lots of broken
things to photograph. All my love, Rose.

I was mad about Rome, until the last afternoon, that is. I had saved St
Peter's for the end. I was reluctant to confront all that power and glory.
The moment I entered the huge dark ugly basilica I knew I should not
have come. But I was drawn by its magnetism. I walked about, tense,
my shoulders hunched as if I were expecting someone to strike me. I
was cringing. It should be sold, I thought. All these treasures should
be auctioned off to feed the hungry.

Tony had told me about the Baldacchino and I dutifully inspected
it. But that too was monstrous and menacing, a grotesque squatting
ogre, an ornate guillotine whose hidden blade was about to fall on
me. Its prelates and gargoyles leered, threatening my liberated soul
with reincarceration. I turned and ran. Oh no, you don't, I said. I had
planned to visit the Vatican Library, but I could not bear the thought
of those murals executed for the princes of the Church. I stood on the
vast steps breathing hard. I felt like I imagined Eva did on that day in
the Museum of Modern Art.

Don't be stupid, I told myself. There are far more wicked institutions
in this world than the Catholic Church. Its invidious heyday is past.
Think of the drug companies, the arms dealers, the Pentagon, the
CIA. All much worse. And minus the art. As I stood looking at the
huge square, criss-crossed at this hour by only a few people, I suddenly
recognized it as one of the locations of my dream. I experienced the
same breathlessness, the same physical weakness. It was a sign. One
of the signs that are always appearing but are invisible to most people.
The world gives them away as presents, and it would be mad to ignore
and ungracious to refuse them. I left the city that night. I did not want
to die in Rome – or anywhere – until I'd found you or exhausted all
the possibilities of finding you. Later for death.

I stepped off the boat at the Dover docks and smelled the cold damp
air that was so like Black Water Road. It propelled a rush of energy up
my spine. I am a northern person. I liked to be covered up in clothes,
wrapped in blankets. I like disappearing into fogs. I guess that was why
Greece had made me feel so exposed. You have to be beautiful to thrive
there. Nudity must feel like your natural state.

275

I walked towards the station with the queasy feeling that accompanies the arrival at dawn in an unknown city. I looked back. There was a narrow band of golden light across the horizon. It was 6 a.m.

I loved the green of the South Downs. I had never seen countryside so *arranged*. It looked as though man and nature, having sat down and discussed their problems, had reached a compromise and this was the result: a kind of DMZ, a humane and rational wilderness. The landscape and the low sky shrank accommodatingly to make a theatre. Nature was scaled down to human proportions. It was the backdrop for a pastorale, a little human drama with a happy ending. In Maine nature was just there, bigger than you. You fitted into it as best you could and without giving much consideration to appearances. There was no question of compromises or arrangements. No agreement had been drawn up, and consequently everything had a raw edge. Patches of homely order were scraped out here and there, tacked on to the tameable margins. That was all you could do.

We arrived at Victoria in a chilly drizzle. I had my plan now and I followed it. I changed the rest of my money, checked my suitcase after removing the winter coat, and went straight to a row of telephone booths. I looked up Zahl. There were several. I copied the addresses and bought myself an *A to Z*. Then I went into a café for a cup of tea and a bun. It was eight-thirty. I looked for the address nearest Cromwell Road. (You see how I remembered everything you said, every little thing.) Vera Zahl lived at 83 Laughton Gardens. I paid for my tea and went down into the Underground. I noticed nothing. I concentrated on not getting lost.

Laughton Gardens is a row of six-storey neo-Gothic brick houses with deep arched porticoes and stained-glass windows on the ground and second floors. The shadows of their high Dutch gables with their poised, open-mouthed lions darken the street. The buildings are interesting but oppressive. They lean towards each other in weary conspiracy as though there were nothing left for them but gossip. They seemed to be whispering about me, criticizing me. I checked the dim doorways, searching for 83. I stood in the portico, each side of which was decorated with more dirty stained glass. I rang the bell. I waited. No one came. I heard slow footsteps across a tiled floor, the unfastening of locks and bolts. The enormous black door swung open.

'Yes?'

Before me was a small woman with crooked legs, gnarled hands, and grey hair piled in a precarious bun. She wore a purple cardigan and a good deal of costume jewellery.

'What do you want?'

Her accent was strong, her voice gravelly but pleasant, her speech nearly a drawl.

'Excuse me, but I'm looking for – '

'Who are you?' Behind the glasses her eyes were sharp and direct.

'I'm a friend of Miles.'

'What Miles?'

'I don't know his last name. He told me he lived here and that he was a friend of yours. He told me about you. He's a medical student.'

'I know him. He is not here.'

'Do you know where he is?'

'No. I am sorry.' She started to close the door.

'You're Mrs Zahl.'

'I know who I am.'

'Well, I'm Rose. Do you know when he's coming back? Is he coming back?'

'You can write to him. Write to him here. I am very busy, Rose. Goodbye.'

The door closed with a solemn click like the door of a church.

18

Madam Zed

'Y ou can't live in a world where it's forbidden to laugh at misfortune.' You told me that once after a bout of hectoring when I had lost patience and chastized you or maybe even cried. You were right. You could not have tolerated such a ban. But I wonder about me. I think I might have done quite well.

You certainly laughed at my misfortunes. I could hear your laughter that morning. I heard it every time I went to Laughton Gardens. It followed me along the street, echoing off the haughty houses that regarded me with contempt. They reminded me of malicious and bejewelled dowagers who had given up washing properly, members of the *ancien régime*, unaware that the guillotine was being sharpened specially for them. Otherwise I suffered no hallucinations. I did not see in strangers your walk, your smile, your sandy hair. I did not trail men like a love-lorn detective. It wasn't necessary. You were right there inside me. You had been inside me all along. Everyone in my life, every love, had been a harbinger of you. That was what I understood when Madam Zed shut the door in my face. No wonder your laughter pursued me.

During that year I did not see you I felt so possessed by you that I actually prayed. Not to God, I wouldn't dream of going to Him with my troubles, but to a sort of amalgam of female deities. NuitIsisDemeterMary. She who is called in a famous book the Great Mother. I don't know why, but I could not let go of the idea that she was still interested in me and might help me. Perhaps she was only my own mother, poor Nora Noonan of Kittery, Maine, daughter of a textile worker and a salesgirl. Whoever she was, she did not put an end to my misery.

I thought about your limbs, your manicured hands and how you walked on them, always performing. I thought of your mouth which made me envy you and want to be you. I thought about going to bed

278

with you. You had this brisk way of making love which made me at first self-conscious, the way the island had. I was used to Travis and Tony, both of whom were tender and took pains. You just got on with it. But then I began to like your intensity. My very nervousness of you contributed to my pleasure. It's not that you were ever clumsy or brutal; you never hurt me. But you were single-minded. I realized it might not necessarily have been me you were rushing towards. It might just have been your excess energy which had to be daily burnt off. Later on you introduced refinements. It turned out you had a sense of choreography, and that was fun. Sometimes you'd talk. That was interesting too, if a little distracting. I had always preferred silence. None of what you said made much sense. But I began to like it, especially the way it came and went unexpectedly.

When we finished you would fall asleep instantly – on your back like a child exhausted from play. Your dreams did not translate themselves into movement. Lying beside you was peaceful, though I seldom slept well.

You were like a rare, though hardly endangered, species, which I guarded not only as treasure but prisoner. As long as you slept you were mine.

You bounded out of bed with the first light, whistling as you wrapped yourself in the green sarong and made the tea which you served me, in bed. Your energy unsettled me a little. It was as if a coiled spring had been suddenly released. Gerald McBoing-Boing, I called you. Gradually I would come round as you practised your Tai Chi or whatever it was on the terrace. When I was finally awake we'd eat breakfast under the eucalyptus tree, usually in a stiff breeze.

Just as I was getting used to you, you fled. I had made the fatal mistake of permitting myself to feel, just for a moment, secure. Believe me, I bore you no ill will. Even now, after everything that's happened, I bear no ill will. Once one understands a person's motivations and discovers the reasons for their behaviour, it's impossible to be angry. This attitude of mine exasperated you, I think, more than anything.

'Christ, Rose,' you said, 'even Candide had doubts occasionally.'

'I'm sorry. I know it's irritating.' And, from your point of view, it has got me nowhere. But I believe it's necessary to stop and try to consider. We cannot all, always, be blindly advancing like you.

When I returned to Laughton Gardens, five months had passed. I had written you letters, but they had neither been answered nor returned. The days were short and the nights were long. I hardly saw the sun that winter. I was lonely, ripe for a desperate act. So one afternoon, after I had bathed and eaten breakfast, I left the flat. I walked the half-block to the market and turned left. I thought I had gone out for eggs and a lettuce, maybe a bunch of anemones if the flower stall was open. Instead I went straight on down the Fulham Road, past the junk shops and the movie theatre where nothing interesting ever played, then past the new cafés with their white interiors, mirrors, and hanging plants frothing green from wicker baskets, past St Stephen's Hospital and the chic Italian restaurants and the expansive upholstery shops. I turned left at Pelham Street and stopped at South Kensington station to get my bearings. It was one of those too-bright windy March days, necessary, I suppose, to dry out this country after a mild sodden winter. But it was cold and I had no gloves, so I stood in the station to get warm.

I came out opposite the V. & A. and proceeded along the Cromwell Road. This was the long way round, but I wanted time to change my mind. I arrived at Number 83, hesitated by the portico and walked on. I went as far as Queens Gate before retracing my steps. This time I marched straight up to the bell and rang it. Light filtered through the stained glass. It was all quite unreal. A young man in great haste burst through the door, nearly knocking me over. He apologized, pushed the door open for me, and ran off, his mac flapping in the wind. I caught the door but hadn't the courage to enter. I let it slam. I waited then rang the bell. Nothing. I rang again. My nerve was about to fail me. Then I heard the footsteps, the same as before, slow, a little unsteady with a short stride that favoured the left foot. The door opened.

'You are early,' she said.

'I'm sorry.' I was so astonished the words just came out.

'Which one has sent you?' She peered at me.

'Which what?' I felt like Alice conversing with the Red Queen.

'Which agency?' She said 'vich'.

'I – there's no agency. I don't know what you mean.'

'Who are you?'

'I'm Rose.'

'You have been before.'

'Yes.'

'But not recently.' Her Rs rolled lazily.

'No.'

She narrowed her eyes and scrutinized me. I noticed she wasn't wearing her glasses.

'You are expecting employment, yes or no?'

'No – but I'd like to talk to you.'

'Talk.'

'It's about Miles. I'm still looking for him. Do you remember?'

'I remember quite well.' ('Qvite'.)

'I wrote to him like you suggested.'

'Many people do.'

'Oh. Then he's still away?'

'He is away. But sometimes he comes.'

'When will he – come?'

'I cannot tell you.'

I stood looking at her. She held all the secrets. All the keys.

'It is not my will. You understand?' Her gaze was direct but not unkind.

'You can't tell me where he is?'

'That is correct. And now, if you do not expect employment, I must return to my work.'

'Will you tell him Rose was looking for him?'

'I will tell him. Goodbye.'

And the big door closed again in my face. I had forgotten to ask about my letters.

That night at the restaurant I stumbled and spilled a tray of plates which, fortunately, were empty. It was 2 a.m. I had been Drexelizing, finishing off customers' drinks all evening, and was by then quite tipsy. I must have mixed half a dozen types of alcohol. The manager took me aside and reprimanded me. Alistair prided himself on being kind but firm with the girls who worked for him. Though he dressed in jeans like the rest of us and affected a casual style, I was beginning to realize that he had a posh accent, also that he looked down on me not only because I was female and had to earn my living as a waitress, but because I was American. I'd been told he owned an interest in the place.

'I'm a bit worried about you, Rose,' he said, leaning the upper half of his long body against the wall. 'I mean, it's nothing to me if you smash some crockery. Everyone makes mistakes. But what if Giles had been in?' Giles was the owner. 'Think about it, Rosie, and maybe cut down on the booze – not for my sake – I've no right to tell you how to live – but for your own. I mean, I care about you and all the girls. I want you to be happy here. Why don't you go home and think about yourself and why you've been doing this lately. I mean, turn it over in your mind, love, and try to see where you're really at.' He smiled. 'We're all pulling for you, you know.' Then he gave me a hug. An embrace to which I did not respond. This was his idea of enlightened behaviour, how to deal with the subordinates. I suppose in his way he was enlightened. But give me an Eddie Manilla any day.

The next morning my head was splitting. I lay in Sally Soames's bed, rueful and crapulent. I had sublet the place from Sally three months before, just after I started working at the restaurant. It was a basement in a little terraced house on one of the shabby streets that ran off the market road. It overflowed with what Hadley would have called frou-frou: exuberant wallpaper in a Paisley motif with matching curtains and shades, ruffly-edged pink-glass lamps above the wrought-iron bed with its flounced spread; ubiquitous cushions, dried flowers, framed samplers with dreary stains and drearier sentiments, prints of cats, old *Vogue* covers and Victorian beauties, china animals and, yes, a beaded bag slung over a mirror. The galley kitchen brimmed with gadgets.

Timidly I asked if I might repaint the sitting-room and was met with an incredulous, horrified refusal. I wanted to paint it white, but Sally Soames hadn't heard about minimalism yet. I hope, for her sake, she never does. So I left everything as it was and made my way cautiously among the furbelows.

Sally was an actress who had been unemployed for several months when I met her. She worked at the restaurant to make ends meet. Then she was offered a part in a touring production of *Arms and the Man*. In Ottawa one thing led to another and she'd ended up engaged. Meanwhile I remained in the flat until Sally had made up her mind about her future. Once again I'd inherited the shell of another woman's life. Only this time I had not been left a cat into the bargain. Better, I thought. No heartbreak.

At three I groped my way to the kitchen to make tea. I returned to bed with it, switching on the Bush radio as I passed. The lights in the ruffled shades went out. Time to put more coins in the meter. It was always letting me down. My fault, really. I never gave it enough to eat. I needed its food for myself. As a result I was constantly scrambling about, searching bags, drawers and dirty clothes for 5 and 10p pieces. I had been told there were ways to fiddle the greedy thing and resolved to find myself a tame petty criminal.

I deposited 50 pence and lay down again. I tried to take Alistair's advice and reassess myself. Perhaps I was drinking too much. I *was* drinking too much. I did it abstractedly, almost without noticing. That is, I've heard, the most dangerous sort of indulgence. I was squandering all my energy in order to pay the rent on this basement flat with its grubby frou-frou. I was tired and tense from waiting too long for you. Drink relaxed me. Once more I was using it as a tranquillizer, though it was not expensive. I just stole it from the restaurant.

In New York I'd never drunk all that much. I preferred grass until it began to turn me paranoid, or hallucinogens, preferably the milder ones. I had not been committed to chemicals either – more of a drug dilettante, I guess. I wandered through fields of drugs, sampling a little here, a little there, whatever took my fancy. But never to excess. I must have acquired a minor cumulative dependency, however, because I missed their being part of the general ambiance, there to be turned to whenever I needed to dream alone or merge socially, to take a rest or to have a small adventure. I remember those trips like brief love affairs. What was to replace them now that I was a refugee in this piddling apartment? The dregs of many drinks.

I intended to stop that now. After today I would go back to work and earn my keep like a good New England girl. Honest work – that's all there is. I still believed, as I had been raised to believe, that sooner or later it pays off. Not necessarily in wealth. We didn't think like that. No Calvinist Elect. Riches were a subject of scorn, immoral, a target for mockery. They put one far from God and man. We made fun of rich people. They were phoneys. We laughed at them. It was part of the So Far and No Further philosophy. No, work pays off in satisfaction, peace of mind, a sense of self-possession and dignity. Whatever glamour there may be is purely internal.

There wasn't much external glamour on the Road. In winter the stall keepers were bundles of damp wool with red noses and purple cheeks flushed by the wind and by the drink with which they fuelled themselves each lunchtime at the market pub. They were loud, fat and friendly. Some had almost delicate features with small noses and sharp azure eyes. They were like garrulous glove-puppets, urban earth spirits. Stalls could be family affairs with two or three generations operating in rota. They knew their customers' first names and called everyone 'love' and 'darling'. I was charmed by them and horrified to discover that Fulham was then a Conservative borough. They had all voted for Heath.

They were out in every kind of weather and shut up their barrows only on Sunday and Thursday afternoons. In addition to fruit, veg and flowers, they sold cassette tapes, old 45s, bedding plants, used Hoover parts, sweets, and baby clothes in dayglo synthetic fabrics. There were printed T-shirts, a fishmonger and plastic toys. At any hour of the working day the Road was crowded with local residents eager to purchase these wares. Those of us with little money and less pride would wait until just past closing time when we might pick up some Cornish greens or potatoes for a few pence or nothing at all, some of them off the tarmac. Most of the customers lived in the surrounding streets or the big council estate near Fulham Broadway. The majority had been in the neighbourhood all their lives and seldom went anywhere else. A trip to Marble Arch was a safari.

Monied young couples were among the first to purchase workers' cottages in the area. Other outsiders had heard about the market and had drifted in for a bargain and a bit of local colour. I'm told the latter now predominate, but when I lived near the Road there were still elderly widows with identical National Health false teeth and crinkly perms given them by neighbours and daughters-in-law. They had names like Kath and Violet and sang along every night in The Goat. Out on the Road they jostled daily with enormous young matrons with stained jumpers and dropsical calves whose feet were squeezed into cutaway slippers; teenagers playing truant and looking for trouble; mothers with too many children wheeling double pushchairs towards the nearest playgroup. And there were people like me, the marginals. We were accepted and everyone was kind to us, even if it was clear that there weren't any children at home and that none were imminent.

My socializing centred around The Goat. I could not afford many movies and there was seldom anyone to go with. I did so a couple of times with girls from the restaurant, but their invitations were not repeated. My phone, or rather Sally's phone, hardly ever rang unless it was some man trying to sell double-glazing or enquiring what colour knickers I had on. The English seemed to me a very neglectful people. There was no one like Hadley or Steve simply to appear without advance notice and say I'm going to a party/film-showing/bar/gallery. Come with me. These people required arrangements weeks in advance, even with their closest friends, and were affronted by spur-of-the-moment invitations. So I went to the pub a couple of times a week. After six months I knew all the regulars: the Vis, the Stuarts, the Gordons and the Alices who arrived each evening at nine and caroused until eleven.

On Thursdays, Fridays and Saturdays, a black man with a husky voice and a spectacularly wicked grin would play the out-of-tune upright as though he wanted to kill it and sing songs I'd only heard in fake-English Hollywood films. Everyone knew these songs and sang them lustily. In between numbers Bruce would consume several pints, fling around sexual innuendoes and generally insult the clientele, who found his performance hilarious and encouraged his abuse. He made his willing white victims laugh and scream. I was in awe of Bruce.

I was also in awe of the Gypsy. I didn't know his real name. I never heard him called anything else. I seldom spoke to him, being too shy to initiate a conversation. His appearance was exotic, especially in The Goat where most of the customers looked as if they subsisted on meat pies and saveloys. But he would have been noticeable anywhere with his glossy black hair and smooth brown skin and his elongated features that were a cross between the Indian and the Semitic. He seemed permanently, deservedly, happy. An infectious smile accompanied the gentlest of manners. It was impossible to guess his age.

A long-haired Alsatian was his constant companion. She was one of the most beautiful dogs I'd ever seen and with a disposition as sanguine as her master's. Her coat was deep and thick and soft, and she was without a hint of aggression. Lena was devoted to the Gypsy who had parapsychological understanding of animals. (He had a job looking after horses at some secret stable on the Fulham Road.) I wanted to tell him about Foxie. If only I had known him or someone like him all those years ago. He would have made Foxie well again, I was sure of it. But not even he could have saved her from Aunt Bernie bent on murder. She'd have despised his magic gifts.

The old ladies were especially nice to me, asking after my family (about whom I felt obliged to spin elaborate lies), obviously worried about my lack of a man, repeating to me the same stories from their not uneventful lives: old loves, dead children, the Blitz. They were sweet. It was the middle-aged matrons I took against. They had coarse laughs and hatchet faces and mean mouths and played the fruit machines with consistent success. Clearly they all went to the same hairdresser. Their eyes were hard and watchful. You could tell they bossed their husbands. They could have passed for transvestites, except that they were nowhere near as sexy.

I became addicted to what I thought of as the pub's quaint spectacle, something from another era in which I nevertheless felt quite at home. No one ever suggested I reassess myself.

This was how I lived during the months I waited for you. I went to work, I went to the market, I went to The Goat. I wrote you two more letters but received no reply. I called Madam Zed and asked for you, but a young man told me you didn't live there. I left no message. I got one postcard from Hadley which I thought I'd answered, but apparently I hadn't. I repaid Aphrodite her $100.

Arty people often came to the restaurant, mainly actors. They were noisy and troublesome, but not unkind, and always left generous tips. Then there were the patronizers, people who made remarks like 'It's jolly sad' and called a plate a 'pleat'. But occasionally we got the wide boys – rich thugs and shady businessmen wanting to impress their secretaries or what Alistair called their 'doxies'. They flashed a lot of money around and usually tipped well, but they were foul. By now I'd grown used to condescension of the genteel variety. These guys were plain rude, and, because they were paying, assumed they could treat us as they pleased. Hadley would have made short work of them.

A typical specimen occupied the corner table that night.

'Get me some Dunhills,' he barked.

I returned with the pack which I opened and placed before him on a small silver tray.

'What's this, then?'

'Your cigarettes.'

'Do they look like my cigarettes?' He held up a pack of Camels.

'You told me Dunhill.'

'No, my darlin'. You *heard* me say Dunhill, but it's not what I *told* you.'

When he started to be abusive I walked off.

Half an hour later I brought him his coffee. I left it on the table and turned to go.

'Here,' he shouted. 'Pour this coffee.'

I don't have to, I thought. Nevertheless I did as I was ordered.

'Not a bad-looking girl, is she?' The doxie shrugged. 'If she'd fix herself up.'

As I leaned over to pour her coffee, he touched his lighted cigarette to my arm. I shrieked.

'Oh, sorry, love.'

His eyes were glazed and insolent. I did not see red. I did not see black. I saw Hadley. And as I tipped the coffee cup into his lap she gave me an approving smile. 'Oh, sorry, love,' I said.

'Never let them get the upper hand,' she pronounced, as I ran for the kitchen. 'Don't let them think they have rights.'

I dashed to the sink to stick my arm under the cold water tap and left Alistair to deal with the wet thug.

I knew only one thing. I was not going back into the restaurant. Alistair entered.

'He burned me on purpose. Look.'

I showed him the mark which was now an angry red.

Alistair sighed and shook his head. 'That's not what he says, love.'

'Then believe him!' I shouted. 'Believe the bastard!'

'You don't seem to understand, Rosie. It's you I'm thinking of.'

By now we had an audience. The whole staff, even the evil-tempered chef, had gathered round. God knew who was serving the customers.

'It's not me you're thinking of, Alistair. It's Giles. It's profit. Profit first, people second. You're just another avaricious businessman.'

'That's my job.' As he got angrier his voice became more and more subdued. An avuncular lecture was coming.

'You're a creep, Alistair. No better than the creep in there. In fact, you're worse. You're a hypocrite and a creep. You are a mega-crud.'

'With regret, Rose, you're fired.'

'Without regret, I'm gone.'

I marched to the door where Hadley stood waiting for me, blocking my exit. I turned around and held out my hand, palm up.

'I'll take my money,' I said.

'Not possible, Rose.' Alistair remained impassive. 'We haven't totalled all the tips yet.'

'That's OK. I know exactly what I'm owed. £24.52, and I'll have it now, please.'

'Why don't you come in on Friday when you've calmed down?'

'Give me my money!' I screamed.

The chef stepped forward. This was behaviour he could relate to.

He pushed Alistair against the steel worktop. 'It's her money. How about you give it to her?'

I was amazed. He'd always treated me with the usual chef-contempt. Perhaps he was glad to be rid of me or even liked the way I stood up to the manager. At any rate, Alistair handed over my tips and I sailed out, nose in the air. I walked all the way back to the flat where I fell asleep in Sally Soames's bed and slept the clock around.

I never told you that story, did I? Are you surprised at my assertiveness? You shouldn't be. There are times when I am not so pliable, as you now know.

£24.52. I could make it last another couple of weeks, but then what? I hated the restaurant but as an alien I was without a work permit, which was why I had drifted once more into waitressing. The police kept tabs on me. They had already paid me a visit. (They terrified me. I could not get used to their not carrying guns, and always expected the worst. I had lived too long in New York.) Whatever I did would have to be occasional, which meant another restaurant, another manager, another thug, another patronizer, another chef. Why not return to New York? At least at Cal's there was camaraderie. But I couldn't leave. You'd come back, I was certain. And when you did I would be waiting for you. Not only that, you would be glad I'd waited.

That night I re-read my letters from Tony, the last of which was dated five weeks ago. I had not answered it. Then I took out the old photographs of my family in the textile mills. I lay on the bed, the stained and stiffened photographs spread out around me. Now is the time, I thought. Now is the time to take a risk.

On Monday I got up at eight, walked to the market, stopped at Mario's for a *cappuccino* and a gigantic cheese omelette, continued to Fulham Broadway. I made my mind a blank all the way to Laughton Gardens. It was my favourite sort of day, the sort I've seen only in England in April: alternating sun and showers, the air balmy but cool, saturated with delicious moisture and smelling of fresh linen. I loved the drama of the fast-moving clouds whose course continually altered the light, and the breeze on which thousands of cherry blossoms drifted. I felt slight but very alive.

I stepped out of the transient sunshine into the chilly brick portico. I knocked for the third time as in a fairy tale. The door opened immediately. This time Madam Zed was wearing her spectacles.

'You have come for the job.'

'Yes.'

'Enter and we will discuss.'

The hall was so dark I couldn't see to its end. A broad staircase with a red carpet and an ornate banister wound up and up into the gloom. The walls were a drab burgundy, definitely at odds with the stair carpet, and unpainted for many years. The overhead fixture cast a feeble glow. I would not have been surprised to hear the flapping of bats' wings. Madam Zed beckoned me towards a smaller set of stairs.

'Please descend.'

I walked into the pool of light at the bottom. She followed me with difficulty, leaning heavily on her left leg and grasping the banister.

'May I help you?' I asked.

'No, thank you.' She hit the floor with a sigh. 'It is my ankle. I had an operation.' She pronounced each syllable slowly and carefully as if it were I and not she to whom English was a foreign language. I followed her to some french windows on the opposite side of the room. Next to the windows was a round mahogany table. The blue carpet was worn but noble. Indoors Madam Zed looked even more intimidating.

'Sit down, please.' She indicated a chair. She sounded as if she were issuing an exhausted command to a hyperactive child.

288

I moved towards a red damask chair.

'No, here, please.' She tapped the table. 'My eyesight is not so good and I wish to see you.'

Her eyes were large and moist and, contrary to her claim, did not seem to miss a thing. Her lower lip was very full and stubborn, as though nature had stinted on her body in order to consign all power to her face. In amusing contrast, her grey hair was tied up with a little velvet bow.

I sat down. I saw that the french windows gave out on to a patio beyond which spread a lush communal garden. I had never seen such an arrangement and did not realize that they were quite common in London. The vision of the garden seemed to maximize my insignificance. Madam Zed rested her hands on the table top which was littered with accounts.

She looked down at them. 'I must do them myself,' she sighed. 'I was never good at maths. I had to learn. That is what happens when you are alone. Suddenly you must do all the things you think you cannot do.'

I too could have told a thing or two about being alone. Instead I just smiled.

'You are called?'

'Rose.'

'I remember. But you are not English.'

'American.'

'You have been educated?'

'Yes, but not awfully well.'

'America has a very low culture.'

'That's true, I guess.'

'You are here to study?' Her eyes reminded me of someone's, I couldn't think whose.

'No, I'm just – living.'

'That can be very agreeable. But you want to work?'

'Yes.'

'You need money.'

'Yes.'

'You are not – fussy?'

'No.'

'Have you been before a maid?'

'No, but I've cleaned houses since I was a little girl.' I thought of the days I had spent scrubbing Aunt Bernie's floor and Eva's stove.

'Why? Didn't you have a mother?'

'Only for a while.'

'I am sorry.'

'That's all right.'

'I had a wonderful mother.' She said 'vunderfool'.

'I'm glad for you.'

There was a pause.

'You have worked hard at unrewarding things. That is sad.'

'I think I was born to serve people.' I didn't intend to say it. It just came out.

'That is possible. Let me see your hand.'

I held it out to her. She grasped it with her own which was badly wrinkled, but soft and remarkably firm. She inspected my lines, pressed the mounts beneath each finger, tested the resistance of the thumb. Then she solemnly folded it up and returned it to me like a parcel delivered by mistake.

'You are stronger than you think,' she said. 'And, like most women, more practical.'

'I hope so.'

'You are led too much by your imagination. You think other people know better than you.'

'Sometimes.'

'It is not so terrible. But one day it must stop.'

I wanted to ask how she knew all this. I wished she would tell me more. But just then all I really wanted was the job.

'I'll try,' I said. She gave me a smile that was startlingly sweet. I was not only impressed but disarmed, and wondered if this was the moment to ask about my letters. Then her smile vanished with the sun on the communal garden.

'When can you begin?'

'Whenever.'

'That is no answer.'

'Tomorrow, then.'

'It is not necessary. The girl is still here, but I will sack her. After four days I will sack her. I have sacked many maids.' She looked at me hard. 'I am rather difficult.'

I'll just bet you are, I thought.

'I like things done – *so*. Can you do them – *so*?' There was a malicious twinkle in her eye.

'Yes,' I responded bravely.

'We will see,' she chuckled.

'Where are you from?' I asked impulsively. I could not place her accent.

'I am Czech, but I have lived many places. The country of my birth does not now exist. It is called by another name.'

I wanted to tell her about the cemetery for dead countries on that back road in New Hampshire. I wondered what she would think of it, whether she would approve or be horrified. For me the connection was an affirmation of my decision to entrust myself to her. The symbolic correctness raised my hopes.

'I must return to my accounts,' she announced. 'You may have the job. Come in one week and I will explain to you.'

I was eager to find out if that explanation contained inadvertent mention of you as well as more information about my hand. She heaved herself up by means of the table edge and walked me to the stairs. She smiled again. 'Now you have come in,' she said, 'you must find your way out alone . . .'

291

19

Two Streets

The stairway in Laughton Gardens rose five storeys to the attic. The steps were built in sets of eight, interrupted by a landing with a small stained glass window that threw patches of red blue and green light onto the worn carpet. At the landing one turned left and climbed another flights of eight steps to the next floor. The sequence went: eight stairs, landing with window, left turn, eight stairs, landing with corridor in which a haze of dust always hung no matter how often I dusted and hoovered. Seventy-four steps in all. I knew the characteristics of each one – which was getting a bald spot on its carpet, which creaked in the middle, which on the left or right, which was accompanied by a loose rung in the carved banister.

With the passing weeks the patches of coloured light moved from the first step to the second to the third, fourth and fifth, then gradually up the wall with its faded motif of peacocks and golden pheasants, stone bridges and pagodas and trysting figures in court attire. How I would have lost myself in that paper when I was seven. What two-dimensional adventures I'd have lived against its backdrop. It would have been like watching a film. I'd have made the Chinese ladies and gentlemen move and talk like my dolls within a scenario more real than life.

Half-way up the second set of eight steps, between the first and second floors, was a bald patch on the paper which was spreading inexorably as tenants idly stripped the frayed ends in passing. To discourage them I tried to smooth the perimeter with sandpaper, but someone's nails were sharp and strong, the efficient tools of a destructive urge. The culprit always managed to find a weak spot at which to pick, flaying the poor wall bit by bit, a slow torture.

The homosexual Maoists in 3B were prime suspects for a while. But David and Jonathan turned out to be not only very nice, but well-behaved, especially David who was five feet-four with a face as beautiful as a child's. His parents were Chinese, but he had been born and raised in England. Jonathan, who was from Chichester, was six feet-one, adored David and regarded him as a great intellect. It was certainly difficult to argue with him. He had an answer for everything. But they were invariably kind and considerate and never went anywhere without each other and their little red books, preaching their leader's theories whenever an opportunity permitted. Theirs was the only room that was always clean, tidy and aired. They could not possibly be guilty.

They were excellent tenants, Madam Zed's best really. What she made of them, I don't know. If she'd drawn any conclusions as to their politics or sexuality she never said. Perhaps her intolerance of her own sex allowed her to indulge the other one whatever its errors or excesses.

Trevor was a strong contender for second-best and might even have surpassed Jonathan and David if he had not played the clarinet. There had been some complaints, but my employer took little notice. Trevor was a good-humoured Yorkshireman and poor as a church mouse. He worked for a small graphics company specializing in animal calendars. He was always smiling and whistling.

The other young men were careless or boorish or snobbish or all three. The state of their rooms and their linen was a disgrace. Even the natty dressers smelled of wet dogs. (I was cursed with Nora's olfactory nerves, all right.) None of them could have visited the laundromat more than once a month. They lived in a fug of stale cigarette smoke, dirty socks and semen. The ones with gas rings were the worse. Their tinned beef-noodle soup or spaghetti rings or hot milk were forever boiling over on to the rings they did not bother to clean. The protein coagulated, the lactose turned black and brittle. They just went on reheating the spillage every time they cooked, adding a further revolting dimension to the atmosphere of their chambers. No wonder Madam Zed required maids to keep the place habitable.

In general they were decent to me, and I was pleasant and respectful to them. (I intended to question them about Miles once I had gained their confidence.) I scrubbed their sinks and lavatories and floors. I hauled baskets of their dirty bedding down the seventy-four steps. (The dumb waiter hadn't worked in years.) I carried up ten-pound packages of clean sheets and pillow cases fresh from the laundry and wrapped in brown paper.

Making the beds was the most pleasant of my many duties. By the time I'd arrived with fresh linen, the windows would have been open for twenty minutes. I'd drag the single beds from the walls and unfurl the sheets with their creases deep and sharp as in a painting by Zurbarán. They floated high over the bed and hovered for a second before descending like an undeserved blessing on the stained mattresses. Aunt Bernie would have approved of these sheets which were of sturdy cotton. No polyester, no nylon, all quite correct with good hems and no loose threads. I would smooth them out and adjust them so that the valance on either side was exactly the same height from the floor. Then I would tuck the linen under the mattress, making perfect hospital corners as Nora had taught me. Next came the blankets and chenille bedspreads which I'd have hung over the windowsill if the weather was fine. I even made hospital corners with the blankets though this was not strictly necessary. I would then beat and fluff the pillows to maximum volume, lay them on top of the spread which I had folded back, then draw the spread carefully over the pillows as though respectfully covering a dead man's face. This done, I would contemplate the bed which looked almost holy, like an altar. I took satisfaction in the sight of it, as though it were a minor work of art. I know it sounds silly, but it helped me to bear what I was doing. The rest of my chores were debilitating and dull, the sorts of things Aunt Bernie claimed there was merit in. Offer it up, Rose, offer it up.

I discovered that the house was badly in need of repairs. There was damp along the outside walls, and the window frames were turning to pulp. Each week I undid the handiwork of a thousand spiders. Several of the bath-tubs leaked and hairline cracks cross-hatched the plaster. The long shadowy hallways and high ceilings were in need of decoration, and there was none of the human relief that a picture or a tapestry brings. On top of everything else, the place was probably a fire trap. Yet for all its disturbing features, it intrigued me. Here I could imagine your earlier life, before you met me, and somehow that was less painful than my memories of Greece.

I never met Bernice, the other maid who came on Wednesdays. I found signs of her presence – a bangle on the edge of the kitchen sink, a Tampax applicator floating in the downstairs loo – but our paths did not cross. Madam Zed saw to that. There was to be no fraternizing among the help. The condition of her leg made the seventy-four steps a challenge. Nevertheless she climbed them once a week to inspect every room (except the two that were locked and never opened) mainly criticizing but often nodding approval. I resented her authoritarian manner. Yet I found myself wanting to please her and, a good-natured minorite, was happy when I had. Aside from these tours I seldom met her except when she opened the door to me at eight-thirty in the morning. She was usually busy with her accounts, some of which, I noticed, occupied the same spot on the table as the first day I entered the ground-floor flat. There was barely space to set down a plate and cutlery, and I don't know where she ate unless she balanced her supper on the arm of a chair.

She entertained a few foreign gentlemen, old friends of her husband, I think, who knew him at Cambridge. They came mainly in the afternoon to drink tea and eat poppy-seed cake and converse in French, German or Czech. Madam Zed spoke several languages fluently. On these occasions she wore her purple velvet hairbow, a Cashmere sweater of emerald-green and a great deal of jewellery, mixing the chunky costume variety with the antique and precious. The men made her laugh, and when she laughed she was quite pretty. Her secret sweetness was unveiled, and I could see how she must have looked when she was a girl on her way to a music lesson in Vienna or later to a psychology class at the Sorbonne.

She had only one woman friend, a Miss Draycott, whom she always addressed as such though they had known each other for twenty years. Miss Draycott struck me as quite mad, with bulging pale-blue eyes and twitchy gestures. She regarded everyone as if they were both insignificant and dangerous, like mice who might run up her leg. Madam Zed was devoted to her.

'She has had an interesting life,' she confided to me.

When my duties took me to the downstairs bathroom, I could hear them through the partially open door. They bickered continually. Voices were sometimes raised. Miss Draycott was the only person allowed to contradict my employer. Perhaps her madness exonerated her. Aside from these visits, Madam Zed was mainly alone. She said she never went out in the evenings. I assumed she read after watching the six o'clock news to which she was addicted. She managed both with a collection of spectacles and the magnifying glass which was perpetually among her papers. I always checked to see which book lay open on the tabletop welter. Most were in German, as were those which lined the shelves of the glass-doored bookcases. German, English, some French. Works on psychology, parapsychology and philosophy. She clearly enjoyed the odd romance for there was a shelf devoted to Rosamund Lehmann, Catherine Cookson, and others. She must have listened to music as well, judging from the record collection which included many 78s, heavy and brittle. Schubert, Mozart, Mahler, Janáček.

'My husband was very fond of Schubert,' she volunteered.

It was he who had paid a fortune in bribes to have the furniture shipped from Prague, following it across Europe to Trieste then to Cambridge. It represented only a fraction of what had graced their huge first-floor apartment. Persian and Baluchi carpets, standard lamps with tassled shades, the Blütner grand, paintings, including a Braque and a Sisley, and the shabby but once magisterial armchairs and couch – they were lucky to have me to keep them dusted and polished and beaten. One of the pictures was a portrait of Madam Zed herself, a present from a friend. I found it most unflattering. Her eyes protruded, her lower lip was exaggerated to almost idiotic proportion. However, her short black curls, restrained by a blue headband, were charming.

I wanted to ask her about her precious objects. The longer I worked for her, the more curious I became. She had stories to tell, I was sure. Even more though, I wanted to ask the *one* question. But I didn't. I was biding my time, waiting for an opening, the right moment. She never mentioned my previous visit or questions. Sometimes they hung in the air between us, but perhaps I was imagining that. She spoke to me only when moved to do so. She was like a child; she did not aim to please or satisfy.

Whenever I came in to dust and hoover her flat, I kept an eye out for my letters. I still believed she had received but never forwarded them. I didn't trust her. One morning as I was on my knees, cleaning the toes of the *chaise-longue*'s lion feet, she looked up from her accounts and spoke to me.

'Miss Mullen.'

'Yes.'

'You asked me about Mr Miles.'

'Yes.'

'I have had a postcard.'

I wanted desperately to go to the loo.

'That's nice. Is he well?'

'He is very well.' She pushed her spectacles back on to her nose and returned to her accounts.

I carried on working. She said nothing.

'Where is he?' I finally asked.

'Who?'

'Miles.'

'Mr Miles is in Africa.'

'Oh. Excuse me, please. I'll be right back.' I walked from the room as normally as I could then dashed for the toilet.

Weeks went by before she referred to you again.

*

My life was divided between two streets. Four days a week I squandered my energies in the sepulchral atmosphere of 83 Laughton Gardens. The rest of the time I spent recovering in Sally Soames's basement, then going out to the Road to wander among peole who smiled at me and of whom I was fond but oddly distanced as though I were watching them in a film. My two worlds were linked by the 28 bus. I went, as the English say, from pillar to post, a divided person with no peace of mind.

After the conversation with Madam Zed my anxiety became acute. I had bad dreams. In one of them you were the young man who had been Aunt Bernie's only suitor, he who had made someone else pregnant but wanted to marry Aunt Bernie anyway and had been refused. I saw Aunt Bernie from behind, sitting in a circle of light at the foot of the cellar stairs. A blue headband prevented her black curls from falling onto her forehead. Her slate was propped on an easel which stood on the earth floor. She was drawing cats, very lifelike but with malicious eyes. You walked down the steps. You had come to charm and entreat. When you approached she turned her back on you and swung full round on her stool. Then I saw that her face was that of Madam Zed, and her eyes were – but I can't remember. On another occasion it was you who wore the disguise. You appeared first as Travis who I could not believe I had found at last. But when I rushed to embrace him, he turned into you and you laughed and pulled faces and vanished just as I was about to kiss you.

I began to suspect a conspiracy. You know paranoia is uncharacteristic of me. But for a while I was convinced that you and Madam Zed were colluding. I imagined you conspiring against me, whispering and laughing as you set new traps and planted false clues. Why did you want to trick me this way and hurt me? What had I done to win your contempt and inspire your malice? What made me such a good victim? I wondered if you were hiding in the house. It would be easy to do. I walked without knocking into Madam Zed's sitting-room, hoping to catch you together, but she was always alone or with her gentlemen callers. Every day, twice a day, I tried the doors to the locked rooms, in case you'd forgotten to turn the key in the latch. But of course you would never forget. I attached hairs between the door and its frame and checked each morning to see if they had been disturbed. They hadn't. I listened, my ear pressed to the dark wood, but there was no sound. You would never make a tell-tale noise. Were you watching me play private eye?

To ease the pain of these fantasies I would go to The Goat and let

Gordon and Stuart buy me brandies and listen to Vi's reminiscences of old loves, and, on the evenings when Bruce turned up, sing along with the songs I had now learned by heart. Then I would read one of the novels I carried home each week from the Fulham library and fall asleep about one to rise at seven and take the 28 bus to Laughton Gardens.

The street had no trees, but it seemed to trap the darkness and damp of night and hold it prisoner all day. Perhaps because the buildings were so much higher than those of the surrounding area and cancelled the sun with each other's shadows. Not once did I feel welcome when I turned its corner. 'Her again,' hissed the houses.

Sometimes I felt afraid of the house. The skin on my back tightened with apprehension when I opened the door. I shrank from its dimensions as though it might swallow me whole. The atmosphere of late afternoon was particularly oppressive, and I hurried through my last chores, in order to be finished and out before dark. I should go, I thought. I should run. But of course I didn't.

Madam Zed and I began to talk, but only at her instigation. Slavs were creatures of moods, she said. They liked to be gregarious and then to withdraw. I tried to accept this explanation of her conduct, but I could not believe she was as simple as that. I tried also to repress my paranoia. You're crazy, Rose, I told myself. (You see, deep down I think I don't know anything. That is why I am obliged to put my faith in phantoms. For years I have been high on pale reflections.)

Inevitably I was drawn into these one-sided conversations. She was not interested in me other than as a good listener. Perhaps I had a boring palm after all. But I was very interested in her. I found her charismatic if also malign. For all her brutal directness, she had a sense of irony which I lacked and which both intimidated and seduced me. You and she had a lot in common.

From these monologues I gradually put her life-story into chronological order, though the episodes never followed any sequence and ended as abruptly as they started. She turned out to be not only exotic but courageous.

'When the Gestapo arrived at our flat, it was naked. My husband had already left and sent our belongings to Trieste.' (I could not understand why she had remained behind.) 'They found nothing, only me. I sat in the flat on the last kitchen chair and I waited for them to come. I said what do you want here, this is my flat. And they said you must come with us now. They were quite polite.

'At the prison I said to my interrogator, do whatever you want with me. Everyone I love has gone. And it was true. My husband was now safe as were my brother and sister-in-law. The rest of my family was in France. They were Catholics. I had no children. The Gestapo had no one to threaten me with. What could they do to me? You cannot hurt me, I said. And they knew this. And I knew they knew.'

'What did they want from you?'

'Formulas.'

I nearly laughed, it was such a cliché.

'My husband was a chemist. A Polish Jew. We were quite rich, you see. This they hated especially, that Jews should be rich. They took all our money. But they could not get the formulas of my husband. He had taken them to Trieste. And now I still wait for my money. The German government is required to pay me for what they stole. This is the law. I have written many times about my money and they promise and they delay. And so I wait and run a boarding house because I have not enough money. But the Germans must pay.'

She would begin suddenly. An event from the past would take hold of her mind and compel her to talk about it. These events did not follow on but were fed to me in a kind of slow release, a leisurely series of non sequiturs.

'I was travelling in Spain and Portugal. I stayed with many prominent people, and they were kind to me because though I was young I was very intelligent and everyone enjoyed my company. There was a famous joke at the time about Madam Franco. At a country house where I was staying a message came that she wished to pay a visit and would arrive the next day. She would expect tea, supper and breakfast. My hostess became very serious and then very busy. All the servants were summoned, and they worked hard for the rest of the day removing the silver and the pictures and the rugs and hiding all the noticeable valuables in the cellar and attic and stables. Madam Franco was notorious for appropriating whatever took her fancy in anyone's house and carrying it off. Naturally it was impossible to refuse her if one wished to continue a rich full life. The greatest fear was that, God forbid, she should arrive unannounced. So all the treasures were put away. But one rug in a small library they forgot, and so she got that. Miss Draycott tells me Queen Mary was similarly inclined.' Her tiny shoulders shook with laughter.

She ended, as she often did, with Masaryk; his reading, his musical tastes, the occasions on which she'd met him: tributes that trailed off into sadness and quiet. I didn't know who Masaryk was, so I looked him up in an encyclopedia in the Fulham Library reference room. He was elected president of Czechoslovakia in 1918 and is considered the father of his country. He hoped to unite the Bohemians and the Slovaks. He also wrote a book on suicide. He was learned, rational, humane. No wonder Madam Zed admired him. It seemed almost impossible for a politician to survive under such a burden of decency and it did not surprise me that he was doomed.

She said, 'You are a good listener, Miss Mullen. You have not too strong an identity.' It was the first compliment she'd paid me.

'When I was let out of the prison I returned to my flat and I found there a German couple. They said what are you doing here and I said this is my flat, get out. But they would not go. The Gestapo had given it to them, you see, and so I had nothing. These two were not terrible people. They were very embarrassed by what had happened and they felt sorry for me, I think. Still, they would not go. So I left my flat and my building and my street. I went to my bank where I had still some money, and I withdrew just enough to buy a jacket and some men's trousers and strong boots. I put on the clothes and threw away my dress and shoes and handbag and bracelets and rings and brooch. I put them in a dustbin and I walked away. I walked past the shop where I used to buy chocolates and past the furrier's where my husband had made me a present of a fox coat and past the jeweller's where he had bought me an emerald ring and past the café where I had gone so many afternoons to drink coffee and eat cakes. The manager knew me well. He was a good man. That afternoon he was standing by the door and he saw me walking alone in men's clothes and with no hat or make-up. We looked at each other but we said nothing. You see, he knew I was saying goodbye to him. I would have liked one of his wonderful coffees then. He would have given it to me for nothing. But I did not dare to stop. I knew I must get out of Prague that day. I did not take money because if the Germans had stopped me and found it that would have been the end of me. I went to the station and bought a third-class ticket. I had never in my life travelled anything but first class.

'I thought only about reaching my husband in Trieste. He might have left, I didn't know, but Trieste was where I must go. I left the train just before the Hungarian border and crossed at night. It was a miracle. There were many miracles. I walked for three months, wondering always if my husband was dead or thought I was dead. I had help from some people I knew in Budapest. For two days I was warm and I could have a bath. But I could not stay. It was too dangerous. So I crossed the mountains. On foot. It was very cold and often I had no shelter or food. Once a border guard helped me. It is unbelievable –

what you discover in people at such times. The enemy shows mercy, a friend betrays you. You expect nothing. You are always surprised. I knew I would come through.

'I had to wait many days to cross in the boat to Italy. The boats were illegal, you see. Sometimes they made it. Sometimes everyone was shot. The man and woman who ran these boats, they were truly saints, I tell you. They were very very brave. They were arrested and murdered a week after I crossed.

'I arrived in Trieste, thin, ragged, dirty. I had no money, so I walked on, wondering what I would do now I was free. I felt nothing, only tiredness. But I was so used to walking, to just keeping going, that I could trudge along not awake, not asleep. Just a machine that walks. I was following the main road that passed through a suburb. A bus came by and stopped. I looked up, for no reason. There on the top deck was sitting my husband.'

I could see him. I could see the man in her photograph with the sharp nose and the smile of a prince, a receding hairline and a high forehead. He turns at the sound of a woman's voice. He looks down. He smiles and rises from his seat, but as he does so the bus lurches and is off. The aisles are crowded, the stairway is impassable. 'Let me through,' she shouts, and a few people try to make way for her but the crush is so great that they can barely take a step backward, despite their good intentions and apologetic expressions. At the next stop she manages to force her way on to the street but when she looks back he is no longer there. He saw her, she is sure of that. She turns back and makes her way against the tide of people who throng the avenue. She tries to focus on every face. She gets a pair of blue eyes, a smart coat, a hat with a sweat-stained band, but no jacket of the type she thought she recognized. For every face she sees clearly, dozens pass in a haze. Why has he not followed her? She has come such a long way. She runs, panting and sweating, until she comes to an open square with monuments and public buildings. There fatigue and disappointment overcome her. She collapses and lies on the pavement as pedestrians pass without noticing or wanting to notice. She watches the clouds as they group, then disperse, only to regroup again. They slowly compose a face, a celestial face so vast that it obscures the sun and sky . . .

'Miss Mullen, today you are not such a good listener.'

'I'm sorry, what did you say?'

'I would like you to go to Daquise for me. A friend is coming to tea.'

301

'Yes, of course.'

'Are you all right?'

'I'm fine, Mrs Zahl, thank you.'

'You are white. You are having your period.'

'Yes,' I lied.

'Sit down, Miss Mullen. Drink some tea. Do you like sugar?'

'No, thank you. Black.'

'That is unusual.'

'My father drank it black.'

'Does he still?'

'I suppose he does.'

She smiled at me. 'Mine also drank it black.'

'I'd like to go to that café in Prague,' I said after a moment.

'And I also, Miss Mullen.' She returned to her accounts.

The following Tuesday morning she met me at the door, dressed for the street.

'I am going to Marks and Spencer, Miss Mullen,' she announced. 'I will be back at one.'

My golden opportunity. I could not get down the stairs fast enough. If I did my work at lightning speed I'd have a full hour to rifle the flat for traces of you. It did not take me long to find them. In the top right-hand drawer of her desk was a small stack of postcards held together with a rubber band. Postcards from Germany, Greece, Bombay, Benares, and all from you. How attentive you'd been, how thoughtful. I could just imagine your delighted landlady receiving them. Not that you were especially gallant. One of the cards showed a picture of an enormous sow being ministered to by an old woman in peasant costume.

'The pig women of Germany salute you!' ran the greeting. Most of them were in that sort of vein.

The ease with which I had discovered this evidence of your fidelity did not, however, relieve my anxiety. No doubt, I thought, these have been put here for me to discover in order to torment me. She has gone out deliberately and left this hoard for me to find. Perhaps there are other clues to your desertion, also planted for my benefit. Well, I will not give her the satisfaction of searching for them. I slammed the drawer shut.

Five minutes later I was opening all the others, removing their contents and examining them in the light that came in from the garden. There was nothing but a few pages of a planned memoir, photos, bills, letters in foreign languages. She must have forwarded my letters or thrown them away or hidden them so craftily that . . . I stopped myself following this train of thought. Rose, I told myself, you're losing your reason. She's just an eccentric old woman. She's interesting, charming, if a little authoritarian. She had a bad time, much worse than you. Your suspicions are base. They are unworthy of you. So stop this nonsense and get on with your work.

I spent the rest of the day on the upper floors and did not see her again for a week. Then one day she surprised me by walking into the bathroom while I was scrubbing the tub.

'You asked me about Mr Miles,' she said.

'Yes.' I looked up. 'I met him in Greece.'

'He never goes to Greece.'

I did not contradict her. 'Why not?'

'He had trouble once.'

'I see. He travels a lot.'

'A great deal. He has the itchy feet.' She laughed her high girlish giggle. 'He has also business. A company sends him, I think. It suits him very well.'

'A company?'

She left as abruptly as she'd come. She was holding a letter in her hand. Suddenly I understood that Miles was your *last* name. I am very slow sometimes.

That night I dreamt about breaking into one of the locked rooms. It was empty. The window was open and an old white lace curtain flapped in the breeze like a fragile dirty sail. Then I noticed a narrow flight of stairs. I wanted to climb them. I knew that they led to the roof. But if I did so would unsympathetic people arrive and drag me away as they had Eva?

In the morning I met Madam Zed on the stairs, but she passed me by with only a nod. The next Tuesday she again sustained a Slavonic mood-swing.

'Miss Mullen, you are a Catholic?'

'Yes, Mrs Zahl.'

'You have been to the Vatican?'

'Briefly.'

'I understand.' She hesitated, waiting to spring it on me. 'I saw there the Pope.'

What had the woman not seen? I played it straight as usual.

'No, but I saw him, really. In his undertrousers, what do you say?'

'Underwear. Were you in his bedroom?'

'No.' She was very serious. 'In the library.'

'The *Vatican* library?' Perhaps I should have visited it after all.

'Yes. He was between the shelves. He thought no one was there, but I was there. I recognized him, though he was wearing ordinary robes. That was Pius XII, a bad man.'

'Very bad.'

'He lifted his skirts and there I saw his undertrousers. They were white and came to his knees. And his red socks also, held up with garters. It was so funny. He took from the shelf another pair of undertrousers and put them on. One over the other. I wonder why. He did not see me, but I saw him. I will never forget these undertrousers.'

'I had a friend who waltzed with the Pope.'

'That is interesting. Was he also Pius XII?'

'No, the present Pope. But he was only a cardinal then, or a bishop – I forget.'

'And did he dance well, the present Pope?'

'Divinely.'

'I am glad.'

She told me many stories during the months I waited for you. Perhaps she told them to you as well. But I mention them in case she didn't. I'd hate you to miss anything.

Then I saw the Sign. I knew a critical event could not be far off. I found a discarded copy of *Time Out* on the bus. I picked it up and leafed through it, idly curious. (Since I never went out, I never bought it.) I checked the film section, and there on the bottom right-hand corner of page 59 was an advertisement for a showing at the ICA of two films by Tony Lasky – *Master and Servant* and *Martyrs*, which had won a prize in a San Francisco festival. And he hadn't told me. But then why should he? I hadn't written in months. The advertisement displayed a still of Hadley and me on the beach, the mirrors behind us reflecting the water, sand and sky. Her hands were on my shoulders and she was pushing me backwards on to the sand. I wore an expression of surrender. We looked exactly alike.

I missed my stop and had to walk four blocks back, clutching the magazine. I sat on the bed and looked again at the picture. I would go to see the films. I had to go. But when I picked up the telephone to call the box office I saw that the *Time Out* was a week old. I called anyway, but the showing had ended the previous Saturday. I asked if they were planning another screening, and the bored girl at the other end said maybe, since they were new to the repertoire. When, I asked. She didn't know. Were the shows well attended, were they a success? She didn't know really.

I tore out the picture, folded it and put it in my wallet. I carried it around with me for a long time until it was brittle and torn. I liked to look at it. It was a Sign.

The following morning I began work where I usually did – on the top floor, unlocking each door, holding my breath and running to the window. By the time I reached the second floor the house was criss-crossed with summer breezes. It gave me pleasure to open this mausoleum and let in a little of the season. I even sang as I carried the brown paper packages of linen up the stairs. On the fifty-second step I realized I had been singing along with something. The sound of a piano was rising up from the basement and filling the house as I had filled it with fresh air. This puzzled me. It was unlike Madam Zed to play records early in the day. She liked to give music her complete attention and considered it a travesty to use it as background noise. Why was she listening now? Perhaps she was entertaining one of her gentleman callers. I continued singing along with 'Smoke Gets in Your Eyes' until I reached the top floor where I was out of hearing range.

When I returned to the third floor, the music had switched to a stride piano in an energetic imitation of Fats Waller. I went down to the second floor. The technique wasn't brilliant but something of the original spirit was present. I descended to the first floor then the ground as the music got louder. The door to the basement stairs was ajar. I opened it and went quietly down. I had this feeling, you see. I opened the door to the flat.

I stood and watched you. I must have waited five minutes before you finally felt my eyes on you and turned to me. I guess you thought I didn't notice the flicker of irritated surprise that crossed your face. You still thought you could hide everything from me because I was a greenhorn and a bumpkin, but I saw. I pretended to let your arch smile win me.

'Well, well. Fancy meeting you here.'

'Hello, Miles. You never told me you could play.'

You picked up a cigarette, took a drag and sent a stream of smoke towards the ceiling. A new vice.

'Well,' you said. We held our respective positions while you looked me up and down like a fox.

'Cheeky maid suits you. Been here long?'

I curtsied. 'Didn't she tell you?'

'She said she had a new maid, but she didn't say it was you. You appear to be weathering the storms better than most.'

'I do as I'm told. I listen. She likes that.'

'Made any movies?'

'Uh, uh.'

You stood up and crossed the room. You laid your hand on my shoulder, a friendly gesture. I froze. I'd wanted you to touch me, but when you did I felt only anger.

'Hello, my darling.'

Still I did not respond. I kept quiet, I met your eyes. I waited to see what you would do and what clever means you would use to persuade me you had not wronged me.

20

Love

Dear Daddy,

I have just been reading about the resignation and imagining you doing the same. Someone said that Nixon is like a rat that you keep trying to kill with a broom. You whack here, you whack there, but you just miss him. He always escapes. He was the President and he subverted the Constitution. He is a criminal, but he will get off scot-free. To some he is a hero, a martyr, even. What does this mean? I really need to know what you think about this.

What Uncle Eugene would have called my new position is working out fantastically. My boss is very kind to me and entrusts to me her most important affairs. She says I am indispensable to her. I was so lucky to have seen that ad in the *Guardian*. She intends to give me a raise at Christmas. Whoever thought I'd end up as personal assistant to such a great lady? Just now our efforts are concentrated on the welfare and relocation of refugees. We are going to Geneva next week for a big conference. The Aga Khan's brother will speak, I'm hoping to be involved with the Vietnamese representatives. That's what I would like best. Failing that, the Palestinians. I can't tell you how wonderful it is to be a part of it all. For the first time, I really feel that my life has a meaning, because I am helping other people.

Did I tell you about the house? It is enormous, with six floors, very elegantly furnished, but not too *de luxe*, with large stained-glass windows like a church. There are always people coming and going, often staying overnight or for several weeks. Tuesday is our busiest day. So many appointments, so many foreign visitors to see. My French and Italian are improving daily. We even have some

Chinese among our colleagues. You should come and see. It is very exciting.

Give my best to Denise and my two little brothers. I'd better go now. I'm required upstairs. A very interesting young Englishman has just arrived and is serving as our medical adviser. He has travelled everywhere, and I enjoy talking to him when we have finished work. He has such original views.

Please write. Be a sport, Vinnie. It's been a long time. I miss you.

Your loving daughter,

Rose.

I fought you at first. I suspected you were trying to bamboozle me, to take unfair advantage of my need to think the best of people. You knew I wouldn't allow anyone simply to be bad. Addicted to emotional salvaging, I am sure that somewhere the good always lurks. Finally, against my better judgement, I decided to believe your story.

You insisted that, in my desperation, I had interpreted Aphrodite's actions as kindness rather than revenge. Furious at your rejection, she tried to make me think the worst of you. That is why she took my money and hid her own, along with the necklace.

'How could someone be that vindictive?' I asked.

'Spurned lovers are raw, dear. All exposed nerves. And Aphrodite was – excuse me, but she was a dreary bitch as well as a fifth-rate artist. Anyway, most people are bitter. We can't all be Rebeccas of Sunnybrook Farm, like you.'

'Is that how I am?'

'Huh, huh, huh.' Malevolent stage laugh. Collusive glance at make-believe audience.

'So the money she gave me was really my money. How bizarre.'

You shrugged. 'Guilt. Morning-after regrets.'

She had even hidden or destroyed your note to me.

'Rich people don't like to be crossed, especially in love,' you said. 'They're frustrated when they can't sue.'

'Then why spend time with them if they're so awful?'

'Exploitation is fun,' came your prompt reply. 'But I'm sorry for what I did, Rose. Sometimes if I think things are getting too complicated I run. It was bad of me. I do know that. Please forgive me.'

I accepted your apologies for the abrupt departure. You'd wanted to come back. You'd even returned, hoping to catch me alone. But you saw me with Aphrodite and assumed the worst. After your fight in Athens she'd forbidden you to go back to the house. You wanted to avoid her wrath, so you left. You guessed she'd poison my mind against you. (Though with your talent for verbal abuse, I found it hard to understand why you'd been reluctant to confront her.) Moreover, I had Hadley's letter to excuse my presence. You knew she wouldn't be angry with me.

My letters never reached you, not necessarily through the fault of Madam Zed. There used to be some weird characters in the building. Your mail had disappeared before. (Mail from whom?) You could only conclude once more that I didn't want to see you. I suggested that someone who really cared for me would have made a greater effort to confirm my feelings. But then men behave strangely, at least the men I know. They don't do the emotionally logical thing. Love makes them hide their love. Look at Travis, look at Vinnie. They certainly loved me and yet – But I did as I always do and convinced myself that tolerance and forgiveness weren't simply weakness in disguise.

My father hadn't so much deserted me as put himself out of reach. Travis had gone, probably for ever, to follow his very American destiny. He'd embraced the life of a wanderer, of this I'd been certain for a long time. He'd fulfilled his function of leading me into a new world and ultimately to you. I was glad he'd done that, although I still missed him and would always be sad that he had disappeared, like so many others, into our huge country where anonymity is so easily come by. He was smoke, air, unrecoverable. But you were not. This time, at least, the Elusive One was staying put, the phantom was incarnated and the past redeemed. (Though in my more lucid moments I conceded I might merely be replacing one obsession with another.) It was as though in capturing you I had captured at last the real Rose, the one who fled. Finding you again gave shape to my life, which may have seemed to others merely a collection of negative episodes, a series of senseless particle collisions. In fact, I reasoned, these events had been incitements to advance, cues from the wings by an unknown prompter. A divine plot had led me to Laughton Gardens and Madam Zed and the fourth-floor room where I spent hours in your company long after I was supposed to have left the building.

I wanted to ask you so many questions, but I waited, unwilling to spoil present happiness with prying. I waited so long that many will remain unanswered for ever.

'Madam Zed calls you Mr Miles.'

'It's my name.'

'You mean Miles is your last name?'

'Yes, dear.'

'Do you have a first name?'

'Yes. Most people do.'

'Is it – Rumplestiltskin?'

'Don't wise-ass me, Rose. It doesn't suit you.'

'Won't you tell me?'

You winked. Whoever has the secret has the power.

'Tell me. Please.'

'Roland.' Hands suddenly around my throat. 'If you breathe a word you'll wish you'd never been born.'

'But Roland's a wonderful name. It's heroic.'

'Hate it.'

'Isn't it funny we both hate our names?'

'Isn't it funny we're both Caucasian? Isn't it funny we're both living in the twentieth century? Isn't it funny we both have a heart, lungs and liver, not to mention other pieces of vital equipment?'

'Oh give me a kiss, grump.'

'No.' You began to pull your repertoire of repulsive faces, all of them combinations of the fatuous and the malign. Mr Hyde, Dracula, priapic dwarf, asylum escapee, Godzilla, orangutan. I have never known beautiful features contort themselves into such a catalogue of grotesques. The performance never failed to both horrify and make me laugh till I hurt. I begged you to stop, but you were merciless. You caught me and held me down on the bed and forced me to watch your grim antics close up. If I shut my eyes you pinched and tickled me until I opened them. Then you bounced the bed up and down so that I thought the springs would give way. I hadn't experienced anything like it since I was four.

I asked why you'd left medical school.

'I haven't left. I'm on sabbatical.' You strode up and down the room, wearing your sheet like a Roman senator.

'I thought about re-applying for my old job at the hospital, but I decided not to.'

'Why?'

'Because I hated my boss. He's a spineless, brain-dead weasel.'

'But what have you been doing all this time?'

'Enjoying myself.'

You described the things you'd seen in your travels, the exotic strangers you met who I was certain had wanted you and run after you and probably had you. I was captivated. I ate my heart out. That was what you wanted.

'August in Morocco was so bleeding hot we were going to bed in the morning and living at night. The flies were terrible, and the only way we could sleep was to wrap ourselves completely in sheets. When evening came we'd go for a swim, stay up all night and eat *kif* cookies and watch the stars and listen to Indian film music on an old 45 record player that belonged to one of the men in the village. Another swim at dawn, then back in the sack and under the sheets. I almost began to like it.

'Anyway, one night a Berber friend appears and says come with me, there's a party on the beach. Moulay will be there. Moulay was the local magician and general bad-guy. (The Moroccans are very superstitious.) So I went along with him down the cliff to the beach. There was a full moon, and I could see the locals gathered by the shore. They were watching Moulay who was waving his staff around and gibbering in Arabic. Finally he threw the staff on to the sand and yelled a command and before our eyes the staff turned into a gigantic snake and wriggled away. The locals ran off screaming.'

'You really saw it?'

'Sure. An old trick.'

We talked about the sea and about swimming, snorkeling and diving. I showed you the picture of Hadley and me on the beach. But you made no comment.

'I nearly drowned once.'

'Oh Miles, when?'

'A couple of years ago. It was early spring, and we'd gone to stay on an island off the coast of Wales where there's a monastery that takes guests. I went for a walk by myself and, it being an excellent day, I decided to have a swim. Current carried me straight out. Very scary.'

'It's hard to imagine you scared. How did you know about the monastery?'

'Oh, Madam Zed goes there sometimes.'

'And you went with her?'

'She kindly invited me. We've made several little jaunts together.'

'Where?'

'We are inquisitive, aren't we? Didn't your aunt ever tell you it's not polite?'

'The monastery intrigues me.'

'Then we'll go. Cup of tea, dear?'

'Yes, please. Do you mean it – about the monastery?'

'Of course I *mean* it. Do you think I'm some sort of *trifler*? I'm deeply offended. Even so, I'll arrange it. I must love you – it makes me so happy to please you.'

The idea of your travelling with Madam Zed disturbed me. I kept wondering where you slept and what you talked about and who paid. It was base of me, I know, but I couldn't help it. I also wondered who'd financed the rest of your globe-trotting.

'Madam Zed enjoys my company,' you said. 'She gets a bit nervous travelling alone so she offered to pay my fare if I looked after her and took care of the practicalities. She adores travel, and it's been hard for her the past few years, poor old dear. She has hundreds of invitations, you know. She has friends everywhere.'

And would she be inviting you again? And would you accept? And would it be soon? You referred to her with such respect. You didn't bother to conceal your admiration. I speculated about what sort of hold she had over you – or you over her. There was definitely something.

During these weeks I seldom saw the two of you together. But when I did you were always solicitous towards her, racing to open doors, helping her on with her coat, allowing her to carry nothing but her handbag. You'd enquire whether she had her keys, her inhaler and her face powder. You ran her errands, even screened prospective tenants. You yourself paid no rent. I knew that you spent afternoons with her – as many as three or four a week – playing chess or backgammon or gin, and that you were invited to meet her European callers. She held you in high regard, really rated you, I could tell. Between you was a secret bond that confounded me and fed my paranoia. I envied you both. You were so fascinating. At least to me.

I was obsessed by your enigmatic relationship. I imagined a blood kinship and looked for physical resemblances. Was she your aunt? Your mother, your grandmother? Both of you had those metallic eyes. You insisted you'd met her only three years ago, but I knew better. Yet if you were related why didn't you acknowledge it? Were you illegitimate? When I asked you gave a stage chuckle and denied any family ties. But there was something about the way you said it. You were lying, I felt sure. Then I was convinced that Madam Zed was the mysterious person who had rescued you and paid for your education. That would account for the affection which you obviously felt for her. Or perhaps her husband had been your benefactor. Perhaps he had introduced you to his wife in the first place? That too would make sense, but how had he discovered you and where? Were you the son of friends killed in the war, unable to escape in time from Hungary or Austria or Romania? You could easily be German or Slav. For a while I settled upon the latter theory. It was a good story with a happy ending and implied hope for the future. All I had to do was force you to confirm it.

Then there was the problem of money. Was your landlady in fact supporting you and was that why you were so gallant to her? And if not, how could you afford the money to take me to dinner?

'Savings, dear. Hadn't you noticed? I'm very careful with money. Mother was a Scot.'

'But you haven't got a mother.'

You made Madam Zed laugh. She loved to look at you. I watched her follow you with her eyes. She took you all in and digested you with satisfaction. You were delicious to her. Her feelings often seemed indecently close to my own. But old women are different, I thought. They may observe and take pleasure in observing, but their minds do not move towards the same goal. And I heard Hadley say, Oh yeah?

'Tell me about your family, Miles.'

'Actually, I was hatched from a giant melon.'

'Why can't you ever be serious?'

'I don't know. You inspire my silliness.'

'You mean, you're not silly with everyone?'

'Certainly not,' you snapped.

'Are you silly with your mother?'

'Rose, do you really think you can trick me with such crude tactics?'

'Worth a try. Do you have siblings?'

'A sister.'

'Only one?'

'Why would I want more?'

'Is she older or younger?'

'Older.'

'Is she pretty?'

'She looks like Princess Anne.'

'I don't believe it. Does she have children?'

'Yes.'

'Then you're an uncle.'

'Leave it out, Rose.'

We kept our friendship a secret. You warned me to be careful about going in and out of your room. Madam Zed must not find out. I suggested my place, but you complained that the decor would make you impotent. Anyway, you hated Fulham. It was dreary and dirty and full of riff-raff.

'Anything is preferable, even my rat-bag room,' you said. And you disliked The Goat. 'You may find it quaint, but I've seen too much of that sort of thing.'

You would come, with reluctance, every once and a while, but mainly we met at Laughton Gardens. Usually I stayed the night. Once I ran into Madam Zed in the hallway at 8 a.m. She was surprised. I lied and told her that one of the boys had let me in, and she gave me a quizzical look and didn't reply. This made me nervous, and my anxiety was fuelled by your cautionary remarks. You implied I'd lose my job if she discovered what we were up to. That she would even be angry with you. Then why stay here? I asked. Why not be safe at my place? For a little while you came home with me, but we soon returned to Laughton Gardens. I think you liked sailing close to the wind. You enjoyed the risk and the secrecy of it. Perhaps I did too. The game was infectious, and we played it with escalating relish, like bad children.

'What if one of the chaps rats on us?' The only ones we trusted were David and Jonathan.

'They wouldn't dare.'

'Why not?'

'They know what would happen to them if they did.'

I wasn't sure how to interpret these threats. You wielded the idea of retribution like a cloak. It was one of your props. What you would actually do if someone told, I hadn't a clue.

We made rules. If we went out in the evening to a movie or a restaurant, you returned with me to my flat. If we didn't go out, I stayed with you. That way entrances and exits were kept to a minimum. Our affair's secrecy only enhanced its wicked sweetness. You were illicit: the brother I hadn't known I wanted, my opposite and my twin. We never invited other people. I didn't care; I didn't miss them. I wanted to have you to myself with no distractions and no competition. Also I have never been one for giving much thought to the future. And so our strange life suited me.

Madam Zed now treated me coldly. Her stories abruptly stopped. I polished and hoovered and dusted in silence while she worked away at the accounts and talked on the telephone in French or German. She paid me promptly, handing over the brown envelope that contained my wages – in cash – every Friday afternoon. Sometimes with a smile. Usually not. She knows, I thought. She is waiting to strike. Perhaps she has already confronted Miles and he has defied her or made some sort of compromise. When I asked if this had happened you denied it. Now I wonder.

You did not deny you loved me, though you seldom uttered the straightforward words. No matter, they were not what I relied on. I counted on the fact that you clung to me. Clung and then withdrew, ashamed of your clinging. When you were distant or surly, I did not complain. I left you alone until the black mood lifted. I had touched your soul. You liked it and you didn't know if you should like it. I had lured a part of you from its dark cave out into the light. You resented the exposure and you compensated with props and weapons: coldness, sarcasm, cruel wit. Lots of teasing and pulling faces until you had exhausted your fund and lay down beside me and held me. You knew I would take it all and that it would break me. My persistence annoyed you. It also touched you.

'Rose, look at me.' You turned my head towards you and held your hands on either side of my face like blinkers, drawing me close until I was nearly touching your nose. 'What do you see?'

'My other self.'

You kissed my fingers which were now permanently bare of varnish as well as dry and red from housework.

'I love your hands.'

'They're horrible. They're not pretty any more.'

'I don't love them because they're beautiful, I love them because they're yours . . . stupid.'

You were like a child or an animal, damaged, perhaps, and scary. But also marvellous. Pure.

We read aloud to each other: Rilke or Sartre or Kafka or Nabakov. Nineteenth-century French novels and the sort of battered old volumes you used to be able to find in London's second-hand bookshops. You read very well, better than I, and clearly enjoyed the sound of your own voice which could be quite dramatic and resonant. I said you could have been an actor.

'Where did you go to school, Miles?'

You glanced in the mirror. 'I have a spot on my back. I'm not perfect.' You gave a stage pout.

'You're as perfect as anyone has a right to be. Who educated you'

'Who educated *you* dear? You say "cirqueeshush" for circuitous and "duplishush" for duplicitous and "egregyus" for egregious. Haven't you ever noticed that?'

I blushed. There were still words in my vocabulary which I had never heard pronounced. I had only, years ago, misread them. Just as there were words whose meaning I was unsure of but had always been embarrassed to ask about. That had not been lost on you, and you had purposely waited for an unguarded moment to enlighten me. I smiled and said I stood corrected.

'You don't even know what anomie means or what a zygote is.'

'Later, Miles.' I went to the door.

'*Rose.*' You sounded like Sister Mildred. 'Don't flounce off on me. I went to Laburnum Road Playgroup, Granby Village school, Radley, the University of Bristol and Bart's Medical School. Satisfied?'

I turned and hugged you, feeling your skin, silky as a cat's, under my fingers. You picked me up in your arms, swung me to right and left like a pendulum then dropped me on to the bed.

'The only thing they understand,' I heard Hadley say, 'is the sound of retreating feet.'

4C's chief delight was a window that overlooked the communal gardens. It was the reason Madam Zed had given you the room.

'Did you ask for it?'

'No, she offered.'

'How long have you lived here?'

'Always.'

We leaned out into the day, our arms resting on the ledge, and savoured the view of the grass and trees and the steeple of St Anne's beyond. Risky, but we could not resist the bright September morning. I could have claimed to be cleaning the room. Explaining my bathrobe on the back of the door would have been tricky.

'Rose,' you said, 'don't work today.'

'I have to.'

'Call in sick.'

'Miles, how can I?'

'Use the pay-phone in the hall.'

I did. Madam Zed answered and I made my excuses.

'I wonder if she believed me.'

'Let's go out.'

'Aren't you expected downstairs?'

'The hell with it. We'll play truant and drop some of these.' You held up a baby food jar full of yellow pills.

We left the house holding our breath lest Madam Zed make an unexpected appearance. Cautiously we eased the door shut until it gave a quiet click. You grabbed my hand and we ran off down the street. We turned into the Cromwell Road, passed the Science Museum then turned left at the V. & A. and entered the park via the Alexandra Gate. We sat down under a plane tree not far from the Albert Memorial and swallowed three each of the pills.

'Where did you get these?'

'Harry.'

'Who's Harry?'

'A friend from medical school. Harry is mad and bad and works for a drug company. Harry isn't above much.'

You took my hand and we lay on our backs under the high canopy of trees and enjoyed the cloud rush-hour and watched the leaves clap their hands, applauding us, with the blue sky as a backdrop. Then we began to talk, and slid by degrees into one of our unresolvable arguments.

'If Aunt Bernie hadn't died,' I mused out loud, 'I wouldn't ever have gone back to Florence, which means I wouldn't have found the seven hundred dollars. And if I hadn't found the seven hundred dollars, I wouldn't have gone to Greece, and if I hadn't gone to Greece I wouldn't have met you and we wouldn't be lying here in Hyde Park.'

'You make it sound so logical – like it was someone's *plan*, as if some cosmic headmaster were checking to make sure we learn our life-lessons properly.'

'I just feel a force, *something*, working away for our good.'

'Rose, there are two thousand diseases of the skin alone. Doesn't that tell you something about the human condition?'

'Yes, but – '

'It must be wonderful to be consoled by such codswallop. Why did you bother to leave the Church?'

'It's got nothing to do with the Church. Catholics are forbidden to be fatalistic. It's a mortal sin, didn't you know? We're supposed to believe in free will. It's a great burden.'

'I'm sure.'

'You're much more fatalistic than I am. You think we're doomed by the gene pool or by conditioning. I can't figure out which.'

'I just think we're nasty pieces of work and that it's better to face the fact.'

'OK, Micky Spillane. Look, it's obvious we're not all nasty. What about children, what about the sick and the poor, those who aren't strong or mean enough to struggle for survival? What about the victims?'

If the underdogs suffer – well, it's not what I personally would like; it gives me no pleasure. But it can't be helped.'

'That's disgusting.'

'Look, four hundred million years ago ninety-five per cent of all species on the planet were wiped out. No one knows why. How's that for victims? What would you have done for them, organize a march to Washington? It's nature, that's all.'

'Then, maybe. Now it's politics.'

317

'Rose, if you knew what really went on in the world you'd kill yourself.'

'Well, that's a nice thing to say . . . Am I that fragile?'

'You bet.'

'OK, try me. Tell me something really horrible and see how I react.'

'OK. You asked for it. We'll begin with the relatively innocuous and work our way to breaking point.'

'Shoot.'

'You like animals, don't you? Let's start with them. Research carried out in your country and mine in the name of medical and scientific progress. Speaking of underdogs, there's no dog more under than a stray mongrel. People deal in them, sell them to labs, make a nice profit too. Anyway in experiments at a medical college in Chicago, tubes made of PVC, rubber or silicone are stuffed down these doggies' larynxes. Then a laser beam is focued on each tube. The laser acts like a blow-torch and sets fire to their throats. Conclusion: there is no laser-safe tube.'

'Oh my God.'

'Quiet. I've hardly begun. Cats next. At Oxford University ten-day-old kittens have their eyes stitched shut and die at six months without having seen daylight.

'You seem to like victims, so I bet you're fond of bunnies. Well, some New Zealand Whites have paraquat applied directly to their bare skin to see how much it will take to kill them. The experimenters watch their slow death and take notes. Scientists certainly are funny people. Now, tell me what you think the life-lesson was for those bunnies.'

'None. I mean, how can I say? It's horrible.'

'Just a warm-up. Shall I go on'

'Yes.'

'Right. Humans now. The Turks have recently developed a very interesting new variation in torture. Instead of beating the defendant to a pulp, they round up his or her family and friends and work them over while the accused sits next door and listens. Guilt adds another dimension to the agony.'

'Miles, where do you learn these things?'

'Some people collect snuff boxes. I collect horror stories. I make it my business, partly for the edification of my fellow man, partly because they're the only things that really interest me.'

'Is that true?'

'It's very addictive stuff, let me tell you. Just wait, it'll grow on you.

Miles predicts it; you too will become a devotee. Anyway, you look as if you could use a good laugh. Personally I find this one the funniest. A couple of years ago both Coca- and Pepsi-Cola decide to introduce plastic bottles for their soft drinks. Pepsi's container is based on polyethylene terephthalate, while Coke goes for the polyacrolonitrile. The Monsanto Corporation runs tests – on animals, of course – to see if the substance is carcinogenic for humans. They say it's OK. Later the Environmental Defence Fund take the case to court where it turns out that the original approval was unjustified. More tests by other companies. More animals get cancer, birth defects, etc. Then the USDA decides that significant quantities of acrolonitrile are leaching into the Coke bottles. Result: polyacrolonitrile banned. Further result: Monsanto is left with twenty million unsold plastic Coke bottles, all poison. Isn't that a wonderful image? Twenty million – a mountain of non-biodegradable toxic Coke bottles. Isn't it a screech?'

'Hilarious.'

'So, after that bit of comic relief, on with the serious stuff. How are you bearing up?'

'Oh fine, fine . . .'

'I have next for your entertainment as fine an example of high-level corruption as even I have come across. Ready? This'll knock your socks off. Unit 731 is a notorious group of Japanese doctors who operated, shall we say, during the Second World War. They were of the Mengele school of medicine. They used prisoners of war to test chemical and bacteriological weapons. Their victims were nicknamed 'Maruta', meaning logs of wood. They were tied to stakes while anthrax and gangrene bombs exploded around them. They were put naked into freezers for frostbite research. The doctors of Unit 731 were very clever. Unlike their Nazi counterparts they escaped prosecution by giving the information obtained by these experiments to the US government who naturally gave them immunity.'

'Wow.'

'And here's where we separate the men from the boys. The Cossacks of Russia used to flay Jews alive and feed their flesh to the dogs. But the Red Indians did them one better. They fried their victims' flesh in strips and made them eat it . . . And in the Inquisition – '

'Stop!'

'OK. We'll leave the Inquisition for another time. But you've got to endure one more.'

'Why?'

'Because I'm in it. There was a big scandal in Germany last year about some barrels of toxic waste that went walkabout. Herr Geisel, a very prominent businessman, was alleged to be the godfather of the operation, but he astutely ducked all responsibility. It was touch and go for a while with lots of press and a few suicides. It's illegal to transport disguised toxic waste across international borders, you see. Herr Geisel, if it was he, simply repackaged the offending substances, changed their labels and paid out thousands in Deutschmarks to various officials who turned blind eyes. He's a kind of poison broker, you see. Anyway, the whole lot was dumped in Belgium – a hideously unsafe spot, but who cared. Then someone's conscience got the better of him and he ratted to the appropriate ministry. Key witnesses conveniently offed themselves, media coverage ceased and Herr Geisel went to the Seychelles. Twenty barrels, unfortunately, were never accounted for. An everyday story of life in the Rhineland.'

'And how did you find this out?'

'Herr Geisel was my boss.'

'But you can't speak German,' I said stupidly.

'Why do you always underestimate me? Of course I speak German.'

'Miles, you can't mean what you just told me.'

'Now you're doubting my honesty. I'll get a complex, and it'll be your fault. Don't you know there are hundreds of toxic middens all over Europe? Schools are built on them, high-rise blocks of flats, and nobody knows until it's too late and they're ill.'

'You know what I'm saying, Miles. What were you doing working for this Geisel?'

'A summer job, dear. Just to tide me over. Some people are deckchair attendants.'

'But he's a monster.'

'So they say, but remember: nothing was proved.'

'He's endangered thousands of people.'

'From which they'll learn a valuable life-lesson, I'm sure.'

'Oh, I see, Miles. You made it all up.'

'Dear, dear, dear. Nobody believes me. And it's a shame, because I know where those twenty barrels are.'

'Where are they?'

'What's the point of telling you? You wouldn't believe me either.'

'Miles, if you really do know it's your duty to report this to the authorities.'

'The authorities? The *authorities*?! Who do you think helped him dump the fucking stuff in the first place?'

'Oh. I see. Of course.' Suddenly I understood your terrible predicament. 'Do they know you know?'

You just laughed.

I repeated my question the next evening as we were having a drink in Finch's Wine Bar.

'Let's talk about it, Miles.'

'About what, sweetiepie?'

'The missing barrels.'

Your face went blank, then you burst out laughing.

'You are the most nelly woman I've ever met.'

'Please be serious.'

You hugged me. 'What fun you are. I do adore you. I was having you on.'

'Miles, are you sure?'

You continued to roar with laughter while I tried to smile. People turned at the sound of your cackle. I felt a fool.

'Don't tease me, Miles. It's really bad of you. I get very upset.'

'Why do you think I do it?'

'I don't know. Why do you do it?'

'For you, you silly bitch. Look, Roseate. At some point in your life you made a decision to see things as they really *aren't*. This annoys me. Because I love you it also worries me. So I'm determined to drag you forward into healthy cynicism. I want to rid you of pastels and paint you in primaries. I want to break your delicate shell and stomp all over it and smash it and grind it into grotty reality. I'm going to soil you. You're in the frame, Rose. Why aren't you grateful to me?'

'I am, in a funny way.'

You stayed at my flat that night. The weather was still hot and we lay with only one sheet over us – one of the few times such a thing had been possible in the year and a half I'd been in London. The three front windows were open, though the shades were drawn, and we could hear passing footsteps on the sidewalk above us. Music came from next door and traffic noises drifted in from the Road, reminding me of the East Village. There was a light breeze. The world was very close; it touched me on all sides. I felt I belonged in it as I had in New York and, years ago, on Black Water Road. I listened to you breathe, hardly breathing myself.

If you moved I was careful to remain still, even if you lay on my arm until the circulation stopped. I felt that any action on my part might shatter the atmosphere like glass. I had forgotten such emotional perfection. I had glimpsed it with Travis but lost it just when it seemed achievable. Now I lived in it as in a beautifully furnished room. I was determined that no false move on my part should lead to my eviction.

You rolled over and embraced me, making satisfied noises. Carefully I laid my arm across your back. I was taking infinite pains.

'Are you all right, Rose?'

'Yes.'

You rubbed your face in my neck. You were so warm, every bit of you. We quickly started to sweat.

'Let's get rid of the sheet.' You kicked it off and we lay face-up in the dark.

'That's better.' You took my hand. 'We have a very private life, don't we?'

'Yes, we do.'

'Do you mind?'

'No.'

'Sometimes I wonder. My misanthropy and everything.'

'I'm fine, Miles.'

'Then we'll just go on as we are.'

'Yes.'

You squeezed my hand and kissed the air, too tired, I guess, to raise your head again. Within seconds you were asleep.

21

Fancy Dress

'She's going away!'
'Where?'
'Eastbourne. Always goes in October. Drops in with the dying season.'
'Alone?' I was afraid she'd asked you to accompany her.
'Nope. With Miss Draycott. They have a few whoops-dearie nights out and walk along the front.'
'When?'
'Next week.'
It was Saturday and you'd breezed in, Gerald McBoing-Boing, unexpected, at nine in the morning. I was propped up in bed with the cup of tea you'd made me. Big-Bang strength, you said.
'For how long?'
'A week.'
'I wish it were longer.'
You began to tidy up my room, whistling and singing, going in and out with dustpans and waste baskets, pirouetting and closing the door with a deft foot, executing adroit gambados and waving a J-Cloth. I watched the saucy swing of your hips. I often wanted to ask if I was too old for you, but considering the age of my rival, it seemed a pointless question.
'Miles.'
'Yes, dear.'
'Why don't we do something? I mean, go away?'
'Can't. Cat-sitting. Axel mustn't be left on his own.'
'Not even for a couple of nights? I've never seen the English country-side.'
'I loathe the English countryside. Tell me, are you trying to build the Great Pyramid out of garbage?'
'I'm in a slovenly phase.'

323

'Your kitchen is a health hazard. I should be getting danger money for this.'

'I have to save my fastidiousness for 83 Laughton Gardens.'

'Rightly so. How's your tea doing? Time for another injection?'

'Yes, please.'

Madam Zed had said nothing of this proposed trip. But then she wouldn't. After teetering on the brink of intimacy, I had slid backwards into ordinary dumb servitude. The barest civilities were exchanged. Otherwise it was silence, accounts and the remains of afternoon teas. Often I'd be scrubbing the bath while the two of you giggled and tippled over your board games. If I was forced to enter the room where you sat opposite each other at the card table trundled out for these occasions, you both behaved, unless you needed something, as if I were not present.

'Miss Mullen, rrrrefill the pot,' she would say imperiously. And I would do it, trying all the while to catch your averted eyes. The pain of your absence was never as sharp as at such moments.

These were the only opportunities I had for observing the two of you together. While I moved about like an automaton, my senses were hyperactive.

Innocuous exchanges assumed enormous significance. I realize now that I exaggerated their importance. But at the time they wrung my heart.

On one occasion – you probably don't remember – you were playing cards and she had asked me to come and dust the insides of the bookcases. They had not been done properly for six months, she said. My predecessor had not been conscientious. They looked fine to me, safe behind their glass doors. But she insisted the books must be removed and cleaned, almost as if she wished to stage your tête-à-tête for my benefit.

For a while you played in silence, except for the neat slap of the cards and the crinkle of papers in the box of Terry's All Gold that lay beside you. You did not offer any to the maid. You sipped your teas, very grave. But I knew she would soon be bored with sobriety and ask me to fetch the port. Once I had done so, you began to speak to each other and soon you were talking more than playing.

'You did that on purpose, you dreadful bitch.'

'You're not concentrating.'

'Rubbish.'

'You are thinking of something else.'

'Don't bully me. I'll get very upset and scream and scream till
I'm sick.'

'When you are not concentrating you remind me of someone.'

'Who, darling?'

'Max Ernst.'

'So glad it's not Toulouse Lautrec.'

'When you don't concentrate you look much – kinder.'

'Remind me to concentrate.'

'He was very handsome, Max Ernst.'

'Indeed.'

'I once met him.'

'Did you?'

'I met also Breton. And Eluard – he whose wife left with the
painter.'

'I assume you're referring to Dali, not Bert the decorator.'

'Dali.'

Pause. Slap of cards. Groans.

'I was very happy in Paris.'

'Wicked cities suit you.'

'I was then a young girl. A student.'

'I wish I'd known you,' you said without a trace of irony as I nearly
knocked over a Japanese lacquer bowl.

'You would not have liked me.'

'That has nothing to do with wanting to know you.'

'You would not have liked me. I was too independent. I was also very
outspoken.'

'*Plus ça change . . .*'

'You would have lost patience with me. You would have looked for
someone bendable.'

'You make me sound like a scrap merchant.'

'This I do not understand.'

Pause. Slap of cards.

'So tell me, Titch, who was your heartthrob way back in the mists
of time? Who did you love?'

'I loved many.'

'Tart.'

'I loved my cousin.'

'Incest too.'

'Do not disturb yourself. He was my second cousin. We were
children together, the same age. Later he came also to study in
Paris and there I saw him many times. He was in love with me

325

and wished to marry me, but I could not decide. I was young and I didn't love him quite enough to give up the good time I was having. You understand?'

'Too well. What happened?'

'He went on holiday to Austria, to an aunt who had a house in the mountains and there he died.'

'How?'

'In a fire. An accident, very mysterious. Perhaps some sparks from the grate blew into the curtains. Or he was smoking in bed. Or the electrical switch – It was so tragic. He was so young.'

She stopped. The doorbell rang.

'Miss Mullen, if you please . . .'

As I left I heard the legs of your chair scrape softly on the carpet. I sensed your moving to her side. When I returned with the delivered parcel, the door to the flat was locked.

On Wednesday Madam Zed left for Eastbourne. I watched from the window of David and Jonathan's room as you carried her bags to the waiting taxi, assisted the two women into the car, then hopped in yourself. You were to accompany them to Victoria and see them safely on to the train, but it wasn't until you returned three hours later that I believed you weren't secretly planning to go with them. That was my mental state.

I waited for you to come and find me, but you didn't appear. I went on working, listening for your steps on the stairs. Finally I went to your room. The door was open and the place was in disarray. I panicked and was just about to race downstairs when you walked in.

'Oh Miles,' I said, not bothering to hide my relief. 'Where were you?'

'Serving Axel his tea.'

'Why is your room like this?' Normally it was immaculate, so clean and tidy that I hardly needed to touch it.

'I've moved into the basement flat.'

'What?'

'Until Madam returns. It was part of the deal.'

I slept that night on Madam Zed's bed. Or rather lay on it, because I could not sleep or even close my eyes. I expected her at any moment to walk in on us. I could not lose myself in making love. I worried my period might come and stain the sheets, or, even worse, the mattress beneath.

I still had my duties to perform (I wouldn't have dreamed of skipping

them) but otherwise I spent every moment with you. After the second
day I relaxed a little and it began to seem as though we had always
lived this way: harmoniously if eccentrically together. Like Greece, it
was exotic, but it was an exoticism of warmth and darkness rather than
light and rocks and sea. Enclosure rather than expanse.

The weather turned gusty, and there were little maelstroms of leaves
on the patio. I watched them through the french windows. I strained to
see the purple sky that omened winter, and wondered if the Channel
storms would drive Madam Zed from Eastbourne.

'What do you think, Miles? She wouldn't come back early, would
she?'

'Once she's settled, nothing can move her. In fact, I'm not sure she'll
ever die. She's decided life is It, and death isn't going to have an easy
time prying her loose.'

'She misses her husband.'

'That doesn't mean she wants to share his state.'

'I guess not. What shall we see tonight?'

'How about nothing. I'm sick of movies. I only go to please you.'

We'd been every night to a film and to supper. I hardly tasted the
food or remembered the movie. I was too aware of your presence to
absorb other stimuli. It even dispelled the fear of Madam Zed. She
ceased to haunt the flat. Only Axel watched me reproachfully.

You always paid for the meals. I tried to contribute, but you wouldn't
let me.

'Save your money, dear. Follow mother's example.'

I argued that you could not possess an indefinite supply, but you
didn't listen, you were very generous. Again I tried to make the source
of your income a topic of conversation.

'When I'm broke I'll get a job in the hospital.'

'Aren't you going back to medical school?'

'When I feel like it.'

'I don't understand. How can you be away so long?'

'Don't worry, Rose. They'll be delighted to have me.'

I wanted to ask again about Herr Geisel. But why risk spoiling these
perfect days? I still think I was right to keep silent, even if the result
is now eternal doubt. I believe we are entitled to personal, temporary
happiness and that this state of grace is worth a few ensuing anxieties.

I persuaded you to play the piano for me. I can't explain how happy
this made me. You always produced a packet of cigarettes for the
occasion and worked your way through études and barcaroles and
bagatelles and 'Stormy Weather' and 'Teddy Bear's Picnic' with a fag

dangling from your lips. You said they helped you to concentrate. You were quite a poser, weren't you? You were no great pianist either but I loved to watch and listen, seated in a far dark corner, audience of one. The goose-neck lamp on the Blütner lit up your face and hands and made the whole scene quite cinematic.

'How did you learn to play, Miles?'

'Don't know. Picked it up. I had a few lessons when I was a kid.'

'Why won't you tell me about your childhood?'

'I'd rather forget it.'

'Did you go to boarding school?' I'd only just learned that these places still existed, swallowing up children whole from the age of seven. I thought they had been eradicated or banned.

'By default. My damned uncle insisted on paying, I didn't want anything to do with school. I wanted to teach myself and get on the road as soon as possible. But the family insisted. I took my revenge and did badly on purpose.'

'But if your grades were bad, how did you get into medical school?'

'I cheated. What would you like to hear now, musically, I mean? You have a morbid fixation on my upbringing.'

'That's because you never volunteer information. You do it on purpose. You like to arouse my curiosity and then frustrate it.'

'You *are* getting to know me. Positively last request, Rose.'

'OK. "Stranger in Paradise".'

You stopped at midnight to avoid complaints from the lodgers. They all knew about your taking up residence with Axel, but my presence was naturally top-secret. We still had to be cautious with entrances and exits. It was the only reminder of restrictions during that week.

After making love in the mornings you'd practise Tai Chi while I cleaned up the evening's mess and cooked your breakfast. I sang you Jackson's song which you'd never heard and which you liked a lot. We had only two nights left.

On the penultimate afternoon you went out to do some errands for Madam Zed and arrived back at six with a bottle of vodka. You said we were going to stay home and celebrate. When I looked out at the harsh rain I felt pleased to be indoors. I put the vodka in the freezer and made a plate of sandwiches. We sat at the round table, cleared a space among the accounts and ate while the rain splattered against the french windows. The atmosphere was cosy and illicit, We switched on the stereo and set about getting smashed. The bottle of vodka was consumed in no time.

'We need more booze.'

'We're all right. It's awful out there.'

'We don't have to go out.' You strode towards the cabinet against the far wall. 'Damn, the old bag locked it.'

'Miles, what are you doing?'

'Looking for the key, of course.'

'Miles, you can't.'

'I can and I will, if only – aha! Just where I thought it would be. She's so predictable. There's a certain kind of woman who always hides keys in a mug of loose change. You'd think she could find a cleverer spot, wouldn't you? She has a tacky domestic side to her nature, you know.'

The doors opened on to a trove of alcohol. No wonder she'd locked it. Jade and amber bottles; liquids pink, mauve, yellow and diamond-clear; labels in gleaming black, silver and gold.

'God, it looks too beautiful to touch.'

'Leave out the scruples, sweetie, and choose your poison.'

'Oh no, she'll find out.'

'I know that, and that is why tomorrow morning I will purchase replacements for whatever we drink tonight.'

'It looks expensive.'

'It is.'

'I don't think we should. Somehow she'll know.'

'You seem to think she has supernatural powers.'

'She does.'

'Very well. I'll take the responsibility. I'll choose.'

You grabbed three bottles and returned to the table. I inspected them in the lamplight.

'What's Poire William?'

'An innocent little yellow pear. It's good with ice. Here, let me.'

You took two glasses to the kitchen where I could hear you smashing ice in a towel. You understood ice. In that respect you were more American than English. It must have been all your travelling. I stared at the bottles, unable to tear my pinned eyes away.

'They're like liquid gem stones.'

'Don't dilate – drink.' You poured me a glass and handed it to me.

'Delicious.'

We clinked glasses, smiling at each other, pleased with our naughtiness. The liqueur, hot and cold at the same time, had an immediate, elevating effect.

'I feel wicked,' you said.

'Want to go to bed?'

'In a while.'

'I'm not sure I like the look in your eyes.'

'You'll learn to love it. Come sit on my lap.'

You were so warm, your inner fires, as usual, banked up higher than mine.

'I fancy a bit of theatre,' you said. 'Let's explore.'

'Where?'

'Oh, I don't know.' You raised me up. 'Around.' You headed for Madam Zed's room. I followed and sat on the bed as you opened the closet door and disappeared inside.

'Miles, don't.'

The bed was in chaos and the floor littered with our clothing. Otherwise the room was as usual, its scores of trinkets and mementoes dust-free after my weekly cleaning. Though I'd been in the room many times, I had never opened a drawer unless it was necessary to put something away. This was sanctified ground. And I had never looked in the closet. Even when I broke into my employer's desk in search of the postcards, I left the bedroom inviolate.

The closet was much larger than I had supposed. A dressing gown hung on the back of the door. It looked so tiny without her that it made me feel guilty.

'Please stop, Miles. It isn't fair.'

'What's fair? God, the rubbish this woman collects. Look at these.' You emerged with hat boxes and an old fur coat.

'I didn't realize she was such a hoarder.'

'Yep. This is the Queen Rat's den, all right.' You produced a large zip-up plastic bag which contained two three-piece suits.

'Hubby's, I presume.'

'Miles, we really shouldn't. Let's put it back while we still can.'

I opened one of the boxes and removed a pink straw cloche with a battered velvet rose. 'Oooh, look at this!' I tried it on before the mirror. Your reflection appeared beside mine.

'It's divine on you.' You pulled aside my T-shirt and kissed my shoulder. This is the point at which to turn back, I thought.

I squirmed and twisted, trying for a better view. You dragged an ancient leather trunk into the middle of the floor.

'This is what I was looking for.'

'Is it locked?' I stood over you while you unfastened the buckles and straps.

'Yes, but I can guess where she keeps the key.'

It was exactly where you predicted – in the middle drawer of the dressing table which was sea-green with gilt edging. Inside a box of earrings. How well you knew her. I was very jealous. Perhaps you weren't guessing after all.

'Open it,' I said.

The inside of the trunk smelled of lavender and cedar and old paper. I removed the piece of yellowed pink satin that covered the contents. We heaped the bed with the clothes, accessories and billets-doux of five decades.

'This would make a healthy bequest to the V. & A.'

I reached for an album of photographs, bottle-green velvet with a heart-shaped mirror in the centre of its cover.

'Wait.' You stayed my hand. 'The drinks.'

We retrieved them, refilled them and commenced to plunder the nether regions of the trunk. The contents were arranged in a faded pastel order: bundles of letters, pressed flowers, greeting cards from 1936, baby shoes (whose?), old linen, photos of the Zahls in their dashing youth – what you called the Miss Haversham all-sorts. I kept my eyes peeled for a tell-tale adolescent picture of you. I was convinced it must be in there.

'Ah!' You produced a packet of letters. 'These are from the cute cousin.'

We read them greedily, consuming more Poire William and Framboise and sharing a joint all the while.

'My, he was keen on her.'

'I'll say.'

'It's so sad.'

You tossed them aside. 'Nothing scurrilous, though. There must be something more interesting. Now, what's this?'

From the very bottom of the trunk you withdrew a flat package wrapped in tissue paper. I made you take great care undoing the Sellotape so that we might stick it back on when our frolic was ended. It was my last rational act of the evening. You became quite rash and wild whenever you'd had too much to drink, which by now you had. And I was more and more reluctant to keep you in line.

'Please, Miles,' I said halfheartedly.

Something in the package winked and gleamed. You held it up, raising your arms above your head then standing.

'It's gorgeous.' I had seen one or two such dresses in the window of Clarisse's antique clothing store on 9th Street (meant for visitors from uptown, not the local girls), but never anything so well-preserved. It was made of sheer black crêpe, sewn all over with silver and black glass beads in undulating patterns that sparkled in the overhead lighting. I examined it, thinking how impressed Aunt Bernie would be with the perfect stitching.

'Put it on. Take the hat off first.'

I removed my jeans and T-shirt and slipped the dress over my head. It was heavy, like the finest chainmail.

'Look at yourself.' You turned me towards the mirror, your hands gripping my arms. 'You're fabulous.'

The dress was sleeveless with a scoop neck and hung straight from the shoulders to just below the waist where its flow was interrupted by a band. The skirt was cut on the bias, sipping into three V-shaped panels so that it flared gracefully. It must have nearly reached to Madam Zed's ankles, but it came to just below my knees. It was completely transparent.

'The knickers must go.'

I removed them.

'Lovely, but you're too pale.'

'Shall I make up my face?'

'Yes, but you need some shoes too, and some jewellery – and something for your hair.'

'Pin it up, maybe?'

'Yeah. Let's see what I can find here.'

I spent what seemed a long while in the bathroom. It was the first time since Aunt Bernie's death that I had masked my face with cosmetics.

'Look what I've found for you.'

You stood behind me and placed a tiara of black silk flowers on my head. It pinched, but it was worth any amount of suffering. We returned to the bedroom.

'There are some shoes, but they're too small for your American gun-boats.' Madam Zed was a size-three. 'Stay barefoot. It's quaint. Now for the jewellery.'

You slid rings on to my fingers, bangles about my wrists, fastened a double string of black pearls around my neck. I started to giggle.

'Stop it. This is serious. Stand back and let me see you. Almost perfect.'

'Thank you.'

'But I'm unworthy of you.'

'You could never be unworthy of me.'

'How can I transform myself?'

'You're not going to make faces, are you? Please don't make faces.'

'You ought to know better by now than to beg me not to do

something. It's bound to make me do it. I have to. I'm compelled. When will you learn? As it's a special occasion, though, I'll spare you.'

You plunged into the hanging plastic bags, yanking out suits, waistcoats, shirts, and ties, and flinging them aside. 'No . . . no . . . no . . . yes!'

You brandished a green velvet smoking jacket of immaculate cut, if the worse for wear.

'Wow. It's terrific.'

'Trousers are all too big. Have to roll the waistband over.'

'How about a cravat?'

'Corny.'

'You look – triumphant.' And a little scary. 'I feel like the two bad mice. What we need now is a party.'

'We are the party. A few bottles, a joint or two, a record player, smart gear, you and me. That's a party.'

'Then let's dance.'

'Hang on. First a drink.' We toasted as we faced the mirror, unable to stop admiring ourselves.

'We're a handsome couple.'

'Glamorous.'

'Amorous.'

'Chic.'

'Unique.'

'We even look alike.' And we were also well and truly gone.

We broke into Madam Zed's collection of 78s and chose a few that seemed suitable for the occasion. Some of them were from the thirties and forties and had that scratchy lyricism I like so much. I chose 'Nice Work If You Can Get It' by the Benny Goodman trio recorded in 1937. Vinnie would have killed for that. Where had she found it?

I held tight to you, my hand against a little throbbing vein in your neck. Barefoot, we covered the wide room, weaving our way among furniture, swaying and dipping, narrowly missing chairs and standard lamps and potted palms. I thought of Nora and Vinnie and the way they had roamed the dance floor at Third Cousin Melanie's wedding, as if it were everyone's obligation to make way for their grace and their happiness. I was four then, but I remembered.

I was afraid I'd start to giggle and had to work hard to control myself. This was fun, but it was also serious, like a rite.

'How Christopher Isherwood we are,' you said.

'You're a great dancer.'

'Naturally.'

'We've never danced before.'

'You never asked me.'

'I needed French courage.'

'Which reminds me. Let's have another drink.'

'We weren't bothering with ice now, and the glasses had a sticky veneer like melted candy. I wasn't worried. I didn't care about anything. I was on that crest that one hits just before sliding down into sickness. But I still had a little bit higher to go. The little bit that is irresistible and that guarantees the sickness. We were operating on the same principle as building an altar and wrecking it.

'I'm dizzy. I have to sit down for a minute.'

'Nope. Not allowed,' and you whirled me faster. I tripped over the magazine rack and we fell, my hysteria peaking and carrying me off like white water on its way to the falls. My state was contagious. You shook with laughter beside me until, calmed a little, you lifted the magical dress above my waist and made love to me on the carpet as hundreds of tiny glass beads ground into my back. It should have stopped there.

The combination of drink and grass had the strangest effect, because we woke after what seemed a short sleep, refreshed, energized and ready for more. God, we had a good time together.

'You never took your clothes off,' I said.

'Oh shit. Am I mussed? Better change.'

'No, you're beautiful in that. Why change?'

'Have to. Miles gets restless.'

I saved the record, which was still going round and round, the needle grinding into its precious surface.

'Hope we haven't destroyed this.'

'Don't worry about it.' You walked briskly towards the door. 'Come on, girl. Back to the dressing-room. More props.'

When I entered with the drinks, you stood naked in the midst of discarded clothes.

'I've looked,' you said, 'but there just isn't anything as good as what you're wearing.'

'Have it, then.'

'You're too good to me.'

'But what will I wear?'

'The smoking jacket, of course.'

'But what about underneath?'

'Wear nothing.'

You raised your arms and let the dress slide over your body.

'Very elegant,' I said. 'Good thing you're skinny.' I noticed a sprink-ling of beads across the carpet. 'But your hair. It needs something.'

I searched the hat boxes and found a purple turban, much mis-shapen and graced with a diamanté parrot brooch. It fitted perfectly, accentuating your oval face and full mouth. You paraded, pouting, before the glass.

'Make-up,' you said. 'Make me up. Just like you.'

I set to work, my hands not as steady as they might have been, but enjoying myself, completely absorbed in altering your seductiveness to the feminine mode. The results showed how well it worked – either way. There we stood, side by side: porcelain beige foundation, midnight-blue mascara, silver-grey eye-shadow, Black Honey blusher. We decided we must become more alike, so I slicked my hair with Madam Zed's baby oil and pinned it severely back. Then I added some clip-on earrings to your ensemble, but you insisted they exaggerated the starkness of your collar bones.

'Cover them with necklaces,' I suggested.

'In that case, we should break out the good stuff.' You went to the sea-green-and-gold dresser. I tripped from the bedroom in the smoking jacket that reached half-way down my thighs. Having rolled back the sleeves, I searched the records, found a Django Reinhardt and put it on. When I felt you stand behind me, I turned and laughed. You'd decked yourself preposterously in layers of gold, silver and gems, like a demented grand duchess.

'I couldn't make a decision, so I wore them all.'

Bangles jingled on your arms. Your fingers and even a couple of toes bulged with rings. When I looked closely I saw how fine the finery really was. You'd stolen her best treasures, all right.

'Play something for me, Miles.'

'Too drunk. Christ, where's the booze?'

I went down on all fours and crawled to fetch the bottle from under the table. (I had no idea how it had got there.) My exposed behind was too great a temptation, and you nudged it playfully with your foot. As I was about to reach for the bottle, I was caught off balance and fell forward, hitting the side of my face on the lion's-claw table leg.

'Sorry, darling.' You rushed to me, clinking and clanking, sat down on the floor beside me and put your arms around me. 'Sorry, Rose. I didn't mean to push you so hard. I really didn't.'

'Oh, look, Miles.' I pointed to the rising erection under your dress.

'Well, well, we have company.' It sprang rigid, holding aloft its glittering transparent tent.

We became hysterical all over again. I'd abandoned any thought of the condition of the flat and was relishing my irresponsibility and the feel of your shoulders and the salty taste of the creases in your neck.

'Ouch!'

'What is it, love? God, what have I done now?'

'Your jewels. They've stabbed me.'

'What a way to go. You've got class, Rose, I gotta admit.'

'Wait, it's caught, it's – ow!' I sat up quickly, not noticing that a strand of my hair was twisted round an amethyst.

'Here, let me. We are having difficulties, aren't we, bunbuns? There.'

'Thank you. What a relief.' It was when I kissed you that I saw the necklace. It was at the bottom of the heap, the nearest to your skin. Being jet, it was outshone by the gaudier overlay, and I might not have noticed it at all if it had not caught the light at a particular angle. I reached for it, but you pulled me back on to the floor and held me there. I let you, too surprised to speak. I tried in vain to catch another glimpse of the beads, but you rolled me over, pulled me to my knees, and made love to me from behind. Did you guess that I'd seen it? *Had* I seen it? As much as my boozy brain tried to twist that perception in your favour, the image remained, stubborn and vivid.

I no longer wanted to be drunk, but it was impossible to alter my state. I was lost and gone. My body felt nothing. It failed to respond to your movements or caresses. I simply endured you, waiting for you to finish so I could see the necklace again. But you jumped to your feet, Gerald McBoing-Boing, and vanished into the bathroom. I followed, stubbing my toe on a chair leg as the room lurched dangerously. Perhaps we were on a boat, the *Aegina*, maybe, in a storm at sea, and I had forgotten. The door was shut and I could hear you singing, something from *Guys and Dolls*, I think.

'Miles!' I opened the door and leaned against the wall to keep myself steady.

'Do you *mind?* I'm repairing my make-up, it's in a terrible state. Anyway, a gentleman doesn't just barge in on a lady, you know.'

'Miles, I want to see the necklace.'

'Kindly leave, or I'll be forced to call the cloakroom attendant.'

Perhaps we *were* on a ship. 'Miles, show it to me.'

'I'll scream, I tell you. Why, you're not even wearing trousers. Masher! Masher!'

'Miles.' I rested my hands on your shoulders. 'I remember it.' You removed my hands and tried to dodge me, but I grabbed the necklace, along with a couple of others, and kept hold of it as you jerked your head violently sideways. The strings gave and beads clattered across the white tile floor. We just stood there, looking at them. Time stopped. I will never be rid of this moment, I thought. It's inside me now, like a virus.

'Good move, Rose,' you said. 'Nice one.' And walked out.

I had seen the necklace. Being so well made, it had survived our scuffle with only one broken link, and lay like a dead snake in the corner. I picked it up and held it close to my face, trying to focus. I felt brain-damaged. It was impossible to reach a conclusion or formulate a decision via the usual mental processes. I was driven by an inner turmoil that would not tolerate stasis, however much I might have preferred it. I stood in the bathroom, my oiled hair hanging in limp strands, my mascara running in streaks, my lipstick all over my face, dressed in a stolen smoking jacket from an era gone for ever. It would have been easier to stay put, staring at the necklace and not being able to think. Except, as I said, for this perverse impulse towards action, however destructive. It was an instinct similar to that which prompted me all those years ago to abandon my aunt and was now propelling me towards the bedroom, the necklace in my hand.

'Miles, I want you to tell me about this.' I dangled it before you as once you had dangled it before me.

'You know I don't react well to demands.' You had removed the hat, and the dress which lay, its magic evaporated, a black heap on the bed. You'd changed into a dressing-gown, but left on the make-up. You looked like a has-been tubercular actor.

'Please tell me.'

'Why?'

I didn't answer. I watched your mischievous expression. For a split-second your gaze wavered.

'Well, I suppose I might as well tell you. You're a nice girl, really.'

You turned your back to me and began fussing with your hair before the mirror. I waited.

'The necklace is mine. It's always been mine. I gave it to Aphrodite as a present when she was my mistress.' (And to whom else?)

'Then why did she say it was hers?'

'Because rich people think that possession is nine points of the law – a view I don't happen to share.' I said nothing. 'I was finished with her and I wanted it back. It's not uncommon for an exasperated lover to turn Indian giver. Come, now, is it really so dreadful? Does it really merit that tragic expression?'

'I don't know. Why didn't you tell me this before?'

'I didn't *feel* like it. I *forgot* about it. I don't *know*.' The words made me flinch, they were spoken with such venom. My indignation was draining away.

'I feel bad about Aphrodite.'

'Don't.'

'I should write to her.'

'Suit yourself. I'm going to bed.'

You threw back the covers, lay down, drew them over you, and switched off the bedside light. Within minutes you were asleep. My resolution was spent and the state of the flat was beyond me. I would have to devote all the next day to repairing the damage we'd done. My present condition was a warning that I would not be equal to the task. I climbed in beside you, keeping as far away as I could. I too lost consciousness immediately, but woke after three hours as the alcohol-sugar rang every alarm bell in my nervous system. Then I remembered: you'd told me Aphrodite had *hidden* the necklace. That's what you'd said when you reappeared in August. If so, what was it doing here?

My stomach was trying to eat itself. My mouth tasted like swamp leavings. A major headache was simmering in my frontal lobes. Anxieties returned, a legion of demons to gnaw at my flesh and brain. Absurd theatrical phrases ran through my head: Hell gapes; This way madness lies; Hither comes the Armada; Thou art a living devil.

At last I passed out. I woke to hear you get out of bed and leave the room. The velvet drapes were drawn, and I couldn't tell what time it was. The phone rang and you answered it.

'The Castle,' you said in mock minatory tone.

Madam Zed, I was certain. There was a ding as you replaced the receiver, then the sound of water running into the bath. I could hear you whistling. I was too sick to move, and lay helpless as the waves of nausea rolled over me. I did not want to be sick while you were in the bath. Even in extremity I couldn't bear you to see me in a repulsive state. Embarrassment, shame: they can be stronger than anything.

After a while I heard your voice across a great distance, talking to Axel in your usual style, as though the two of you were disgruntled old gentlemen grumbling together at your club. Then silence. Then the slamming of the front door.

At noon I dragged myself from bed and gulped down two Alka-Seltzers. I hadn't been sick after all. I wished I had. I made a cup of tea and sat at the table, Axel on my lap. My employer was due back tomorrow. I must cover our tracks today. But it was after three before

I could bend over without feeling that the world was coming to an end. I made some cinnamon toast and that seemed to work. I listened for the door, hoping you'd return and lend a hand. It was a big job. But I was forced to begin without you.

By five I was nervous, but I kept going. The contents of the trunk, including the dress, now ravaged, had to be replaced in a semblance of the order in which they had rested for decades. It was like trying to mend a shattered glass. Not humanly possible, but, as usual, I did my best. Then there were the clothes, the littered floor, the contents of the drawers, some of which still lay scattered in the bathroom. I had no idea where each item of jewellery belonged, and by six I was in a panic. So I moved on to the other rooms. The condition of the necklaces would have to be explained. By whom? I wondered.

I worked away at repairing the damage we'd done, preoccupied with your treachery, if it was treachery; your wickedness, if it was wickedness. My mind orbited the problem like a satellite coming no nearer a solution, just going round and round. Clearly you'd lied about the necklace. But it was not the necklace that worried me so much as the fact that I had finally caught you out in a lie. Here was positive proof that you were worse than just a mischievous tease, that you were in fact capable of real malice. A shadow was cast upon you, one that no amount of light could dispel. It was a confirmation of all my fears.

About what else had you lied? About your Scottish mother and medical school; about laboratory animals and kinship with Madam Zed; about breast screenings and Herr Geisel; about loving me? I pictured you in military uniform, your slicked hair, your immaculate skin and clothes, your shiny boots, the pitiless expression of your eyes, your mouth hard and scornful. Your evil had risen to the surface, masking the beauty behind. You were a CIA agent, a mercenary, a vivisector, an arms dealer, a toxic waste peddler, a misogynist. The images were so extreme, so ludicrous, that I started to laugh. Neither were they one hundred per cent inappropriate. No smoke without fire. Yet surely one lie did not demolish your character or negate our relationship. A misplaced necklace did not confirm that I had given myself to a monster. No, but it did resurrect doubts, the ones I had buried for three months, implications I had chosen to ignore. I had fallen for a scoundrel, a cool scallywag who manipulated women, encouraged them to become dependent, then abandoned them.

I ran up to your room, leaving the door to the flat wide open. I found you on the bed fast asleep. You had been reading – a book of plans for

Ancient Greek temples. I spoke to you but you did not stir. Surely you were pretending, and in a moment would leap up, jump on me, tickle me, pull grotesque faces.

What about all the horrors you'd teased me with and then denied? I could not reconcile them with the sight of your dreaming face. I accused myself of paranoia, of a deranged mentality, of a bad hangover. I wanted to touch you and make everything real again, but I didn't dare. I listened to my heart, afraid the sound would wake you. You slept on, or appeared to. I didn't know what to do. I wanted to ask you again about the necklace, Madam Zed, and all the stories you'd told me, but I couldn't face a confrontation. She would throw us out, I would be banished, you would be banished; Adam an Eve eighty-sixed from Eden. Maybe it was for the best.

You opened your eyes and looked at me with indifference – as if I really were just the maid.

'Yes?' you said lazily.

'Did you – have you?'

'I'll do it later.' You closed your eyes again.

Downstairs I went on setting the place in order. At eight I went once more to check on you. Your room was empty, your clothes neatly folded on the back of the chair. I was exhausted. I looked in the mirror and felt that old urge to pull faces before it, to distort my features until they formed a fitting expression of my inner state. I saw that my hair was still slicked with oil, but I didn't care. My mind ground to a halt after reeling all day between your light and dark halves. I made a decision. I walked to the end of the road and took a taxi back to Fulham.

We'll sort it out, I thought, when I woke the next morning. That whole ugly scene was simply the result of the Poire William. Hadn't you said it was devastating? I smiled at the image of us cross-dressed and drunk. Two bad mice.

I'd left the flat immaculate (or so I imagined) and even managed to repair the jet necklace with a small pair of pliers. The rest of the jewellery I'd pushed as far to the back of the drawer as possible. I'd never seen her wear them. It would be months before she discovered they were broken. And by then . . . I assumed you had replaced the liqueurs, so I was not alarmed when I met Madam Zed at the top of the stairs the next morning. She stood as though she had been waiting for me.

'Come with me, please.'

I followed her downstairs. She stood by the table heaped with accounts, just like the first time I'd entered that room. She was full of tiny majesty.

'Did you have a nice vacation?' I asked.

'Very nice, thank you.' She held out a brown envelope.

'What's this?' I smiled.

'Your wages.'

'Thank you.' The envelope felt fat. 'Isn't this too much?'

'It is three weeks.'

I understood.

'I must let you go, Miss Mullen. You know my views. Maids do not mix with lodgers.'

I started to speak, but she stopped me with a raised hand.

'No talk. It is too bad, but you must go.'

'I'm sorry Mrs Zahl.'

'It is not discussable.'

I left my mop and bucket in the middle of the carpet and walked out.

22

Two Days

'Really, Rose, if you don't answer this letter, I'll just have to give up on you.'

It took a while to make sense of the last line. Then I re-read the envelope's postmarks and forwarding addresses and understood what had happened. Hadley's letter had followed me across London, languishing for weeks in the sorting office and finding me at last in Laughton Gardens. Apparently she had written before. How unlike Hadley, I thought, to have been so persistent. She must have mellowed – or even missed me.

The postmark was New York, the 5th of February. I consulted the calendar above the kitchen worktop. It was now the 20th of March. I hadn't much time. I wrote a hasty note and posted it on my way to the Europa. I asked the clerk to send it express and felt prodigal and lighthearted. Something unexpected had happened.

I forced myself not to think of Hadley while I did Madam Zed's shopping. My concentration had been poor recently, and I found that if I were to perform my duties to the best of my ability it was essential that I shut off that part of my mind that liked to whirr anarchistically away. I had trained myself to don a set of mental blinkers in order to focus exclusively on what was before me. This way I held my inner and outer lives in equilibrium. Over the past year I had achieved a measure of calm.

So when I come out of the shop I was able, with a good conscience, to let fantasy off the lead. I pictured Hadley now, nearly four years older than when I had waved to her from the window of the departing bus. Her complexion would be drier, perhaps with a few lines, her figure not as good since the birth of her first child. But her eyes and her smile would dazzle. She would be very demanding and laugh a lot. I would introduce her to my employer. We would have tea. The child would play on Madam Zed's sitting-room floor. It would be very jolly. Kit might even arrive in the midst of . . .

She would not understand my life. She could not tolerate the retreating part of me, the Frances to whom she had never been formally introduced. Even in New York she'd been irritated by it, always goading me to be more of a Rose. What would she make of my situation? She'd flee. She would indeed give up on me. Or she'd be fascinated, creature of extremes that she was. I hadn't realized how much I missed her, how her friendship confirmed and upheld me, even now. I'd thought of her often, usually as someone past and gone. But all the while I must have known she would strike again.

How would I break the news of her to Madam Zed? That sounds silly, I know – as though a visit from abroad were an earth-shattering event. It's just that our life was so routinely quiet. There was the physiotherapist, and there were the gentlemen callers, the ranks of whom had been sadly reduced. But they were so much a part of our existence as to create no interruptions and certainly no surprises. Now here was this foreigner from the past, a very volatile and tangible ghost. What would a frail old woman make of such a potentially disrupting influence?

Don't be daft, I told myself, it's no big deal. If my employer disapproves of my friend I can simply invite her up to 4C. Of course it's cramped, not with my belongings, which are very few, but with those other things, things left behind – all those books on astronomy and chemistry and Ancient Greece. Not the sort of place for a two year old to enjoy an uninhibited romp. We could always go to Daquise, but it would be nicer to be private. In the end the flat would be preferable. Cheerier, too, despite its lack of teatime light. I decided to persuade Madam Zed to let us stage the reunion in her flat.

That was where I spent almost all my time anyway. 4C was only for sleeping and for novel-reading on the nights when I was unable to sleep. Since I lived at Madam Zed's any normal person would concede that it was practically mine. So how could she object? But the idea of confronting her, even about such a trifle, made me nervous. When I opened the door and walked in with the groceries, the sight of her at the table, seated in her wheelchair with a book at which she peered through a rectangular magnifying glass, made me even less inclined to broach the subject. She looked up at me, her large eyes misty but bright beneath the points of a pink chiffon bow which held in place what was left of her hair. I put the bag in the kitchen and returned to face her.

'We're going to have a visitor.'

'Good.'

'Not someone you know.' Silence. 'A friend of mine.'

'Who is this friend?'

'Her name is Hadley, and we were great mates when I lived in New York. We were very fond of each other.'

'And so you are still fond?'

'Yes. She has a child.'

'And why not?'

'I mean, she'd like to bring the child. I'd like to see him.'

'She must bring the child.'

'You don't mind.'

She shrugged and smiled.

'I'm a bored old woman. I need distractions. Even bad ones.'

'Oh, it won't be bad. Hadley's very lively. Very amusing.'

'I am glad. Will you take me now to the toilet?'

I wheeled her to the bathroom, helped her up, set her down, waited, then helped her up again. It was an easy session, and in no time I had her back at the table immersed in *The Robe*. I performed such functions from 8 a.m. until 8 p.m. when one of the night nurses came on. I fed and bathed her, read her the papers, clipped her toenails, administered her medication which I also fetched from the chemist, went to the Czech butcher's to buy her Moravian sausages, learned to make her favourite noodles with poppy seeds, butter and sugar, watched the soaps with her, played gin rummy, answered her correspondence and wrote variations on that letter to the German government demanding the return of her stolen money. I also did the house accounts and paid the maids whose tenure was invariably short. None of them, she said, was like me; none as willing or as conscientious. Nevertheless I found the business side difficult. I was not an organizer. I need someone to indicate what must be done, since I am usually too preoccupied with my inner life to notice. Once I know the rules, I can follow them with a semblance of cheerful obedience. In this guise I served the tea and the Night and Day cake to her guests and joined them sometimes when they spoke in English, listening as they quibbled over the dates of Czechoslovakian royal succession or discussed events in Poland or told tales of border crossings amidst a storm of bullets.

'Miss Mullen is a gem,' they said.

I admit that at first I felt trapped by the iron routine of Madam Zed's daily life. I knew that an invalid's existence must be well ordered, but the rituals of illness weighed on me. There were few variations in our procedures. If the weather was fine she would spend an hour or so in the garden. On these occasions, her book would fall into their lap or slide on to the grass, and she would stare into the dark foliage as though communing with its chlorophyllous mysteries. Nothing she found there appeared to surprise her. I would come to fetch her, reluctant to disrupt her contemplation. I would stand apart until she turned, aware of my presence. She seemed eternally awake.

But the truly great events were the shopping expeditions to Marks and Spencer or Barker's, when I would push her in her wheelchair all the way to Kensington High Street; or further afield to Fenwick's or Selfridge's and, at Christmas, Harrods. The latter excursions required taxis and were carried off in a flurry of lists, loose buttons and last-minute details which bred extravagant anxieties. Then would come the carefully considered purchases: woolly underwear, Cashmere cardigans in fuschia and aquamarine to keep her warm beneath the sturdy pinafores which were all she could wear. Then presents and cards for surviving cousins and in-laws in Brno and Tel Aviv. Then tea and sandwiches in one of the upstairs restaurants with tartan curtains and brittle smiling mannequins moving among the customers who were dressed like tidy, well-scrubbed refugees. I had not realized that dowdiness on such a scale still existed. However, I saw it surpassed in Eastbourne where we'd made a bleak pilgrimage the previous October. I was replacing Miss Draycott who had died that summer, completely mad at last, and who had left the majority of her estate to my employer. The money generated elaborate fantasies of the Italian Lakes, St Paul de Vance and even Iceland, but these had yet to descend to the level of firm arrangements. I didn't pin my hopes on them. I was happy, in a way, as I was. I didn't lust after exotic lands. People I'd known had gone off in legions to India and Bali, but these places didn't call me. Really, Rose, I thought, you are not a very adventurous person. But that is not entirely true. My adventures have been of another sort.

The stroke had affected only her left side, incapacitating the arm and leg but causing no pain and leaving her speech and brain unimpaired. Despite its effects, Madam Zed was full of plans for the future: she would undertake journeys, she would walk again by her eightieth birthday, she would write her memoirs. She would re-read all of Proust and set up a hostel for runaway girls arriving in London. I listened with half an ear, having listened many times already. But I was moved by her optimism and her persistence. When I commented on her outlook, she replied that that was what Jung had rightly advised old people to do. She was lucky, she said. She found such an attitude easy to adopt; it was her natural approach to life.

What puzzled me most was her desire to have me back. I'd found temporary employment at the Pizza Express on the Fulham Road, and had been working four miserable evenings a week for a few months. When I could stand no more I left and found a pleasanter job stuffing junk mail through letterboxes. At least I was outdoors. After several weeks of this I received a telephone call from a Miss McKlusky. She said she was ringing for Mrs Zahl who would like me to visit. I said yes. My curiosity was strong. And so I went along to Laughton Gardens the next afternoon.

It was shocking to see her so diminished. She had shrunk into her small frame which listed to one side of her captor wheelchair.

'Miss Mullen,' she said in her gravelly voice. 'You don't look well.'

'I've been working hard.'

'It is not good for you. You must leave your job.'

'Actually, I need the money,' I replied a little irritably.

'Of course. I will pay you.'

'You!'

'I need help, as you can see.'

I glanced at the nurse.

'She's only temporary. I am not satisfied with her.' She still did not spare the feelings of her minions. 'None of my nurses has been satisfactory.' She paused then chuckled. 'It's not their fault. I am hard to please, aren't I, Miss McKlusky (pronounced "McKlooosky")? That is what she says. I am hard to please.'

Miss McKlusky was not to be drawn and kept her eyes firmly on the pages of *Woman's Own*. Madam Zed chuckled again. Her eyes positively sparkled. I smiled in spite of myself. She looked like a malicious crippled fairy.

'So.' Very serious again, very formal. 'Will you come?'

'Why are you asking me? Me in particular?'

'Does that matter?'

'Yes.'

'Because you know where is everything. You are trainable. And you are kind.'

I'm not kind, I seethed. I'd take great pleasure in strangling your wrinkled chicken throat.

'Axel likes you.'

Had she decided to pretend that the demolition of her flat had never taken place?

'I don't know,' I said.

'You will live here. It will not be expensive for you. You can save money.' She smiled again. 'Or you can throw it away.'

346

Bossy cow.

'Where would I stay?' And why was I asking?

'Where would you prefer?'

'4C. It has a good view.'

'It has a good view.' She nodded. 'The man in 4C will be removed.'

'Please don't do that.'

'He is never there in daylight. What is the view to him? You can arrive on Monday?'

'Yes.'

The hell with it. Why shouldn't I? Junk-mail delivery wasn't very edifying.

She did not refer to my dismissal nor to the events, whatever they were, that followed. Weeks passed and she did not mention them, and I was damned if I was going to ask her. Let her be inscrutable. I no longer wanted to discuss the matter. But one thing was sure. She did not ask me back because I knew 'where was everything'. She wanted my company, we shared certain memories, had certain affections in common. All right, Madam Zed, I thought, but you might be sorry.

Then I softened. Maybe she'd missed me after all and regretted her hasty decision to fire me. Clearly she needed me, though she'd never have put it that way. Wasn't this the kind of opportunity I'd looked for that first year in New York and been denied? I'd wanted, or thought I'd wanted, to look after someone. Well, here was my chance.

Despite her iron resolve, she'd grown sentimental since her illness. She cried easily, not over her present state, but over people and events from the past. Once as I was writing a letter to the Germans, I looked up to see her collapsed face wet with tears running from those eyes which continued to remind me of someone, I wasn't sure who.

'Are you all right, Mrs Zahl?' I didn't make a fuss. She wouldn't have liked it.

'I am thinking of Masaryk,' she said.

She complained that her eyes were bad. 'It was the lights of the interrogator. Soon I won't be able to read.'

'I'll read to you.'

'Thank you.'

She free-associated. She'd be talking about the new Pope when all of a sudden, without preliminaries, we would be in Amsterdam in 1952 or a garden in Lisbon overlooking the steps to the harbour; a flood in Africa, a dance in Nice. Lately she'd begun switching in mid-sentence to German or Czech, which I found unnerving and could not get used to. But in consequence my job was not as dull as it might have been.

Her fractured tales relieved the depression that comes of being trapped in linear time.

I wanted to ask again about my palm; I was convinced she had seen a catastrophe or some secret corruption. (There was a rotten spot in me, a soft spot. I was not, like my employer, consistently sound.) But I did not broach the subject. Occasionally she expressed an interest in my childhood, in particular my life with Aunt Bernie. She pitied me, I guess, for being the product of a low culture. The subject of Roland Miles did not come up. Though she sometimes referred to you in the third person. 'When *he* and I went to the monastery . . . It was a book which I gave to *him* . . .' I found this chilling, but still I did not attempt to draw her out. *He* had sent her three postcards which she did not offer to show me. I received none. But I disdained to rifle her drawers in search of them. I left my employer's belongings strictly alone unless instructed to do otherwise. We never discussed you. Yet you were always there, an invisible presence in the room, a force that united us.

Madam Zed was intrigued by what I told her about Hadley. I fed the fire of her interest, rationalizing that it was good for her as well as for me. I told her about Kit and finding the first word and how he had become a writer and how Hadley and I had been Underground film actresses in New York. She was fascinated by the fact that the Underground was a social phenomenon and not a means of public transport.

'Is it like Solidarity?' she asked.

'It's not as structured. In fact it had no structure.'

'Is it like Mr Dostoevsky's novel?'

'Sometimes.'

'Then it is quite nasty?'

'Also sometimes. But mainly fun.'

'It is anarchistic?'

'Very.'

'Hedonistic?'

'Quite.'

'And does it still exist?'

'You'll have to ask Hadley.'

'I will ask her.'

She was only half an hour late. I'd expected her to be later. I was nervous as I went to answer her ring, walking slowly at first, then taking the stairs two at a time once I was out of sight of Madam Zed.

'Hi there,' she said, her head cocked to one side, her left hand holding that of a child who was trying to drag her down on to the doormat. 'Rose, this is Danton.' The child took no notice of me but continued to tug at her arm and whine. He was very chic in black Osh-Kosh and pink jumper. On his feet were tiny cowboy boots. I don't think he liked the atmosphere of 83 Laughton Gardens.

'You look very nice,' I said to him.

'He chose it all himself,' replied his proud mother who was also looking very nice in a Byblos coat and a pair of boots I'd seen in the window of Kurt Geiger. But there was still something reassuringly messy about her.

'Can we come in?' I didn't realize I'd been staring.

The child was crying halfheartedly. Hadley explained that he was jet-lagged, and scooped him up, balancing him on her hip. I thought of the scene in the film where she'd pushed me down onto the sand. I remembered how physically strong she was. I could not make a connection between her and this child.

'Come and meet Mrs Zahl.'

'Can't I talk to you first?'

'No, first meet her. She'd like to see Danton.'

'OK.'

I'd given her a sketchy account of my circumstances, but her expression told me she was not prepared for the sight of my employer hunched in her wheelchair. As always, though, she rose to the occasion.

'I'm Rose's friend Hadley?' she said, lifting the end of the sentence to make it sound like a question.

'I am pleased to meet you,' Madam Zed replied in what must have sounded to Hadley like a growl.

Hadley introduced her son whose whingeing continued, and answered Madam Zed's polite enquiries about age, development and preferences in colours, ice-cream and TV programmes. I stood in surprised silence, watching them flirt, curiously left out.

'I haven't seen Rose for four years,' she announced. She placed her free arm around my shoulders and hugged me hard so that I leaned into her double embrace.

'And do you find her changed?' The three of them scrutinized me.

'Mmmm. Yes. We don't look alike any more. What do you think, Rose?'

'I really don't know.' I was very uncomfortable. 'I haven't had time to think about it yet. I feel shell-shocked just being in the same room with you. You look great,' I added hastily. And she did.

'I feel like hell. Always tired, not like I used to be.' She flopped into a chair, holding the squirming child against her to prevent his wrecking the sitting-room, which was clearly what he had in mind, and periodically covering his head with smacking kisses. Her patience impressed me. She was a good mother, I could tell.

'Your life's changed.' I stated the obvious.

'Everything's changed.'

'And do you still live Underground?' asked Madam Zed in all seriousness.

Hadley laughed. 'Well, it's where my heart lives.'

'You mean it is no more?'

'The Village is a carnival for tourists.' She addressed me. 'And your old neighbourhood is inhabited completely by junkies. You should see it. 2nd Street has been burnt out by the property speculators. The windows are all covered with corrugated iron. The ethnic groups are being moved way uptown or even further. There's a theory that they're being sent to gas chambers or incinerated, and that somewhere up the Hudson there are mass graves.'

'My God.'

'The *Voice* is like *The Times*. There's no money for the Cinemateque, but plenty for artists and galleries. You wouldn't believe SoHo on a Saturday afternoon. New York is just for the rich. There are even some deposed monarchs with entourages of people who ought to know better just falling over themselves to get photographed with them. Everything's about money. Culture is over. It's just so boring.'

I could feel her wanting to add that she wished there were someone interesting to go to bed with.

'Cal's has been taken over by people from uptown and Long Island. Nobody goes there any more and nobody knows what happened to Clyde. There's no place to go any more – besides two or three clubs way downtown. We don't see anyone.'

I didn't believe this for a moment.

'What about making movies?'

'Some get made, I guess, but I don't see them. I got a little tired of all that preciousness. I wasn't alone. It's not the same.' She sighed. 'Oh, I forgot, Drexel's dead.'

'What?'

'He *over-did* it.' She indicated her left forearm.

'I see. When?'

'Six months ago. I really miss him. There's no one else to talk to and have fun with. I'm so fed up. I just went to bed for two weeks after the funeral. I ate ice-cream and watched television and read movie-star biographies.' She nuzzled the child. 'Yes, we just watched television,

350

didn't we, Danny, didn't we, didn't we? Nasty old television with your poor old mom.'

I thought of all the busboys and wondered what had happened to them now that they were no longer lighting up the kitchen, tables and toilets at Cal's. All of a sudden I missed Drexel too. Not like I wanted him to appear in the room with us. I simply wanted to know he was somewhere in the world being impossible. Keeping the naughtiness quotient high. I missed them all. I missed Tony and Steve and Star and the Hadley and the Rose who used to be. I experienced the in-comprehension which until then I had only known when looking at photographs of myself as a small child. Where had we all gone? Even those of us who were still alive were somehow missing. How could we have let that happen? How could we have let anything change? I felt that nothing could ever replace that time in New York. I felt spent, like I'd used myself all up, or maybe somebody else had used me. I wonder who.

'And there are all these horrible scandals?' Hadley went on. 'Like the Love Canal?'

'What's that?'

'You haven't heard of the Love Canal?' She was amazed. 'The Love Canal is at Niagara Falls. Honeymooners – get it? Well, forty years ago this chemical company – I think it's called Hooker – dumped massive amounts of benzene and PCBs into the river and the government only just found out about it. The president declared the site a national emergency. I can't believe you don't know about it.'

'I lead a sheltered life.'

'Maybe that's no bad thing. At least you're spared the people obsessed with ecological catastrophe. After dinner everyone sits around and plays Ain't It Awful. They all try to one-up each other with stories of poison, war and death instead of art, gossip and sex. The seventies will be remembered as the decade when we all got scared, when we first heard about the collapse of the eco-system, when we found out the planet was sick and that we'd infected it. We should all have died in 1968.'

Hadley had now switched to her new set of acquaintances. It seemed she did go out occasionally.

'They're all so trivial. I get really angry and lose my temper and walk out. They all hate me. It's not fashionable anymore to be confrontational.' She laughed and hugged Danton. 'They're just pests, pests, pests, aren't they, Danny?'

'Peths, Peths, peths.' He clapped his hands then turned and slapped his mother in the face. 'You peth!'

'I am not. I just bought you a new jacket, so be nice to me.' He was her little doll.

'It's teatime.' I went to the kitchen and left them to gossip. Hadley appealed to Madam Zed. I could tell. That defiant toss of the head was something she could relate to. I listened as they discussed Madam Zed's illness. Hadley asked very direct questions. She didn't pretend not to see what she saw. She was sympathetic but not condescending. Her attitude was matter-of-fact with no hint of wanting to squirm away or resenting an old woman for being tiresome. She found it easy to talk to people. She was genuinely interested. Her generous spirit was still intact.

'Look, Danton, how wonderful!' she exclaimed as I carried in the tea tray. It was I, not Hadley, who wanted to squirm away.

The subject of Kit finally came up. His third novel was doing well. No more waiting for the first word, though his initial patience had been amply rewarded. They were getting rich. Of course nowhere near as rich as the unacceptably rich New Yorkers, but rich enough for them. They had an apartment on 1st Avenue with a view of the United Nations building.

'It's about a *doppelgänger*,' she told us. 'A double. Like that Poe story.'

'William Wilson.'

'That's it.' She laughed. 'Only it's not as good. It's not too bad, though, is it, Danny? Daddy's silly book isn't *too* bad.'

'Daddy dumb.'

'Hey, only I get to say that.'

'And is this double wicked?' asked Madam Zed.

'It's up to the reader to decide. Kit's never judgmental about his characters. He refuses to be the omniscient author.'

Danton's unruliness escalated into violence, and when he broke his cake plate Hadley decided it was time to leave.

'We're having dinner with some people tomorrow night,' she said as we stood at the door. 'I don't know whether they're awful or not. Why don't you come with us? Kit would like to see you.'

I accepted. We stood for a moment longer while the taxi idled on the street.

'She calls you Miss Mullen.' Hadley was incredulous.

'She's from another world, another planet, almost. Anyway, she's not always so formal. Sometimes I'm Rose. But not in front of callers.'

'When did she have this stroke?'

'About two years ago.'

'You weren't with her then?'

'No. She was alone. She'd lost someone she loved very much.'

'Oh. Well, she's nice. Crazy but nice.'

'Get her to read your palm.'

Hadley made a face. I waited until the taxi left and watched her and Danton waving to me out of the back window.

It had been months since I'd gone out to dinner. I had nothing suitable to wear, found my reflection in the mirror unsatisfactory, and glanced with regret at the copy of *Cousine Bette* that lay open on my bedside table.

We ate in an expensive restaurant near Piccadilly whose name I can't remember. The surroundings alternately dazzled and bored me. Ditto for the company, which consisted of Kit's English agent and his wife, a bottle-blonde with hard black eyes, and another writer whose name I didn't recognize and to whom I explained apologetically that I only read books on astronomy and Ancient Greece.

Neither Kit nor Hadley were bothered that I didn't fit in. They had a just-do-it attitude towards socializing which works or it doesn't. The English don't understand this. The others either didn't like me or wished, for my sake, that I wasn't there. But the discomfort was lost on the two New Yorkers.

Kit was kind and attentive to me as always. Hadley never stopped laughing, at what I could not work out. Back at their hotel he gallantly offered to take Danton upstairs to bed leaving Hadley and me in the bar with our bourbon and sodas.

'They *were* awful.' She smiled. 'I'm sorry.'

'It was interesting – what I could understand.'

'What do you mean? All they talked about was money.'

We turned to the past. Tony, she said, was still in California, lecturing on films at UCLA, the hero of a small group of staunch admirers. We'd stopped corresponding completely. Maybe I'd try again.

Star was married and living in Vermont with a painter. Steve was running a small production company. Jackson had disappeared into the San Francisco gay underground.

'Bike boys,' she snorted. 'Shooting amphetamine and getting himself smeared with shit. He'll end up dead too.' She listed other tragedies. I listened, very depressed.

'Rose,' she said suddenly, 'why don't you have a lover?'

'Please try to be more direct, Hadley.'

'Well?'

'No one's asked me lately.'

'You mean you wait to be asked?'

I shrugged.

'Well, you'll never meet anyone working for Mrs Zahl, you know.'

'Probably not.'

'You're getting too introverted. Why don't you leave England?'

'I like it here.'

'You can't like it. I mean, what do you think will happen to you? She might die. Does she have any money? Where would you be?'

'Don't know.'

'Rose, I'm not saying you should develop killer ambition, but don't you want to go forward a little?'

'No.'

'God, you're a beatnik.' She laughed. 'Just a genteel beatnik.'

'I just want to help someone who really needs me.'

'Then help us.'

'How?'

'Come back to New York. You'll never get anywhere here. Come with us. Really.' She pressed my arm. 'We have a big apartment with a spare room and I'll need help with this baby. Oh, I forgot to tell you. I'm pregnant again.'

'Congratulations.'

'You can work for us until you find a job. We talked about it and we decided it would be good for all of us.'

'Did you?'

'Oh Rose, don't give me that resigned British sarcasm. Don't you know it's all they have left?'

'Probably.' I wondered why everyone felt licensed to boss me around.

'I know New York's vulgar, but at least it's alive.'

I stared into my drink.

'You *really* don't have anyone to go to bed with?'

'Not at the moment.'

She described an affair she was having with a musician. I listened politely.

When she'd finished I said, 'Why didn't you wait for me in Greece?'

'I'm sorry about that. Kit and I had a fight. Besides, I assumed you were having fun somewhere else.'

'As you would have been if you were me.'

'OK, OK.'

'I did meet someone, actually. At Aphrodite's.'

'Who?' Her eyes lit up.

'An Englishman. Quite young and – interesting. He – '

'Not Roland Miles!'

'Yes.'

She burst out laughing. I was a little annoyed. She laughed and laughed. Finally she caught her breath. 'I fucked him!' she gasped.

'What?' Everyone in the bar turned towards us.

'That's what Kit and I fought about. That's why we left. Oh, I just love it!'

Her laughter rose again and broke all over the room, filling the corners, dashing itself against the bar.

'He said he didn't know you.'

'He did? Oh my God, how funny. I'll split in two.' She calmed down a little. 'What did you think? He's pretty cute. Did you have a good time?'

'As a matter of fact, yes. Was he really Aphrodite's lover?'

'Wasn't he everybody's? Is he around? I'd love to see him. On second thought, better not.'

'He's gone.'

'Just as well. Kit was so mad at me. Hardly spoke till we got back to New York. I just could not resist. I took one look at that mouth and that walk and – I even liked him, sort of. Know why?'

'Why?'

'He reminded me of you.'

23

Advent

Sister Dympna used to tell us that there was some good in everyone, a little bit, a speck, she insisted, even in the most abject sinner. God, she said, in his infinite goodness, was incapable of creating anything totally evil. When a small brave soul (it wasn't me) raised her hand and asked didn't that mean that God wasn't omnipotent, she was made to stay after school every day for a week. I sought confirmation of this little bit of goodness idea from Aunt Bernie, who, not surprisingly, sided with Sister Dympna. There was indeed good in everyone.

'Even Hitler?'

'Even Hitler.'

'You mean he might have gone to heaven?'

'If he'd been given Extreme Unction and made a good confession.'

I returned to Sister Dympna and, yes, it was possible, though unlikely. If we were truly sorry for our sins and made our last confession – provided a priest were handy or, at a pinch, any near-by person – we would be forgiven and join our Blessed Saviour and His Mother in heaven.

'Even Hitler?' I asked.

'Even Hitler,' she nodded, though she looked a little worried.

The idea bred a fantasy which I nurtured for years: the Führer in a dramatic death-bed scene; deep in the bunker, some humble parish priest, who could not believe his luck, kneeling over him, the two men illuminated by a celestial spotlight; the Act of Contrition, barely audible; the absolution, the winging of his snow-white soul towards paradise. Think of it: Hitler in heaven. Hope for us all, even the least and the worst. I would imagine it until I made myself sick.

A few days after Hadley left I remembered the tableau. Only this time Hitler had your face. Isn't that funny? Why I never told you I don't know. You would have laughed.

The day after Madam Zed fired me I called and called. As usual no one bothered to answer the phone. I half-expected you to just turn up, to swoop down on my flat and begin cheerfully knocking it into shape, chastising me about my sloppy habits while serving me tea and toast in bed. But you never came. Finally Jonathan answered. I'm sure he could tell by my voice that I was embarrassed. You weren't there. He checked your room and said it was empty except for the books. The door and the window were open, the bed stripped. You'd definitely gone.

That was when I decided to give up, get the job at the Pizza Express, read novels, and drink. The despair was necessary, I know that now, but at the time life was hard to bear, no matter how cunningly I reasoned. I'd given up my acquaintances from the restaurant. They just weren't interesting. At night I went to The Goat. I felt comfortable there. I became an acolyte in the cult of failure. I had built my altar and wrecked it. So what.

I resolved to be realistic at last and not make up stories to excuse you in advance. I was angry that you had left me holding the bag. I became almost a normal person with a normal quantum of rage. I vowed to stop roseating, to stop forcing every wrong to work out right, even if it meant tampering with the evidence. You were not going to get away with murder this time.

For months I nurtured my bitterness. But I could not sustain the effort. I guess I just don't have the equipment. Soon I was up to my old tricks with myself. (I can't live long without consoling rationalizations.)

What if you had done all this on purpose? Showing me the necklace – everything. You'd said once that you meant to purge me of that American gullibility which makes us putty in the hands of any ambitious manipulator, any old snake-oil salesman pedalling justifying, soothing or lucrative lies. You were trying to make me a healthy sceptic. You were determined to cure me and cures are painful. In the end I opted for this explanation, though it did not ease my hurt.

Then there was your sin of omission about Hadley. Perhaps you were just being sensitive, assuming that your affair with her, however brief, would wound me. You kept it a secret, trusting she would do the same, at least for a while, long enough for me to have got over you, perhaps.

Coming to terms with your ratting on me to Madam Zed (I guessed it was you who told her) took longer. As for disappearing, it was your style.

You were the only being true to your nature, which I accept, although it is a mystery to me; which I accept *because* it is a mystery to me.

Someone was still working away at the patch of wallpaper. The bald spot had grown in my absence and now reached nearly to the fourth-floor landing. I pictured you, sneaking out to tear off another strip with your clean sharp nails, then retreating to the locked room to snicker as I puzzled over your occult message. As for the postcards you'd sent to Madam Zed, I knew all along they were meant for me. You'd heard of her illness, you'd guessed that she would call for me and I would come and that she would be compelled to tell me you'd written. Behind these communications I heard you whispering to me. I first noticed it as I was arranging the pulley that lowered and raised her into the bath. I thought I was imagining it and put it down to the gin she and I had drunk half an hour before. Then another postcard arrived and the same thing happened. I was alone in my room. I was reading and getting sleepy when I heard you and woke up with a start. I couldn't make out your words. I only knew that they were addressed to me. After three similar incidents – on the stairs, in the kitchen, outside one of the locked doors – I decided that I was not hearing things. I knew what the whispering meant: you were returning. I must only stay quiet, read the signs, and wait. It was necessary, as usual, to have faith.

For a while I suffered a repetition of my earlier paranoia and went searching for you all over the house, trying the doors to the locked rooms, looking for means of entry via the roof. I woke at three in the morning to the sounds of your laugh, the piano, the voices of you and Madam Zed in conversation. I searched for clues to your presence in the bathrooms (difficult, since you always left them spotless). Once I found a few hairs. No one else in the building had such fine, sandy-coloured hair. I imagined Madam Zed holding you against your will as a punishment for consorting with the help. She was keeping you prisoner as a means of torturing me. I hated the malicious old harridan. I hated you for hiding from me. Again I pictured you both as conspirators plotting my moral, psychological and even physical destruction. I watched the garden from the upper rooms, hoping to catch you together. I was miserable and sick, sick in my mind. Then I began to see the signs.

Usually they arose out of the most ordinary circumstances. I soon developed small rituals, not only to encourage myself when I slid into doubt, but to facilitate the manifestation of these omens. Some were based on superstitions I'd evolved when I was a child. They were comparatively crude, I know, but nonetheless effective in pacifying me. If the telephone rang between 1 and 2 p.m., you would be back in two weeks. If it rang again before two-thirty, we would have a happy reunion. If I laid down six cards and one of them was the Ace of Hearts, all difficulties would be resolved and we would be together for good.

Some signs were arranged, you see. They were basically tricks. But soon I learned the superior method of simply letting them surprise me. Five milk bottles on the steps of Number 81 proved I was not just imagining everything. The hieroglyphs were ubiquitous once I'd learned to translate them. One day there were twelve milk bottles on our doorstep. One plus two equals three, the harmonious triangle. The runes could not have been better. The same afternoon I saw two herons winging their stately way towards St James's Park, a superlative omen which nourished my psyche for days. I was so excited I wanted to tell someone, but there was no one to tell. Then came the music. Themes and phrases would suddenly arrest my attention, sending me messages in harmony and counterpoint.

On the morning of the 3rd of September, I was listening to the 'Overture' to *Fidelio* on my Bush portable. *Fidelio* was my favourite opera then. When I went downstairs to say good morning to Madam Zed, she informed me that she had received a letter from a friend she'd not seen or heard of in twenty years and whom she'd assumed must be dead. The friend's name was Leonora, Beethoven's sublime heroine. I had to sit down to catch my breath.

Motifs reached for me out of nowhere, precisely echoing my state of mind at that moment. Everywhere I looked there were messages for me, hidden but findable as in some complex but innocent children's game. They sprang up all around me, erupted, bloomed, prolific as wild flowers or mushrooms.

I thought of Eva and her obsession with symbols and miracles translatable only by herself. Perhaps I too was born to be an interpreter of glyphs, a Sensitive, after all.

Sometimes the fur on Axel's cushion formed rudimentary images – a geometric pattern, a castle, a tree. I found things in the dustbin for which there was no logical explanation – a brand-new belt, a bouquet of fresh Sweet Williams, a pumice stone, a watch. I believed you had come in the night and planted them to bewitch me. They were answers to the questions I never stopped asking, confirmations, denials, signals and warnings. Like Travis and Frank I found them everywhere: magic in dustbins, signs on the stairs, symbols washed up with increasing frequency on the beaches of my small coast, carried by primordial currents from far and near. Therefore I was not surprised when you turned up.

Aside from the messages, life had been quiet. I looked after my employer with dedication and ran the house conscientiously if not brilliantly. I went one evening a week to The Goat and took the 28 bus home or walked if the weather was fine. I had a kitten, Musetta; my very own cat after so many surrogates, though I'd loved them all. She stayed the nights with me and in the daytime had the run of the house. She was about six weeks old when I got her, a tortoiseshell like Foxie (another omen), though her fur was longer and it looked as if her eyes would be green. She was an adorable delinquent, who gambolled and pillaged and flirted shamelessly with everyone. She was a free spirit, a sterling example of self-reliance.

There had been no messages for a few days, no billets-doux addressed to me and signed 'Yours truly, Fate'. The milk bottles did not assume any interesting formations, the parked cars were not significantly distributed, no evocative strain of music caught my ear when I least expected it, echoing my thoughts. Life gets pretty four-square without such visitations. I was consoled by the weather, leaning each morning and evening over my windowsill to gaze at the grey spire of St Anne's and the goldening garden where the work of thousands of spiders decked the soft decay. The fall is a slow process here – a graceful demise rather than the high drama of New England, a terminal patient enjoying to the last breath the sweetness of existence.

It was All Saints, my favourite day of the year, the day on which I would like to have been born, and a day which offered the probability of superior omens. If I had been baptized Rose and born on All Saints, life would have made much more sense.

Except for the lovely weather which came so generously through the french windows to find us, we were pretty gloomy. So when I saw the look in her eyes that morning I knew it meant only one thing. She sat with the postcard before her on the table. Her golden eyes danced and she smiled at me.

'He says he is coming.' She pushed the card towards me, the only one she'd voluntarily shown me. I picked it up.

Dear Titch,

Well, I'm broke. Why else would I be planning to turn up on the doorstep of Number 83 on the 4th of November? Now what's this I hear about you lazing around in a wheelchair? If there's one thing I can't abide it's sloth, so don't expect any sympathy from me. I intend to kick you into shape in short order. Lumpy custard for you, girl, so watch out. Longing to see you, though I suppose by now you look like a mouldy old cabbage.

Eternally,

Miles.

'Very nice,' I said and handed it back to her. The postmark was Hamburg and it was dated four days ago. She told me to prepare a room on the first floor. Not the maid, me.

Despite the advance notices and my faith in your affection for us, I was surprised to find myself unnerved at the prospect of seeing you again. I had to sit on the bed, and when I at last collected myself I found I had twisted the sheet so badly in my clenched hands that I was forced to go to the linen closet and get another. For the next three days I hardly ate or slept. Then the weather broke.

When I opened the sitting-room door you were bending over her, your mac dripping on to the carpet, your travelling bag beside you.

'Hi,' you said.

I nodded, then ran off to the bathroom to get hold of my nerves and my anger and stop myself behaving like a ninny. I pep-talked myself, issuing commands to cast off my cowardice and face you and fight like an American. How I wish I were better equipped for combat. In the end I calmed down and returned to the sitting-room, though I was damned if I would offer to make tea. You were slumped in the red chair, your legs languorously crossed, smoking a cigarette. You looked darker, but not from the effects of the sun. It was something under the skin, something seeping through. It was dirt, no, of course it wasn't. You were manicured, as usual, your shirt was blue-white, the little pores around your nose all open and clean. Still, there was a new dinginess about you. Dark rings circled your eyes which had lost their metallic brightness, though they darted towards the source of the slightest movement. Your clothes were expensive. How could you be broke? Your surface was smooth as ever, but a grey pigment had mixed with your composition.

I was glad to find you less than perfect. It made you a little more real and therefore a little more vulnerable. Could it be that you had lost some of your power to blind me? Maybe, Rose, I thought, but don't count on it. Still, I meant to keep up a better front than I had in the past. I wasn't simply going to let you back in with a smile. I had no intention of making a fuss, especially in front of Madam Zed, but this time you should be made to pay for your crimes. Pay a little something at least.

I observed the two of you from my place on the couch. Madam Zed did not take her eyes off you. She seemed to be watching your neurons at work, trying to see into your cells. At last she was being properly entertained. You were her favourite company, as you were mine. You spoke without interruption, the spotlight full on your soiled glamour. I grew acclimatized to your presence as you talked on and on about Africa. What had happened to Hamburg?

'We were taken to the poorest part of the city, the part the tourists never see. There were so many beggars I ran out of change in thirty seconds. Not that there was anything to buy. The so-called market was selling wormy oranges and week-old bread. My friend said it came from the backs of the bakeries and restaurants. It was what nobody else would touch, the bottom of the food chain. So these poor souls would bring half a loaf and sell it for the equivalent of about a quarter of a penny. It would then be broken into four pieces and sold for half a penny each. That was the level of the local economy. There were no women around. I mean none. But plenty of donkeys, all sweltering in clouds of flies and regularly thrashed. The garbage donkeys were the worst. They – '

'Why don't they revolt?' I felt obliged to say something, just to prove I wasn't afraid of you.

'Donkeys aren't very well organized, dear. Besides, they've always practised passive resistance.'

'I mean the people. How can they endure such an existence when just down the road in the big hotels – '

'Their spirit is broken, like the garbage donkeys.'

I kept quiet after that.

Madam Zed was listening with her whole being. She asked questions and nodded and looked pleased. Your tales gave her the vicarious pleasure she had once taken neat in her travels. She still enjoyed her life and therefore she was not defeated. I wondered how you saw her, this tiny woman with her twisted body, huge eyes, a pink chiffon bow in her hair and a Solidarity badge pinned to her Kelly-green cardigan.

Suddenly you stopped talking. 'I think I'll retire now, love. The flight was aerial Bedlam.'

'Go.' She waved her hand at you as though shooing away an adored child.

'Come this evening. We will eat.' She looked at me. 'All of us.'

The first time we sat down at a table together was peculiar, but the two bottles of Bordeaux you'd brought helped relax the initial tension. Not that you ever needed much to loosen your tongue. The drink and the food (I'd bought an Indian takeaway) weren't really compatible, but no one cared. The sound of rain and the dancing candlelight harmonized our peculiar reunion.

Madam Zed's hand was very shaky that night, and one or the other of us had to steady her glass for her while she drank.

'I'm a very fortunate woman,' she said, growing sentimental with wine. 'I've had a wonderful life.'

You patted her shoulder. 'We'll soon put a stop to that.'

She smiled. Tears filled her eyes. 'You could be my son,' she said, and turned to me. 'And you could be my daughter.'

There was a drained silence. We couldn't look at each other.

'Would you like your raspberry yoghurt now?' I asked.

'No. I will go to bed. I am too silly. Will you help me, please, Miss Mullen. I cannot wait for the night nurse.'

You began to clear the table. I could hear you singing and doing the washing-up as we went through our evening ritual. Some of it had to be skipped since she was practically asleep. As I was tucking her into bed she touched my arm.

'Rose,' she whispered. 'Give me a kiss good-night.'

I touched her forehead with my lips, not unlike the way I had touched Aunt Bernie's in her coffin. I pressed her hand. 'Good-night. God bless you,' I said.

The sink, the draining board and the table were immaculate. You sat in the red chair, a clean ashtray and a fresh pack of cigarettes beside you. The creases in your trousers were razor sharp.

'I see you've had a rise and a promotion.'

'No thanks to you.'

'Now, now.'

'You might have come to see me before you left.'

'I was in a hurry. I don't always have control over my life.'

'I don't think I believe that.'

'Don't, then.'

'Why didn't you stand up for me? We were in it together after all.'

'How could I save your bacon when I couldn't even save my own?'

'You mean she was – '

'Furious.'

'Well.' I sighed. 'I can't blame her.'

'Nonsense. Look how everything's worked out for the best. You might be right after all about turning bad into good. Maybe you really do have a talent for it. Look at you – you're much better off than you were two years ago.'

'It hasn't been too bad,' I answered. 'Are you smoking full-time now?'

'Yeah. Wanna make something of it?'

'You're free to do as you please. We all have the right to destroy ourselves.'

'That's very indulgent of you. But then I'm a very indulged person.'

'Why? Who else indulges you?' I smiled and sat down opposite you in the blue chair. We'd always called these furniture twins Labour and Tory.

You opened the pack of cigarettes. 'That's for me to know and you to find out.'

'Then you're welcome to your knowing.'

You smoked and stared at the ceiling.

'Where have you been, Miles?'

'The rose wants dusting. Africa.'

'But whereabouts?'

'All over. I'll tell you.'

No you wouldn't.

'Then you're staying?'

'Yes, dear.'

Silence.

'You know I live here now?' I made it sound a bit like a warning.

'I assumed.'

'Does that bother you?'

'Of course not. I'm delighted. Now, would you like to come and tuck *me* in?' You held out your hand. I didn't take it.

'I'm waiting for the night nurse. She'll be late.'

'Then I'll wait with you. Any more wine?'

I filled your glass. I was still the servant, at least in the confines of this room. Roles and poses; how they stick, stick, stick.

'You're glad to see Madam Zed?'

'Naturally.'

'Are you glad to see me?'

'I'm always glad to see you.'

'Sure. Any particular reason you're here – apart from having no money and needing a warm place to hibernate?'

'To spend Christmas with you, of course!' you exclaimed indignantly. 'I love the holy season. Advent's my favourite time of year.'

I sighed.

364

'Can we get ashes smeared on our foreheads?'

'Ashes are for Lent – as in Ash Wednesday.'

'How stupid of me.' You struck your forehead. 'Miles to brain, come in brain. I suppose we can't make our Easter Duty together?'

'No.'

'Promise we can later.'

I didn't answer. Why should I? You weren't serious.

'Promise, Rose.'

I kept quiet, just looking at you.

'*Please.*'

'Oh, all right, goddamnit.'

'Thank you.'

You came and sat on my lap.

'Forgive me, Rosie.'

'What, again?'

'You know you want to.'

'I *don't* know, actually. I'll just have to see.'

The weeks before Christmas: my memory of them is photographic. I can see the patterns in which the dust falls, number the hairs in eyelashes, compute each convolution in a Paisley fabric. Fresh detail springs out at me from the Chinese wallpaper, I discover a new and unnamed colour in Musetta's coat, can read the smallest print on billboards yards away. Particulars swarm so intensely around me that I wear sunglasses in the street to dilute the rich reality brew. Your presence animates everything. How am I to concentrate on my duties when the world is pressing so hard against me? And yet I do. I am devoted to you both. Nothing is too much trouble for me. Is it this concentration on another that brings the world so sharply into focus? A pressure has been lifted from a part of my brain – that, or it has closed up shop. Self-consciousness withers away. I see everything but myself. It is a blessed relief.

I no longer felt excluded from your games. When the Terry's Chocolate Orange was divided, segments found their way to the couch where I sat mending or scouring the papers for the news from Poland or for features I thought would interest and amuse her. We ate together, watched Television together. We were a family. Your attentiveness to both of us was touching. You would massage her tumid feet, taking infinite pains over the flesh that had given her so much trouble. You carried out the rubbish, insisting it was too heavy for me, and did the washing-up. You kneaded my shoulders after a tiring day and scrubbed my back in the bath and brought me cups of tea, and biscuits. You were so good to me, so thoughtful. You gave me a bracelet made of water-buffalo tusks, assuring me the animal had died a natural death. You said you'd bought it in India specially for me. You presented me with a pair of earrings, and with an oyster-coloured silk blouse with which I had nothing worthy to wear.

Often we just sat together as families do, not speaking, absorbed in a private present. Occasionally Madam Zed would lapse into one of her strange monologues about Cambridge or Prague, or an oft-repeated incident on her walk to freedom. There were even a couple of lectures on Czechoslovakian history. We should remember 1620, she said: the dire date of the country's annexation by the Hapsburg Empire. Other times she'd do that eerie trick of taking up a long-past conversation in Czech or German.

'Ever get the feeling the old girl's not quite the ticket?' you whispered.

I liked our silences best. I loved looking up and seeing you in the Tory chair. I delighted in your features and attitude, in your shadowed beauty. I would wait until you sensed me watching you and you looked up and our eyes met. Amazing, they telegraphed. What are we/you doing here?

You were at home every night, though you often went out from midday until suppertime. I never asked what you'd been up to, but you volunteered the information that you were making arrangements to return to medical school. You'd begin in the spring. It was all so promising.

Ever since that night Tony and I saw *Les Enfants Terribles* at the New Yorker I'd had a secret fantasy which now you helped me to fulfil. I'd experienced something of this dream with him, but it did not last. I myself shattered it. Yet here it was again, true and complete. I wanted to be alone in a room with a bed and someone I loved, never to leave this room, but to feel life progressing without us – out there, outside the walls – and an arcane life of our own inside. (The sense of exterior activity is essential if womb is not to become coffin.) I wanted to create a crucible with another who was also myself, and to shut out the world, once and for all. You and I and 4C and the fourth thing, the X-factor that included us and was more than us – the sum of our psyches and what they could generate. The genie of the room.

'Wouldn't it be wonderful,' I said, 'never to leave?'

'Yes.'

We set about building our holy place, our altar and shrine. We did it with books and decor and drink, with sex and music and darkness, with our treasures and our toys.

'It looks like a cross between a brothel, a gypsy caravan and a Bedouin tent.' You feigned contempt, but in fact you loved it. 'Oh, and a nursery school.'

With my new authority came permission to open one of the locked rooms which contained nothing more sinister than ancient drapes and bedspreads and a few tables and chairs. There was no stairway to the sky. I mentioned the furnishings to Madam Zed who could remember nothing about them and would never again be capable of climbing to the fourth floor to inspect them. I asked if I might use them for my room. It was, I said, a bit like a dormitory and I wished to add a more personal touch.

'Have them,' she said. 'What do I care for a lot of old curtains?'

We took them off to the cleaners, and they turned out quite nicely: a rich, red-brown damask, which had faded in parts to coral, and a grey-green velvet, thin in patches. We used them to cover the walls and ceiling and to block out every bit of sunlight. Who needed the view of a church steeple that was always the same? We rose at 4 a.m. and went to Bermondsey market and the junk market in Shoreditch. We found a stone garden urn for £2, a metal chair that was torture to sit in, a blue-glass shaded lamp, a reproduction of a Piranesi, an engraving of a gloomy Scottish castle. We went to second-hand bookshops and clothing stores where we found some interesting editions, a Victorian Paisley shawl, battered candlesticks whose paint had interestingly chipped and faded, and a maroon satin dressing gown that was straight out of Tennessee Williams, and more candlesticks. You bought me a bee-keeper's hat in which I looked wonderful and which I wore most evenings in the room. We were stock-piling, creating an emotional bunker.

One afternoon you arrived home with the *pièce de résistance*: an enormous mosquito net which we draped above the bed. Its arrangement took hours, but the result was a vision. We crawled inside it and made love.

When the room was finished we took formal possession of it, intending to leave as seldom as possible, aside from fulfilling our obligations to Madam Zed. We spent every night in our claustral environment. We had fun, we had a ball. Were you happy? Did you ever get tired? I guess you can't answer that.

*

'Turn round, Rose,' you ordered one morning when I was first to rise.

'Why?'

'Your ass has dropped.'

'Oh. Does it look awful?'

'It's rather endearing.' You settled back, your arms tucked behind your head.

'I wonder when it happened.'

'Yesterday. It's a mistake to think age comes gradually and gracefully, you know. It's a bastard – always takes you by surprise.'

'Thanks for telling me.'

'What's a friend for?'

I did think of you as a friend, one who educated me and showed me myself, no matter how painful. You would not allow me to fall, like most people, asleep on my feet. I knew I had been right to choose the Elusive Ones.

'Miles, tell me something, and please be honest. Is it you who's been peeling off the wallpaper? Was it you all along?'

'Hee-hee-hee.'

Sometimes we'd stay up and play Scrabble. (It turned out you did like the game after all.) These were long, silent, bitter contests that went on until four or five in the morning, each of us burning to win and speaking only to recite definitions from *The Shorter Oxford Dictionary*.

We still read aloud to each other. Your favourite book at the time was an account of a White Russian exile's wanderings in Siberia and Mongolia during the twenties. There were adventures in forests and on rivers, encounters with magicians, ghosts and animal spirits. The author's political views seemed a bit paranoid to me, but this didn't bother you.

On one of our family evenings, after a couple of whiskies, I summoned the courage to ask Madam Zed about my palm. This time she did not refuse me, though she was not exactly eager. She turned my hand over and over, examined it in the lamplight, her own shaking a little.

'Look, the fate line is broken at the head line which dips all the time towards the mount of the moon. The plain of Mars is full of boxes and crosses. You have a turbulent middle life. There is a crisis. You stop, and you do not go on.'

'You mean I die?'

'I cannot say. Death is not predictable and one should not try. It is unethical, an invasion of privacy. I am not a commissar.'

I didn't understand this at all. 'Why do I stop?'

'It is your choice.'

'Well, that's all right then.'

She gave a little shrug.

'You think too much,' she said. 'And you are stronger than you think.'

I took no action to avert the predicted crisis. Let it happen, I thought, we will make something good out of it. Anyway, what action could I have taken? As usual, I heeded only the subtle. The obvious I ignored.

We prepared for Christmas. It would be the first I had celebrated in years and I was actually excited. All those happy secrets – no wonder people liked it. I felt almost re-admitted to the human race. You and I went to the Road and purchased a large tree for Madam Zed's sitting room and a small one for us. We bought ornaments and crackers, fairy lights, the lot – and all as naff as possible. We were determined to give her a good time and shelved our cynicism until after the New Year. For us Christmas would go on for a month, beginning with St Nicholas's Day when Czech children hang up their stockings.

'At Christmas,' she said, 'we have three visitors: an angel, a devil and St Nicholas. The devil is to punish bad children, the angel is to plead mercy for them and St Nicholas to act as a judge.'

'Sounds like the three of us,' you said. 'I'm the devil, Rosie's the angel, and you, dear Madam Zed, are the judge.'

'That is appropriate,' she answered.

The smell of the tree made me homesick. It reminded me of the Maine woods, the New Hampshire mountains; of balsam pillows from L. L. Bean and those incense burners in the shape of log cabins that we all used to keep in our bedrooms. The metal chimney held the conical piece of pine-scented incense so that, when you burned it, it looked as if someone was living in the little log cabin. I called my father.

We set up the tree and made a big performance of trimming it. She sat in her wheelchair taking regular sips from a glass of sherry and criticizing everything we did, while her Richard Tauber 78s crackled on the stereo. Oh, she was entertained all right. That night we repeated the process in 4C, keeping an eye on Musetta who was resolved to smash the tree ornaments and eventually did. We sprayed the poor fir with aerosol snow, garlanded it with angel hair and fairy lights and crowned it with an electric angel whose wand flashed on and off. Our one socket bulged dangerously with plugs. We'd decided that everything must be in the worst possible taste. It was an altar of sorts, a charming offence, a Woolworth apparition.

'I have nothing for my children,' Madam Zed said sadly on Christmas Eve after we'd given her a potted palm that was a present from us both. 'Only these.' Two envelopes lay before her on the table with our names written in a spidery hand. Each one contained a cheque for £100. I accepted mine with reluctance. I wasn't sure whether she could afford such extravagance.

'And now I am going to bed,' she announced. 'You two must stay up and watch for the Golden Pig. If you see it, wake me.'

'Well, Rosieposie, how are you planning to spend your loot?' You were stretched out on the bed. It was eight o'clock. A Greek gentleman had called on Madam Zed and would stay with her until the arrival of the night nurse who was being paid triple time.

'I'll buy something for the room, and I guess I should send a present to my half-brothers. God knows what they like.'

'You're not awfully fond of these half-brothers, are you?'

'Does it show? I try to be fond, though I hardly know them. I'm fonder than I used to be. I speak to them on the telephone now – and Denise as well. I already sent my father a biography of Parnell.'

'How is your father?' You'd never asked before.

'Not so good. His heart's giving him trouble, and being Vinnie he refuses to give up the French fries and lobster rolls and beer. He looks like an Irish Buddha. He's still a blue-collar nihilist, though, I'm happy to say.' Denise kept me well-supplied with photographs of her and Vinnie bursting from their Bermudas, Budweisers in hand, flanked by husky friends and the barbecue. 'I'm worried about him. He has no common sense.' Musetta crept under the mosquito netting and jumped into my lap. 'I should go and see him, I guess.'

You grabbed my hand. 'No. Stay here.'

'I wasn't serious. How could I leave?'

'I wouldn't let you.'

'Really?'

'Of course not. It's too much fun being Hansel and Gretel.'

'You don't think we'll end up in the oven?'

'We're already there. Look, I've got a present for you.' You handed me a small white packet.

'Another one?' You'd already given me a book on archaic Greek art.

'It's for both of us really.'

'I see. Something naughty.'

'We've been far too Christian and good. It's more than body and soul can stand. We deserve some sin. Let's drop some.'

'What is it, another of Harry's specialities?'

'Rose, I get the feeling you don't trust me.'

'I wonder why.'

'Harry said it's something new on the market. They give it to the dying.'

'The *dying?*'

'Well, that's all of us, isn't it?'

'I guess.'

You brought in a bottle of champagne from the window ledge. It wasn't very cold. Christmases in London are usually warm and rainy. The heating was on low, but the room still felt overheated. In a way I liked it. We closed the window. We'd had enough Christmas spirit seeping into our élite surroundings. The point of the room, after all, had been to create a space where there were no atmospheres or influences but our own. Distilled Miles and Rose: Essential, hermetically sealed, pure.

Every bit of exposed flat surface was covered with candlesticks. Thirteen flames swayed in gentle syncopation with the flashing fairy lights. We could hear the soft dripping of molten wax. A lovely sound. (I spent one afternoon a week scraping it from the furniture and carpet, half a mouldering Aubuson which we'd bought for a song. Sometimes the place made me think of Eva's apartment and then I wasn't quite so comfortable.) You asked would I please wear my bee-keeper's hat, you were so fond of it. I put it on and climbed back under the mosquito netting with you, doubly gauzed. Through the haze the candle flames became lion-headed chrysanthemums, the fairy lights were All-Sorts stars. You, the room, everything, was enveloped in a coral-coloured mist.

For a while I felt wonderful. Everything was funny, there was so much to say. We lay on the bed and laughed and played with Musetta. We made, for once, as much noise as we liked. The house was empty of lodgers. They'd all gone home for the holidays, even David and Jonathan, and the only other ears in the place were five floors below us. Then you mentioned India. You mentioned it in connection with a journey you'd made three years ago. It was not the first time your dates and events failed to tally. I'd learned not to let it upset me, but this time I felt I could not let your inconsistencies simply slide past. I'd never get used to being lied to.

'Miles, you went to India on *this* journey.'

'What makes you think that?'

'You told me so.'

'A misunderstanding, dear.' Aside to imaginary audience: 'She's been known to misunderstand me before.'

And suddenly I wanted to know. My curiosity was sharp, and my desire for satisfaction would not be controlled. It galvanized my tongue and made it speak words for which I would otherwise have bitten it.

'Miles, where *did* you go?'

'I do hate it when you take that tone with me.'

'I don't care. I don't care if you hate it. Where did you go and how did you get the money to go there?'

'Steady on. You know I don't like being grilled.'

'I do know, but I'm tired of mystery.'

'Rubbish, you love the mystery. I'm your demon lover, your eldritch Miles. You'd be bored with me if I were honest and normal.'

'Wrong. I don't want a demon, I want a human being who tells me what really happened.'

'Don't be stupid. Humans have no more probity than demons, and they're far less intelligent.'

So it went on, with your parrying my every attempt to get under the skin of your cheeky persona. It was infuriating. Normally I would not have been able to withstand you, but Harry's *de luxe* death-bed special and my repressed inquisitiveness were a hot combination.

'You tell me you were one place, and it turns out you were in another. You say that you faked medical results and that you didn't, that you have a mother and that you don't, that you were in the pay of a public enemy and that you weren't.'

'Americans are so literal.'

'I can't even believe what you say about a fucking necklace.'

'Language, language.'

I marched to the door, though where I'd have gone if I had opened it I had no idea. Downstairs to tell Mummy?

'Rose,' you drawled loudly, 'come back here.'

I came back.

'Sit down, my darling.' You patted the counterpane and looked friendly.

I crawled back under the mosquito netting, reluctant to surrender my huff.

'I do appreciate the confusion into which a life-style like mine can throw a nice straightforward girl from the sticks. Uh-uh-uh! Don't storm off again. I'm not being facetious.' You took my hand. 'I admit my existence is a bit outré, so unlike the home life of our own dear Queen. But do bear with me.' I began to relax. 'I don't keep you in the dark on purpose, you know. Only because I think you prefer it that way.'

'I do *not* prefer it that way.'

'Please don't shout. My nerves are frayed. I'm already grinding my teeth. Maybe this stuff isn't all Harry said it was. Maybe he lied or switched labels. I wouldn't put it past him. He's a very sick boy.'

'Why take it, then?'

'Well, if I'd known it was going to start World War Three I'd never have suggested it. I was only trying to please you.'

'Then go on with what you were saying. That will please me much more.'

'OK. I realize you're upset and I agree it's right that I should clarify matters. Set the record straight, you know. Honesty is, after all, the best policy.'

'Don't play cute,' I said, 'just tell me.'

'I went to Africa this time. You're right, India was before. That's where I was – West Africa. That is, after I went to Germany. I visited Herr Geisel first, to sort of talk over old times. Reminisce. I knew I was going weeks before I left but I never told you. I wasn't sure what to say. I knew you'd try to prevent me, but I hadn't decided whether or not to lie. I was spared the decision by subsequent events. (By the way, I did not tell Madam Zed; she guessed. I gather your tidy-up was rather haphazard. There were several tell-tale clues. Careless of you.) Where was I? Oh yes, Hamburg. Dear Herr Geisel. A sweet man. He was ever so pleased to see me. He regretted he could offer me nothing in the way of employment, but he did suggest an Italian colleague who ran a similar operation to his own. The Common Market is a wonderful thing, my dear. Even with the handicap of being British I can legally seek work throughout the Continent. Anyway, this wop's company was looking for a sales engineer with my sort of experience. I won't explain what that entails, it would bore you or upset you and you wouldn't understand anyway. But I predict there'll be more and more of us. Exalted dustmen in suits and ties. Waste disposal is the coming thing. Just wait. So he hired yours truly. My charisma distracted him from certain other shortcomings. Salary and benefits were attractive. Expenses and a company car. Not bad for a drop-out medical student. Certainly an improvement on the hospital office.

'Well, off I went to West Africa where the local officials welcomed me with open arms. Charming people. Their white teeth gleamed in the tropical sun at the prospect of all those lira. They were a sight to behold. Warmed the cockles, it really did. The deal was clinched, so I went on a little jaunt to Morocco. Now there is a country with a really attractive bureaucracy, not to mention the magnanimous Hassan II. Then it was back to Hamburg, only to be informed that UN moles had been complaining about our little shipment. Two hundred drums of toxic industrial waste leaking into a vacant lot next to a slum. Children splashing in the noxious orange puddles, people vomiting, developing skin rashes, running sores, eye problems. Whoops!

'My employer, who is not an unreasonable man, says OK, mate, we'll shift her. Return flight to Africa for RM, a few irate citizens and a couple of righteous officials unhappy with their bribes and we're off again. This time a bit further down the coast where the inhabitants weren't as fussy.'

'You mean they took them?'

'Natch. Those people are starving, love. Think they're worried about a couple of leaky barrels? They didn't give a fuck. In fact they were grateful. It was a heartening experience. I mean, I saved lives! I deserve a citation, come to think of it, even a medal. But don't get me wrong, I'm not complaining. Virtue is its own reward.'

'Miles, stop.' I clapped my hands over my ears.

'I wish you'd make up your mind, didums. I'm only doing as you asked. Really, women are very demanding. Here am I, trying to set your mind at rest and all you do is get shirty. And after we agreed that honesty was always the best – '

'Shut up!' I screamed.

You laughed. You shook with laughter. I'd never seen you laugh like that, with your whole body.

'Oh, you are a petal,' you gasped, and held out your arms to me. 'Come here, Rosie, come to Miles.'

I let you hold me against you. I lay there stiffly as your spasms continued.

'You're such a dummy. Oh, I do love you to bits.'

'Then why do you tell those awful stories?'

'Why do you believe them? We go through this every time.'

'Because – oh God, they seem so real. I mean, you're right. People are evil. And what about Herr Geisel?'

'There isn't any Herr Geisel. He's just another product of my fertile imagination.'

'Really?'

'Oh Christ, don't look at me with those Irish eyes full of Irish weather. *No-there-is-no-Herr-Geisel.*' You raised two fingers. 'Scout's honour.'

'Don't make with the honour. You told me you were thrown out of Cub Scouts after one week.'

'What a memory.'

We started to laugh. We couldn't stop. I think it must have been the drug, because, viewed objectively, the situation wasn't at all funny. I pulled away and wiped my eyes.

'I'll ask once more, then. What were you doing for the past two years?'

'Now, who's tormenting who? All right, I'll come clean. I was working for Mother Teresa.'

I began to laugh again. 'Tell me about it.'

'How voracious you are. I feel like Scheherezade. I shall be worn to a frazzle. My tongue will wither in my mouth, but never mind. I'd do anything for you, you dreadful woman, *and* you know it.'

'Let's have it, then. All of it, this time.'

'Very well, oh whiplash of my emotions. I know when I'm licked. Poor Scheherezade. Poor Miles. I confess out of sheer exhaustion. And it's nowhere near as bad as you thought. I was working in a laboratory in Dorset. I only went to Germany to see an old mistress who runs a centre for youthful junkies.'

'Which laboratory?'

'It's called Porton Down.'

'That place! That's the centre for chemical warfare.'

'It ain't a book about bunnies.'

'That's where they do sick things to animals to find out how to kill people.'

'You're better informed than I thought.'

'My God, did you – '

'Stop! I know what you're thinking and I didn't do it. Not for long anyway. The pay was terrible.'

'What *were* you doing?'

'Oh, very simple things, really. Don't worry, no fires in doggies' larynxes, no blinded kittens. I'm not that advanced. I only looked after the animals – monkeys and rats, mainly – checked their responses, their rate of deterioration; how long it took them to die, in other words. Come to think of it, it wasn't as boring as I thought at the time.'

'You mean you – '

Uh, uh, uh. Don't leap to conclusions. It wasn't that lurid. Quite a few died immediately and peacefully.'

'Miles, is this true?'

'Oh yeah.'

'I mean the real truth.'

'Isn't that what you wanted?'

'Tell me what happened – what they did to the animals.' Now I was into it I was unrelenting. Some perverse part of me insisted I pursue this topic to the end of the line, last stop, all off, get out.

'If you insist. You won't like it, but maybe it will teach you a lesson once and for all. One thing first: chemical and germ warfare aren't just intended to kill, but to kill in a particular way. The military want to find out the specific nature of the weapon's effect. It's really quite refined, which is why they have to test over and over again on animals.'

'So what do they do?'

'You want examples?'

'Yes.'

'OK, but don't blow your Irish stack at me. None of this was my idea. I was just a bystander . . . They do things like spray baboons with nerve gas. They blind rabbits and monkeys with laser beams, shoot monkeys in the eye, practise battlefield surgery on pigs. (Did you know that the greatest advances in surgery were made as a result of operations carried out in the field during the Second World War? You're right, you know, there's a little good in everything.) Mind you, I did feel that some of the wounding experiments were a waste. You know how I hate extravagance. Now you'd think they'd realize, being soldiers and doctors, that if you shoot someone in the head with a 3.2 mm steel ball, they'd die almost instantly. But you see, they're intrigued by that, *almost*. They want to know what happens in the interim. So they shoot all these rhesus monkeys. I mean a grapefruit would have done as well. Supposedly they were anaesthetized. Some more than others, it turns out. In fact they survive between two and a hundred and sixty-nine minutes, and in most cases the drug has worn off. Of course that was the intention. They want to observe the after-effects and for this purpose, they argue, the victim must be conscious. Otherwise the experiment isn't complete.'

'But they haven't even the excuse that the experiments save lives.'

'No, indeed. It's called a Higher Form of Death. You must have heard the expression.'

'But can't anyone do something about this horror? The English are supposed to love animals. It must be reported somewhere. Surely people *know*.'

'Actually, they don't. There are two reasons for this. First: Porton

Down feels the general public is too emotional to understand either the reasons for or the importance of this research. You see, the general public is a lot like you, Rose – sentimental and irrational. People would get upset. In a way, they're kept in ignorance for their own good. Second: most of the experiments are top secret. Not even the RSPCA can prosecute because military research is protected by the Crown. I find that interesting, don't you? We in England do not have a Freedom of Information Act like you enlightened Yanks. England is the most secretive country in the world. I thought you knew that by now.'

'You tortured innocent creatures. You weren't forced to, you chose to.'

'No creature's innocent.' You lit a cigarette, as though this were your final word on the subject.

I felt ill.

'Were there any – cats?'

'Would you rather they used babies? Get serious, Rose.'

You're very quick. You caught my wrist in mid-air before I could land the blow.

'Don't *hit* me, darling. I don't *like* it. Something *snaps*.' Your grip was so hard I cried out. 'You want to play *games* with me but you can't take the *pace*.' As you let go you pushed me backwards so that I hit my head against the bedstead.

'You hurt me.'

'You'll live.'

'You're teasing me again, aren't you?'

'Why should I tease you? If you want to know the truth I'm bored with teasing you. It's stopped being fun.'

'You're a creep, Miles.'

'Sticks and stones will break my bones, but names will never hurt me. Isn't that how it goes?'

Behind the flippancy I could see that you were really cross, otherwise you would not have joined me in the exchange of stupid insults from which all sense of humour was absent. It wasn't only animals and babies and germ warfare that had me so agitated. I was tired of being teased and tormented for your pleasure. I wanted to know what you really meant, what you were really up to. I wanted to know your reasons for saying such things and treating me the way you did. I wanted you to be serious and tell me the truth for once. Just once. We got very worked up. The atmosphere was moving from sour to poisonous and neither of us was attempting to control it. The argument, as arguments do, became circular, an indication that soon it would sink to an even lower emotional plateau.

The situation deteriorated to the point where I actually said: 'You only like me because I'm a convenience.'

'What makes you think I like you? You're not very exciting. You aren't even beautiful. And Bernice was much better in bed. Come to think of it, she was pretty fetching in the black dress too.'

The nearest candle guttered against a winking backdrop of fairy lights. The combination gave a stroboscopic effect which made your face look haggard and mean. I looked the same way, probably: ugly. I hated myself, but I hated you more and I was not afraid of you. I felt strong, and though I knew it was a transient state, I was determined to use my power while it lasted. Time to wreck the altar.

A second later you sat looking at me, astonished – for the first time, really surprised – with three long red scratches across your cheek. I stared at you, hardly believing what I'd done. You lifted the mosquito netting, bounded out of bed and, with a single movement, swooped down on Musetta where she sat cowering beside the Christmas tree. You caught her in your manicured hand and flung her with all your might against the opposite wall.

I didn't scream. I didn't say anything. I bent over her limp body where it lay on the floor, the neck broken, definitely dead. The room seemed to pulsate like a giant heart, the furniture swelling and shrinking with every breath.

'Why did you do that?' I whispered.

'Because I don't hit women.'

'You murdered her. She was innocent. She was without sin.'

'Then she'll go straight to little pussy-cat heaven. Or hasn't she been baptized?'

Every sadness and wickedness of my life flowered again in that moment, a vile resurrection. I knelt beside Musetta trying to breathe, slowly, in-out, in-out, using the rhythm of the expanding and contracting room to stop myself fainting. If one of the stories were true – even only one . . .

'Get out, Miles,' I said.

'With pleasure.' You went to the door. But when I saw your hand on the knob, I jumped up, tore off the bee hat and threw my arms around you, not in supplication, but in the certainty that I could crush and kill you. I wanted to wrap myself round you like a boa constrictor, harder and harder, until your breath, like Musetta's, was all spent.

I caught you off balance and we fell to the floor. You struggled in my arms, but I would not let you go. I held you with all my strength. Mothers have been known to lift automobiles off the bodies of their injured children. That was the kind of strength I had.

I lay on top of you, pinning you so that I looked straight into your eyes. They were the eyes of a wolf, a lizard, a deep-sea fish that swam before me until the moment when you tried to move backwards, flung out an arm, hit the Christmas tree and sent it toppling on to the floor. Some of its lights went out. Others winked crazily as we struggled on the carpet, our arms and legs entwined.

Only they were not your legs. The animal's eyes which had looked into mine were complemented now by fur, rough and brown. The fur concealed claws that tore at me, the feathers that followed, talons. But I gripped you tighter around the waist and would not let go. Not even when I felt the grate of the scales and then the slimy moisture on my arms. You exuded some chemical substance as you continued to bite and claw. The smell came from that new grey that had invaded your skin. I could not claw back for fear of releasing you and having you escape me. I clung to you through each metamorphosis, even as we slid down that grassy bank into a black lake without a bottom; even when you became a giant wave that tumbled me to shore and ground me over and over into the rocky beach and my mouth and lungs filled with brackish water so that I thought I would drown. The temperature dropped and the room was covered in hoarfrost, the curtains and netting magically white and glistening. I embraced a snowdrift. I shivered and froze, but I would not release you. We were lifted by a hot wind that whirled us in shrieking circles like Paolo and Francesca. The howling split my eardrums, but I held you fast until the wind dropped and we plunged downward, spiralling through the firmament, and fell into an enormous crypt. Buried alive, I held you still, a decomposing corpse in whose eyeless sockets could be read the end of every dream. Light came at last, a pinky-orange glow; the pink of anemones, sea coral, ancient stucco, internal organs, that is like the blood of air, the most beautiful of colours. The colour of heat and love and animate life. My favourite colour. The room was bathed in it. I saw your face now, and it was *your* face, and you smiled at me and kissed me and in that moment I let you go.

You jumped up. Oh, I thought, that is the light: the Christmas tree and the candles, all real and human and not sepulchral. That is what I remember thinking.

You shouted at me. How did you have the strength left to be angry? But you weren't angry, were you? You dragged me to my feet. My knees buckled. When I saw the flames I supposed the hallucinations were beginning again. Then I understood: it was the flames that were the source of the beautiful light. I looked for Musetta, but the smoke hurt my eyes and made them water. I'd forgotten she was dead and that you killed her. You used a blanket to beat the blazing tree. That's right, I said, that's the right thing to do. Then the curtains caught fire, then the mosquito netting.

I'd never realized how fast a fire spreads. You kept on shouting at me. It was impossible to breathe. Finally I unbolted the door. Now I heard what you were shouting. I ran to the pay-phone at the end of the corridor. I knew the Hotel Pearl was a firetrap the first time I saw it. I called the New York Fire Department, but the line was busy. I dialled 999. I heard your footsteps behind me and your voice saying – I can't remember. What was it? That you were going to save Madam Zed, probably.

The hall was filling with smoke. Far, far away I could see the dancing flames, orange and black. The ceiling was a lowering sky and the trees were crashing all around me. The sight of them was paralyzing. Then came the scratching. Then the scratching stopped. 'This is the crisis,' I said aloud. 'I'm going to die in a fire.' I called for you to save me. I knew you could if you really wanted to. I called again, but you didn't answer, or you did answer and I didn't hear you. More scratching. I couldn't bear the sound and finally it drove me out. Clutching the banister I groped my way towards the stairs, or maybe that was earlier. Each time I try to remember what happened events shuffle themselves like a pack of cards. I was crazily aware of the Chinese wallpaper. Where was everyone? I called for David and Jonathan, for Irene, for Phyllis and Clovis, but there was no reply. I had completely forgotten about Christmas.

When I reached the top of the stairs, I looked back at our room. Or perhaps I looked back earlier when I was running for the telephone. How unreliable perceptions are. For a split second I could make out the number 4C on the door which had been firmly closed. Then it's all right, I thought. That is what you are supposed to do in a fire – close doors. The door is closed. Everything is all right. Slowly I descended the stairs.

24

Night

Today, the 30th of November, 1978, as I was reading aloud from the *Listener*, I glanced at Madam Zed to make sure she was still awake. She was, and watching me with golden eyes. At that moment, exactly then, I realized whose eyes they were and why they have always seemed so familiar. They are Foxie's eyes. They are. I know it's crazy, only I can't help seeing in my employer the reincarnation of my oldest friend. Absurd as the idea may be, it will not go away. I have been forced to accept it along with a thousand other absurdities. Strictly speaking, of course, it is impossible for Foxie to have been born again in Madam Zed. But I am not all that bothered any more about what is possible.

You'd say I adopted the fantasy in order to help myself bear all that has happened. That I am telling myself stories to keep myself sane, and that these very stories will finally undermine my sanity. Maybe. But they are Foxie's eyes.

My employer's behaviour has been quite peculiar lately. More than usually so. The other day she informed me that she owned a castle in Hungary on a mountain called the Rosenberg.

'That means hill of roses. A beautiful name.'

'Yes.'

'But I don't like to go there.'

'Why?'

'Because it is too big. It makes me nervous.'

'I don't blame you.'

I used to feel the same way about this house. It resurrected childhood fears of big empty mansions and factories and temples; that certainty of something in the attic, something in the cellar.

Who is in the cellar? We are in the cellar.

Other times she lapses into Italian or German and expects me to understand what she's saying. I've grown used to this now. I act as if nothing out of the ordinary were going on, though I try not to patronize

381

her, which would be base of me. It is a little disconcerting, however, when she speaks to me as though I'm someone else. For example, she informed me yesterday that I was from the continent and that I was a Jew. I denied it and tried to reason with her, but she wasn't interested and wouldn't have it.

'I'm Irish-American,' I said.

'No,' she answered, patient but firm. 'You are not American, you are Jewish. You were born in Austria before the war. You must not be ashamed. Do not try to hide it. I know you. You are pretty. You have a good character. What is there to be ashamed of? Here we accept Jews. My husband is a Jew. Here you do not have to pretend. There is nothing to be afraid of. Here you are safe.'

Now I just let her call me whatever she wants.

This morning she told me over strong black tea and a sugary bun that she intended to leave me the Hungarian castle.

'Please don't.'

'You are Rose. You should live on the Rose hill.'

'That's very kind of you but I don't think I should accept. I'm not suited to castles.'

'But you are in a castle already. And it suits you very well.'

I don't know whether I believe these fantasies or not. Often the look in her eyes makes me think she is having me on, enjoying her little games as always, and faking an extravagant senility for the fun of it. This is quite possible. Vera Zahl has always been a naughty girl.

There is little chance that she will walk again. We keep up the pretence, however. It's very important. It would be a mistake to let our spirits flag. We talk about her memoirs. We have even made a crude chapter-plan which she studies for hours, unable to read a word of it. Of course it will never be written, but I encourage her. It's good for old people to have projects. The hostel for runaway girls has had to be dropped, however. Shelved, I should say, rather than dropped. Funds are low. It has turned out that Mr Zahl was badly underinsured. And she simply carried on paying the premium without taking into consideration – But it's far too complex and neither of us are any good at maths. She was meant to be index-linked. We can't understand what happened. And after all those years of poring over the accounts. Why didn't she see? Was she even reading them? *Could* she read them? Sometimes she gets upset about it, but I console her.

'We will survive,' I say.

Miss Draycott's legacy has been drained away on expensive repairs. General Accident is claiming we failed to take proper precautions, that the place was a fire trap and that what happened was inevitable. I know from my own experience that this was probably the case, yet there are other, more relevant, causes to be considered: the Christmas tree, the candles, cigarette butts, the overloaded electrical outlet.

I don't think the company can make their charges stick. If they do, we won't be able to cover our losses.

So we economize. Some of the jewellery, including Aphrodite's necklace, has had to be sold. I couldn't bear to tell Madam Zed the real story. I'm glad the necklace has gone, and I hope Aphrodite will forgive me. Of course the Germans may pay. Replies to our recent letters have been encouraging. The future is not completely black.

I have moved into the basement. I sleep on the foldaway bed while she keeps the bedroom. Another economy. The night nurse seemed a needless expense. The two upper floors have been gutted, well, nearly gutted. Work stopped once it became obvious that we could no longer afford the builders. A tarpaulin still covers part of the roof. I hope it has survived the recent gales. I should go and check, I suppose. But I'm not exactly eager to venture upstairs. I'll go next week. I'll wait for a nice day.

No one lives upstairs now. The lodgers are gone. Jonathan and David came round a few times, but we haven't heard from them in several weeks. They kept saying how lucky it was, it being Christmas and everyone away. Then they'd remember and there would be a painful silence. It's strange to think of all those empty floors and empty rooms. But the quiet is lovely, we both agree. And of course there is nothing to clean. Responsibilities in general are reduced. The pile of accounts has dwindled to no more than a few papers which she shuffles about on the odd mornings when she thinks her energy has come back.

Something else happened today. Denise called. She has only telephoned me once before, when my father had his first heart attack. I have spoken to her often, but it is always Vinnie who initiates the communication. She called to tell me he is back in hospital. That he was in intensive care, but now he's fine. Sort of.

'It kinda hits you when you see them with all them tubes. I walked in and says, "Woah, just a minute here!" Really bummed me out, y'know? But what do you think? Twenty-four hours later and he's asking for a BLT. This morning it was chocolate butter crunch like I make it at Christmas. "OK, my lord and master," I says. What a guy, huh? Doctor said he was out of his cotton-pickin' mind. But you know Vinnie. Got his BLT in the end. Nurses are all crazy about him. It's like a goddamn party in there.'

Relations between us have improved. I'm even having Greggy to stay next summer, though where we'll put him I don't know.

She asked about my face. 'They lookin' after you OK?'

'Fine. I'm fine.'

'Any pain?'

'Not now.'

'What they say about it?'

'They say I'll be fine.'

'Well, that's good, Rosie. I'm real glad to hear it.'

'You haven't told Vinnie, about my face, I mean?'

'Not yet. I did like you told me. You coming for Christmas?'

So that's how it was with Vinnie. 'I'd like to. But it's hard to leave her.'

'Yeah, I know. Hey, what a year, huh? Year of my life!'

'Mine too.'

'Shame you're such a ways away. But listen. Find someone, honey. To take your place. Hire a nurse for a week or something. Zahl can afford it, I bet. And we'll give you a hand if you're broke.'

'Thank you, Denise. I'll try, I really will. Only I don't know whether –'

'You try.'

'OK.'

'And hey, Rose, I gotta really lotta great photographs for you.'

I thought about Vinnie and Denise. They'd had fun together. I envied them. I pictured him in his hospital bed, punctured and plugged. I should be there with him, I knew. Divided loyalties are my speciality. I'd spoken to him about two weeks before when he had sounded tired but insisted he was 'tip-top'. We talked about politics a little, about the twin spectres of Mrs Thatcher and Ronald Reagan. He said he'd been amassing damning evidence on that air-head and was planning a full-scale assault as soon as he was better. Might even take his findings to the newspapers. I asked about Aunt Bea. He replied that according to Bobby she was, despite her frailness, more sprightly and cheerful than ever. She'd managed to forget everything. I was afraid he'd cry and I couldn't bear that so I switched the topic to the weather. How was it in London? he asked. Rain, I said. Gales. Damp and chilly. Then suddenly his voice broke and he almost whined – something my father never ever did.

'Why don't you come back to a good country?' he asked.

I have decided to go out tonight. John volunteered to come at eight after I've made the supper and done the washing-up. John lives at Number

384

75 and often spends an evening with us. He is one of our few regular visitors.

'I'm going now.' I leaned over her and she pressed my hand in her shaky one.

'It will be all right. I have a good companion.'

'Don't worry, Rose. I'll see she behaves herself. Any nonsense and – ' He rapped the table three times.

'Goodbye, my dear.'

I left them with the Scrabble board. (They allowed foreign words, proper names, abbreviations, the lot) and the television which flickered away, ignored like a senile old relative.

It was raining and there was a north wind, so I took a bus to The Goat. It was just beginning to fill and was smoky and cosy. I hadn't been in a couple of months. I was losing my need for the place, if not my affection.

Violet waved to me from her customary corner. The Gypsy stood at the bar with Lena beside him, her head resting on his foot, her coat lush and sparkling with raindrops. He talked to me about the horses. I imagined them in their blankets, shifting their weight from hoof to hoof, deep in their stables somewhere off the Fulham Road. It was a nice image. I just listened, not saying anything. He was a magical person – magical like people I used to know on the Lower East Side before it became the East Village. Without being at all aware of doing so, he cultivated the uniqueness of his nature. He simply concentrated on that and it made him beautiful. He was mysterious, yet he wore no disguise. Part of his mystery was that he wore no disguise. Perhaps that's why I've always found it difficult to talk to him, why I can only listen and watch.

'Your scar is better,' he said.

Instinctively I looked in the mirror behind the bar. My face still startles me. Nevertheless I smiled at my reflection. I watched the Gypsy touch the red fish-shaped mark on my cheek with his fingertips.

'I can give you something for that. And the arm. I'll bring some next time I come. When will you be here?'

'I don't know. What will it do?'

'Make the skin heal a little bit faster, that's all.'

'It won't take the scar away, will it?'

He shook his head sadly. 'No, nothing can do that. But this will help make its surface smoother.'

'Good.' I sipped my brandy. 'I've got used to my scar. I sort of like it. At least nobody else can be mistaken for me. And I won't look like anybody else, will I?' I smiled at him.

The Gypsy found this very funny. He laughed and laughed. He bought me a drink. He obviously thought I had the right attitude, and that made me glad. Then the bar got crowded and he began talking to one of the stall-keepers. I joined Violet. She had saved me a place between her and Ann who was talking about the rumour that developers were trying to have the Market moved south of the river to be housed in a vast concrete assemblage. For whose good, we wondered.

'They won't never do it,' Marge said confidently.

'They do as they please,' Vi insisted. 'And what you and me want don't matter.' Everyone nodded gloomily but with a certain satisfaction. 'They do as they please,' she repeated and consulted her audience with her eyes. More nods. This brought a ritual ending to the conversation.

'All right, love?' Vi turned to me. 'How's your dad?'

'Back in hospital.'

'Shame. You going to see him?'

'When I can.'

'Well, don't leave it too long, love.' She looked at me hard then patted my hand.

I promised her that I wouldn't. But I could see the future. I'd say I was going, would want to go, would make arrangements, and then be forced to cancel them. I'd go on doing that until one day it would be too late. I wish things could be different, but with my responsibilities, how can they? Divided loyalties. But I'll try to do my best by both of them.

I lost track of the dialogue. But they were used to my silences. They let me just be with them. They understood it was all I wanted.

It was while I was sitting there that I decided to stop writing to you. I know where you are, and I know that this time you will not come back. But at least I know where you are. The nine-month death gestation is long past. It is the reason I didn't go to the funeral. There was no point as long as I thought you were still around and, in a way, still alive. Plus I had no desire to meet the mother who had abandoned you and been the cause of your warped character. Or not.

For the past year writing to you has been a way of still pursuing you. My last pursuit and my last confession. I have made it for your pleasure and, I admit it, as a way of keeping you with me. I thought if I entertained you, you might want to stick around longer. Crazy. You made your flight and have gone where I cannot follow. And now you really are the face in the clouds that looks down with such detachment on all the sorrows of this city.

NIGHT

I can't talk to you any more. For a long time now you have not been listening. I've just been talking to myself and all of a sudden it makes no sense. That afternoon in the little church you told me I would never amount to anything until I confronted my shadow by making a full confession. Well, now I've done it. I wanted to keep my promise at last and to thank you for this precious scar for which I am so grateful. I wanted to repay you and now I have. I have freely given what you once cruelly, teasingly, tried to extract: my confession, complete and entire; my secret and my truth. The real Rose.

I hope you enjoyed it. At times even I enjoyed it. But it has got to stop. You took your secret with you into the fire, but I don't care. In fact you're welcome to your secret. The mystery is not solved, but at least it is finished. Nothing has worked out as I wanted, yet I am not unhappy.

For a while I convinced myself that you tried to save me. Perhaps you did, and perhaps I'll convince myself once more that this is so. Maybe I tried to save you. I was certain I had as I watched the fourth and fifth floors burst into flame and the genie of the room go up in smoke. I stood on the cold pavement, and there was no one to wrap me in a grey blanket, to give me a hug and a kiss. Just the night nurse who rightly spent every second with Madam Zed. But I've thought about that Christmas Eve for so long that I have blown a mental gasket. I don't know how else to describe it. I cannot wring any more significance from the event. Death puts an end to reasoning. That is its only mercy.

No doubt the world will seem a bit four-square and bare-boned without all the omens and lurking implications. It will be, for a while, a desert. But what I've forgotten is that a desert is beautiful. Geometry is clean. I've misinterpreted what Travis taught me, I guess. The altar wasn't about the fun of destruction, but rather the idea that everything should have its chance. I got the altar all wrong. Oh well.

The bell is ringing, it is time to leave. But Bob is lenient. Everyone stays past closing time. A few customers furtively purchase an extra short. Some have their personal beer mugs refilled. There will certainly be one more song. But I must go. I said I'd be home by eleven-thirty, and I intend to walk all the way. I don't know when I'll return to The Goat. I say good-night to everyone, like a child to multiple parents before climbing the stairs to bed. Except that I have no parents, no stairs, no bed. Things are fine.

Outside the rain is turning to snow. But the snow does not lie and each flake vanishes as it meets the ground. Dead on arrival. It may stop by the time I reach Laughton Gardens. There is no killing winter here.

Spring will come soon and, shortly, a new decade. It is something to consider. Something to look forward to.

I walk quickly along the Road. I hurry my pace, not for fear of being late, but for the pleasure of the exertion. I even, for a couple of blocks, break into a run. Shop-front neon flickers and goes out. At the S-bend the road widens. Cars, slick as fish, pass in succession under the street lamps. A low-flying sky skims the chimney pots. An ordinary night, except for the snow.

I close my eyes and I am nine years old, walking the streets of Florence, accompanied by the souls of Foxie's children. I open my eyes. I am back on the Road. Turning left at the intersection. My shadow before me on the shimmering pavement. The black halo of my umbrella. I live in light.

A NOTE ON THE AUTHOR

Mary Flanagan was born in New Hampshire and now lives in London. She is the author of the widely acclaimed short-story collection, *Bad Girls*, and the best-selling novel, *Trust*.